SOUTHERN CHASTITY
AN EROTIC NOVEL

L. D. CUB

This is a work of fiction. While some of the characters, organizations, and events portrayed in this novel are real or have been based on reality, they are part of a story that is a product of the author's imagination and are used fictitiously. Any resemblance to actual persons, living or dead, events or locales is entirely coincidental.

Copyright © 2021 by L. D. Cub.

All rights reserved. Printed in the United States of America. No part of this book may be reproduced in any form or by an electronic or mechanical means, including information storage and retrieval systems, without permission in writing from the publisher, except by a reviewer who may quote brief passages in a review.

ISBN: 979-8-737-09086-9

Book and jacket design by L. D. Cub

Published by Locked Cub Stories

For all my fellow locked men.

TABLE OF CONTENTS

Chapter 1	How Did I Get Here?	1
2	Meeting John	7
3	My First Steps	17
4	The Trial Period	31
5	The Contract	43
6	The Decision	59
7	My Last Day Uncaged	73
8	The Start of My Service	85
9	Sub Brothers	103
10	Interviews	113
11	Cleaning Day	131
12	The Weekend	147
13	My First Session	167
14	Getting Into the Routine	179
15	Flagging Yellow	193
16	The Visitors	207
17	Bear Pride Atlanta	231
18	Memorial Day Weekend	251
19	The Cabin in the Woods	271
20	The Pool Party	293
21	Kenny's Boy	313
22	Summer in the City	329
23	Jay's Graduation	341
24	Max's Initiation	353
25	My Work Trip	367
26	The Gay Pride Festival	377
27	Beach Bums	395
28	Visiting Key West	411

29	Office Service	427
30	Bo's Graduation	441
31	The New Sub	457
32	The Christmas Party	471
33	Winter Wonderland	493
34	Meeting Alex	507
35	Concluding My Contract	523
Epilogue	Life as a Collared Sub	537

FORWARD

This story takes place between the years 2015 and 2016 and draws upon some of my actual experiences as I explored a subordinate role under the tutelage of a local dominant in Atlanta, Georgia. While the character of John is based on this man, it also incorporates aspects of other dominants I have known. Some literary license was also taken to craft the narrative. Similarly, many of the plots, sub-plots, and minor characters have their basis in reality but have been adapted and enhanced through the writing process. Thus, the reader should treat this as a work of fiction.

This was my first novel and it was released originally as a serial through the Nifty Erotic Stories Archive. Many readers offered comments and suggestions on edits for content, context, grammar, and syntax. I considered these as I compiled the various parts into one narrative for publication. Thus, fans of the original story may find minor changes have been made for clarity. However, mistakes happen, and I beg the reader's patience for any errors that may have slipped through as this is a self-funded endeavor.

The acts that are performed within the story involve some high-risk sexual behavior. In the real world, I always advocate for the use of condoms and safer sex practices. I also encourage the use of PrEP (pre-exposure prophylaxis) for all men who have sex with men to reduce the incidence of HIV transmission. However, even with PrEP, many sexually transmitted diseases circulate in the community. Please know your status and see a doctor regularly to protect yourself and others.

Finally, while many of the experiences in this story relate to the BDSM (bondage, discipline, dominance, and submission) dynamic, I am by no means an expert or fully experienced in this realm. Some license was taken when crafting the story and I welcome any feedback from more experienced individuals on how to better illustrate the lifestyle. However, I firmly believe that a healthy BDSM experience is grounded in communication, trust, and respect.

CHAPTER ONE

How Did I Get Here?

Hi! My name is Matt. I am a chastity sub that looks to service other men whenever I can. I know you read about such things in stories all the time, but I am not the typical young and skinny guy that is always featured or desired (it seems). I'm in my 40s, weigh about 240 lbs (109 kg), have a height of about 5' 10" (1.78 m), pretty hairy all over, though I keep my pubes trimmed (to avoid my cage pulling anything), size 8.5 feet (euro 41), have a full beard I keep trimmed neatly at about a medium length, have brown hair (with some white streaks in my beard) and green eyes. Most people would describe me as an older "cubby" type, for those familiar with the bear scene. And, as a symbol of my role, I am permanently in a metal chastity cage that is only removed once a week for a brief cleaning.

So, you might ask yourself, how did I become a sub in permanent chastity? Well, I have always had a submissive streak. Growing up, I would always defer to the more dominant of a group. That usually was my twin brother Steve, who is also gay and the yin to my yang. He has always been more dominant and took charge most of the time. Now, before you ask, yes, we did fool around as kids. I mean, kids explore. But it was not like you see in porn. It was just mutual masturbation and such. He was a bit more hung than I was and I always loved watching him explode though. But, going into college I did not limit myself. I was rather endowed myself (measuring about

1

7 inches by 5.5 inches in girth (17.8 cm x 14 cm), so I topped as much as I bottomed, but I still had this lingering need to want to please dominant individuals. Sex with a dominant man was so much more satisfying to me.

After college, I had a string of relationships that never worked out and I started to explore some kink over time. I got into leather and role play and of course and I took the opportunity to be the sub whenever I could. It was my friend Chris that first introduced me to the concept of chastity. We had a game night, and he came over and mentioned that his boyfriend put him in a chastity cage, and he had it on at the game. He showed everyone and I was fascinated. We got to talking later that evening and he let me know where he got his online and we discussed measurements and such. I ordered one as soon as they left.

When it came in the mail, I tried it on, and it was a head rush. I have always been a massive precummer, to the point I often leave huge wet spots in my pants if I am turned on. I instantly started dribbling precum after it was locked on and I got so horny thinking about not having access to my cock for a bit. I left it on and started looking at porn and made it about an hour before I had to take it off and jack off. It was an intense experience to be sure.

I had Chris and his boyfriend Rick over for drinks the next week and mentioned that I had got a cheap chastity cage and how much it turned me on. Rick smiled and said that Chris had taken to wearing it for days and it had spiced up their relationship. Rick then asked if I wanted him to hold my key for a while to try it where I could not just unlock it when I wanted to. The thought turned me on immediately, but I was a bit nervous. He encouraged me to go get it and put it on. So, I went to my room to retrieve it and as I turned Rick was in the doorway.

"That's a nice cage there Matt. Now hand it to me and drop your pants." Rick said.

I was a bit taken aback but very turned on. Rick was a hot muscle bear-type guy that I had always found attractive and we often played with Chris, usually taking turns loading Chris's ass up. But this was the first time I was in a situation where Rick was giving me an order. I did not waste time, though, and gave him the cage and keys and dropped my sweatpants to reveal my hardening cock.

"Well, that won't do," he replied. "What works for Chris is a cold washcloth. Go into the bathroom and get you one wet with some water."

I turned and went into my on-suite and grabbed a clean washcloth out of the closet and got it wet with the cold water from the tap and wrung it out good. When I came back into the room, Chris was with Rick and had ice in his hand.

"Hey bud, put some ice in that cloth as well, the colder it is, the quicker you can get rid of your boner," said Chris.

I took the ice from Chris and wrapped it in the washcloth and put it on my cock. It did not take long for my erection to subside and Rick got down on his knees and put the cage on me. He inserted the lock and clicked it close and then put the keys in his pocket as he got up.

"There you go!" Rick said. "I like the look of that on you, Matt. Chris, why don't you drop your pants too, no use in keeping your cage under those clothes."

Chris grinned and dropped his pants to reveal his cage and took his shirt off as well. Rick undressed to reveal his massive cock that was starting to swell.

"Now that I have two chastity boys here, why don't you two help me out?" Rick asked. "Chris, I need my ass eaten, and Matt, get on your knees and suck this cock."

I was so fucking turned on at this point that my cock was straining in the confines of my cage. But I dropped to my knees immediately and started sucking on his hot cock and fondling his massive balls while Chris was behind him with his tongue deep in his ass.

Rick was moaning in pleasure and asked if we could move to the bed, which I gladly agreed to. He laid down and I knelt over him to continue to suck him. Chris laid beside him and they made out while

I did. I was precumming so much there was a line of liquid from my cage and pooling on the bedspread. Chris noticed this and got some on his finger.

"Damn Matt!" Chris exclaimed. "I know you were a leaker, but you are turned on by this aren't you?"

I grunted as I attempted to deepthroat Rick, who was arching his head back and growling and grunting. He grabbed my head and started to face fuck me and I did my best not to choke on his thick meat.

"Chris, bring that ass over here and Matt, grab some lube, this cock is going in your ass," Rick said.

I went over and grabbed some lube and some poppers from the side table and Chris got up and swung his legs over Rick and put his ass in Rick's face, so he had good access. When I got back on the bed Chris was already moaning and I put some lube on my hand and started getting Rick's cock ready. I had cleaned out in preparation for their visit because we do occasionally play around, but I was not expecting to do this locked up.

After I got Rick's cock ready, I turned facing away from Rick and Chris so I could best take the downward curve of his member. Sliding my legs under his outstretched legs, I knelt back and slowly let his cock enter me as I took a hit of poppers to help. It took a minute, but I was able to finally get him balls deep and I started to ride him. I could hear Chris moaning in pleasure and Rick occasionally grunt and groan as well.

He got Chris off him and told me to turn around and ride him face to face. So, I rotated around and sat down on him again.

"That's a boy," Rick said as he grabbed my cage. "You like riding a real man's cock, don't you?"

"Hell yes," I replied.

"Hell yes, Sir, boy!" Rick barked back.

"Hell yes, Sir! I do! I love your cock!" I immediately replied.

Chris had a grin from ear to ear as he laid next to his boyfriend who was now in complete control of my cock and ass.

I continued to rock back and forth when Rick grabbed my hips. "You want my load, boy?" Rick asked.

"Yes, Sir! I want your load, Sir!" I replied.

Rick tensed up and forced me down on his cock as he exploded. I felt his cock pulsing as his seed went deep and he let out a huge growl that was muffled as Chris leaned over to make out with him.

We sat there for a moment as Rick recovered from his orgasm. After a bit he had me get off him and Chris immediately went down on him to clean up the remains of the cum on his cock, sucking on Rick's balls after.

"Thanks for that, Matt," Rick replied.

"No, thank you! That was hot! Can I have the key to take my cage off now? I need to jack off myself after that," I replied.

"I don't think so, Matt," Rick said. "You were interested in this, so you can leave that on till we leave later. OK?"

I was so hard in my cage and needed to cum, but I agreed, and we went into the living room to have our drinks and watch some TV.

They stayed for about three hours, but it was getting late and they needed to leave to get home and feed their dogs. So, they went to get their clothes and get dressed. As they came back into the living room, Rick approached me.

"Here is your key, Matt," Rick said. "But I challenge you to keep that on as long as you can tonight. Text me if you can make it till bedtime."

"Sure, I can do that," I replied. I mean, I thought, it was only another few hours till my bedtime anyway.

As they left, Chris whispered to me that he found the whole evening hot as hell and I told him I agreed. We exchanged some hugs, and I closed the door behind them. I went to clean up and realized I still had Rick's load in me. As I thought about the session we had, I started to try to get hard again and the strain led me to start to precum again. I figured I needed a distraction, so I went and watched some TV for a while and when it got close to 10 pm, I snapped a pic of my cage and sent it off to Rick.

He replied, "Good boy. I enjoyed loading up that ass of yours. I am proud of you for waiting till bedtime. Now, go drain those balls."

I texted back, "Thank you, Sir!" with a smiley emoji and immediately got the key and unlocked and removed the cage.

My cock got hard immediately and a huge spurt of precum came out that was apparently trapped by the cage. I used it to get my dick wet and sat on the bed and started to jack off with my right hand and play with my nipple with the other. They were directly wired, and I was rock hard in just a few seconds.

Normally, I have pretty good stamina and can go for a good five minutes or so before I need to shoot. But, this time, I felt my balls lifting and my cock started shooting cum out just sixty seconds after I started jacking. I collapsed back on the bed at the same time and growled loudly.

When I came to my senses after a few minutes, I noticed that I had shot so far that it was all in my beard and had gone over my shoulder and onto the pillow behind me.

"Damn! That was intense!" I thought to myself.

As I got into the shower to wash the cum off my body and Rick's load out of my ass, I could tell that this chastity thing was something I wanted to explore more.

CHAPTER TWO

Meeting John

It had been about a week since the Tuesday that Rick and Chris had been at my place and I got to explore a chastity experience. It left me wanting more. I had been texting them both over the past few days asking him questions about how they got into the kink, if there were others we knew that were into it, and some dirty talk as well telling Rick at one point I wanted to do it again sometime.

On Sunday, Rick texted me and asked me if I would be willing to meet him at a local restaurant for lunch. He explained that he had a friend that he wanted to introduce me to. I asked what place he had in mind and he mentioned the Mongolian grill located on the west side of Atlanta. I loved stir fry (especially all you can eat), and the place was not too far from my apartment, so I told him I was in and he told me to meet him there at 1 pm.

The restaurant is attached to a small mall with an entrance inside the mall itself. When you enter the mall, some benches sit in front of the restaurant and that is where I saw Rick sitting with another man. I have already mentioned that Rick is a big muscle bear of a man. Six-foot-tall, 250 lbs (113 kg) and looks like he could bend iron in two if he wanted to. His friend was similarly built, but maybe not as fit. You could tell he had a little bit of a belly over his muscles, but just as furry and his chest hair was peeking out of his t-shirt that he was wearing. My mouth was watering.

"Hello, Matt!" Rick said as he stood up. "This is my friend John."

John got up as well and extended his hand to shake. He had a firm grip and a deep voice. Man, this guy was fucking hot, I thought.

"Nice to meet you, Matt," said John.

"Likewise," I replied.

"I already put us on the waitlist, and they handed me this gizmo that is supposed to light up when it's our turn. It should not take too long," Rick said.

I nodded a bit uncomfortably. I am a pretty outgoing guy, but I can be a bit awkward around people I do not know. Perhaps sensing this, John spoke up and asked me how I knew Rick and I mentioned that I had been friends with his boyfriend Chris for several years before they met. John mentioned that he had met Rick at the Atlanta Eagle a few years ago during their monthly leather weekends and they had hit it off pretty quickly.

Before I had a chance to reply, the gizmo started buzzing and flashing indicating it was our turn to be seated. We entered the restaurant and the server showed us to our table. She asked if we had been there before and we all said we had, so she gave us leave to go and fix our bowls to be sent off for frying. I was the first to get back to the table followed by John.

"So, Rick tells me that you had a little fun last week with him and Chris," John said.

"Yes," I replied a little shyly, "we occasionally meet up for drinks and to socialize and to play around as well."

"Ah," John replied, noting I was being a bit hesitant. "How did you enjoy being in chastity and treated as a sub?"

I was not expecting such a direct question, but as I was about to answer Rick came back and sat down.

"So, have you told John about how much fun you had locking up your cock and riding mine?" Rick asked with a grin.

"We were just getting to that in fact," John replied.

I took a drink of the soda the waitress had left at the table for each of us and replied, "I have to admit it was a pretty hot experience. I was leaking precum the whole time."

"That's for sure. It ran down and was all over me and the bedspread," Rick said laughing a bit. "John here is a pretty experienced dominant. He trains and has collared and owned boys in the past. I figured since you were interested in learning more about the lifestyle, you might benefit from talking to him."

"Have you ever been a sub for a guy before?" John asked.

I told him about my experiences growing up. I told him about my boyfriend I had once that was pretty dominant and how we role played a lot in the bedroom. However, I had never really explored the fetish to any great detail and had only had my chastity device for a short time.

"Well, chastity devices can be fun, and I do make them a part of boys I work with, but there is a lot more to it as well. I am curious, you said you like to top as much as you like to bottom and you have role played, but what turns you on more? Are there aspects that you find you want to explore more?" John asked.

I told him I had to admit that I found playing with a true dominant to be very fun. I was much more willing to be the bottom and liked it when someone else set the scene and told me what to do.

"And whose pleasure is most important in a dom/sub relationship you think?" John asked me back.

I thought a bit about this before I replied. "Well, I think it should be pleasurable for both people. But I can see where the dom should be put first. I think it would be hot to put a lot of effort into pleasuring a guy and to get as much pleasure out of it from the sub role by doing so."

John seemed intrigued and pleased. "That's a good answer boy."

It was the first time he had addressed me as 'boy' and I admit I smiled when he said that. John saw me grin and smiled back and turned to Rick and said, "This one may be a good candidate."

I did not know what he meant, but the waitress brought out food at that point and so we started to dig in and Rick began to talk about some things he had been dealing with at work. From there the conversation went to current events and things going on around town. At one point, I mentioned my job that allowed me to work from home about half the time and how liberating it was to not have a dress code or even be in my underwear all day. We laughed about that. It was a pretty nice time and I got comfortable around John. You could tell he was a dominant in the way he held himself and the way he talked, but he was nice as well. He was approachable, I thought.

"Well, I need to take a piss," Rick said as he stood up. "I'll be right back." He squeezed John's shoulders a bit and gave him a wink as he left.

"Matt, I will be honest with you," John said after Rick was gone. "Rick and I go to the same gym and had a conversation about you the other day. He mentioned you were interested in chastity and exploring it and were pretty turned on when he dominated you."

I nodded and smiled sheepishly.

"Well, if you are interested," John continued, "I think you might be someone I would be willing to take under my wing and train and let you explore some aspects of the kink. What are your thoughts about that?"

I grabbed my drink to have something to hold on to and I replied, "that could be fun, but I would want to discuss limits and such."

"Of course! It is very important that we discuss what things you are interested in, not interested in, what limits you have, and what limits I set. But, before we get to any of that, I want to see how disciplined you are," John replied.

"Ok," I said.

"Well, Rick tells me you just got your chastity cage. What is the longest you have worn it for?" he asked.

I told him that it had only been about six hours the time that I played with Rick and Chris. Since then, I had worn it a few times during the week, but the six hours was about the most I had ever done.

"Do you have any places to go after lunch today and are you working from home tomorrow?" John asked.

"I don't have anything planned at the moment and I was going to head back home and play video games. I am working from home tomorrow," I replied.

"Then I want you to put your chastity cage on when you get home and take a picture and send it to me," he said. "Then I want you to take the keys and put them in a container with water and freeze them in the freezer. I want you to take a picture of this when you put it in and about an hour later to show me, they are still there and freezing inside the block of ice. I want you to stay in chastity overnight and then text me in the morning when you wake up with a picture of you in your cage. Do you think you can do that?"

Nervously I said I could. It was a big step, but if the keys were in the ice, although I could not get to them immediately, I could always find a way to thaw the ice and get at them if I needed to.

"I will warn you," John continued, "sleeping in a chastity cage the first night can be frustrating. I have had boys that had very sleepless nights due to attempted erections. It helps to sleep on your side with a pillow between your legs and have a cold washcloth handy to soften things up if you get too hard."

"I understand," I replied.

"If you make it through the night and send me a picture of yourself still caged and another with the key still in the ice, then I will know you have some discipline, and we can discuss the next steps. How does that sound boy?" John asked me.

"I understand and I am willing to do it," I replied.

As if on cue, Rick returned from the restroom. "So, have you tried to collar him yet, John?"

John laughed, "it's a tad bit early for that, but he's going to cage himself up overnight, so we will see how he does."

"Good idea! You might want to text Chris. He had a hell of a night the first time I made him wear his overnight and I had to make him sleep on the couch. Might be worth asking him for any tips. He is a pro at it now," Rick said to me with a grin.

We continued to eat and after we were done, we walked out, and I hugged Rick and he left. John then turned to me and we exchanged numbers.

"Looking forward to your text later boy. Don't disappoint me," John said.

"Yes, Sir," I replied.

John grinned and said, "good answer."

He waved and headed back into the mall and I exited to get to my car.

The drive back to my apartment was interesting. I was hard the whole time and I could tell I was precumming again because my pants were wet. I was turned on. It was intimidating as well, though. This would be the first time I had ever worn the device that long and I did not know if I would be able to do it. It was at that point that I realized that I never jacked off in the morning like I usually did. The last time had been before dinner yesterday. When I got into the parking lot of my apartment complex, I texted John to tell him I got home and I would be putting on the device soon, but to ask if I could jack off quick before.

"No, boy. No cumming. I want you to lock up as soon as you get inside," came the reply.

I was frustrated, but it was still a turn-on, so I got inside and grabbed some ice and a washcloth and got my erection down to a point that I could put the cage on and close the lock. I then grabbed a water bottle I had and put the key on some thread and suspended it in the middle of the bottle and screwed the lid back on over the string to help it hang there. I took a picture of my locked cock and then put the water bottle with the key in it in the freezer and snapped a picture of that as well.

"Good job, boy. Now wait about an hour and a half and send me a picture of the water bottle again once it is starting to freeze solid," John texted back.

It was 3 pm at this point and I had nothing more to do. I decided to watch some Sunday sports games and I started texting Chris to tell him what happened and ask his advice on sleeping with the cage on. I think he was as turned on about everything as I was and he reiterated sleeping on my side with a pillow will help, but he also told me that I will still wake up several times and just to be prepared. I replied I was working from home, so I didn't have to worry about being too sleepy or disheveled looking. Chris told me that was a good thing with a big smile emoji. He also told me it would be a good idea to lubricate the ring with some lotion as well to avoid any chafing or pinching. That was good advice, I thought, and I put a bottle of lotion next to my bed for later.

At about 4:30 pm, I checked the freezer, and the bottle was pretty much on its way to being solid. I took a pic and sent it off to John then grabbed some chips and a beer and went back to my game.

I got a text back about 15 minutes later. "Boy, now that you have followed my instructions, I want you to sit and think about what kinks and fetishes you have always been interested in and why. I want you to start an email to me and put as much detail into it as possible. If I decide to move forward and work with you, this will be helpful to me as we set guidelines, boundaries, and goals for you. Do you think you can do this?"

I replied that I could, and he sent me his email address to send it to. So, I pulled out my laptop and started to think about anything that I had ever seen in a porn that interested or excited me. I thought about the relationships and sexual experiences I had over the years and put down what I liked and what I did not like and things I always wanted to do or explore. I got into the assignment and before long I had written a nearly two-page essay. But I figured that it was better to be thorough and I saved and emailed it to John before returning to my sports game.

Chris texted me after I had eaten to see how I was faring. I told him I had that blue balls feeling, and I wished I had jacked off this morning, but I was ok. He replied with a 'LOL' and told me to text him if I had any problems.

As I got ready to sleep that night, I took off all my clothes and noticed how crusted my underwear was. I had precummed a freaking ton since the cage when on. I grabbed my caged dick and full balls and squeezed them and then went to brush my teeth and get into bed.

I had grabbed an extra pillow from the closet and stuck it between my legs. Sleeping on my side was not a huge issue. I use a CPAP to sleep at night and am normally on my back or side but never on my stomach, so I figured that would work well anyway. I put on my CPAP mask, got as comfortable as I could, and prepared to get as much sleep as I could.

About two hours later I awoke to my dick straining against the cage and some discomfort. I sat there a moment hoping it would go down, but it didn't. I realized I had not used the lotion before I went to bed, so I took my mask off and got up, and used a cold rag to help the erection go down. I then grabbed the lotion and rubbed it on my balls and around the ring. I could already tell it was a bit sore in a few places, but I pulled my scrotum around and readjusted till it was comfortable again and then laid down to sleep again.

I woke up three more times that night and had to get up once more to cool my engorged member and reapply the lotion. But, when 7 am came and my alarm went off, although I was groggy from lack of sleep, I was proud I had made it. I went into the kitchen and took a picture of my locked cock next to my watch showing the time and of the key in the water bottle and sent them to John.

John texted back soon after. "Very good boy. I am impressed. Not many people make it the first night or follow instructions as well as you have. I also liked what you emailed me yesterday. You can defrost your keys and unlock and cum now. Text me after you are done with work and we can discuss the next steps."

I was very happy. I took the bottle out and put it under the tap and let the water run for a while. Seeing that it was not going fast enough, I got a pan out and started to boil some water and put the bottle in that to speed up the process. It took a while, but I got enough of the water melted to get the key out and unlock my cock.

I got hard immediately, and I looked down to see the imprints of the cage on my skin and a few red areas, but no sores or blood or skin broken, which was good. I went back to my room and grabbed my handy Fleshjack toy and stuck my cock in it and jacked off till I was shooting my load. I was so horny that I did it again about ten minutes later.

Feeling that my balls were finally well-drained, I turned my attention to a hot shower and started brewing some coffee to keep awake for the workday ahead. I was exhausted but strangely ready to do it all again.

CHAPTER THREE

My First Steps

It was a typical Monday at work. I had some paperwork to look through and some calls to make, but I was exhausted. The lack of decent sleep from the chastity cage waking me up constantly overnight made it difficult to focus. By noon, I was on my second pot of coffee and thankful that I was able to work from home today.

As I took a break for lunch, I was feeling horny again and decided to jack off a third time. Yesterday's adventure in chastity had me pent up. I was grabbing a sandwich when Chris texted me.

"So, how did it go last night?" he asked.

I realized I had forgotten to message him when I woke up.

"It went ok, I guess," I replied. "I was up several times during the night, but I did make it till the morning. John let me unlock and cum and I've done it three times so far today. LOL."

"Well damn Matt! Sounds like you got turned on by it. I know it's a kink we play with from time to time and it can be very hot," Chris said.

"Yeah," I replied, "I seem to be getting into it."

"Just be careful," Chris replied. "It can be a-dick-ting as well. LMAO"

"Uh-huh," I replied with a smiling emoji after.

The rest of the workday was pretty much normal and when I logged off the computer, I went and grabbed a soda and sat down, and pulled out my phone to text John.

"All done with work here," I said.

About ten minutes later I got a text back from John. "Sounds good boy. You up for dinner on me? I'd like to talk face-to-face."

"Sure," I replied.

"Good," he said. "Meet me at Jason's Deli across from where we ate last night. I'll be there at 6:30 pm. Text me what you want to eat, and I will order it for you. Also, bring your chastity cage with you. You can leave it in your car."

"Sounds good," I replied, and I texted him what I wanted as well.

It was 5:15 pm now, so I had time to clean up and get dressed. After I jumped in the shower, I checked my cock again. I had been paranoid that I might have got a sore or irritation from the cage given how much it kept me up last night, but it looked normal. No issues or irritations. Of course, I was getting hard again thinking about being in the cage and I started jacking off in the shower. My cock soon erupted with threads of cum leaping to the side wall of the shower and running down as the water mixed with it and washed it away.

"Ugh, that is four times today. Man, that got me horny," I said out loud to myself.

After I was all clean, I toweled off, brushed my teeth, and got my trimmer out, and did a little clean-up trim on the beard to make it less ragged-looking. Then, I rubbed some beard oil in and combed it through, put on some deodorant, and got dressed in some tight jeans to show my ass off a bit and one of my t-shirts.

I grabbed my shoes and headed back into the living room and noticed it was 5:45 pm. It would take me about 15 minutes to drive to the restaurant, park, and walk inside, so I had some time to kill. I decided to re-open the email I had sent John last night to go over what I had come up with in terms of things I was interested in exploring and what my experience level had been in various kinks.

John:

As I mentioned to you at dinner, I have had some experiences and explored a few kinks and fetishes. I would say up till now I have been 40% top and 60% bottom, but that is mostly because, well I am above average endowed, and some people just like to bottom with me. I prefer to be more subby in the bedroom and even when I top, I am not aggressive and usually, people ride me. I have some leather at home including a harness, wrist straps, and vest that I have worn to the Eagle on leather nights. I am very orally inclined and love to suck cock and eat ass. I'm a very tactile person as well and love to rub hands over someone and such.

I have always been fascinated by the dom and sub dynamic. Although I have never explored it fully, I would be interested to learn what it is like to be a true sub. In other words, in a situation where the dominant is in control of what happens and directing the sub to fulfill his pleasures. I'm into bondage as well, and although my experience is limited, have enjoyed being tied up with a little light torture including floggers and paddles, for instance. Strapping me down to a fuck bench and having the dom have his way with me is a bit of a fantasy. Wax play might be fun, though with my fur that might be a mess.

I do have some limits, though. I don't ever want to see or do anything with things like blood or scat. I am not a pain freak either, I have very low tolerance, so I need a safe word and limits on too much pain. My tits are extremely sensitive and directly connected to my cock. So, nipple clamps are insanely painful and usually off-limits.

I would like to work on my gag reflex. Although I love sucking cock, it is annoying choking on a nice one. Maybe I just need lessons on how to do it better. I also would love to learn more techniques to please a partner as well and things that can make their toes curl, for instance. I always am up for learning new things for sure whatever it is.

If I were to explore any of this, though, I would need to request some level of privacy. I have a twin brother who is not into the kinks I am into and having pictures floating around of me in situations could be confused with him. Having said that, I have no issues going to bars and making out with people, groping, and talking about sexual stuff. That is no issue at all. I hope that makes sense.

I will say you are hot as hell. I have known Chris and Rick for a while now, but have spent more time with Chris since I have known him the longest. I appreciate you talking to me and being nice about everything. I have to admit it has been a bit of a turn-on being caged and not having immediate access to the keys. I am sitting here dribbling precum as I type this out in fact.

Anyway… I hope that is enough for you.

Matt

After re-reading what I wrote, I wondered what John thought. He seemed like a nice guy, but I did not know much about him other than what was discussed yesterday at lunch. He was a friend of Rick's so that went a long way, but I still had some nervousness deep down.

I went and got my cage from the nightstand and noticed there was some dried precum on it, so I washed it with some dish soap and dried it well and stuck it in the little bag it came in with the keys, and headed out to the car to drive to dinner.

When I walked inside the restaurant, I saw John by the window to my right and I waved and came over. I sat down opposite of him. He was in a business suit which made him look even hotter.

"Glad you could meet me, boy," John said.

"I am happy to," I replied. "I like your suit!"

"Thank you very much," John said. "This is my normal work attire. I am a lawyer and work downtown. I have not had a chance to get home and change yet. So, tell me about last night. How did you sleep?"

"Well, I will be honest, it was a bit tough," I replied. "I woke up several times. Chris told me to use some lotion around the base ring to help with discomfort, but I had forgotten before I went to bed. So, the first time I woke up I put some on. However, I woke up several times after. It seems my body was just popping erections all night long."

John grinned. "Well, that is to be expected and pretty common, honestly. Your body has natural nocturnal erections, and you were probably turned on by the cage as well."

"That is true," I replied with a half-laugh.

"So, I read what you wrote to me," he said. "It sounds like you are inexperienced but wanting to learn. Let me explain more about myself. I have trained and collared many boys over the years. Most graduate after a year of service to me and are collared by a dominant master. Some have decided to move to more of a dominant role as they got older and others have left the scene or moved away. I am not looking for a partner or a boyfriend."

Rick took a drink of his iced sweet tea and then sat back and continued.

"I have a boy graduating from his service term with me this Saturday, so I will have an opening to take on another very soon. Rick and I had been talking at the gym and he suggested you might be a good fit to take the empty slot. I normally have three boys training with me at a time. Currently, in addition to the one graduating this weekend, I have one named Jay that has been in training with me for about six months, and another one named Bo that has been with me for three months. They have designated days they come by my house and have protocols they follow. I have a dungeon in my basement that is private where we explore things that please me and that they are interested in. It also helps them to learn about kinks and techniques that a lot of dominants like to explore. They also have chores to do around the house and tasks that I have them do during the week so they can learn to be a good house sub. We have weekly discussions on their progress and where they need to improve as well. I also require chastity of all my boys, and we work on extending the time in chastity as they near the end of their training period. How does that sound to you so far?" John asked me.

"That sounds interesting," I said.

I was starting to realize that this guy was the real deal, and this was not a casual thing for him. I was a little nervous, but deep down I was interested.

"Do you ever have situations where your boys are there at the same time?" I asked.

"Yes," John replied. "As I mentioned, they all have duties and tasks to perform around the house and they are to make themselves available for my pleasure. Many times, this involves collaborative work. I also have new boys partner with more experienced ones or even ones that have completed their training in the past to learn and grow. I do have parties at my house, on occasion, for my dominant friends and the boys not only help to coordinate and run the event, but they also serve as the party favors. I also will occasionally have the boys come on the same day if there are things they need to work on, and it would work better in a group environment." John replied.

We were interrupted as the waitress brought our food and I took the opportunity to grab a drink from the soda fountain as well.

When I returned, John asked me, "So what are your thoughts, boy? I want you to be honest with me."

"It sounds like it might be interesting. But is there any way we could do a trial to see if I am comfortable?" I asked.

"Of course!" John said with a laugh. "I need to ensure you are a good fit for my time as much as you are comfortable submitting around me. Would you be interested in having a little session tonight?"

I was kind of surprised he was asking to start this soon, but I was also turned on about the thought of working with him as well. I replied, "Sure that sounds like fun."

"Good. And you brought your cage with you, correct?" John asked.

"Yes," I replied.

"Yes, Sir," John corrected me. "Your first lesson is the proper way to address a dominant. If you continue training under me, I will expect you to be courteous and address me and any other dominant or friend of mine as 'Sir' or 'Master' at all times no matter where we are or in what situation."

"Yes, Sir," I replied. "I understand."

My cock twitched a bit when I said that.

"Good deal, boy. Then eat up and tell me more about yourself," John said with a smile.

We had a good dinner and I told him about my work, where I grew up, how I came to be in Atlanta, and about my family and such. He told me about his life and career as well. He was born and raised in Birmingham, Alabama but had been in the city for about fifteen years and practiced at a law firm downtown. He told me he had a house and a nice bit of private property that was perfect for entertaining.

The more we talked, the more comfortable I felt around him, but you could also just sense his authority. The way he carried himself and the way he talked and acted, you just knew he was all dom and used to being in control. I liked that.

After dinner, we left the restaurant and as we got to the parking lot, he gave me his address and told me to follow him there. He did not live too far away either, which was good.

When I pulled up to his place, I was impressed. It was at the end of a cul-de-sac and surrounded by trees on two sides. The left side had a neighbor, but a high fence was present that protected the privacy of the backyard. The yard sloped down on the right and there was a side door. I would later learn that this was the main entrance to the basement level of the house and gave access to his dungeon area and also allowed you to access the backyard that had a large in-ground pool and a pool house on about a half-acre (0.2 hectares) of land.

He pulled into the garage and had me pull behind him and park in the driveway.

"Grab your cage, boy, and follow me," he told me.

I grabbed the chastity cage out of my glovebox where I had it stored and followed him as he made his way to the right and down a small hill to the side door.

"If we continue to see each other, this is where you will enter. You will never use the front door," John said.

He punched a code into the door and the lock opened and he showed me in. A short dark hallway greeted me, but the lights came on automatically when we entered. To the right was a set of cubby holes with four colored bins in them (red, green, yellow, and black) behind locked clear doors. Three of them had nameplates above them. The one with the red bin said 'Jay', the one with the green bin said 'Bo', and the yellow one was labeled 'Johnny'. I assumed these were for the use of his current boys. The black bin had no nameplate. At the end of the short hallway was another door.

"Ok, so let's start talking protocols," John said. "The first thing I require of my boys is that they strip down and take off all their clothes. I do not allow boys to be clothed in my house unless I specifically tell them otherwise. These bins to your right are where my boys place their neatly folded clothes and anything else they bring with them like their phone and keys. It is the only space in my house that belongs to them and no one uses them but the assigned boys. The black bin is for potentials, so that is the one you will use tonight."

John reached over and pushed in a code at the side of the door that contained the black bin and the door swung open.

"Please turn your phone off before you put it in the bin," he said.

He then waited and I realized that he meant that I needed to strip now, so I started undressing nervously. I put my shoes and socks in the black bin first followed by my pants and shirt, neatly folded, and then my underwear on top. I put my keys and phone in next (after turning it off) and placed the bin back in its cubbyhole. The only thing I had left was my cage and keys in a small carrying bag.

"Well done, boy," John said. "Now, put your chastity cage on and just hold on to the keys for now."

I opened the bag and took my cage out and quickly put it on before my cock had other ideas and started to get an erection. I put on the lock and closed it and pulled and adjusted my balls till they were comfortable and then put the carrying bag in the black bin with my clothes.

John reached over and closed the door to the cubbyhole, and I heard it latch.

"Now, follow me," John said.

He led me through the second door which opened up on a large room painted a dark brown with one wall completely covered in a mirror and the opposite side had blacked-out windows and a sliding door that led out into the back yard. There were black racks, drawers, and shelves on the walls with all sorts of sex equipment including gags, whips, hoods, floggers, dildos, and other things I had no idea what were used for. There was a fuck bench, a Saint Andrews cross, a sling, and other equipment in the room as well. The floor looked to be rubber padding in most places with some black painted concrete on the side of the room we were in. To my right, in one corner, was a small table and one chair. On the floor to the left of me against the wall were three painted squares of red, green, and yellow. In the corners near the ceiling were cameras as well. It was a very well-equipped space.

"What do you think, boy?" John asked.

"I'm amazed, Sir!" I replied. "I have never seen a setup like this!"

John grinned. "Well, this is my main dungeon area. I can open the doors here on the wall to the right and have access to the pool and backyard for any parties I might throw. There is a bathroom to your left and the door next to it leads to a staircase up to the main level."

"What about the cameras?" I asked.

"Those are for not only security but for also monitoring the space, so I know when my boys come in and out, and for recording sessions as well. I like to record most sessions, but it is never shared publicly," John replied. "Ok, well now that you have seen the dungeon, let me show you upstairs."

He opened the door to my left to reveal a staircase and I followed him up to the main level of the house. To my right was the main living area and to the left was a hall to the front door. In front of me was a small reading room with bookshelves and a small desk and this led to the kitchen and dining area that extended back and connected with the living area again. It was a nice open concept design. Another staircase to my left led up to the second floor where the bedrooms were.

John took his shoes off and placed them on a rack to my right and took off his suit coat and hung it on a hanger on the rack as well. He then went into the living room to sit down and I followed behind him. "I do not allow my boys to sit on the furniture," he said. "You can sit on the floor in front of the couch here."

He pointed to an area to the right of a coffee table and I sat down on the floor cross-legged as he found a spot on the sofa.

"So, are you ok so far? Are you uncomfortable being naked in front of me? Has anything you have seen so far scared you in any way?" John asked.

"No, Sir," I replied. "To be honest, I have no problem being naked. It is a little weird being so with just this cage on, but I am fine."

"That is good to hear," John said. "I think you are pretty good-looking. I know a lot of doms look for young, hairless twinks, but I like a furry boy with meat on their bones and older boys tend to be better at following the rules. I am willing to take you on for a trial period till Wednesday evening. During this time, you will remain in chastity and I will give you daily assignments to do at home. This will include reflective writing like you did for me yesterday as well as some other tasks as well to see how obedient you are. If you are successful and please me, then we can talk about moving forward more formally. If at any point you want to stop and end the session, we can leave it on good terms, but know that it will mean I may not consider taking you on in the future, though."

He paused and allowed me to speak and I said, "I understand, Sir."

"Good boy," John replied. "Now, on the table, there is a box. It is a Bluetooth combination box that I can open with my phone."

As he said this, John picked up his phone and pressed the screen and the box whirred and popped open.

"If you agree to this trial session, I want you to put the keys to your chastity cage in the box and close and lock it," he said. "I will let you take the box home with you. If you need to end the session, you can text me and I will open the box and you will have access to the keys. If there is an emergency, you can do the same. If you do not want to start the trial, then close the box, stand, and leave the way you came."

He then watched as I took my keys and placed them in the box and closed and locked it.

"Very proud of you, boy," John said. "This is your first step. I think you can be molded into a really good sub if that is what you are willing to become, but we will see how things go from here."

He reached down and undid his pants and slid them down and I saw the bulge under his boxers start to grow. He reached in the front slit and pulled out his cock, which was every bit as thick and long as Rick's was. He began to stroke it and it grew to its full 8 inches (20 cm) and at least 5.5 in around (14 cm) in girth.

"Come here boy and show me how well you can suck a man's cock," he said.

I got up and came over to him and knelt in front of him and licked the full length of his cock. Precum had started to form at the tip and I sucked on this, taking in the sweet-tasting nectar. I brought my tongue down till my nose was deep into his bush and breathed in his scent, which was intoxicating. I began to take in one orb and suck on it and then the other. I worked my way back up his shaft and then took it in my mouth and worked up and down slowly.

John was groaning in pleasure. "Damn, boy. Rick was not kidding when he said you knew how to give a good blow job. I won't have much to teach you there."

I grinned and then continued to work up and down on his shaft using my hands as well and cupping and fondling his balls. I choked and coughed a bit, but it did not stop me from continuing.

John arched back and extended his legs and he let his feet stretch as he enjoyed the sensation. The precum was readily flowing from his large cock and I was in heaven slurping it up.

John grabbed my head and guided it slowly up and down his shaft. He brought me down to near his balls and I choked a bit again. "That's ok, boy. Take your time. Learn to take it all. You need to learn better breathing techniques. We can work on that."

This went on for about fifteen minutes before I felt his balls start to lift. He grabbed my head and forced me down just as he erupted and the cum shot to the back of my throat. I choked a bit and coughed, but I did not let any of it slip out. He kept cumming and I felt the shots hit my throat and upper palate. He growled and moaned. As his dick stopped pulsing, I let it slide from my mouth, swallowing all of his load in the process and not wasting a drop.

"Damn, boy," John said as he looked down at me. "That was amazing, and I am glad to see you did not leave any behind."

I had a grin on my face. "Thanks, Sir. I enjoyed that as well."

"Very well," John said as he stood and pulled his pants back up. "Stand up and face me."

He placed his hands on my shoulders and looked at me. "For any dom and sub relationship to work, there must be communication from both parties. I want you to be honest with me and speak your mind when I allow you to, and I promise to stay within the boundaries we may set should I take you on full time."

"I appreciate that Sir," I replied.

He removed his hands and gave a slight slap to my ass. "Good, well take the box with your keys in it and I want you to leave the way you came through the side door. The code for the black bin with your belongings is 7789. You can dress when you get to the entrance hall, just be sure to close the door to the dungeon before you leave. I will text you later with your first task."

"Thanks, Sir, I look forward to it," I replied.

I crossed the room and went back down the staircase into the playroom and back into the small hall closing the door behind me. I got my clothes out of the black bin and redressed and headed back outside to my car to drive home.

As I was driving, I reached down and felt the cage. I was already getting hard at the thought of having the cage on not for just one night, but for two nights this time and the keys were much harder to get to as well. Before, I could have just melted the ice whenever I wanted, took the cage off, jacked off, and put it back on, and refroze the keys had I wanted. Now, there was no access to them without texting John. This was going to be interesting.

CHAPTER FOUR

The Trial Period

It was 9 pm or so when I got back into my apartment. I normally go to bed about 10:30 pm or so, and given how bad I slept last night, I was exhausted. About 15 minutes after I got home, I got a text from John.

"Did you make it home ok, boy?" he asked.

"I did, Sir," I replied. "Getting ready for bed soon."

"I understand," John said. "While we are in this trial period, I want you to start following some protocols at home. I want you to strip and fold your clothes and leave them next to the door whenever you come home. You need to get used to being naked and comfortable in your cage. Please do that now and send me a picture."

I had taken my shoes off by the door, but I returned to the threshold and stripped down entirely. I had to pull on my balls a bit to get them adjusted right in the cage, but once I was comfortable, I moved away from the wall a bit and held up the phone and snapped a picture and sent it off.

"Good boy," John texted back. "I will periodically text you for a picture. I expect a response within a reasonable amount of time. The quicker the better. If you are working from home, you will be naked. If you are in the office, you will find a private place and pull out your chastity cage for the picture. I want you kneeling if possible."

"I understand, Sir. I can do that," I replied.

"Second, for this trial, I don't want you to sit on any furniture in your house. You may sleep in your bed, but I want you to get used to sitting on the floor," he said.

I had returned to the living room and was sitting on the couch when he sent this, so I got up and sat down on the floor in front of the couch and replied that I understood that as well.

"Finally, tonight's task. From your picture you just sent me it appears your living room needs straightening up. I want you to vacuum the area completely, dust, throw away any trash and make the place as spotless as possible. Do the same for your kitchen, bedroom, and bathroom and then send me a picture," John texted.

I groaned at this. I hated cleaning but he was right, the place was a bit of a pigsty. I texted back "Yes, Sir," and then put my phone down to go grab the vacuum. I figured I would do that first to get that out of the way since it was late, and I didn't want to annoy the downstairs neighbors.

The kitchen just needed the dishes done and a wipe down of the surfaces. I put everything in the dishwasher to save time. The bedroom took a while as I had to fold several loads of laundry and put those away. While I was doing that, I noticed I was having to adjust my cage a lot. It was a cheap cage, so I guess it was expected to not fit as well. I was not going to come out of it, but it was pinching a bit here and there.

After my bedroom was presentable, I went into the bathroom and turned on the light. I got on my knees and scrubbed the toilet first, then I moved on to the shower and sink, bagging up the trash as I went.

It was almost 11 pm by the time I was done. I figured it might be late for him, but I texted John pictures of the clean apartment. At this point, I was exhausted and a sweaty mess. I turned the shower on just to rinse down quickly and after I dried off, I collapsed on the bed. I remembered to put some lotion around my balls where the base ring to the chastity cage was and then I put a pillow between my legs, my CPAP mask on, and fell fast asleep.

I was so exhausted from the night before and from spending a few hours cleaning that I only woke up twice during the night. The first time I had to use a cold washcloth to help my erection subside, but the second time only took a little adjusting of the cage while I was in bed. When the alarm went off at 7 am, I was still a bit tired, but much more rested than before.

I checked my phone and noticed that John had sent me a message at 6 am telling me that I did a good job on the cleaning and that he would check in on me later. So, I got out of bed and took a long hot shower. I was about to get dressed when I remembered the protocol of no clothes in the house. So, I took what I was going to wear and put it on a chair next to my apartment door and then went to the kitchen to put the dishes away from inside the dishwasher from the night before and then start breakfast.

After I was done, I looked down and saw a stream of precum dangling from my caged cock. Normally, I jack off when I wake up, but that was not happening today. I caught the dangling rope of fluids and licked it off my fingers and then grabbed some paper towels to clean up the rest. I decided to make a quick breakfast as a distraction.

I scrambled some eggs and made some toast and poured myself a glass of orange juice. I was about to sit down at the table to eat when I remember the other protocol of not sitting on the furniture. Ugh. This was going to be annoying. So, I just ate standing at the kitchen countertop. When I was done, I put the dishes in the dishwasher and went to the door to put my clothes on and head off to work.

This was the first time I had worn my chastity cage under my clothes in public. It did not make a huge bulge in my pants, but I was self-conscious about it all the time. Fortunately, I have a desk job, so I was able to keep hidden most of the time. It was about 10:30 am when I got a text from John asking for a picture. I closed my office door and pulled down my pants and knelt on the floor for a selfie and sent it off within 60 seconds.

"Very well done boy. Very fast too. I am pleased. I hope you have a good rest of the day," John replied.

I grinned when I got the message and pulled my pants up and was just sitting down when my coworker came in the door to ask me something. In the back of my head, I panicked a bit and realized how close I came to being caught, literally, with my pants down. I needed to be sure to lock the door next time.

The rest of the day was pretty mundane. I was done a little early, so I headed back home to beat the traffic a bit. As I was getting to my car in the parking lot, Chris texted me.

"Hey bud, Rick is going to be late getting home tonight. Do you mind if I stop by and hang out a bit?"

I replied, "sure" and was just driving out of the lot when I realized that I was not allowed clothes on in my apartment nor was I to sit on the furniture. I panicked a bit and found a place to pull over to text Chris back.

"Hey, there is just one thing. This John guy that Rick knows is key holding for me for a few days, so I have my cage on and he has some specific protocols I have to follow as well."

"Well, that is hot," Chris replied. "What do you have to do?"

"Well, I am not allowed clothes on in my apartment and I can't use the furniture except the bed," I texted back.

"Damn! You already sound like you are in training!" Chris replied with a laughing emoji. "I don't care though. I have seen you naked you know."

"LOL. Well, that is true. Ok, well as long as you understand," I replied to Chris.

"I'll be over about 6 pm and I will bring pizza," Chris texted.

"Sounds good to me!" I replied.

When I got home, I stripped down and folded all my clothes and put them on the chair next to the door and went to the kitchen to grab a beer and relax. I sat down on the floor between my couch and coffee table and watched some TV till Chris arrived.

I heard a knock at the door about 6:10 pm and saw it was Chris through the peephole with a pizza in his hands. I let him in, and he looked at my naked and caged cock and replied, "Look at you being all subby and cute!"

"Yeah, yeah. I know," I replied.

Chris reached down and squeezed my caged balls and said, "Damn, you only had that thing a few weeks and you are already giving the key away, I'm seeing a whole new side to you sexy!"

I blushed. "Thanks, but this is a lot to take in the first time. John seems to be nice and I feel I can trust him. Hell, I gave him control of my keys. But the protocols are something new."

"Eh. You can handle it. I know people a hell of a lot kinkier than you are bubba," Chris said with a laugh. "Let's eat, I am hungry!"

I grabbed some plates for the pizza and Chris took his to the couch. I sat down next to his feet and ate at the coffee table.

"You know, I could get used to you in chastity at my feet," Chris said with a smirk rubbing his foot in the crack of my ass.

"Uh-huh," I replied sarcastically as I turned around to face him. "I seem to remember you in chastity too."

"Oh, I know. But I am not now, and it is kind of hot. I think you might need to turn around and get on your knees and give me a blow job right now."

I looked up at him and he put his plate on the side table and gave me this look and pointed at his crotch which was bulging. Not wanting to be a bad host, I grabbed a drink to wash everything down and turned around, got on my knees, and undid his pants. Out popped his cock fully hard and dripping.

"Damn Chris. You are turned on, aren't you?" I asked.

Chris nodded and leaned his head back and I went down on him. He has an average-sized cock, so it was a lot easier to deep throat, but I always loved his balls. They are massive and fun to play with. I took my hands and started to move up and down his shaft and forced my face down on his cock on the downstroke to take him in fully. I continued to stroke his cock and moved my mouth down to suck on his big balls and nibble on them, which I already knew drove him wild.

Chris bit his bottom lip and was groaning and reached down and grabbed my head and pulled it off his cock.

"You think I can fuck you, Matt?" Chris asked.

"Sure, I am game, but why don't we go to the bedroom so I can use the bed," I replied.

So, we headed back, and I handed him the lube and hit some poppers and leaned over the side of the bed. Chris took no time in mounting me and I felt his balls slapping mine pretty soon after. The problem was my balls and cock were trapped inside the cage and the slapping of his huge sack sent stimulation into my groin. I could not get an erection, but I swelled to the full extent of the cage and I felt precum start to dribble out.

Chris's cock had a slight downward bend, so every thrust brought the head across my prostate. The sensation was fucking wonderful and I reached down between my legs and grabbed the cage. I felt my swollen member behind the bars and precum coated my hand. All I wanted to do at that moment was stroke my shaft.

Chris had a hold of my hips and was pounding me furiously when I felt him tense up. "Fuck!" he yelled. I put my hands by my sides to steady myself as I felt him slam home and his cock started pulsing rhythmically, dumping his load deep in my ass.

After a few more strokes back and forth, he leaned on his arms on my back and let his cock finish releasing its seed. When he finally pulled out, I heard a plop from the cum and lube escaping and landing on the floor.

"Woops!" said Chris laughing. "I think I overfilled you! Sorry about the mess on the floor."

"No need to be sorry," I said, rising from my crouched position. "I can clean that up."

I walked over to the bathroom and felt the cum dribbling out of my ass and down my legs. I grabbed a towel and wiped it up and then wet it a bit to return and clean the floor. Chris grabbed the edge to wipe down with as well.

"Damn Matt!" said Chris as I was putting the towel in the dirty hamper.

"What is it?" I asked.

Chris was pointing at the bed. "Look at that wet spot!"

He was right. I had precummed so much from the fucking that there was a huge wet spot on them.

"Well, you know I precum a ton and I am locked and horny as well," I said with a laugh grabbing my cage and showing how strained I was inside it.

Chris noticed and walked by me into the bathroom and turned on the cold tap and soaked a washcloth on the counter. He brought it back over and wrapped it around my caged cock and I jumped a bit, but I did start to soften.

"The struggle is real," Chris said. "I've been there."

After my cock had returned to its flaccid state, we went to go back to eating and as I sat down, I got a text from John. He wanted a picture of what I was doing. So, I sent him one back of me sitting down on the floor with my pizza. Chris's bare legs and soft cock were in the background behind my head and shoulders.

"Who is that behind you?" he asked.

I replied that it was Rick's partner Chris and that he had just finished fucking a load into me.

"Good, boy. Sounds like you are already being of service. Enjoy your evening and check your email later," John replied.

"Was that John?" Chris asked.

"Yeah," I replied. "He likes me to send him pics when he requests them."

"Was he ok with what we just did?" Chris replied.

"It's not like we are dating or anything. Yeah, he told me it was good I was being of service," I responded.

"Ok. That's cool," said Chris as he reached down and fondled himself.

After we finished dinner, we played some video games for a while. Chris was occasionally playing with his cock and eventually, he was hard again.

"I think we need to take a quick break," he said. "You need to suck a second load out of my cock."

I turned to see him at full mast with a devilish grin looking down at me.

"Damn, boy," I said. "What's got into you?"

"Umm… the last time I checked, the one that wears the chastity cage is the boy," he said pointing at me, "and that means you should be ready to take loads whenever."

I laughed. "Ok, you win, but I think this is giving you a bit of a power trip."

"Hey," Chris said with a smirk, "don't ruin this for me. I don't get to top much."

I got up on my knees again and took his cock into my mouth. I could still taste a little bit of the lube and my ass from the last time we played. I did not care, though, as I do love to give blowjobs.

Chris leaned back and stretched his feet out and I used my hands to move up and down on his shaft as I bobbed on his head. I reached up at one point and played with his nipples and that got an immediate reaction as a spurt of precum came out and I sucked it down.

As I was moving up and down and deep throating him, I felt his balls move and knew he was close, so I sped up a bit until he was shooting in my mouth. I made sure to stay on him till every last spurt was swallowed and then I sucked a little bit more till he jumped and shoved my face off.

"Hey!" he said. "You know I am sensitive after I cum!"

I was laughing. "You know you love it."

Chris leaned back and put his arms on either side of the back of the couch and stretched to cool off some.

"Seriously, though, thanks," he said. "That was freaking amazing."

"Hey!" I said pointing at myself. "Chastity boy ready to serve here."

"I am starting to see that," Chris said with a wink.

It was getting close to 9 pm, so Chris got up and went and got his clothes on. As he grabbed his keys, I gave him a kiss and a hug and thanked him for the pizza. He grabbed my ass a bit and thanked me for the fuck and then he left.

After cleaning the apartment up a bit from dinner and the activities, I went to my laptop and checked my email. John had sent me a task to complete.

> Boy:
>
> For your task this evening, I want you to define the terms sub and dom. I want you to be as detailed as you can be. I want you to think, though, what these terms mean to you, or what you would like them to mean to you.
>
> Send me your response along with a picture of yourself on your knees with your hands behind your back and your head bowed.
>
> Have a good evening - Sir

This one took a bit more thought. I started by doing some research online and reading articles from the mainstream press and BDSM sites. It was fascinating to see common threads in some areas and widely different views in others. However, I was able to put my thoughts together eventually.

> Sir:
>
> I have been sitting here thinking over what at first looks like a simple thing to define. I have been reading definitions online and also thinking about how I feel about the terms as well. Dom to me means the one that has more authority. The sub has the role of giver and the dom the receiver. I see the dynamic as the sub giving of himself to please the dom and in doing so gain pleasure through the giving. I know for me, if I were to take on a total sub role, that is what I would like it to be. The more I have read, though, the more I understand what you told me about the importance of communication. You must be honest and straightforward with your dom as a sub. You need to listen to them and make sure their needs are met for a healthy relationship to work.
>
> Boy

Satisfied with my email, I set up my camera with the timer and took my picture kneeling with my arms behind my back and my head bowed and attached it and sent it off.

I went back to watching some TV and played some games a bit before getting up to get ready for bed. As I was brushing my teeth, I got a text on my phone from John.

"Good answer boy. I appreciate your thoughts. How is the chastity going?"

I messaged him back that I was doing ok and that last night was not as bad as the night before.

"I am glad to hear that," John replied. "I will be working from home tomorrow. After you are done with work, I want you to message me and I will have you come over and we can remove your cage and then discuss the next steps."

I replied, "I will, Sir!"

I got into bed and only woke up once during the night this time. It seemed my body was rapidly adjusting to sleeping with the cage on my dick.

CHAPTER FIVE

The Contract

My day in the office on Wednesday was pretty normal. John asked for a picture around lunchtime and I remembered to lock the door before taking it this time. The whole afternoon I was straining in my cage and making a mess of my underwear. I had to go to the bathroom a few times to clean up all the precum. The thought of getting out of my cage and jacking off several times was something I was looking forward to.

I texted John as I headed out to the parking lot after work. "All done, Sir."

"Sounds good, boy. Come to my house and park in the driveway. Enter through the side door using the code 1998. Strip naked and put your things in the black bin. The code for that bin is 7789. I want you to go into the dungeon area and kneel next to the table on the right when you enter the room. Put the lockbox with your key in it on the table as well," John replied. "I will have the cameras on downstairs, so I will know when you are there."

"Ok, Sir," I texted back. "I should be there in thirty minutes."

When I arrived, I followed his instructions. Upon entering the dungeon area, I looked to my right and the low table I saw before was still there with a chair on one side. Figuring that chair would be for John, I knelt on the opposite side of the table, placed the lockbox that contained my key on the table, and waited.

It was a little cool in the room, especially given this part had just a black painted concrete floor and my balls were contracting a bit but were constrained by the cage from getting too small. As I knelt there totally naked in the quiet of the room, I felt vulnerable. I looked to the corners of the room and knew the cameras were on. I figured John was just watching and waiting and taking his time.

After about 15 minutes, I heard someone coming down the staircase and the door into the room opened and John came inside. He was casually dressed in sweatpants and a t-shirt and was in his bare feet. I noticed they had tufts of hair on them as well, so although I had never seen him fully naked, I figured he was a pretty hairy guy. In one hand was a manilla envelope and in the other was a glass with ice in it and what I assumed was whiskey or something similar.

"Good to see you again, boy," John said as he crossed the room and sat down in the chair opposite me.

"Hello, Sir," I replied.

"So, tell me, how did you survive the two nights of chastity and the rules I gave you at home to follow?" he asked.

"Honestly, Sir, it was not too bad. I had to remember and catch myself a few times with the rules, but I obeyed them. As far as the cage, last night I only woke up once, so it seems to be getting better. I will admit, though, I am ready to have this off and jack off several times, though," I said with a laugh.

John's expression did not change though, and I quit laughing quickly.

"Well, I am glad to hear that you are adapting to the cage," he replied after a pause.

John placed the envelope in front of me and leaned back in the chair and took a drink from his glass. The ice clinked a few times and had a light echo in the quiet room.

"I have been thinking about you a lot today. You have impressed me, boy. As I have said, I will have an opening soon and am willing to take on a new sub for training and I think you might have what it takes; however, I can see there are some things we need to discuss first," John said.

"Ok, Sir," I replied looking down at the envelope and back at him.

"I need to know you are interested and committed to the training. This is not something I do as a whim or every so often. I look at it as a service agreement. I am willing to take you on to train and mold you, but you have to fully embrace the training and follow all rules that are set forth."

John took another drink from his glass and put it down on the table and leaned forward.

"I need to know, are you interested in entering into a formal arrangement with me?" he asked.

"It is an intriguing offer, Sir," I replied. "But I would like to know more about what you are thinking about."

"Well, that is what the envelope is for," John continued. "Inside is a standard contract that I offer to all boys that pass the initial test phase, which you have done. I will not alter anything in this contract, but there will be an addendum added that will be crafted with your input that covers any limits you might have."

I looked down at the envelope wondering what was in it and just how detailed this arrangement was supposed to be. I had just got into chastity a few weeks ago. I had just been playing around before I met this man. But it excited me as well. I was feeling a rush. Was this the hormones raging because I have not had an orgasm in a few days or was this something I was truly considering?

John grabbed his drink and sat back again. "Open the envelope boy and read it over. I dated it for this coming Sunday, so we will have a chance to discuss it today and you can take it home and think about it before making any final decisions. I am going to go back upstairs and refresh my drink. When I return, we can talk more."

He stood and left the room and I reached out and broke the seal on the manilla envelope and slid out the paperwork to read it.

SUBORDINATE SERVICE CONTRACT

This subordinate service contract (hereafter referred to as the "Agreement" or "Contract") dated Sunday, March 8, 2015, is between the undersigned (hereinafter called "the sub") and John Dante, hereafter referred to as "Sir", and pertains Sir's rights as key holder and trainer for the sub.

Section 1: Roles

The sub will always address Sir with this title and nothing else. As the sub's trainer, Sir will promise that in his presence he will tend to the sub's physical safety and emotional and mental well-being and will always adhere to the precepts of this contract with the sub as long as the sub is in his service. Sir accepts the commitment to treat the sub as detailed in this contract, to train, discipline, punish, and reward the sub and use the sub as Sir sees fit. Sir accepts the responsibility to use his power to mold and shape the sub, assist the sub to grow in strength, character, confidence, and being, and to help the sub become better in all areas of life.

The sub's primary purpose is to serve, obey, and please Sir and others in a manner that Sir sees fit. It is understood that the sub will have a designated time to visit and serve Sir as outlined in the ADDENDUM to this contract. While in Sir's presence, the sub shall follow any rituals and guidelines as established with the understanding that breaking a ritual or guideline will lead to some form of punishment. The sub agrees to follow the direction and commands given as it pertains to his daily life, to include, but not limited to, the following: gear and clothing or lack thereof; extracurricular and social activities; household chores; personal grooming including hairstyle and body hair; and to be in chastity (see next section). These specifics will be laid out in the ADDENDUM to this contract. The sub will always respond to the sexual needs of Sir. The sub will at all times act in a manner that is respectful of Sir, to include manners of obedience, loyalty, and honesty.

Section 2: Chastity and Service

As the sub's key holder and trainer, the sub gives Sir the right to determine how the sub is used and when. A key aspect of the sub's service is chastity. Sir will secure the sub's genitals, hereafter referred to as his nub, in any sort of chastity device of Sir's choosing. The sub will wear the device as a symbol of its commitment to the service of dominant men. However, Sir will provide a Bluetooth lock box with a spare key in it for the sub to take home. If there are any emergencies, the sub can contact Sir at any time and Sir can unlock the device if Sir deems the issue serious enough. The sub may not attempt to remove or circumvent any device with which Sir fits the sub in except in emergencies as described. Any attempt to do so may serve as a breach of the contract and Sir will have the ability to punish or release the sub from service at that time.

The sub must keep himself clean and well cared for so that the wearing of the device is not impeded on health grounds and the sub can continue to be locked up. This includes keeping the sub's nub washed regularly and inspecting it for any rashes, sores, or any other health issues. The sub may also submit to prostate milking to keep the sub's prostate healthy. The sub may request such a session at any time; however, the timing is solely at the discretion of Sir. At least one milking session must occur every two weeks.

As the sub's key holder and trainer, Sir will lock up the sub's nub to deprive the sub of the ability to regularly play with itself, attain erection or orgasm through stimulation to his nub. It is the goal that the sub understands and embraces the idea that selfish self-pleasure is not its main goal. The sub will reorient its mind to enjoy the pleasure experienced by the men the sub services. Additionally, the sub will be encouraged to learn how to orgasm from anal stimulation alone. The sub is to look upon its locked nub as a symbol of service. The sub is expected to keep Sir informed of its experiences in wearing its device. The sub will take pictures and report in for Sir as requested as quickly as possible.

As a sub, it agrees to have the privilege of having daily access to its nub and personal self-gratification denied and will be grateful for the service it will perform for other men. To facilitate this change, the sub will be given short locking periods in its chastity cage followed by releases and a manually stimulated orgasm. Over time, these periods of chastity will be increased. At the end of a year schedule to be added as part of the ADDENDUM to this contract, the sub will be expected to submit to permanent chastity and be given one last manually stimulated orgasm from its nub as part of its graduation to full sub status.

The sub's body will be used for the pleasure and satisfaction of Sir and other men upon their request. The sub is expected to service Sir and give him pleasure through the use of the sub's ass, mouth, and/or body. However, Sir also agrees that the sub will not permanently hurt the sub in any way nor will Sir permanently mark the sub, as this is the right of the Master that eventually will collar it (see next section). At any point, the sub can call out and request a "time out" if the sub feels that things have gone too far using the safe word "TELEPHONE". However, this may also serve as a breach of the contract and Sir will have the ability to release the sub from service at that time. Sir will abide by the ADDENDUM drawn up and attached to this contract detailing the sub's hard limits.

As part of this arrangement, Sir agrees to keep the arrangement secret in the sub's public life. However, if Sir and the sub are together at a public or private event, the sub is not entitled to have its subordinate and neutered status kept secret. In such a case, Sir may decide to inform anyone as he sees fit, have the sub display itself and/or its nub, and have the sub perform tasks.

At least once a month, Sir will unlock the sub's nub and remove the chastity device for a deep cleaning. At this time, the sub will have its arms bound and will be blindfolded. It is not to see itself out of chastity for the duration of this contract. If it is at the end of a locking session, Sir will manually manipulate the sub's nub to full orgasm. While out of the cage, the nub will be inspected and shaved, and/or trimmed per Sir's wishes.

As a sub, it will always be grateful and take pleasure in the fact that Sir has taken the time to train it in the proper way to please dominant men. The sub should always thank Sir for securing its nub in chastity and let Sir know how grateful it is to embrace its new life.

Section 3: Training, Collaring and Future Service

Upon signing this contract, the sub will receive a training collar provided by Sir. It is not to be removed, except in emergencies or in case of medical necessity. It can be hidden under clothes while at work, but it is expected to be displayed at all other times.

It is the ultimate goal for the sub to be trained to a point that it becomes a permanently locked sub so it can enter into full-time service to a dominant man or Master. Sir will always plan duties, tasks, and expectations for the sub so that this ultimate goal may be reached. As such, Sir will train the sub to experience various kink activities that it might be required to perform or be involved in. This includes CBT, flogging, whipping, bondage, discipline, sensory deprivation, wax play, watersports, and other kinks as agreed to by Sir and the sub. The sub will also learn to service Sir through household duties and acting as a footstool or a piece of furniture.

Should the sub reach a point of permanent chastity one year after signing this contract, the sub will receive a graduation collar indicating full status as a trained sub that can be recognized by other dominant men. Indeed, it is expected at a future time that the sub will be taken in and owned by another dominant man in the future and will leave the service of Sir. At this point, this contract will become null and void.

Section 4: Punishments

The sub and Sir agree that appropriate punishments are necessary for the growth of the sub. The following is a list of potential punishments the Sir can use on the sub with the understanding that the list can be altered or added to at any time depending on the effectiveness of the punishment. Punishments may include writing assignments; timeouts/isolation/forced to stay in a room or other location alone for an extended period without any form of electronic devices: e.g., iPhone, iPad, Laptop, and TV; CBT; whipping and/or flogging; spanking; and public and semi-public acts. Hard limits will be honored as detailed in the ADDENDUM to this contract.

Section 5: Alteration

This contract may not be altered, except when both Sir and the sub agree. If the contract is altered, the new contract shall be printed and signed, and then the old contract must be destroyed.

Section 6: Suspension

Under certain circumstances, events, and conditions, suspension of this contract may be wanted, warranted, and executed for a determined period. Sir will determine if a suspension is warranted.

Section 7: Termination

Under certain circumstances, events, and conditions, termination of this contract may be wanted, warranted, and executed, but must be an absolute last option when no other recourse is possible. Sir will determine if termination is warranted.

SIGNATURE OF "THE SUB"

I have read and fully understand this contract in its entirety. I agree to enter into service with Sir. I understand that I will be commanded, trained, and punished as a submissive, and I promise to be true and to fulfill the pleasures and desires of my Sir to the best of my abilities.

_____ Signature

SIGNATURE OF SIR

I have read and fully understand this contract in its entirety. I will accept the sub into my service and will command him, train him, reward him, and punish him as a submissive. I understand the responsibility implicit in this arrangement and agree that no harm shall come to the sub as long as he is in my service.

_____ Signature

This was not a joke, I thought as I finished reading and put the paperwork down. He is serious about this. Parts of the contract had me nervous and I also had no idea if this was something I truly wanted to even consider. As I sat there, I heard John coming back downstairs, enter the room and then cross the room to sit down in front of me again.

"Well, boy," he said, sipping his drink, "What do you think?"

"This is a lot more detailed than I expected Sir, I will be honest," I replied.

"Oh, that I am sure," John said. "Most boys I present this to have blank stares when I return and are sometimes shaking. That is why I have built-in time for you to think about this. Today is Wednesday and the contract is dated for Sunday. You have that amount of time to think this over. I will unlock you before you leave, and you can return to your normal life and do not have to follow any protocols I set up for you the past few days. We will not speak, and I ask that you do not text me as I will be preparing for my boy's graduation ceremony this week here at the house. Take this downtime to think this over carefully."

John paused to take another sip and I continued to quietly listen to him.

"I do; however, want to take some time right now to give you a chance to ask any questions you might have right now," he said.

"I think I need time to read this over some more, but I did want to ask that if I decide not to do this, or if I do and then end the contract early, will I still be able to see you?" I asked.

"Not in a sexual context, no," he replied. "I will be happy to acknowledge you in a social setting if you choose not to be in my service, but that will be it."

"I understand, Sir. What is this part about an addendum?" I asked.

"Ahh. Very good. You have paid attention. As I mentioned to you before, I will respect any hard limits you might have. On Saturday night, if you plan to come here Sunday and sign this contract, I want you to email me any hard limits you have when it comes not only to sexual play but also any interactions as well. For instance, I have had some boys that are highly claustrophobic and cannot handle being bound in small spaces. I have had boys that refused to drink piss or boys that were deathly afraid of things like needle play. I need to know anything you find as a hard limit. This does not mean we will not try some of them to see if we can make you more comfortable in experiencing them, but it will not be a line I will push you initially," John replied.

"I understand, Sir," I said, with some nervousness still in my body.

"The addendum will also be where I will detail the length of your chastity sessions and when you will be released for manual manipulation of your nub," John added.

"Finally, along those lines, if I understand this right, once I sign this contract, I will be put into chastity, and from that point on I will be blindfolded and bound when I am given a chance to orgasm. Does that mean it is possible I may never see my cock again out of the cage once I sign?" I asked.

"You are correct," said John. "That is why you need to think very carefully on this and determine if this is truly what you want. Only the very few can live up to the caliber of a sub I expect. Indeed, often I have to take in boys from other parts of the country that are up to the challenge."

I swallowed hard and sat quietly there for a moment after he finished.

John placed his glass down on the table to break the silence. "Well, boy, I am looking forward to seeing what the future holds for you, but in the meantime, you need to be rewarded for your successful completion of my trial period."

He clapped his hands together and stood up and told me to rise and led me across the room over to a leather-covered table. It had space in the middle where I assume a cock could dangle down if you were on your stomach. It also had places in the corners with restraints as well.

"Hop up here face-up and get comfortable," John said. "I am going to restrain you, but I promise you are in for a fun and enjoyable time."

I got up on the table on my back and he pulled my arms back to the corners and tied my hands and arms down. He did the same with my ankles and legs. At this point, he flipped up a segment of the table under my feet and then reached under and released a lever that allowed him to tilt the table at about 20 degrees. My weight slid a bit till I was resting on the segment he had under my feet. I was as comfortable as I could be, but I could not move.

John went over to the side of the room and grabbed a device that was on a box on wheels. It looked like a big pump with tubes and what looked like what you would put on a cow to milk it. He plugged it in and flipped some switches and then turned to me.

"So, have you ever had a milking machine used on you?" he asked me.

"Umm, no. What is that?" I replied.

John grinned. "Well, you are in for a ride my boy. This device not only creates a suction on your nub but also gently massages you as well. It will feel wonderful at first, but it is relentless. It will continue to stroke you till it brings you over the edge and you will have a strong orgasm as it drains your balls dry. The tubes will extract your semen and collect it in a container here on the side. But the fun does not stop there. It will continue to work on you for as long as it is turned on. The last guy I had on this machine had three orgasms and by the fourth, he was shooting blanks and begging for it to stop."

I was turned on by this and a bit frightened at the same time.

"To make it interesting, I will make a bet with you. If you can make it to three orgasms, I will give you 50 dollars. If you make it to four, I will give you 100 dollars and I will add 100 dollars to any orgasm after that. You decide when you need to quit. How does that sound boy?" John asked me.

Now, this sounded like a challenge I was up for. "Ok, I am game!" I said with a grin.

John went over to the table and pushed in a code and the lockbox opened and he retrieved my key. He then returned and unlocked the lock on my chastity cage and removed the device. He took a second to explore my cock and balls to ensure everything was ok.

"You are a little red in places here, but no skin is broken. However, I think you need a different device for a better fit, so I will make sure we have that for you on Sunday if you choose to return," John said.

He then brought the tube over and used some lube from a container with a pump on it to massage my cock. I got hard instantly, and he brought the tube over and placed it on my cock. He flipped a switch and the device started moving and sucking. He had to adjust some strings and connections that held it over my body so that it was not moving around a lot and had a good fit, but eventually the suction took hold, and the feeling was incredible.

It felt so silky and smooth and the sensation was out of this world. The device would slow down and speed up on a pre-programmed routine and I was groaning and writhing as much as I could in my restraints.

John brought the chair over and sat down and watched as he sipped his drink. The whole thing was being taped, he knew, and this would make for some fun viewing after.

I had not cum in several days, so I knew it would not take long, and sure enough, only about five minutes later my balls jumped, and I growled in pleasure as the device extracted the first load. I watched as my cock continued to pulse under the suction of the machine and my load was drawn up in a tube to be deposited in another container. I collapsed, but the device did not stop.

"Well, boys," John said, "That's number one!"

I stayed hard in the device and the continued massaging and sucking immediately made me squirm. I am very sensitive after I climax and had I not been tied down I know I would have ripped the machine off instantly. I cried a bit in a little pain but mostly pleasure and it continued to work.

It took about ten minutes of sucking and slurping and massaging my shaft, but I could feel the sensation again, and when it came, I screamed as the second load was pulled from my cock and shot up the tube. It was much more intense than the first time and I was even more sensitive after.

"That's two!" John said with an evil grin.

"Oh, fuck," I replied. "I don't know about this."

"Take a deep breath boy, you can do this," John replied.

My cock went a bit limp after the second load, so John had to get up and hold the device firm against me so it would not move. Thus, it continued its relentless pulsing and suction, eventually getting me hard again after fifteen minutes.

John reached over and turned a knob and the device sped up and increased its suction a bit. I yelled and groaned as it forcefully worked to compel my balls to release what remained of any stored seed. Eventually feeling the sensation build and my cock erupt a third time.

"Holy fuck!" I screamed.

"That's three," John said. "You just earned yourself fifty dollars boy!"

"Motherfucker!" I screamed and the device continued to pull at my very sore and drained cock. My balls were on fire as well. I did not know how much more I could take of this.

"So, are we stopping?" John asked.

"No!" I cried. "Keep going!" I was in pain but pleasure as well. The sensation was the most intense I have ever had, but I wanted to see what my limit was.

"Impressive, boy," John said. "Most impressive."

John had to reach over and hold the device again and change the speed and suction to stop it from falling off as I got soft again. The remnants of my last load were sucked away, and you could hear a slurping sound from air getting in and some of the residual cum and lube interacting with the device.

It took a good 20-25 minutes, but I eventually got hard again. Not fully hard, but enough that I knew my cock was trying. I was so sore, and my balls ached, but I had to try. John turned up the speed and the suction and sat back as the machine did its job.

When the sensation hit my body, it was no longer pleasure anymore, it was pain. My cock tensed up, my balls leaped up and what would have been a fourth load came out, but it was mostly dry and more milky than white. I screamed in pain and told John I could take no more and to stop it.

John grinned and reached over and turned off the device and removed it once all the remnants of my semen had been drained away. As he removed the device, my cock, red and sore flopped to the side and I cringed.

"Holy fuck that was intense," I said.

"Well, you earned yourself 100 dollars today. Very well done. Most guys don't make it past the second one," John said. He moved the device over and went and got a wet washcloth to wipe me down.

After he was done, he said, "I'll be right back. Just take deep breaths."

He left the room and went upstairs. When he returned, he had a bottle of vodka in his hands which he placed on the floor next to the table. He returned the table to a horizontal level and then took my restraints off. He helped me get up and sit on the side of the table and handed me a 100-dollar bill with a smile.

He then reached around and pulled the container off the side of the device that contained the loads that had been extracted from my balls. He removed the lid and looked at the side where there was a measurement listed.

"Looks like about 12 ml of semen there, boy," John said. "That is a pretty impressive production. One thing you will learn if you decide to sign the contract is that I do not allow waste of semen or precum, mine or yours. There is a little lube mixed in here because it is needed for the device to work, but it is safe for consumption. However, I find a little vodka cuts the taste."

He reached down and added about a shot of vodka to the container and swirled it around to mix it well.

"I needed to wait a bit for your semen to melt, as they say, but it should be all mixed there now," John said as he handed me the container. "Drink up boy. Time to recycle that seed."

I swallowed the shot in one gulp, and it burned a bit going down, and had a slimy taste, but was not too bad.

"Very well," John said. "Your chastity device and keys are on the table over there along with the contract in the folder. Take them with you and think things over. Again, I do not want to hear from you until Saturday night. If you plan to come over, then send me your addendum ideas for the contract and if you do not plan to come over, then maybe I will see you out at the Eagle sometime."

He helped me off the table and as I went to get my cage and the envelope, he went about cleaning up the table and the device. I went back into the small hallway closing the door behind me and as I got dressed to leave, I started thinking about the big decision I had in front of me.

CHAPTER SIX

The Decision

When I got back home from John's house and walked in the door, I started stripping down before I realized that I did not need to do that anymore. I was surprised how fast I had adapted to the protocols that John had given me. I left my pants and socks on but did remove my shirt and sat down on the couch for the first time in a few days. My chest hair was still a bit matted from the sweat that I built up from the intense time with the milking machine and I ran my hands through it and then adjusted my sore balls.

After catching my breath, I put my cage on the table beside me and stared at the manilla envelope containing the contract for a moment before putting it on the table as well.

"I can think about that later," I said to myself.

I pulled my socks off and threw them on the floor and went into the kitchen to reheat some leftovers. When I brought it into the living room to eat, I instinctively sat on the floor again and put my food on the table.

"Well," I said to myself. "One thing you have learned is that you train quickly."

I laughed and finished my dinner and played some video games.

The following day Chris messaged me at work. "How are you doing bubba? You still locked up?"

"Nope!" I replied. "That session ended yesterday. I am back to my old self again."

"Sweet! You up for coming over for some playtime followed by dinner and drinks? My ass needs some attention." Chris followed that by a devil emoji.

"Grins. That sounds good to me," I texted back. "I can be there about 7 pm if that is ok."

"See you then stud!" Chris replied.

After work, I headed home to change and got to Chris and Rick's apartment right on time. When I entered, Chris was running around in his jock, which is pretty usual for him, and Rick was sitting on the sofa in his socks, undershirt, and boxer briefs playing a game.

"How are you doing there Matt?" Rick asked without changing his focus on the monsters he was fighting on the TV.

"Not too bad. Little wore out from work, but otherwise good. How are you all doing?" I replied.

"Well, I am working my tush off getting things cleaned up around here," Chris said, poking his head around the corner from the next room. "That one has been playing video games since he got home."

"Whatever," Rick replied. "I bring in the most money for this household anyway."

"Ha!" Chris replied as he re-entered the room. "It's a good thing you have a decent cock to be useful in other areas, Rick."

"You know it," Rick replied. "Thick and girthy and ready to breed that ass."

I rolled my eyes at that comment while I took my shoes off and put them by the door.

"Matt you come with me, this one will be busy for a while," Chris said.

I followed him back to the bedroom and Chris helped pull my shirt off and take my pants and underwear down.

"Now lay down there and let me suck on you for a while," Chris said with a sexy tone.

I collapsed on the bed and he crawled up between my legs with his ass handing off the end of the bed and started to work my cock, which made me groan. Fortunately, the soreness from yesterday's activities had subsided and I was enjoying the stimulation. I was flexing my feet and listening to the joints pop which I love to do when getting a blow job.

Just then Rick walked in. "Well, that did not take long," he said with a grin.

Rick pulled off one sock and then the other, tossing them with one landing on the floor and one landing on the corner of the bed. He then took his t-shirt off revealing his furry, muscled chest, and threw it on the bed. Dropping his underwear last, I saw his engorged member working its way to full staff.

Rick bent down and started eating Chris's ass while Chris went down on me. That got a huge groan out of Chris and he started to go to work on my hard cock.

After Rick got his ass good and wet, he started fingering Chris. First, one digit then two, and then three. Chris was moaning more and more each time and grinding his ass back on Rick's fingers as he pushed them in.

"Fuck me, babe," Chris said as he came up from my cock.

Rick grabbed some lube from the side table and coated his cock and aimed it for Chris's ready and waiting hole. As he slid his large, thick cock in him Chris gasped and put his head in my crotch for a moment to catch his breath.

Once Rick was balls deep in him, he sat there a moment and then started thrusting fully in and out of Chris. "Fuck yeah, babe," Chris said. "Fuck my ass good."

Rick smiled and groaned as he worked his cock deep into Chris's ass, feeling his big balls slap before pulling out and slamming back in again. Slowly at first, but then picking up the pace as Chris moved backward to meet him on the forward stroke and pulled away for the backstroke.

Chris was in heaven and he continued to work on my cock as well. He knew just how to use his tongue and manipulate my balls with his hands to send me into ecstasy. I threw my head back and groaned in pleasure, which encouraged him to get into it more.

Rick was working up a sweat and it beaded on his forehead and started to run down the fur on his chest and abdomen. The smell of sex moved throughout the room and I recognized the aroma of Rick's musk. It was intoxicating. This man was so fucking hot. Chris made quite the catch when he nabbed this one.

Between the slaps and thrusts, I heard Rick begin to pant. "Are you ready for this load?" he asked Chris.

"Blow it in me, babe," Chris replied as he backed off my cock and prepared.

Rick slammed his cock into Chris twice and then on the third time kept his shaft balls deep as he erupted his seed, flooding Chris's insides.

"FUCK!" Rick yelled as he came down from the orgasm high.

Rick reached over and grabbed his shirt he had thrown on the bed and wiped his brow and chest. He then pulled out and leaned down and kissed Chris's back gently and nearly lost his balance as he walked over to lay on the bed next to me.

"That was hot," I said to Rick, looking over at the hair matted to his sweaty chest.

"Well, it is your turn now," Rick said with a grin. "He's pre-lubed for sure."

Chris lifted his head off my cock and gave me a grin and I got up and moved around him. While I did so, he flipped over and put his legs on my shoulders, a position that was better suited for me since I am shorter than Rick.

I was hard as a rock from Chris's great blowjob and had no trouble entering his ass that was sloppy with Rick's cum. I slid in pretty quickly to my root.

"Damn, Rick!" I said. "This is not sloppy, this is flooded."

Rick laughed and winked at me as I started to grind into Chris. I leaned over some and pinned his legs back as far as I could. Chris was pretty bendable, so it was not an issue.

I immediately switched into top mode and started dirty talking and having fun slowing and quickening my pace as I churned Rick's cum in Chris's ass to a froth. But as I was doing so, I had a flash of the contract in my head. It was dated for Sunday and if I was to sign it, I would not see my cock out of a chastity cage again and I would not be fucking again either. This might be one of the last chances I had to load someone up.

It was a bit of a mind trip, but Chris snapped me back to reality when he asked if he could flip over on all fours. I pulled out and let him and then climbed up on the bed to mount him doggy style and continue to pound my cock into him.

I was having so much fun and getting lost in my head that I jumped a bit when I felt a finger in my ass. I turned and it was Rick. He was hard again and smiling.

"Sorry," he said. "I'm still horny and I love your furry ass."

"Mount up stud," I said. "You know I love being in the middle of a fuck sandwich."

Rick didn't waste time lubing my hole and Chris moved down a bit so I could hang a little closer to the end of the bed for better access.

I felt Rick's cock enter my ass and I paused as he slowly worked his way in. Then I coordinated my thrusts so that I could enter Chris on the forward thrust and back up on Rick's dick on the backward thrust. The stimulation on my prostate was just what I needed to send me over the edge and I pretty quickly added a second load to Chris's well fucked ass and the contractions my ass made as I pumped my cum into him drove Rick over as well and he flooded my ass with his load as well.

Rick and Chris collapsed on the bed to catch their breath and I sat on the side. I reached down and picked up Rick's sock from the side of the bed and could not resist bringing it to my nose and taking his scent in. I have to admit, I am one of those piggy guys that loves a good man's musk.

"Had those on all day today, Matt. Must be pretty rank," Rick said.

"Oh, I don't mind," I said, turning and giving him a wink. "You smell good."

Chris rolled his eyes. "Ok, you two, enough with that shit. I'm hungry!"

He leaned over and made out with Rick a bit and thanked him and then went and grabbed some towels for us to wipe down. Rick put his underwear back on and I threw on my pants and we went back out to sit at the dining table while Chris went to the kitchen to finish making the spaghetti he had in a pot and bringing it out to us.

After dinner, Chris took the dishes into the kitchen to clean up and I went into the living room to sit down on the couch. Rick followed and sat next to me.

"So, how are things going with John?" he asked.

"It's been good. He had me caged for two nights as part of what he calls a trial period. That ended yesterday. I met him at his house, and he told me he was interested in taking me on as a trainee and gave me a contract to look at. It's pretty detailed and has some things that have me a bit nervous," I replied.

"Ahh… the contract," Rick said with a grin. "You must have impressed him to move to that stage."

"Oh, so you know about that?" I asked.

"Oh sure," Rick replied. "I've known John long enough to see several boys contract with him for training and go on to graduation as well."

"Can you tell me more?" I asked.

"Well, it's not a decision you should take lightly," Rick said with a more serious tone. "John has been training boys for a long time. He is fair but firm and he knows how to mold a boy into someone that can be collared by a dominant for the long term. I've seen the results of his training, and the boys that train with him are completely different people on the other end for sure."

"I guess the thing that is making me the most nervous are some of the more stringent parts of the agreement. For instance, he expects those in training to stay in chastity for longer and longer periods and be permanently locked within a year. It also states clearly that you are not allowed to see yourself out of chastity at any point, so it looks like once you sign the contract, you never see yourself unlocked again. That's a huge deal," I said with some nervousness in my voice.

Rick put his arm around me and brought me in close for a hug. "Well, I would not have introduced you two if I didn't think you might be a good fit for him. I know you do top from time to time, but I also see how much you enjoy bottoming and you get subby around dominant guys when we have been out at the Eagle, for instance. I can see you becoming quite the catch for a good dom. But you are right, some sacrifices come with that."

"Thanks. I know what you mean, and I'll be honest, the idea isn't something I have dismissed. I'm just going to have to think about it," I said.

"I'm sure you will make the right decision and personally, I think you would look awesome in a chastity cage full time," Rick said looking at me with a big grin.

I groped his groin and felt his soft, but large cock. Devilishly, I said, "I bet you would."

"Ho-ho!" Chris said as he came into the room with a laugh. "Are you molesting my man, Matt?"

"Hey! He's hot, what can I say," I said with a wink at Rick. "But he only has eyes for you."

Chris grinned. "Yeah, I'm a lucky guy."

"Me as well babe," Rick said as he and Chris kissed.

We played some video games before it was time for me to head back home. It was a work night, after all. I went and got my clothes from the bedroom and was sitting on the bed putting my shoes on when Rick came in.

"I know you are still mulling your decision, Matt. Would you be interested in meeting a sub that John has trained?" he asked.

"That might be good," I replied. "Do you know of one?"

"A good friend of mine collared one of the boys John trained and I was texting with him just now. He'd be willing to bring him out to the bar tomorrow night after work if you want to talk and ask questions," Rick said.

"That would be awesome, actually," I said with a grin.

"Perfect. I will get things set up and text you the details," Rick said.

I stood up and hugged him. "Thanks a bunch."

The next day was Friday and work was a mess. We had some projects that people had gotten behind on and I was trying to sort it all out. As usual, I was the one doing most of the work. At about 4:30 pm, I got a text from Rick.

"So, it is all set. Can you meet us at Woofs at about 7 pm?" Rick asked.

"Sure, that is no problem," I replied. "I will see you all then."

I walked into the bar just a little late due to traffic, which is bad in the city, especially on a Friday night. Across the room in the back bar, I saw Rick waving to me, and I came over to his table. Across from him was a tall, bearded, muscular man, probably in his late forties if I had to guess, with a tight t-shirt on that showed off his chest and dark-colored jeans with boots. Next to him sat a younger man with some scruff on his face who looked to be in his twenties. He had a red and black chainmail collar around his neck with a padlock and a gold tag that said 'Boy Dan / CHASTITY SUB / Collared by Sir Greg'. He was dressed in a t-shirt as well, but his jeans were tight, and he had a pretty noticeable bulge in his pants that I figured was the chastity cage.

"Matt, this is my friend Greg," Rick said, gesturing to the larger man.

Greg stuck out his hand and I shook it. He had a firm grip and a deep voice replied, "Nice to meet you Matt. This is my boy, Dan," he said putting his hand behind the boy's back.

Dan extended his hand, and I shook his as well.

"Nice to meet you, Matt," Dan replied.

"Well, take a seat here next to me Matt," Rick said. "I got a pitcher of beer here if you want to share."

"That would be awesome. Thanks!" I said, grabbing an empty glass and filling it up.

"So, Rick tells me that you are considering training to be a sub under John," Greg asked me.

"Yes, Sir, I am," I replied.

I don't know why I added the 'Sir' in the sentence, but it just seemed like the right thing to do. Dan smiled, though, and seemed pleased.

"Well, Dan here finished his training about six months ago and I collared him right after he graduated," Greg said as he slapped his hand on Dan's shoulder. "He's the best sub I have ever had, and I expect he will be around for the long term with me."

Dan looked back at him and said, "Thank you so much, Sir. It's been an honor serving you."

"When do you have to make a decision, Matt?" Greg asked me.

"Sunday," I replied. "Well, actually Saturday night since I have to send him some things by email."

"The addendums, Sir," Dan said to Greg.

"Oh, that's right," Greg replied. "Dan here showed me his contract when I was interested in him. Well, it's a big decision, no doubt. Not everyone is cut out to be a true sub boy. I advise you not to go through with it unless you are committed."

"Oh, I understand, Sir," I replied. "It is a big decision."

Just then there was a little commotion at the front of the bar, and it looked like someone people knew walked in.

"Oh hey!" Rick said excitedly. "That's Tom. I have not seen him around in a long time. Let's go say hi Greg and let these two talk, if that is ok that is."

"Sure, I have not seen that guy in ages, and it would be good for these two to have some time alone," Greg said. "Feel free to be open and honest about anything Dan."

"Thank you, Sir," Dan replied.

Greg and Rick grabbed their beers and headed over to the other side of the bar and I moved over to sit closer to Dan.

"So, what was it really like training under John," I asked.

Dan took a drink of his beer and sat it on the table.

"It was the most intense, but rewarding experience of my life," he said. "I had always been very subby, I guess is the best way to put it. But I learned that there were a lot more aspects to it than just what happens in the bedroom. It's a whole new way of thinking and acting around people and a new way to think about what is important in your life as well."

"And you are in permanent chastity now?" I asked.

Dan laughed and grabbed my hand and put it on his crotch. "Yup, the last time I had a manual release from my nub was six months ago."

I felt the hard cage under his pants. It had to be metal and it felt pretty damn secure. My cock twitched a bit as I brought my hand back.

"But that's just a symbol of service," Dan said. "Don't get me wrong, it's a head trip. I went from days to weeks to months of chastity before I went permanent, but I also learned to have pretty mind-blowing anal orgasms when I'm fucked. I honestly forget it's there most of the time. The real struggle is learning to emphasize others rather than yourself."

"How so?" I asked.

"I intuitively know when Greg needs a massage, a blow job, or when he just needs alone time, and I should just clean the house up," Dan said. "I make sure his every need is met and I enjoy it. Honestly, I experience almost akin to an orgasm when I can please him and bring him to climax or satisfy his needs. I don't need to jack off anymore or look around for short-lived pleasures. I have what I need in him if that makes sense."

"Sounds like you have a very close relationship," I replied.

"We do," Dan said. "But it is not a boyfriend or husband type of relationship. Greg has a guy he is sort of dating, and if it becomes more serious, then I will be his boy too. But it still is a special relationship, and he values me."

"Interesting," I said. "Were you nervous when John gave you the contract?"

Dan laughed. "Oh, hell yes I was. When Sir handed me that envelope and I was reading it, I nearly freaked out. The thought of long-term chastity alone was daunting, but the idea of total submission was not something I had seriously considered at all at that point."

"What made you decide to go through with it?" I asked.

"Honestly, I just wanted to challenge myself. I was intrigued by it all and I figured, if I failed, I failed, but at least I gave it a try," Dan said.

"Well, that is a good way to put it, I guess," I said.

"So, how many loads did he pull out of you on the sucking machine?" Dan said with a grin as he picked his glass up to take a drink.

"Ha!" I laughed. "Four. But I had to stop after that, my dick and balls were killing me."

Dan laughed back. "Yeah, you did better than me. I could not make it past three. My poor nub just was too sore."

Dan put his glass down and turned to me a bit more seriously. "But, honestly, Sir only takes in a few boys a year. That he offered the contract to you means he sees promise in you. Take it as a huge compliment, whether you decide to do it or not."

"Thanks, Dan," I said as I picked my glass up and clinked it against his. "Cheers!"

"One other thing," Dan said. "If you decide to go through with this you will have the ability to partner and work with those that have graduated from Sir's service. I'd be happy to mentor and help you if you want. But you should also rely on your sub brothers that Sir is also training. Bond with them, they will be there for you. I know my sub brothers Ryan, Hunter, Johnny, and Nick are still some of my closest friends and even though most are all collared now we still keep in touch."

"Thanks for the offer," I replied. "That would be awesome."

Dan showed me his phone and said, "Here is my contact info. Feel free to text me if you move forward."

As I put the info in my phone, Greg and Rick sat down and we ordered some food to have with our drinks. I asked Greg about his experience in the scene and how he met Rick. Dan discussed how much he was enjoying serving Greg. We discussed kinks and the scene and what was new in the city. It was a great conversation and evening. At about 11 pm, though, we decided it was time to head out.

We exchanged pleasantries and Dan hugged me and whispered in my ear, "good luck fellow sub. You can do this."

I replied thanks and we all parted ways.

The next morning, I wandered into my living room naked after jacking off in my bed and nearly hitting the wall with my cum. Feeling satisfied and calm, I decided it was time to open up the contract again and look it over in more detail and mull my decision over in my mind.

I sat down on the sofa and brought the table closer and spread out the paperwork before me. The more I read and re-read the more I got not only turned on but nervous. It was a lot to take in, but Dan put my mind at ease in a lot of ways. I could see myself in his situation, to be honest. That was not something I was averse to. He also had a great point. I could always drop out of the contract. It would be a huge failure to be sure, but it was not like I did not have options. If it was too much, then it was too much.

I slowly started to talk myself into it and by lunchtime figured that I would move forward. However, if tomorrow would be the last time I would see myself out of a chastity cage, I was damn well going to make sure I came a lot today.

CHAPTER SEVEN

My Last Day Uncaged

By Saturday afternoon, I had finally taken a shower and put some clothes on. I returned to the living room and pulled out my laptop. I had decided to move forward and accept John's contract for training. He had asked me to write down what my hard limits were and email them to him by this evening. I had plans to head out to the Atlanta Eagle tonight for bear night, so I decided I better get this out of the way now.

The first thing I wrote down was blood and feces. I had no interest in dealing with any scat and blood nearly made me faint. I knew there was no way I would ever make it as a nurse, like my brother was, for damn sure with those issues.

The second thing I wrote down was severe pain. I can deal with a little pain, especially when bondage is involved. I had gotten flogged before and spanked with a paddle, but I had no interest in rising to the level where it was unbearable.

The third thing I wrote down was nipple torture. My nipples were hard-wired to my cock and were very sensitive. Just lightly playing with them was enough to get me hard and dripping and biting and pinching them, let alone clamps and such were extremely painful.

Finally, I wrote down permanent marks, scars, or body modifications. I know it was sort of implicitly noted in the contract that this would not occur, but I wanted to make it clear in the addendum as well.

I tried to think of anything else I wanted totally off the table, but nothing came to mind, so I emailed it off to John and went to gather my laundry to bring it round to the back of the complex to get it started.

It was a warm March day in Atlanta. There was some rain in the area, but the temperature was 70 °F (21.1 °C), which is not that uncommon in the South. I was in shorts in a t-shirt and walked around two of the buildings and the pool area to get around to the laundry area on the side of a third building.

When I walked in the door to the small room, the eight machines they had in there were empty, which was a nice surprise. I had everything in a couple of machines pretty quickly and I was sitting there watching the suds go-round when one of my friends, Kenny, that lives in the complex a few buildings over came in to wash his clothes as well.

"What's up Matt?" Kenny asked me.

"Hey bud," I replied. "Not much. Watching my socks chase my shirts as usual."

"I hear ya there. Laundry day is always so exciting," he said sarcastically rolling his eyes.

"Can you believe this weather? It was in the 50s yesterday and now it feels like spring," Kenny said as he put his basket down and started to fill a machine.

"Yeah, that's Atlanta for you. I am used to it by now," I said.

Kenny laughed. "Well, I am from Detroit. It is a bit different up there. I don't miss shoveling snow though."

After he had things loaded up and started, he sat down next to me on the bench in the center of the room.

"Are you planning on going out tonight?" he asked.

"Yeah, I'm headed out to the Eagle tonight. What about yourself?" I asked.

"Naa. I can't. My straight cousin's been staying with me all week. He is between apartments and can't get into the new place until next week. He's ok, but I don't trust him there by himself for long," he said.

"Damn. That sucks." I replied.

"No doubt! He's sharing my bed as well, so I have not had anyone over since last Friday and have to sneak into the bathroom when I can to jack off. It is annoying."

"Ok, well that is bad," I said. "When was the last time you got off?"

"Wednesday," he said.

"Fuck dude!" I exclaimed. "You got to be ready to burst!"

"Don't remind me," he grimaced. "I have been seeing this cute, subby chaser guy. He is all bottom, which I fucking love, and he gives great head and I love to eat and pound his furry ass. He pushes all my dom buttons. But he lives with roommates, so I have not had any outlet there either."

Kenny was grabbing his crotch at this point and I noticed he was getting hard thinking about it.

"Well, you know I would be happy to suck you off, if you want," I said with a grin.

"What, here?" Kenny asked, acting surprised.

"Sure!" I said as I went over to the door to the laundry and closed and locked the handle.

"Umm, what are you going to do if someone tries to get in?" Kenny asked as I came over and knelt in front of him and undid the front of his shorts.

"Meh, they can wait. Besides, there have been plenty of times this place has been out of order," I replied.

Kenny doesn't wear underwear, so I pulled his pants down to his ankles and started sucking on his soft cock. He is a cute ginger cub with a goatee. Short, fuzzy, and chubby with a huge set of balls and nice thick uncut cock and a fire crotch with a very intoxicating scent that I have always loved, though we don't get to play much.

His cock didn't take long to swell to its full extent as I went down on him and massaged his balls. He was a big precummer like me and I could taste the sweet and salty taste of it on the back of my tongue.

"Fuck, dude!" Kenny growled.

He kicked his flip flops off and his shorts, took off his shirt, and swung around to lay down on the bench and put one leg on either side as I continued to suck on him.

"God, I needed this," he said. "Just go slower boy, I want to enjoy this."

"Of course!" I said backing off and then stroking him slowly and moving down to take his balls into my mouth and breathe in his scent that made me hard as a rock as well.

I reached under his furry ass and used my middle finger to probe his hole a bit which elicited a moan and even more precum flowing from his fat cock.

"Be careful there," Kenny said. "You know I don't bottom much."

"Don't worry," I said, "I'll be gentle."

As I worked my finger in, I felt him relax a bit, and his cock pulsed and released some more precum into my mouth.

"Damn this feels good!" Kenny said as he stretched his legs out on the sides of the bench and curled his toes.

I added some more spit to my finger and started to work into his hole more. I moved around deeper until I felt his prostate and started to gently rub it in circular motions. At the same time, I took him deep into my mouth and used my tongue to explore his cock and the inside of his foreskin as well.

Kenny groaned louder, "Fuck yeah, boy! Suck daddy's cock."

Kenny was enjoying this, so I removed my finger and then moved up his chest using my tongue to lick his fur and when I got to his nipples, I slowly started to nibble at them while I gently jacked his cock. This caused him to start producing so much precum that it was dribbling down his shaft and acting as a great lube.

"That's a boy," Kenny said.

He let out a sigh between his groans and brought his arms up behind his head. This put his pits on display, and I moved up to bury my face in them. I did love his natural musk and I breathed it in between licking with long strokes.

"Take it in boy," Kenny said. "I know you like my scent. Get that all over your beard and face."

I rubbed it all over and licked and breathed in some more before moving back down to his cock and taking it in deeply. I put my finger back up his ass to get at his prostate again as well. Kenny's body shuttered a bit and his legs jittered. He closed his pale blue eyes and bit his lip as he moaned. I could tell he was enjoying this.

"Dude, I am going to blow if you keep that up," Kenny finally said.

I grinned and went to work massaging his prostate with my finger and started sucking a little faster. I had every intention of draining that three-day load from his big balls fully.

Kenny outstretched his legs fully and arched his back just as his ass muscles contracted on my finger probing his prostate. He was about to cum. He grabbed the sides of the bench and threw his head back and groaned and his cock flooded my mouth to the brim. He came so much I coughed and choked sending it down into my beard and up my nose.

"Fuck boy!" Kenny exclaimed as I withdrew my finger and used my hands to stroke and get the last bits of cum out of him.

He was panting there on the bench trying to catch his breath and I watched his furry ginger belly lift and fall. His thick cock slowly deflated with a little bit of remaining cum at the tip dribbling out.

"Damn, I needed that," he said as he swung himself back upright and grabbed the remaining dribble off his cock and licked it off his fingers. He then laughed as he saw the cum in my beard. "Looks like I coated you a bit."

I was laughing as well. "Yeah," I said as I used my hands to collect and lick up the remains of his load. "It kind of went up my nose as well."

"Ha!" Kenny said as he reached over and helped to grab a few places I missed and fed them to me.

I put my head into his crotch one last time to suck the tip of his cock and then got up to go unlock and open the door as he pulled his pants up.

"You know you are good at that," Kenny said to me as I returned to sit on the bench, and he was buttoning his shorts and putting his flip flops back on.

"Thanks! I do enjoy it," I said with a grin and handed him the shirt he had tossed on the floor.

He reached over and stuck his hands down the back of my pants and probed my asshole with his finger.

"One of these days I need to fuck that ass too," Kenny said, giving me a wink.

For the next couple of hours, we caught up on some of the local gossip as we waited on the machines to finish and then later folded our clothes.

I ended up finishing first, so I put everything in my basket and told Kenny I would catch him later.

"Sure thing bud," Kenny said. "And thanks so much. Let's do it again soon!"

I decided to play some video games and watch some TV after I got back to the apartment. About 6 pm, I got a ding on my phone indicating a new email. I checked to see that John had replied to the addendum suggestions I had emailed him.

> Boy:
>
> This looks good. I have added this to the contract. If you decide to take my offer, then I expect you to text me at 11 am tomorrow to confirm. You are then to be at my home at 2 pm sharp.
>
> Enter through the side door and on the top of the shelves with the bins will be a piece of paper with the code to the yellow bin lock. You are to strip all your clothes off, fold them neatly and place them and your keys in the yellow bin and close and latch its door. This will be your bin for the entire time you are under contract, so don't forget the code.
>
> After your belongings are put away, you are to kneel in the hallway with your hands behind your back and bow your head and wait till I come to get you. Do not enter the dungeon area until I tell you to.
>
> You do not need to bring anything else with you. Leave your phone in your car. I will have the official copy of the contract and addendum to sign at the house.
>
> Sir

It was all becoming a lot more real at this point. Still, I was not planning on backing out. I wanted to move forward and challenge myself. Plus, I still had one night of freedom to have some fun.

I decided to make some ramen with some pulled chicken for dinner and afterward called up my friend Paul to see if he was going out tonight. He said he was, and we agreed to meet at my place and go together. He barely drinks, so usually, he is my designated driver.

After playing some more video games, it was getting to be about 10 pm and Paul said he would be at my place by 10:30 pm, so I went back into the bedroom and laid out my normal bar wear including tight jeans, black boots, harness, and black leather cap. I had a black t-shirt I wore over my harness.

After Paul arrived, I hopped in his car and we headed into town and drove around the neighborhoods behind the Eagle till we found a spot to park. When we walked up to the back deck of the bar, we noticed a pretty good crowd. I told Paul I would grab a drink and would be hanging out on the upper back deck and he told me he would look for me there later on.

I walked up the staircase and walked through the back door on the upper deck area. The music was already going from the dance floor from the front of the bar and there were some really hot guys walking around. I took my shirt off and adjusted my harness a bit and then tucked my shirt partially in my back pocket.

As I was waiting in line for a beer, someone came up behind me and put their arms around my waist and grabbed my crotch. I looked around to see Chris grinning back at me.

"How ya doing stranger?" he asked coyly.

I laughed and said, "not too bad sexy!"

Chris grinned and backed up a bit. "I was wondering if you were going to come out tonight."

"Is Rick with you?" I asked.

"Oh, he is around somewhere. He has his friends and I have mine. You know how it is," Chris replied.

We grabbed our drinks and headed back out to the upper back deck and stood near the railing.

"So, did you make a decision regarding John?" he asked.

"Yeah," I replied. "I am going through with it."

Chris's eyes widened a bit and he grinned. "Look at you being the bold sub!"

I laughed. "Well, the idea has intrigued me and I'm up for a challenge."

Chris raised an eyebrow and leaned into me. "Looks like we need to get you a few blowjobs tonight then before that cock of yours is off-limits."

I gave him a devilish grin back and we continued to drink and talk with some people around us.

Around 1 am I was getting pretty wasted. We had moved to the side of the upper deck that had some benches to sit on. Chris was just as wasted and was playing with my nipples which made my cock instantly hard in my pants. One of the cubby guys we had met that night and had been hanging out with saw the bulge and reached down and felt it.

"Looks like someone is hard-wired," he said.

"You are welcome to get down there and find out," I said as I unzipped my pants.

The cub smiled and got down on his knees between my legs and pulled my hardening cock and out went down on me. He was obviously just as drunk as I was and it was not the best blowjob I have ever had, but he had a good technique and pulled a load out of me pretty quick. I grunted as the last spurt of cum came out of my cock and he raised his head and took a swig of his beer to wash my load down.

"Thanks," I said, and I leaned in to make out a bit with him tasting my load mixed with the beer on his lips.

Chris reached down and pulled my underwear up but left my pants unzipped. "Save that for a bit and let me know when you're ready again. I want to give you your last blow job."

I smiled and zipped my pants. "Just give me a little recharge time," I said.

I managed to navigate the increasingly crowded bar that night to get one last beer. I knew that would be my limit. When I returned to the bench, Chris started rubbing my crotch and asked if I was ready. I grinned and unzipped my pants again and he pulled out my cock and got on his knees in front of me.

Chris knows how to work a cock and this blowjob was much more intense than the first. He was working my shaft with his hands and fondling my balls. I was in an alcohol haze and threw my head back and groaned. The cubby that sucked me off earlier saw and came over and started making out with me and played with my nipples. That got me leaking precum a ton and Chris was happily swallowing it all.

Between the cubby's tongue exploring my mouth, his massaging of my nipples, and Chris's deep-throating abilities, I was in heaven. It didn't take me long to get close to the edge again.

"Oh fuck!" I yelled as I blasted into Chris's mouth and he swallowed every drop. He milked my cock with his hands and mouth and massaged my balls to get every last bit out.

The cubby leaned in for one more kiss and said, "that was hot, dude."

I thanked him and put away my cock and zipped my pants up while Chris stood up and managed to sit down next to me without falling over from his drunk state.

I put my hands around his shoulders and leaned over to his ear. "Thanks, Chris," I said.

Chris looked over with his glazed eyes and gave me a peck on the lips.

Rick and Paul found us a little after 2 am and decided it was time to get our asses home, so after hugs all around we parted our separate ways. Paul dropped me off at my apartment and I managed to make it inside and pass out in my bed.

CHAPTER EIGHT

The Start of My Service

I awoke and found myself sprawled out on the top of my bedsheets. At some point, I had the good sense to kick my boots off and put my CPAP on as I can't sleep very well without it. Otherwise, I was still in my bar clothes. I had lost my t-shirt at some point so apparently, I came home in just my harness and jeans, but I didn't remember much after leaving the bar.

I rolled out of bed and noticed that it was a few minutes before 11 am. It then dawned on me that John had asked me to text him at that time to confirm if I was coming over to sign the contract or not. I looked for my phone and found it on the floor and picked it up and sent him a text that I would be there at 2 pm as requested.

John texted me back, "See you then."

I put my phone on the charger, took my harness off and threw it on the floor, and then collapsed back in the bed.

About noon I awoke again and managed to drag myself out of bed and into the kitchen to grab a sandwich and a soda. As I sat there eating, it dawned on me that the blowjob I got from Chris might be the last one I ever received. I looked down to see my pants bulging and realized my cock was engorged from just the thought. I pulled off my pants and jacked my cock off till I was shooting my load all over my chest. I rubbed the cum in my chest hair and savored the feeling of the orgasm before standing and going to the bathroom to get cleaned up.

While I was in the shower, I masturbated again and shot a second load before washing up thoroughly and stepping out to dry off. I stood in front of the mirror and had a thought, so I went back and grabbed my phone and took some pictures of myself completely naked. I figured I might not get a chance again to see myself uncaged.

I decided to just wear some jeans and a shirt since John had not specified anything specific. I grabbed my tennis shoes and put them on and then looked at the clock. It was 1:30 pm at this point and it was time to get on the road. I picked up my keys and headed out to the car to drive over to John's.

I had to stop at the gas station on the way, so I was pulling up into his driveway at a few minutes to 2 pm. I noticed there was a car in the street and another in the driveway next to me, so I did not know what to expect when I got inside.

I went around to the side door and punched in the code and entered. The door to the dungeon area was closed and it was quiet. On the shelves to my right was a small piece of paper with the number 9475. I went to punch this code into the door that enclosed the yellow bin and noticed that it was labeled 'Matt' already.

Once the bin was open, I stripped all my clothes off and put my shoes in first followed by my keys and then my neatly folded clothes. I closed and locked the bin door and then got down on my knees on the floor and put my hands behind me and bowed my head.

I had been there about fifteen minutes and I was getting more and more nervous as I waited. I could always get up and leave if I wanted, I thought. There would be no shame in that. But I stayed where I was.

Eventually, I heard someone walking around in the dungeon area and the door in front of me opened. I could not see who it was as my head was bowed, but I saw the bare feet of the person walk in and stand in front of me and I recognized them as belonging to John.

"You may look up, boy," John said.

I lifted my head to see that John had on black leather chaps and a black with blue-trimmed leather jock on whose front portion looked to be snapped on. He had leather suspenders that attached to the jock and rain on either side of his chest and up and over his shoulders. It was a very hot look, and I could not help but start to get an erection.

John was emotionless as he told me to stand and follow him into the dungeon area.

"I have the cameras on in here, boy, to record your first day under my service, so please act accordingly," John said.

As I entered, I saw two people on their knees with their hands behind their backs and their heads bowed. They both had chainmail collars with padlocks around their necks, wore chastity cages, and were each within painted squares on the floor. A younger, larger, cubbish-looking guy was kneeling in the green square and a thinner, hairy, otter-type guy was kneeling in the red square. I assumed these were the two other subs that John was training, meaning that the thinner guy was Jay, and the bigger guy was Bo according to the nameplates on the bins.

John closed the door behind me and directed me to my right to the low table. On it was a stack of several pieces of paper, which I assumed was the contract, a pen, and a long box. I walked around and kneeled on the floor behind it opposite the chair he sat in last time and John took a seat.

"Before you is the contract that you have agreed to be bound by. I encourage you to look it over, but nothing has changed from the copy I sent you home with. However, behind this is the addendum that I have drawn up based on your email to me of your defined hard limits. Please take a moment to read all the paperwork and then you may speak if you have any questions," John said.

I started reading through everything and he was correct that the contract was identical. The addendum read as follows.

ADDENDUM TO THE SERVICE CONTRACT

This addendum to the SUBORDINATE SERVICE CONTRACT (hereafter referred to as the "Agreement" or "Contract") dated Sunday, March 8, 2015, is between the undersigned (hereinafter called "the sub") and John Dante, hereafter referred to as "Sir", and pertains the agreed-upon hard limits of service submitted by the sub to Sir, his defined rules and responsibilities, and the detailed chastity schedule during the term of this contract.

Section 1: Hard Limits of the Sub

The sub has detailed the following hard limits that he does not want the Sir to cross while he is under contract.

a. Blood and feces. Sir agrees that no act of service will involve the sight of blood or will draw blood from the sub. Additionally, Sir agrees that no form of fecal material will ever be present during, or a part of, any form of service while the sub is under contract.

b. Severe pain. Sir agrees that no act of service will involve debilitating or severe pain. The sub has agreed that some pain is possible and acceptable while under contract, but the sub may utilize the safe word "TELEPHONE" at any time when the pain exceeds his limits, and the Sir will honor this request.

c. Nipple torture. Sir agrees that severe and debilitating pain from nipple play will not occur. As with subsection b above, the sub has agreed that some pain is possible and acceptable while under contract, but the sub may utilize the safe word "TELEPHONE" at any time when the pain exceeds his limits, and the Sir will honor this request.

d. Permanent marks, scars, or body modifications. Sir agrees that no permanent alteration or modification of the sub's body will be requested or performed while under contract without the sub's implicit agreement.

As a consequence of this section, any punishments administered to the sub for any reason will be limited and bound by the sub-section details.

Section 2: Rules, Personal Grooming Habits, Duties, and Responsibilities of the Sub

While under contract, the sub will be required to maintain a professional appearance commiserate with the type of sub that Sir trains. The sub will be a reflection of Sir while in public and private and is expected to be polite and respectful of others, especially dominants. To ensure that this occurs, the following rules apply to the contract.

a. The following general rules apply to the sub for all sessions at Sir's house.

1. The sub will arrive promptly at Sir's house when requested. If he is late, then the sub will be given punishment.

2. The sub will enter Sir's house through the side door and will immediately undress in the hallway and place all folded clothing in the yellow bin assigned to him along with any electronics, keys, or personal items. If this is not done satisfactorily, then the sub will be given punishment.

3. The sub will then enter the dungeon area and kneel on the floor within the yellow square against the wall with his hands behind his back and his head bowed. The sub may sit on legs to reduce strain until Sir arrives in the room, at which point he must be on his knees fully. No matter who else is in the room when the sub arrives, he will remain quiet and will not speak. If this is not done satisfactorily, then the sub will be given punishment.

4. At all times the sub will not speak unless given permission. Violation of this rule will involve punishment.

5. When the sub is permitted to leave, the sub will return to the side entrance hallway, retrieve his belongings, and leave quietly through the side door.

b. The following general rules apply to the sub's appearance and grooming habits.

1. The sub's head and facial hair will be maintained in a neat and professional appearance while under contract. The sub will not be allowed to have a long beard or long hair. The head hair should be short to medium in length, cut over the ears, and squared off in the back. The beard will be no longer than 1 to 1.5 inches (2.54 to 3.81 cm) in length and will be well maintained.

2. The sub will be allowed to maintain his body hair; however, his groin area should be trimmed short to avoid issues with his chastity cage. The sub is allowed to shave his groin smooth if he so wishes, but it is not required by Sir.

3. The sub may retain his current wardrobe and dress normally during the day, but at home, if no family or underage members are present, he will be naked at all times and will strip as he enters.

4. When at social locations or events such as gay bars, parades, and parties, the sub will wear tight jeans that show off his ass and his training collar will always be visible.

c. While at Sir's house, a part of the service duties of the sub will be maintenance and care of Sir's home. This can include household chores, general cleaning, and small projects. These will always be performed naked, but the sub will be permitted shoes or work boots if the projects are outside and protection for the groin area will be provided if the task requires.

Section 3: Chastity Sessions

As part of the contract, the sub will have his genitals, hereafter referred to as his nub, in any sort of chastity device of Sir's choosing. The sub's time in chastity will be increased according to the following schedule.

a. Session One: Sunday, March 8, 2015, to Sunday, March 15, 2015 (7 days)

b. Session Two: Sunday, March 15, 2015, to Sunday, March 29, 2015 (14 days)

c. Session Three: Sunday, March 29, 2015, to Sunday, April 26, 2015 (28 days)

d. Session Four: Sunday, April 26, 2015, to Sunday, June 7, 2015 (42 days)

e. Session Five: Sunday, June 7, 2015, to Sunday, September 6, 2015 (91 days)

f. Session Six: Sunday, September 6, 2015, to Sunday, March 6, 2016 (182 days)

On the release day, the sub will be bound and blindfolded and Sir will manually manipulate the sub's nub to orgasm. All fluids will be collected, and the sub will be expected to swallow them all. The chastity cage will be reinstalled before the sub is unbound. Should the sub complete this schedule, then the sub will be given one last manual manipulation on March 6, 2016, before permanent chastity begins. Once this contract is signed on March 8, 2015, the sub will not see itself out of chastity again.

Should a sore develop, or a health condition occurs that warrants removal of the device, the sub will wear a special sock that will cover its nub and will be under the direction of Sir as to cleaning and hygiene until such time as the chastity cage can be reinstalled.

Section 4: Alteration

This addendum may not be altered, except when both Sir and the sub agree. If the addendum is altered, the new addendum shall be printed and signed, and then the old addendum must be destroyed.

Section 5: Suspension

Under certain circumstances, events, and conditions, suspension of parts of this addendum may be wanted, warranted, and executed for a determined period of time. Sir will determine if a suspension is warranted.

Section 6: Termination

Under certain circumstances, events, and conditions, termination of this addendum may be wanted, warranted, and executed, but must be an absolute last option when no other recourse is possible. Sir will determine if termination is warranted.

SIGNATURE OF "THE SUB"

I have read and fully understand this addendum in its entirety. I agree to enter into service with Sir. I understand that I will be commanded, trained, and punished as a submissive, and I promise to be true and to fulfill the pleasures and desires of my Sir to the best of my abilities.

_____ Signature

SIGNATURE OF SIR

I have read and fully understand this addendum in its entirety. I will accept the sub into my service and will command him, train him, reward him, and punish him as a submissive. I understand the responsibility implicit in this arrangement and agree that no harm shall come to the sub as long as he is in my service.

_____ Signature

After I had completed a review of the contract and the addendum, I placed them on the table and John asked, "are there any questions?"

"No, Sir," I replied.

"Very well," said John. "Take the pen and sign your name to the contract and the addendum."

I picked up the pen and took a deep breath and signed in both places and then I handed the pen to John and he signed them both as well. He then took out a manilla envelope and put the paperwork in it and placed it and the pen on the table.

"I will make a PDF copy of this for you and email it to you tonight," John said. "You are now under contract as one of my boys as of now. Please study this contract and addendum very closely after you return home. You must follow the rules set forth for you at all times."

He then picked up the box on the table and opened it to reveal a black and yellow chainmail rope collar with a lock. It was similar in design to the ones the other subs wore, though theirs were color-coordinated with their bins and squares with one red and black and the other one green and black chainmail. In addition to the small master lock, there was a round silver tag with black lettering that said 'Boy Matt' in large letters. Below this, in slightly smaller capital letters it said, 'CHASTITY SUB' and on the final line it said, 'Sir John, Trainer'. On the back, it said, 'I am in training to learn to serve men'.

John placed the collar around my neck and locked it in place.

"Rise, boy," John said. "Follow me."

I got up and followed John. He went over to a cabinet on one of the walls of the room. It had many drawers in it. From one, he pulled out a measuring tape and started to measure the circumference and the length of my soft cock. He then searched through several drawers and selected a metal base ring that would fit and a cage to go with it. He then grabbed a screw and a small device and turned around.

"This is what is called a Jailbird device," John said. They are very high quality and are made by a company called Mature Metal. I like them because they do not rust, they fit my boys very well, and the owners give me a discount since I buy from them regularly. This will be your starting device. Over time, you will find that your nub will decrease in size due to an inability to achieve erections. I assure you this is temporary, so if you decide to violate and or end the contract, you will return to normal size after a short period out of chastity. Due to this shrinkage, I will put you into a device with smaller cage lengths as the year progresses."

John bent down and pulled my balls and cock through the base ring and then put my cock in the cage portion and put it over a post on the base ring to secure it in place.

"The other reason I like this device," John continued, "is because it comes with a security screw option. You will not need a lock to keep this cage on. However, I will be applying Loctite purple on the threads so that it is secure and does not come out through normal wear. The screw can only be installed or removed with this special key in my hand. I will hold one of the keys and an identical copy will be placed in the Bluetooth lockbox for you to take home in the case of emergencies."

John took the cap off the Loctite purple and coated the threads and then installed the screw in the chastity cage and ensured it was tight. He then adjusted my balls and made sure everything was fitted correctly.

"And with that, you are now officially one of my boys," John said. "Please go over to the wall and kneel in the yellow square with your hands behind your back and your head bowed like your sub brothers."

I walked over to where the other two subs were kneeling and knelt in the yellow-painted square on the floor next to Bo. John put the Loctite away and closed all the drawers. He then grabbed the Bluetooth lockbox and placed the screw key in it and closed and locked it and then left the room for a moment.

It was silent in the room and all I could hear was the breathing of Bo and Jay beside me. We did not speak, and I was getting a little uncomfortable on my knees on the concrete. It was then that I noticed that Bo was sitting back on his legs and I remembered in the Addendum that we were allowed to do this while John... while Sir... was out of the room, so I relaxed a bit and sat back on my legs.

When I heard John coming back down the staircase, Bo immediately sat up on his knees properly and I followed suit. The door opened and John stood in front of us.

"Boys, please rise and face me," John said.

We all three got up at the same time and faced forward, John had grabbed a glass of whiskey and took a drink, and then crossed his hands over his chest.

"Jay, come forward and introduce yourself," John said.

Jay stepped forward and turned to face me and said, "My name is boy Jay. I am your sub brother and have been in training under Sir for six months." He then returned to where he was standing before.

"Bo, please come forward and introduce yourself," John said.

Bo stepped forward and turned to face me and said, "My name is boy Bo. I am your sub brother and have been in training under Sir for three months." He then returned to where he was standing before.

"Matt, please come forward and introduce yourself," John said.

I stepped forward and turned to face Bo and Jay and followed the same response they gave me, "My name is boy Matt. I am your sub brother and have just started training under Sir." I then returned to my original position.

"Excellent work, Matt," John said. "You will be working often with Jay and Bo. These two are indeed your sub brothers. Think of them as your family. You will be given their contact information and are free to text each other. You will find them an excellent source of information on what I expect and how to behave. Jay is your elder brother as he has been here the longest. You will have tasks that you will perform with them and I expect you to support them as they support you."

I was happy to hear that I would have these two to rely on. I knew I had a lot to learn and I figured their insights would be very valuable.

"Jay and Bo," John said. "Please recite the creed for Matt."

Immediately Jay and Bo spoke in unison, "I am a sub in training under the supervision of Sir John. My goal is to serve men in the best way I can and derive pleasure from that service. My chastity cage and collar are a symbol of that service and I desire one day to be in permanent chastity and receive my formal graduation collar as proof of my commitment."

"Good boys," John said. "You are both well on your way and I am very proud of you. You may now leave."

Jay and Bo then stepped forward and moved by me and exited into the side door hallway and closed the door behind them.

"As you can see, Matt," John said, "you have much to learn, but you have two sub brothers that can help you. Your first task before I see you again will be to memorize that creed. You will be expected to recite that at any time or place of my choosing. Is that understood?"

"Yes, Sir," I said. "I understand."

"Good," said John. "Now please stand with your feet slightly apart with your arms behind you and look straight ahead."

While I stood there, John took another sip of his drink and then went over to the side wall and put his glass down and grabbed a camera, and then returned and took several pictures of me.

"As you see here on the wall," John said, pointing to two pictures that were hanging over the table that I had not noticed before, "I keep current pictures of the boys I train displayed here. I will add yours next to Bo's on the end and if you complete your contract, your picture will be moved up to my private office upstairs where the rest of the photos of my graduated subs hang in honor."

John returned the camera to the shelf and then came over and stood before me.

"Up till now, we have had an informal relationship, Matt," John said. "Now that you are formally one of my boys, you will find my tone towards you and how we interact to be different. You will always refer to me as Sir. The contact in your phone must be named that as well. You will always refer to yourself as 'boy Matt' when you are called to identify yourself. Finally, you will always refer to your genitals as your nub. Only men have cocks. You are a sub and subs have nubs. Is that understood?"

"Yes, Sir," I said. "I understand."

"The first few weeks are always the hardest," John said. "You will have slip-ups and I will not be as harsh on you during this time. However, after two weeks, you will be expected to understand the rules and your responsibilities and punishments for infractions will be fully enforced. Is that understood?"

"Yes, Sir," I said. "I understand."

"Your designated day for training is Sunday," John said. "Every Sunday at 2 pm sharp you will enter and strip, put your belongings in your bin and you will come in and kneel in your yellow square until I come for you. We will have things that we will work on one-on-one and I will help you expand your horizons. Is that understood?"

"Yes, Sir," I said. "I understand."

"Your first chastity session, as detailed in the contract you signed, will last seven days," John said. "Next Sunday, when you come for your training day, I will bind you to the table you were on the other day and you will be blindfolded. I will manually manipulate your nub till you orgasm. I will collect your fluids and feed them to you. You will then be relocked in your chastity cage and unbound. You will not be manually manipulated again until the end of the second session after that, which is 14 days in that case. Is that understood?"

"Yes, Sir," I said. "I understand."

"As I told you, you will never see yourself out of your cage again," John said. "You are not allowed to use a toy such as a vibrator to bring yourself to orgasm while in your cage. The only way you are allowed to orgasm is through the manipulation of your ass by a man. Thus, if you are being fucked and you happen to orgasm then there is no problem. If a dominant fucks you with a dildo and you happen to orgasm then there is no problem. If, however, you use a dildo in your ass to achieve orgasm on your own, then you have broken the rules and will be punished. You are to see yourself as an instrument for the pleasure of a man. Pleasuring yourself takes away their use of you and their dominance over you. It is a form of stealing. Is that understood?"

"Yes, Sir," I said. "I understand."

"There are many other things you will need to learn," John said. "But that is enough for today."

I stood quietly trying to determine what was coming next and also trying to remember everything that John told me.

"Is your ass cleaned out boy?" John asked.

"No, Sir," I replied. I thought to myself that I should have remembered to do that in preparation for anything, but I never even thought about it.

"In the future, you will always come clean and ready, boy," John said. "Please go to the bathroom to your left and prepare yourself. There is an attachment in the shower to help you and towels are under the sink. Please return and kneel in your spot when you are ready. I will return."

With that, John turned and grabbed his drink and opened the door to the staircase and went back up to the main floor.

I turned and went into the bathroom and proceeded to use the Shower Shot to clean my ass out and prepare myself for anal play. Once the water ran clear and I felt I was ready, I grabbed a towel under the sink and dried off and hung it on the towel rack to dry. I returned to the dungeon area and knelt in my yellow square and awaited John's return.

After about ten minutes of waiting, I heard John come down the staircase and enter the room. He told me to stand and directed me over to the other side of the room where there was a fuck bench. He adjusted it down a bit and had me get on it. I then heard him pump some lube into his hand and he used his fingers to start to open me up. Once I was ready, I heard him unsnap the front of his jock to let his thick cock out and I felt the tip of it on my ass.

"Boy, I only fuck the boys I train," John said. "It is a privilege to take my cock and I want to welcome you properly."

With that, he started to move, and his cock entered my ass. The girth was apparent immediately and I groaned as he inched forward.

"I don't want to hear you speak, boy," John said. "This is for my pleasure. You may make sounds, but please muffle them as much as you can, or I will be forced to gag you."

I tried to concentrate on not making too loud of a noise and not speaking. I held my breath as well, but as his cock continued to impale me, I found it very difficult. When he finally was balls deep in my ass, I had to let out the air and groan lightly.

"Damn, boy," John said. "I am going to enjoy this ass."

And with that, he pulled out completely and pushed back in, slow at first, but then he picked up speed. The pain hit me right away. Nothing I could not handle, but the sheer thickness and length of his cock was something I was going to have to get used to. I grabbed ahold of the sides of the fuck bench as it groaned and squeaked and tried to steady myself against his pounding.

John was relentless. He grabbed my hips and pounded me for all it was worth until he started sweating and it dripped down his hairy chest and onto my back. I heard the sounds of the smack of his balls against my ass and the liquid sound of the lube lowering the friction as his cock slid in and out of my ass without abandon.

This went on for at least 15 minutes. He would take breaks and adjust his speed, but he was a fucking machine. Finally, I felt him tense up and he pounded my ass even harder till I heard him groan.

"Fuck, yeah boy!" John yelled. "It's time to mark that ass with my seed!"

His cum erupted inside my ass. I felt his cock pulsing as he held his cock inside me to ensure that it was deeply implanted. Once the pulsing stopped, he withdrew slowly and smacked my ass with his hand. He then grabbed a butt plug and inserted it into my ass and made sure his cum did not leak out. He then wiped the sweat off my ass with a towel and told me to get on my knees and clean his cock.

I got off the fuck bench and almost lost my balance at first from the rough fucking. My asshole was sore, and the plug was very filling. But I immediately got on my knees to see his cock hanging low and some remaining cum dribbling out. I took it into my mouth and reached up to grab it as well. John swatted my hands away, though.

"No boy!" John said. "Use your mouth alone."

I sucked and licked his cock and shaft until they were clean. The taste of his cum was wonderful and I could not get enough of it.

When I was done, he stepped back and snapped the front of his jock back on to contain his cock. "That is all for today, boy," John said. "You may dress and leave. Remember the stipulation in the contract about not having any clothes on at home. A pdf copy of the contract is already in your email box. Read, study, and know it by heart. I want you to leave that plug in your ass until you get ready for bed so you can fully enjoy your first breeding as a sub."

"Yes, Sir," I said. "I understand."

John turned and went back upstairs, and I headed for the side entrance hallway to dress and head back home.

The drive home was intense. I felt so full with the plug in my ass and the cage on my nub was something I was going to have to get used to. This cage was more comfortable than the cheap one I had, but it also was a bit shorter of one as well, so there was no room for growth on my nub. That was very apparent when I was getting fucked by John as I could feel my nub straining in the cage to the point that it hurt a bit.

When I got back to my apartment and entered the living room, I remembered to strip naked except for my cage and the plug in my ass. I went over to the table and grabbed my laptop. I was going to sit down but thought the better of that as I was still sore and that would only drive the plug into my ass deeper. So, I stood at the kitchen counter to open the email from John and download and read over the contract I signed. This was going to take some time to devote to memory. He also attached a copy of the creed to memorize as well as the contact info for Bo and Jay, which I put into my phone for use later.

I reached down and explored my caged nub for the first time in its new home. A mix of emotions ran over me. I was excited, nervous, and turned on at the same time. I would have loved to have jacked off right then, but that was never going to happen again, possibly. This was going to be a long journey for sure.

CHAPTER NINE

Sub Brothers

It was about 4 pm when I got back to my apartment from John's house. I had been spending some time looking over the contract and the creed when I got a text on my phone. I looked down to see that it was from Jay, my new sub brother.

"Matt, this is Jay. I wanted to welcome you to the family and wondered if Bo and I could come over to your place and talk?" Jay asked.

"Sure," I texted back. "Here is my address."

I sent him my address and directions to my apartment and about 30 minutes later I got a knock on the door. I went over and saw it was them through the peephole and let them in. Jay and Bo walked in and immediately stripped naked and folded their clothes next to the door. Jay had a small box he put on the floor as well.

"This is a nice place!" Bo said.

"It isn't too bad," I replied as I went into the kitchen. "It is a bit overpriced, but for this area, that is pretty common. Would you both like a drink? I have some Coke."

Bo was adjusting his cage and collar and looked up and said, "yeah, that would be great."

Jay walked over to the kitchen counter and leaned on it and said, "yeah, I'll take one too."

I leaned over to grab three cans from the lower part of the fridge and opened them and handed them to the guys.

"I noticed the plug there Matt," Jay said. "Sir always breeds new boys on their first day. I know I was walking funny for about a day. How is your ass feeling?"

"Ugh," I said. "I'd be lying if I said it was not sore. Sir is not small for sure."

"You got that right," Bo said with a laugh. "But you will get used to it."

I directed the guys back over to the couch. "Feel free to sit there. It is ok."

They both took a seat and I gently sat opposite of them in a chair, adjusting a bit as the plug pushed in farther.

"Well," said Jay. "Are you overwhelmed yet?"

I laughed. "Well, it is a lot to take in. I'll be honest that I had not expected to be sitting naked in chastity, with a cum filled and plugged ass, talking with two people I have never met before in my living room when I woke up today."

They both laughed as well.

"But I am excited to get started," I said. "I want to challenge myself and getting the chance to explore some things I have always been interested in intrigues me as well."

The guys both nodded at me as they drank their sodas.

"I had the opportunity to meet and talk to a guy named Dan that just graduated from Sir's program not too long ago and he put me at ease with the decision."

"Oh, Dan!" Jay said. "He is great! He graduated right before I was taken on and I got a chance to mentor with him when I was starting. He has a great master now."

"Yeah," I said. "I met Greg and Dan at the bar on Friday night."

"Well, listen, Matt," Jay said as he placed his drink down on the table. "I know you are just meeting us today, but Bo and I will be working closely with you in the coming weeks and months. We each had mentors and sub brothers we relied on and it's the only way to stay sane and grounded throughout the training."

"That's for sure," said Bo. "I have been with Sir for three months and if it had not been for Jay here and my other sub brother Johnny that graduated already, I don't think I would have made it. It is a lot to remember and, well, old habits die hard."

"What was the toughest thing for you, Bo?" I asked.

"The chastity portion," he said. "I guess we all would likely say that, but I messed up big time at first."

"How so?" I asked.

Bo was a bit embarrassed. "Well, it was about halfway through my first week. I was horny as fuck and I could not take it anymore, so I was humping a pillow on my couch just imagining playing with a friend of mine and the stimulation was enough to make me cum all over the pillow. I knew I had messed up and I felt ashamed. Johnny made a surprise visit to bring some things to me and he noticed the cum on the pillow and made me promise to tell John what I had done. I didn't blame him for keeping me honest, because I probably would have never admitted it otherwise. So, I told John and I was punished, but I learned my lesson. Things like that happen. You just have to learn to grow and move on."

"For me, it was all the formal protocols," Jay said. "I was a bit of a slob and not very punctual of a person. I have had to work on my appearance, my work ethic, and being respectful of the time of not only Sir but everyone else as well. My sub brother Nick, who Bo here replaced after he graduated, was the elder boy around when I started, and he took me under his wing and helped me a ton."

"What do you think will be your biggest challenge?" Bo asked me.

"Remembering everything," I said. "I have a horrible memory and it takes me a long time to get things down."

"We can help you with that," Jay said.

"For sure," Bo replied as well. "You will have all of this down in no time."

"Speaking of protocols, Matt," Jay said. "You need to have your hair and beard trimmed to meet Sir's requirements. Your pubic hair needs some work as well. I've brought some grooming equipment with me if you are willing to let us help you."

"Umm... sure," I said, not expecting that suggestion.

"Can we set up in the kitchen?" Bo asked. "It might be easier with the three of us."

"Sure," I said.

We all got up and Jay grabbed the box that contained two trimmers, one large one with colored guards to go on it of various lengths and a smaller one. Bo put a chair in the middle of the space. Jay found a place to plug in the larger trimmer and got behind the chair and then handed Bo the smaller battery-powered trimmer.

"Come over here and stand in front of me," Bo said.

I came over and Bo knelt to be eye level with my nub. He turned on the trimmer and told me to stand still and he went to work shaving my pubic hair down to a much shorter length.

"You have the option to go completely smooth," Bo said, "but that can be a hassle, especially using a razor around your cage every day. Using a trimmer like this you only have to do it weekly and it is pretty easy to do."

Once he was satisfied that everything was trimmed neatly, Jay handed him some scissors and he got any remaining hairs that remained.

"All done!" Bo said. "You are up Jay!"

"Sit here in the chair Matt," Jay said.

I sat down and he turned the trimmer on and put a number 5 guard on and went over my hair with it to get it down to a shorter length. I had not had a haircut in about two months, so there was a lot to cut. He squared off the back and made sure the hair was off my ears.

"That looks much better," Jay said. "It is time for your beard now."

He moved around to face me and leaned down some and his chastity cage almost landed on my knees.

"I love your beard, by the way," he said. "The streaks of white give you a bit of a daddy look. Well, a subby daddy look." Jay laughed at that last remark.

"I have a one-and-a-half-inch guard on here, so it should not look too much different, just cleaned up some. I know some people are very personal about their beard grooming habits. Do you trust me?" Jay asked.

I was nervous, but said, "yes. Go ahead"

Jay went over my beard and after he was done, he grabbed the scissors from Bo to make some final touches on it.

"There we go," Jay said. "That looks much better. Just be sure to shave your neck regularly as your hairline is pretty low."

"Yeah, I have been neglecting that," I said.

"Go into the bathroom and see what you think," Bo said. "You might also want to take a quick shower and rinse the hair off. We will clean up in here."

"Thanks!" I said as I went to the bathroom.

I was pleased with the look. It was very cleaned up and did not cost me a thing. My groin looked a lot less bushy and the cage stood out a lot more. I stepped in the shower quickly to wash off any of the remaining hair and then dried off and returned to the front. The kitchen had already been cleaned up and you could not tell we had been in there. In the living room, Jay and Bo were sitting on the couch talking.

"You look a lot better," Bo said as I came into the room.

"Thanks!" I said. "I appreciate all this."

"If you are interested," Jay said, "Bo and I meet up once a month to trim each other and you are welcome to join us."

"Most definitely," I said. "I'd like that."

"Well, unless you have other plans," Jay said, "would you like to start reviewing things with us? I'd be willing to pay for pizza for dinner if you want."

"That sounds great!" I said.

I went and got my laptop and went over all the rules, responsibilities, and expectations that were listed and the guys quizzed me on things and suggested little ways to remember some of the specifics. We also went over the creed several times and by the time the pizza arrived I was feeling a lot better. I put my pants on briefly to meet the delivery guy and took them off again to bring the food into the kitchen where we all grabbed some slices and brought them into the living room.

"I appreciate how much you all have done for me today," I said.

"Not a problem at all!" Jay said with a grin. "That's what we are here for!"

"Think of us really as your brothers," Bo said. "You can text either of us at any time for any reason. If you need to talk or if something is bugging you, just reach out.

"Thanks!" I said. "So, my specified training day is Sunday afternoon according to Sir. What about you two?"

"Well, I come on Tuesday nights," Jay said.

"And I come on Thursday nights," Bo said.

"But you will sometimes be there on our nights and there will be other nights you will be there as well," Jay continued. "This is your first week and Sir will be sending you things to look at and do via email. I will tell you he will expect you to keep your apartment clean at all times and we have to do the same. Next week you will be on a normal schedule. We all come by on Monday and Wednesday evenings for chores around his house. Friday and Saturday are usually yours to spend as you see fit, but there are special events."

"Sir mentioned that," I said.

"Yeah," Bo said. "I started my training under Sir in early December. Sir had a Holiday party on a Saturday between Christmas and New Years' and Jay, Johnny and I had to not only get everything set up, but we had to help run the party and had to be available at any time for any party-goer to use for their pleasure."

"Ugh, that party," Jay said. "I got fucked so much I could barely sit down the next day."

Bo laughed, "that is because you have that irresistible bubble butt. But my ass was pretty sore as well and my jaw was a bit out of wack from that one hung dude that kept face fucking me."

"Oh, I forgot about him," Jay said. "He liked you. I never had to do anything with him."

"Yeah," Bo said. "And poor Johnny was flogged to hell."

"That was his thing though," Jay said. "He was a pain freak."

Bo laughed, "that's for sure."

"Anyway," Jay continued, "so if your day is Sunday, then expect to be there on Monday and Wednesday nights too. Never book anything on those days if you can help it."

"I understand," I said. "That is fine. I don't normally do things during the week anyway. I like going out to the Eagle on Saturday evenings, though."

"Oooo... me too!" Bo said. Feel free to call me up next time you want to go, and we can carpool."

"Cool!" I said.

"I lead a pretty boring life," Jay said with a laugh. "But I might join you both out on occasion."

Seeing that they were both done eating, I grabbed the plates and went to the kitchen to clean up a bit.

"One thing we should discuss," Jay said as he got up and came to the counter and Bo followed him.

"Sure," I said, "what is it?"

"We are your brothers," Jay said. "But we are also responsible for each other as well. If any of us breaks the rules, we have to own up to it to Sir and it is expected that if we do not, and one of us knows about the rule-breaking, we have to report it. Otherwise, we have to join in the punishment."

"I understand," I said.

"Yeah," Bo said. "As I told you before, Johnny saw my infraction and he was obligated to report it if I did not. It's not about snitching, it is about being honest with ourselves and growing as a person."

"I get it," I said. "We have to be responsible for our actions and I would not want to see either of you punished for something I did."

"Ok," Jay said. "As long as you understand. Feel free to confide anything with us but realize that we are each other's keepers as well."

"Not to change the subject," Bo said and pointed to my cage, "but Matt, you are leaking there brother."

I looked down to see that a stream of precum was coming out of my cage and dripping down to the floor.

"Fuck," I said reaching down with a towel to clean up. "Sorry. I am a natural leaker and the stimulation from this damn plug and the fucking I had earlier is taking its toll I think."

Jay laughed. "It's ok brother. You should have seen Johnny. He was the same way."

"Yeah," Bo said. "He had to even wear pads that are normally used for bladder leaks to keep him from making a mess in his pants at work. Especially when he was in chastity for several months at a time."

"That is not a bad idea," I said with a grin. "The one thing I am noticing, though, is that having this metal cage on means I have to adjust it a lot as it hangs down."

"Oh, you can fix that," Bo said. "I'll send you a link to a strap you can get from Amazon. It attaches to the cage base ring and goes around your waist and it helps a lot if you have that issue. Sir is fine with you wearing something like that as well. Johnny wore one all the time for support."

"Thanks," I said. "I would appreciate that. I can order that tonight."

"Ok," Jay said, "As much as this has been fun, I need to be getting home. You ready Bo?"

"Sure!" Bo replied.

"Thanks again for coming by guys," I said. "I am looking forward to getting to know you better."

We all hugged and then the guys went and put their clothes back on and headed out.

After the guys left, I vacuumed the place and cleaned my bathroom up a bit. I decided it was good to get into a routine of cleaning up. My phone went off at one point with a text from Bo with the link to that support strap for the cage, which I ordered immediately. I went and sat down and played some video games and then decided to get ready for bed.

Given all that had happened today, I just wanted to take a nice long hot shower to relax. I let the water start warming up and pulled on the plug that had been in my ass for almost six hours now. A glob of cum ran down my leg when it popped out.

"Damn!" I said. "Sir loaded me the hell up!"

I got in the shower and cleaned up well and let the water and steam help relax me. I instinctively reached down to jack my cock and felt the cage there instead.

"Fuck," I thought to myself. "This is going to take some getting used to."

CHAPTER TEN

Interviews

My Monday morning was going about as it usually did, slowly. I had a lot of things that piled up, mostly because I had let them, and I was buried in a task when my phone went off. It was a text from John.

"How is your first day in service to me going boy?" he said.

"It's going ok, Sir. I am proud to be in your service, but it's a slog at work. I'm buried under paperwork."

"I understand," John replied. "Strip and take a picture of me to show me that hot body."

I went over to the door and closed and latched the lock and then took my clothes off and knelt on the floor of my office and set up the camera to snap a picture with the timer. My hands were behind my back and I faced forward. After I saw it and was pleased with the focus and framing, I sent it off to John.

"Very good, boy," John said. "Check your email after dinner tonight for a task."

"Thank you, Sir," I replied.

After work, I was walking back to my car when I got a call from my twin brother Steve.

"What's up, bro?" I said.

"Hey," he replied. "Not much. Work has been a bitch. They had me on call over the weekend and I had to go in to cover for some people. I'm just exhausted and it's only Monday."

"I hear that," I said. "It's not been any better here, but I managed to whittle down the paperwork a bit."

"I got ya," Steve replied. "Well, I was calling to see if you wanted to come over for dinner. I'm making a chicken casserole and it would be nice to catch up."

I was tired, but I did miss seeing him, so I told him I would come over, but I could not stay too late. He asked me to pick up some beer for him and I got over to his place about 6:30 pm.

I used my key to get into his apartment and saw Steve in the kitchen with his 'Kiss the Cook' apron on. He always had that on when he was in chef mode.

"Heya Matt!" Steve said. "Did you get the beer?"

"Right here," I said.

"Good," he replied. "Open one up for me."

I sat the beer on the counter and pulled one out, unscrewed the top, put it in a koozie, and handed it to him. I then moved around him and put the rest in the fridge.

"You don't want one?" he asked as I reached in for a soda.

"No," I said. "I'm just tired and I'm not in the mood."

"No worries," Steve said, "I get that."

He was still in his scrubs from the hospital. He had taken his shoes and socks off and put the apron on, but that was as far as he got. He worked in the radiology department at Emory Hospital, a job he had taken about six months prior for a lot more money than he was making at the ER at the hospital near us in Cobb County. But it did keep him busy and we did not get a chance to see each other as much.

Steve and I were identical twins. Even as we got older, it was tough to tell us apart. Sometimes I put on a bit more weight and sometimes he did, but even our beards had the same white streaks. The only real difference was some birthmarks he had on his chest, which I did not have. When we were little, it was the only way my dad was able to determine who was who.

As much as we were the same, we were very different. Yes, we were both gay and had similar tastes in men, but he always excelled in the biological sciences and I hated them. I did well in the natural sciences and history, and he hated that. I was fine in an office doing a desk job and he was happier on his feet in a hospital. He liked playing football in high school and I was the band geek. I liked quiet vacations on the beach, and he did destination ones that involved adventure.

These differences also came into play in our sex lives. He was all dominant and nearly always a top and I tended to be mostly a subby bottom. He had had a few girlfriends in high school and fucked quite a few after but thought of himself as mostly gay. I had never been with a woman and never had any interest in doing so. But, mostly, he was the secure one with his sexuality and I was the one that always had issues growing up. Thus, he was my bigger brother that was always there for me even though we were only separated by a few minutes in age.

They say twins have a sixth sense when it comes to each other. That you can tell when one is sad, or something is up. That was true for us in a way, and I think Steve intuitively knew something was different about me. That was pretty much confirmed when I took off my dress shirt to help him with the cooking and he saw the collar around my neck.

"Wait a moment," Steve said, pointing with a spoon in his hand. "That is new."

"Yeah," I hesitated, trying to determine how this was going to go.

Steve leaned in and read the silver tag on my collar.

"Chastity sub?" Steve asked, totally surprised. "What the hell does that mean?"

"It means I'm wearing a chastity device," I said. "And it means I have started to train under a guy to learn more about being a sub."

Steve just stood and stared at me for a moment. I think he was trying to determine what to say, but the words were escaping him.

"Don't be freaked out please," I said. "I just did this yesterday, so I am just getting used to it myself."

Steve turned to finish putting things in a pan and placed them in the oven. He then turned around and grabbed his beer and took a swig, leaning on the counter opposite of me.

"So, tell me how you met this guy," Steve said.

I explained the past two weeks in as much detail as I could. I told him about playing with Chris and Rick and how I met John. I told him about the trial session and then the contract and the collaring ceremony yesterday afternoon. The whole time he sat there and just drank his beer without much emotion. I was having trouble reading him for one of the first times in my life.

When I finished, Steve spoke. "Well, that is quite the tale. I've always known you were much more subordinate, but I know you can be vulnerable at times too. Please just be careful, that is all I ask."

"I will bro," I said, relieved that he was being ok with this. "I want this. I want to challenge myself and push my boundaries and I trust Sir. I also really like my sub brothers as well."

Steve shook his head and smiled a bit. "Sir, huh? Sub brothers? You are into this. Ok, you got to show me the cage. I mean, come on."

I blushed a bit and unzipped my pants to show him the chastity cage. Growing up we had just about the same size penis, though his was a bit longer and girthier than mine. Knowing what I had and seeing it all packed in a small package shocked Steve a bit.

"Damn bro!" Steve said. "Better you than me. I could never do that."

I zipped my pants back up and said, "Meh, I'm still learning to get used to it."

"Well, just promise me you will talk to me if anything seems weird," he said.

"Oh, I will," I said, and I pointed at the stove. "Now, you better stir that mac and cheese before it burns."

After dinner, we chatted a bit more, but I was ready to get home and I knew I needed to check my email for a message from John. I hugged Steve and we parted ways and I got back to my apartment at about 8:30 pm.

Once I entered and had stripped all my clothes off and folded and put them next to the door, I went over to the couch and opened up my computer. I had one email from John that came in about an hour ago.

> Boy,
>
> One of the first tasks I have new boys that train with me perform is to interview one of my graduated subs and their master. I talked to my friend Greg and he said he and his boy Dan had already met you. I have set up an appointment for you to meet them both at Greg's home tomorrow evening. You are to arrive there at 7 pm and do not be late.
>
> In preparation for this meeting, you need to review the attached form. I expect you to have this completed and

submitted back to me via email tomorrow evening after you arrive back home from Greg's home.

Remember, you are now one of my boys and a reflection of me. Be respectful. You will strip when you enter his home and fold your clothes and put them to the side just as you do in your home and here. You will address Greg as 'Sir' and while Dan is a sub boy, he has graduated from my service, so he is the alpha sub, and you are the beta. You will show deference to him if he asks you to do anything.

Have a good day tomorrow and I look forward to your report.

Sir

I had forgotten to message Dan to tell him that I had accepted John's collar and service contract. I decided to text him after I finished reading the email and confirm I would be at his master's place tomorrow.

"Looking forward to speaking to you again," Dan replied. "If you can record voice, I suggest recording our conversations with your phone and then writing it up after when you get home. That is what I did, and it was a lot less of a hassle."

"That's a great idea," I replied. "I can do that."

Dan sent me the address for tomorrow evening and told me to be sure to eat before I arrived and then wished me a good evening. After I put my phone down, I opened up the attachment John had referenced.

INTAKE INTERVIEW

Questions for the Sub

1. What made the sub decide to enter into the training contract with Sir John?
2. What were the sub's most challenging aspects of their training?

3. What was a low point the sub faced and how did he overcome this?
4. How did the sub grow over the year of his training?
5. What advice does the sub have for the trainee during his contract period?
6. How did the sub find his master?
7. What has the sub found most challenging as a graduated and collared sub?
8. How does the sub define his role with his master?
9. Where does the sub see himself in ten years?

Questions for the Master

1. How did the master hear about Sir John and his sub-training program?
2. What aspects of the training program have proved most valuable for his collared sub?
3. What does the master look for in a sub?
4. What responsibilities does the master have for his sub?
5. How does the master define his role over the sub?
6. What advice does the master have for the trainee?

It all appeared to be pretty good interview questions designed to help me understand why Dan came to be where he is now, but also what Greg was looking for and how he and Dan interact. I was looking forward to the session and would be interested to see how things played out.

For now, though, I was tired. So, I propped my feet up on the table and played some video games to unwind, and then got ready for bed. The night before I slept through the night and only woke up once briefly from where my balls had caught in the cage a bit. I was adapting quickly to the cage and looking forward to when I could sleep without a break.

Tuesday went by pretty quickly. I had to go to the bathroom a few times to adjust my cage, but I was doing ok. My amazon order of the strap to help support the cage showed it would be in later in the week, so I figured that would help a lot. However, I was leaking precum a bit in the cage. When I sat a certain way in my chair, pressure hit my balls and it stimulated me to the point where I would start to dribble. I had grabbed a sock on the way out the door in the morning and had put that in my pants to help and that seemed to keep me from making wet spots in my pants, but I needed to figure out a better solution.

By the end of the workday, I had things pretty squared away, so I left a few minutes early to grab some dinner on the way home and still have time to change into casual clothes before going over to Greg and Dan's place.

The address I was driving to was in Sandy Springs, on the northside of Atlanta, but traffic is a bit of a nightmare, so I was really worried I would be late. Fortunately, I knew some shortcuts taking some of the side streets and I pulled up to their gated community with just a few minutes to spare. I buzzed their number and the gate opened and let me in. I took the road around and found their two-story condo on the second street to my left and I pulled into their driveway.

After I walked up the steps to the door and knocked, it opened to reveal Dan. All he had on was a jockstrap that supported his chastity cage, clearly visible in the white mesh, and his collar.

"Great to see you again Matt!" he said.

"Good to see you as well!" I replied.

When I entered, I took off all my clothes down to my cage and collar and folded them on top of my shoes next to the front door. I held on to my phone so I could record the interview tonight, but I put it on silent mode.

"It's really good to see that collar on you, Matt," Dan said. "Congratulations."

"Thanks," I said. "And thanks for talking to me at the bar the other day. It put my mind at ease and helped me make my decision."

"I am glad I could help," Dan said. "Come with me."

Dan led me through the living room and into the kitchen in the back. It was a small place, but nice. The living room was in front and there was a small half bath on the left as you walked down the hall. In the back was the kitchen and dining area with a nice deck off the back. A staircase went up to the left when you walked in the front door and at the top was a landing that led to two bedrooms, one in the front and one in the back, and a full bathroom in the middle.

Greg was in the kitchen sitting at the table with some coffee reading the news on his iPad when I entered. He had on a tank top and was wearing some pajama bottoms and was in his bare feet.

"Nice to see you again, boy," Greg said looking up at me. "You look much better in the cage and with a collar."

"Thank you, Sir," I said.

Dan sat down opposite Greg and pointed to the floor next to the wall.

"You can sit there," Dan said. "Sir does not allow subs in training on any of the furniture."

I got on the floor and sat cross-legged and looked up at Greg.

"So, how are you feeling about everything so far, boy?" Greg asked.

"It has been good so far," I said. "I am just getting started, but I am spending time memorizing all the rules and learning what is expected of me."

Greg finished off the last of his coffee and then said, "That is good. You need to know your place and how to behave. Dan here learned very quickly from what I understand. I hope you learn a lot from him."

Greg stood up and then turned to look down at me.

"I am going up to relax a bit. You can interview Dan down here. When you are done, Dan will show you upstairs and we can continue the conversation there."

"Thank you, Sir," I said as he turned to leave.

Dan got up after Greg left and took his cup and saucer from the table and went to the sink and washed them and put them back up in the cabinet. He then got the coffee pot and cleaned it out too. When he was done, he went back over to the table and sat down turning the chair to face me.

"I hope you are not nervous," Dan said. "I know I was when I did my interview when I was starting. Like I told you before, I want to help if I can, so please feel free to be open and honest."

"Thanks a lot," I said.

I pulled out my phone and turned on the recording and then pulled up the questions that I had to ask Dan.

"The first question," I said. "What made you decide to enter into the training contract with Sir John?

Dan sat back in the chair and thought for a second. "Well, I grew up outside of Memphis in a place called Germantown. It wasn't too bad, but not an open place if you are gay and into kinks, for sure. I attended the University of Memphis out of high school and that is where I had my first experiences with guys. I would answer ads on craigslist or meet people on campus through friends and I felt drawn to men that would dominate me. It was a huge turn-on. When I neared graduation though, I wanted to get out of town."

He paused and scratched his chest before continuing.

"So, I started looking at craigslist ads that were in other cities and I talked to folks on social media sites catering to the BDSM community. That is when I ran across the ad that Sir John had put up stating he would have an opening for a boy in his training program. It was a pretty detailed ad with a lot of what was in the contract we signed, and I was drawn to it. I reached out to him and after a few phone interviews, he flew me here to Atlanta for a few days for a trial run and I stayed in his pool house out back. It went well and he agreed to take me on. He also got me set up with a job here locally as well, so I was able to start the training that September in 2013 after I graduated."

"So, you started fresh here then," I said.

"Yeah," said Dan. "But I do not regret it. It was a great experience for me."

"Along those lines," I said, "What were some challenging aspects of the training, and did you have any low points you had to overcome?"

Dan crossed his arms over his chest and leaned his head back on the wall.

"Oh, I faced a lot of challenges," he said. "I mean, first off I was young, I was only 22 at the time and so green when it comes to sexual experiences. My sub brothers Ryan and Hunter were older and much more experienced. But they helped me a lot and I think the biggest issue I had was being willing to fully trust and be open to Sir John's training, requests, and guidance. I was hesitant a lot at first and made a lot of mistakes, but I grew quickly."

Dan looked down at me and said, "one good piece of advice is to know that he has your best interests at heart and to do what he asks without question. Open yourself up to new experiences, it will be worth it. Trust your sub brothers and rely on them to help you through. Hunter was the elder brother for me when I joined and he was my rock I relied on in many instances in my first three months, especially being a new kid to the city."

"So how did you grow over your year of training and what other advice do you have for me?" I asked.

"Oh, I made leaps and bounds of progress I would say. I'll admit, I rapidly evolved into a bit of a pig, sexually," Dan said with a laugh, groping his cage under his jock a bit as he thought.

"But I learned to crave seeing the satisfaction and pleasure that comes over a guy when you are servicing him. Hearing them grunt and growl when they are breeding you, seeing the pleasure on their face when you suck a load out of them, knowing they are relaxed and well taken care of as you clean up the house or give them a massage, these are intoxicating for me and I look to please men like my Sir wherever and whenever I can."

He leaned on his legs and faced me and said, "that is the biggest advice I have for you. Learn to enjoy that as well and you will be a much better sub."

Dan stood and walked over to get a glass of water and then returned to sit at the table.

"Well, the next questions involve your Sir, Greg. How did you find your master and what is most challenging as a graduated and collared sub? Also, how would you define your role in the house and where do you see yourself in, say, ten years?"

"Humm," Dan said as he sipped his water and leaned back in the chair again.

"Well, I met Sir at one of Sir John's parties. He took a liking to me pretty quick and was fucking the hell out of me one holiday party. Later, he asked to borrow me and Sir John agreed, and we had some trial sessions here at his house where he determined if I would be a good fit for him."

Dan leaned down to face me again.

"I found him very attractive and loved the way he treated me and the things he wanted me to do for him, but there were challenges. He has specific boundaries he sets with a sub. We are not romantic, and this is not a normal boyfriend or partner relationship. I am his sub, and I am here for his pleasure and to keep the house clean. I would not say I am a slave, because I am allowed to have my own life and see other people, for instance, but Sir is my primary focus. That was very tough for me at first, especially after I was collared because I initially wanted more of a close relationship with him, but over the past six months, I have found my place and I am happy."

"And where do you see yourself in ten years?" I asked.

"Hopefully still serving Sir," Dan said. "And, of course, any partner or partners he ends up having. He has also discussed getting a bigger place one day and taking in another sub, so I might be the alpha sub one day too. But, if he decides to let me go in the future, I will likely seek out a similar arrangement. This is something that makes me happy."

I stopped the recording on the phone and looked up at Dan.

"Thanks so much," I said. "This has been great so far."

"Well," said Dan, "then it is time you go up and see Sir then."

Dan went over and rinsed and washed the glass he had been using and then dried and put it away, then he told me to get up and I followed him back into the living room and up the staircase. At the top of the landing, he told me to wait and he went into the back bedroom to talk to Greg and let him know I was ready to interview him.

Dan came back out after a few moments and said, "he is ready for you. Go in and stand to the right of the door near the wall. I will be downstairs when you are done."

Dan squeezed my shoulder and then returned downstairs.

I walked across the hall to the bedroom which was lit by two lamps in the back on either side of a large king-sized bed which provided the room with a warm glow. On the bed, Greg was sitting with one leg outstretched and the other bent. He was propped up on several pillows and had been reading something on his iPad, which he put away. He was completely naked, and a large soft cock was nestled in a bush of dark hair with a trail of light fur that ran up his muscular chest. He had one arm behind his head and the hair from his armpit was matted a bit.

I have to admit, my nub started to swell as much as it could in the cage and a bead of precum started to form, which I felt and grabbed and swallowed quickly as I stood next to the door against the wall facing him.

"How did the interview with my boy go, Matt?" Greg asked me.

"Very good, Sir," I said. I could feel another dribble forming at the end of my nub as the head started to squeeze between the bars of the cage.

"Looks like you are a leaker there," Greg said, noticing my swollen nub and the large drop forming.

"Yes, Sir. I always have been," I said as I reached down and collected and swallowed the precum again.

"That is normal, do not worry," Greg said. "So, what questions do you have for me boy?"

I looked at my phone and turned the recording on again and then looked at the questions I had for him.

"First off," I said. "How did you hear about Sir's training program and what aspects have you noted as being valuable for Dan?"

"Well, John and I have known each other for a long time. We train at the same gym with your friend Rick as well. So, I have been to his house many times, I have seen many of his subs and attended parties where they have serviced me. However, Dan caught my eye. Apart from his wonderful ass, which is a great pleasure to fuck, he has a good attitude and is very attuned to my needs. He often is doing something before I ask him to, and he never backs away from me when I ask him to do something new. I have found that John's program helps to produce well-rounded subs that are experienced in so many techniques and fetishes and yet are moldable and follow rules without question."

Hearing a pause in his answer, I asked, "and what do you look for in a sub? How do you define your roles and what responsibilities do you have for him?"

"I do like younger boys," Greg said. "That is just one of the things that turns me on. But I have had older boys in the past as well. I look for a well-disciplined boy that is self-sufficient yet ready to meet my needs. He also needs to understand that I am not looking for a partner or a boyfriend. I want a servant for the house and to please me, but also one that will serve those that I date and bring in the house as well. As a dom, I define myself as the one in charge. This is my household and my needs come first. I treat my sub with respect, but his needs are secondary to mine. He can have autonomy, but it cannot infringe on my expectations or things I want to see done, for instance."

"And what advice would you have for me?" I asked.

"Learn everything you can boy," he said. "Explore as many kinks as John can expose you to. Seek out opportunities to practice with other men and learn to be the best sub you can be. Become a sub that can anticipate what a dom needs and be there to provide it. Most importantly, respect the men you serve and draw pleasure from the service you provide."

I turned off the recording and said, "Thank you. That is good advice."

"I know you are just starting boy," Greg said, "but I can see you have the raw talent and attitude you need to progress. I'll be honest, Rick, John and I talked about you at the gym yesterday and John is looking forward to molding you into a better sub."

I blushed a bit and said, "Thank you, Sir."

"John also said you know how to give good head as well," Greg said as he got up and moved to sit on the edge of the bed.

He started to stroke his cock, which started to grow.

"Kneel before me boy and pleasure me," Greg said.

I put my phone on the floor and walked over and knelt in front of the large man. His cut cock was long and thick and glistened as a bead of precum formed at its tip. I reached up to grab the base of his shaft and pulled my thumb under his balls into his bush. I then placed the head of his cock in my mouth and slowly started to lick and suck, savoring the sweet taste of his juices.

Greg grabbed some pillows and put them behind the small of his back and leaned back on his arms and looked down at me.

"That's a good boy," he said. "I want you to savor a real man's cock."

I started to go down on him and use my hands to move up and down on his shaft as well. I licked down the length of him and put my nose deep in his bush and smelled his musk. It was pungent but intoxicating. My nub was straining so much it cut off the ability for any precum to come out.

I took in one of his balls and rolled it around with my tongue and did the same to the other. They were massive and I bet could breed a boy well. Greg was moaning while I did this and reached down and grabbed the back of my head, forcing me back into his crotch again.

"You like that scent don't you, boy?" Greg said.

"Yes, Sir," I replied.

"It's a man's scent," Greg said rubbing his crotch over my beard and marking it. "You'll be wearing it home boy."

He let me get back on his cock and I continued to work his shaft with my hands and mouth. I adjusted my head a little bit so I could try to get more of it in my mouth, but I was struggling. I continued to fondle and sniff his crotch as much as I could.

This went on for about ten to fifteen minutes. He would occasionally tell me to back off and would grab his cock and slap its entire length on my face. Sometimes a little rope of precum and spit would fly over my head and face, landing in my hair and beard. Then he would force me back on him and I would continue.

Eventually, he grabbed my head and shoved me down as much as I could go. His thick cock filled my whole mouth and his head hit the back of my throat and made me cough just as he erupted and cum started spewing down my throat, up my nose, and out onto my beard.

He kept cumming too. It seemed to last forever and was running down my beard and onto the fur on my chest. I struggled to breathe a bit.

When he finally came down off his orgasm, he pulled my head off and I gasped for air. I was covered in his cum and musk. He reached down and used his fingers to feed me some of the cum on my face and then he rubbed the rest into my beard and chest hair. He squeezed the last out of his softening cock and fed it to me as well.

"Very well done, boy," Greg said. "John and Rick were not kidding when they said you knew how to orally please a dom."

"Thank you, Sir!" I said with a grin.

Greg put the pillows back at the headboard and moved back to his original position.

"You may go now, boy," Greg said.

"Thank you, Sir," I said.

I started to get up and I felt my nub move. The head had swelled so much in the tight space it was in that it squeezed the urethra completely closed and trapped a large amount of precum deep inside me. When I went to get up, the movement caused the tube to reopen and at least a teaspoon of precum came flowing out of my nub. I was able to grab it just in time before it hit the floor and collect it all in my hands and swallow it.

Greg was watching as I was doing this and smiled. I then turned and reached down to grab my phone and headed downstairs.

Dan was in the living room when I came down. He saw the matted chest hair I had and the bits of dried cum in my beard.

"Looks like you had a successful interview there," he said with a grin.

"Yeah," I said with a slight laugh. "I guess you could say that. He marked me pretty well. I can still taste and smell him."

"His scent is intoxicating, Dan said. "I'm a lucky boy to serve him."

Dan looked down and saw some last bits of precum dripping from my cage. He reached down and grabbed it and licked his fingers.

"You got a little leaky too!" he said with a grin.

I blushed a bit. "Yeah, that is pretty common for me."

"Just wait till you are in permanent chastity," Dan said with a chuckle. "You will be constantly leaking."

I turned to put my clothes on and head back home. After I put my shoes on, he leaned in to hug me.

"As I said before, feel free to reach out anytime. I'm glad to help," he said.

"I appreciate it," I said as we embraced.

I turned to leave and headed back out to the car. As I got in, I looked in the rearview mirror and saw the state of my beard. You could tell I had just been coated with a load. It was a good thing I just had to head home. But I did not mind it at all.

Once I got back home, I came in and stripped down, and went over to my computer to type up everything and send it off to John. It was a good day, I thought.

CHAPTER ELEVEN

Cleaning Day

As I got out of bed Wednesday morning, I realized I had not been woken up by my nub all night. That was a welcome change, I thought to myself. I picked my phone up and noticed a text from John.

"Boy, be at the house at 7 pm," he said. "Eat first and then come in and take your place in the yellow square and wait."

I knew from my conversations with my sub brothers on Sunday night that Wednesday was a cleaning day. I wondered if I would be seeing them, but at the moment the main thing on my mind was getting cleaned up for work.

After I took my shower and placed my clothes for the day beside the door, I reheated some sausage biscuits from the freezer in the microwave and grabbed some cereal and milk as well as some orange juice. I was sitting forward near the edge of the chair at the kitchen table and my caged nub was hanging off the edge. I groped myself a few times and I immediately swelled in my cage. My balls had a deep slight ache as well.

This was the longest I had gone without blowing my load and I still had several days to go. I had felt this aching sensation before. I called it 'blue balls'. I had experienced it before if I had not cum in a day or two. My balls would just feel heavy and a bit sore and if I just busted a nut, it cured it. Since that was not happening till Sunday, four days away, I was going to just have to deal with it, if I could.

After I was done with breakfast, I brushed my teeth and checked myself in the mirror, and then I went to the door and dressed, and headed out for work.

The day was long and included a lot of paperwork. My eyes were getting a little sore by the afternoon and I got up to go to the break room to grab some coffee. As I was sitting there drinking, my phone dinged with a text message from Bo.

"How is your week going, brother?" he said.

"It is going well," I replied. "I had an interview with Sir Greg and his boy Dan that graduated before Jay."

"Oh, I have met Dan before," Bo said. "He's a nice guy. I hope you learned a lot."

"I did, actually," I said. "It is nice to get the perspective from not only subs but doms as well. It seems like there are a lot of different personalities and expectations that you have to prepare for."

"That is for sure," Bo said.

"Sir told me to come over tonight," I said. "Will I see you there?"

"Yup!" Bo replied. "It is a normal cleaning day for us. He's probably going to have you follow us to see how things are done."

"I figured as much," I said.

"Cool! Well, I will see you later then," Bo replied with a smiling emoji after.

I put my phone down and finished my coffee. I liked Bo and Jay, I thought to myself. I had only known them a short time, but I just felt comfortable around them. It was making this whole experience something I was able to handle. I needed to see about hanging out with them more.

My coworker broke my train of thought as she stuck her head in to ask me something. So, I threw away the disposable cup and returned to my office to complete a few tasks before the end of the day.

After work, I picked up a salad on the way home with some sliced chicken on top. I figured it would be something that would be quick to eat and give me a little roughage and protein. I needed to start to eat a little better. The junk food had gotten a bit out of control lately.

When I got home, I stripped down by the door and then went into the kitchen to eat. I was reading a bit of the news on my laptop to kill the time as well. I had got back to my apartment about 5:45 pm and I needed to leave by 6:40 pm to make sure I got to John's place with time to spare. As I was finishing my dinner, I heard a knock at the door which startled me a bit as I didn't expect anyone to be at the door.

I looked through the peephole and saw it was Kenny. I panicked a bit. Should I throw on some pants to greet him? According to the rules I was not allowed to wear clothes inside my house unless there was family around, someone underage or someone that I didn't know, and it would not be appropriate. But I knew Kenny. We had played several times and I had just sucked him off in the laundry the other day. I could also act like I was not there, but that felt wrong as well.

I decided to crack the door a bit and lean around with my head.

"Hey, Kenny. What is up?" I asked.

"Hey Matt," he said. "Listen, I know this is probably not the best time, but I saw you come home a bit ago when I was getting back myself and, well, frankly, I just needed to talk to you about something. Do you have a moment?"

Now I was freaking out a bit in my head. Was I ready to let him see me naked and in my chastity cage?

"If you are busy," he said, "I understand."

In the back of my mind, my subconscious was asking me, "What would Sir want you to do?" And I knew the answer. He would want me to not be ashamed of my appearance or who I am.

"No, it is completely fine," I said, opening the door just a bit more. "But I don't wear clothes at home, is that going to bother you?"

"Not at all," Kenny said. "You got to be comfortable in your own home for sure!"

"Cool," I replied, and I opened the door to let him in.

As Kenny walked by me, he saw my chastity cage, and then as his eyes went back up to my head, he saw the collar on as well labeling me as a 'chastity sub'.

"Well, this is new isn't it?" He said, gesturing with his fingers.

"Yeah," I said as I closed the door. "I was collared by a local dom the other day and I will be training under him for a year. He has a lot of protocols like being naked at home and keeping the place clean, but he also requires his subs to be in chastity as well."

"Hey, that is cool," Kenny said, which surprised me a bit. "You know I am a top and I've had boys in chastity play with me before. It's a fun kink. I like your collar too."

"Thanks!" I said walking back to the kitchen to clean up a bit after dinner. "So, what did you need to talk about?"

Kenny walked over to the counter and leaned on it. "My cousin was supposed to be moving out at the end of the week to get into his new place, but they called him yesterday and told him they had a water pipe burst and it flooded the place. They won't have one ready for a while."

"Fuck!" I said. "What the hell is he going to do?"

"I don't know, and while I love him, I can't have him staying with me anymore, I need my life back," Kenny said. "I know you said once you knew someone that worked at an apartment matching company. Do you still have that connection?"

"Oh, yeah!" I said. "Kit works at one down the street. I can call her quick and see if she can help."

"That would be awesome," Kenny said.

I told him to come into the kitchen and sit at the table and I grabbed my phone and called Kit. She answered and had a few options that would be available by Friday and I put her on speakerphone and Kenny answered some questions on budget and such and we got a plan in place to send some options to his cousin.

After we hung up, Kenny looked relieved. "Dude, you saved my life. Thanks so much."

"Anytime bubba," I said. "And, if you don't mind me asking when was the last time you busted a nut?"

Kenny grinned. "Last Saturday when you sucked me off!"

"Fuck dude," I said. "That was four days ago. Those balls need better care than that. Come over here to the living room, you are getting serviced right now."

Kenny's grin widened and he followed me into the living room, and I helped him take his pants down and he sat on the couch. He was already hard as a rock in anticipation and I figured this would work to my advantage since I could not take too long as I needed to get over to John's place.

I pulled on his shaft a bit watching his foreskin retract and reveal the red and glistening head of his cock below. I licked it and sucked on it and Kenny immediately threw his head back and stretched out his legs.

"You don't know how much I need this right now," he said.

"Oh, I have an idea," I said, thinking about my caged blue balls.

I worked his shaft and moved up and down on it, reaching up to run and caress his belly and fur. I moved my hands under his hips and grabbed onto his ass a bit for better leverage and started to pick up the pace and deep throat him as much as I could.

Kenny was moaning at this point and put his hand on my neck, guiding me as I pleasured him.

"Fuck, boy," he said with his eyes closed. "Daddy needs to cum in that sweet mouth of yours."

I backed off his cock just long enough to say, "give it to me daddy," before continuing to bob up and down on his engorged cock.

Kenny reached down with both hands and grabbed my head and face fucked me as the orgasm overtook him. I forced my head down on him just as his balls erupted and sent his cum deep down my throat and into my mouth. Pulse after pulse came and I did my best to swallow it all before a small amount ran out the side of my mouth and into my beard. The man was pent up.

Kenny collapsed and as I backed off and licked the remains of his load off his softening cock, I saw his belly rise and fall as he tried to catch his breath. His eyes were still closed, and he reached up to wipe his mouth from where a little spit came out when he yelled at his climax.

When he was fully conscious again, he looked down at me and rubbed my head and hair. "Thanks so much for that. I fucking needed that so bad."

I grinned and laughed a bit. "Well, anytime you need to release some steam you know where I live. Now that I am in training to be a sub, I guess it's a good idea to provide service where I can."

Kenny chuckled at that and gave me a wink. "I am going to remember that."

He put his pants back on and hugged me and then headed out the door. I went back into the bathroom and rinsed my beard off a bit to get any remaining cum out and then combed my hair. It was time for me to leave, so I went back to the front door and dressed and headed out to John's house.

When I pulled in the driveway to John's I saw the same two cars there that I noticed last weekend, so I figured Jay and Bo were already here. I got out of the car and walked around and down the hill to the side door and entered. I stripped down and put my things in my yellow bin and then closed and latched the door and then I entered the dungeon area. Jay and Bo were already there and kneeling in their spots. Without speaking, I closed the door behind me and knelt in the yellow square painted on the floor with my hands behind my back and my head bowed and waited.

After a few minutes, I heard footsteps on the staircase and the door opened and John's bare feet came into view in front of me.

"You may look up boys," John said.

I looked up to see John in his boxers and t-shirt and a glass of bourbon in his hand.

"I was pleased with your interview report, Matt," John said as he looked down at me. "Did you find the experience worthwhile?"

"I did, Sir," I replied. "You trained Dan very well and I learned a lot from his interview. Greg was equally as helpful, and I was able to orally please him after as well."

"Yes, I know," John said. "Greg was highly complementary of not only your attitude but your service. You made me proud."

I grinned at that statement.

"Starting next week," John said, "you will be expected to be here on Monday and Wednesday evenings no later than 7 pm. Bo and Jay know this routine very well as these are designated cleaning days here at the house. I want you to shadow them today and learn what needs to be done."

"Jay," John said, turning to look at him. "As the senior boy in the house, you will oversee Matt and make sure that he is brought up to speed on everything. If he fails to remember or do anything correctly next week, then you will share in his punishment for failure. Is that understood?"

"Yes, Sir," Jay said. "I understand."

"Rise boys and recite the creed," John said.

We all got on our feet and placed our hands behind our backs and raised our heads and faced forward. In the back of my head, I was glad that we had practiced this routine and stance several times at my house while the guys helped me memorize what I needed to say.

We spoke as one, "I am a sub in training under the supervision of Sir John. My goal is to serve men in the best way I can and derive pleasure from that service. My chastity cage and collar are a symbol of that service and I desire one day to be in permanent chastity and receive my formal graduation collar as proof of my commitment."

"Very good," John said. "I am very pleased you have learned this already, Matt."

John took a sip of his drink and looked at us each for a moment.

"Well, I have work to do upstairs in my office," he said. "Jay, you are in charge now. When you boys are done, you have my permission to leave."

John then turned and headed back up the stairs and when he closed the door, we all relaxed.

Bo turned to me first. "You nailed the creed. Well done!"

"Thanks," I said. "But you all are the reason. I appreciate all the help the other day and I have been going over it every day since."

"Ok Matt," Jay said to me. "On cleaning days, we all arrive by 7 pm and kneel in our spot as you did today. If anyone is late, we are all punished. At 7 pm, if Sir is home, he will come down and greet us and have us recite the creed. If he is working late or is not home for any reason, then after ten minutes of waiting, we are to rise and recite the creed on our own."

"OK," I said. "So far so good."

"The next step is to come over here," Jay said as he and Bo led me across the dungeon area to the far side.

On the left wall near the end, the mirrored surface was cut differently and there was nothing in front of it. Jay pushed on a spot on the mirror and it opened inward to reveal another room. We walked in and Jay turned on the lights.

It was a standard-sized room for what you would normally use for a bedroom, though there were no windows. To my left were two doors. One led to another bathroom and the other was a closet. In the room were cages that were large enough for someone to be locked inside on their hands and knees, but you would not be able to stand up. Along the wall to the left were shelves that had towels, bottles of lube, and other boxes that were sealed as well.

To the right, as you entered was a whiteboard. On it, John had written our names and below this, chores were listed.

"This room is used for isolation and punishment," Jay said. "So, if you are ever told to report to the isolation room, this is where you will come. You will close the door behind you and kneel on the floor in the center of the room and wait. The closet over there has all the cleaning supplies, vacuums, and rags to dust with. We will grab what we need in a moment. The bathroom beside it is only to be used when you are servicing Sir. Sir will explain more when you have your one-on-one days."

"I understand," I said with a little concern in my voice.

"Here on the whiteboard Sir will list the things we have to do," Jay said. "Most of this never changes, but it is a good idea to check the board every cleaning day to make sure nothing has been added or changed. The first thing written is what you do on Mondays and the second is what you do on Wednesdays."

"Ok. I got it," I said as I read the list on the board.

Jay --- Master suite / master bath

Bo --- main floor bathroom / study

Matt --- kitchen / living room

"So, if I understand," I said, "I will be cleaning the living room today."

"Correct," Jay said. "Today you will be straightening that area up, dusting, vacuuming, and making it look spotless. If you notice, the rooms we are responsible for are based on seniority. The most senior sub is the only one allowed to be on the upper floor of the house and to clean. That would be me. Never go up there, Matt, unless Sir specifically tells you to."

I nodded my head and said, "I understand."

"You and Bo will also have the additional duty of cleaning the basement dungeon," Jay said. "I have the additional duty of cleaning Sir's private office upstairs. We clean and straighten up these additional rooms on both Mondays and Wednesdays. Put off the dungeon till last and Bo can help you when he finishes his duties."

"As you can see," Bo said, "it is pretty straightforward, and we are usually out of here in an hour or two."

"Ok boys, it is time to get to work," Jay said.

I followed them as they went across the room to the closet. We each grabbed a vacuum and a bucket containing cleaning supplies and rags.

I then followed them back into the dungeon area and up to the main floor.

"Bo," Jay said, "help get Matt started. I will come downstairs and check on his progress after a bit."

"You got it, Jay," Bo said as Jay continued to the second floor.

"Ok Matt," Bo said. "You got the living room here to the right. I have the study here in front. One thing that you should know is if you get the study, then you are also responsible for just dusting and vacuuming in the small guest room you will find on the other side of the kitchen there past the door to the garage."

So, Bo and I started cleaning on the main floor while Jay was upstairs. It only took about 35 minutes to complete and then I headed down to vacuum and straighten up the dungeon area and Bo came down to help me soon after. By 8 pm, we were all putting things away.

"That wasn't too bad," I said.

"Naa," Jay said as he closed the door to the cleaning closet, "it is worse after-parties, but normally it's just light cleaning."

"So, are we free to go?" I asked.

"Yup!" Jay said. "I have some errands to run so I am going to head out now."

As Jay went back into the dungeon area and headed for the entrance hallway, Bo turned to me and asked, "do you have anything else to do tonight?"

"Nope," I said. "Nothing planned."

"Why don't you come over to my place then," Bo said. "We can hang out and talk."

"That sounds good," I said.

We walked out of the isolation room and closed the door behind us. We then crossed the room and went into the entrance hallway and got our clothes out of the bins and got dressed. Bo gave me his address and then we headed out to our cars.

Bo's apartment was a little farther south of mine, but it only took about 25 minutes to get there from John's place. I followed behind him and parked in the lot beside his car. His complex had about 10 buildings, all three-story with a breezeway in the middle of each building and an iron staircase in the breezeway that you climbed to get access to the floors. Bo was on the second floor of a building on the back of the property, so he had trees behind him.

After climbing the stairs and entering his apartment, we both stripped down, and Bo showed me where to put my clothes on a table next to the door.

"Would you like a coke?" Bo asked.

"Sure!" I said.

Bo walked to the right across a small dining area to the kitchen behind it. The kitchen was a galley type with the stove and fridge on the back wall and the dishwasher and sink on the other. Above the sink was a cutout and counter that looked out into the living area to the left. Down the hall between the living area and the kitchen was a bathroom at the end and you took a left to get to Bo's bedroom. It was small but looked nice. There was a sliding glass door that could be opened onto a small porch as well from the living area.

"Come over here and sit down," Bo said as he handed me the can of soda and directed me to the living area.

He sat on one side of a couch and I sat on the other and we adjusted to face each other.

"Well," Bo said, "talk to me. How are things going?"

"It's going ok," I said. "I am still trying to take it all in. It's been a whirlwind of a couple of weeks."

"I can imagine," Bo said. "You will be surprised how routine it gets over time, though."

Bo reached down and adjusted his chastity cage. He pulled on his balls and moved the ring a bit.

"How is your cage fitting?" he asked after he was done.

"Not bad," I said. "I ordered that strap you suggested, and it is supposed to be delivered tomorrow. But the main issue I have is the precum dribbling. I am having a horrible time avoiding wet spots in my pants at work."

"Yeah," Bo said. "That is a constant battle for some. I am fortunate that I don't leak as much as you do."

"I have tried using a sock down my pants but that tends to make a bit of a bulge," I said.

"As I mentioned to you the other day, you might end up having to try using something like Depends for Men," Bo said. "It's a pad they make for occasional incontinence. You know, like small dribbles and the like, but it might be good for your issue. It worked for Johnny."

"I'll try anything at this point," I said. "I have been able to suck off a few of my friends the past few days. That was a nice distraction."

"That's a good thing," Bo said. "You get to provide a service to others and a way to burn off some of the pent-up energy you have. I just started my 91-day session in chastity last week, so I expect I'm going to be seeking out a lot of cock in the next few months."

"This seven-day session has been tough on me," I said. "I have a huge case of the blue balls and my release is not till Sunday. I can't imagine three months in chastity yet, let alone six months or permanent chastity."

Bo chuckled, "you learn to deal with it. It isn't pleasant, but you will manage. Plenty of other boys have graduated before you and have as well."

143

"That's true, I guess," I said. "So, what's your story? Are you from Atlanta?

Bo laughed, "nope! I am from Texas. I was born and raised in Corpus Christi."

"Where is that?" I asked.

"On the coast about 120 miles north of the Mexican border."

"Oh, nice!" I said.

"It wasn't too bad," he said. "The summers are freaking hot as hell, but you get the breeze off the bay. I do miss taking the SPID out to Padre Island and having fun on the Gulf Coast, but I like Atlanta a lot more. There is much more of a gay scene here and, frankly, just more to do in general."

"How long have you lived here?" I asked.

"About five years," he said. "I moved out here after college for work. I handle building servers and technology shit. It pays well, so I don't complain. I just hit 30 years old this past January and don't have plans to go anywhere. Well, unless someone collars me after I graduate and pays to move me that is."

Bo chuckled at that last remark.

"Do you think that might happen?" I asked.

"It's always possible," Bo said. "Nick, the sub that graduated and whose spot I replaced, was collared by a master named Adam. Jay told me Adam lived in Seattle and moved Nick out there before Christmas. They still message each other on the phone."

"Oh wow!" I said.

"Yeah," Bo said. "I mean, it is your decision to take the offer of a collar by a master, but it's not always here in town."

"It might be fun to move somewhere new," I said, "as long as it wasn't in the middle of nowhere that is."

"True that," Bo said with a laugh.

Bo pulled out his PlayStation and we played some games for a while and continued to chat. By 10 pm, though, we decided to call it a night. We both had work tomorrow and Bo had his one-on-one day with John after. I walked over to the door and put my clothes on, and Bo hugged me, and I headed home for the evening.

CHAPTER TWELVE

The Weekend

Thursday and Friday were pretty normal days. John sent me some more emails with reflective assignments that asked me to continue to put myself in sub headspace and think about what my roles should be, how I should please a dominant, and how dominants have different needs and expectations.

My week in chastity was going ok as well, though the ache in my balls was worse. Not a pain that indicated that there was something wrong, but that feeling like I just needed to jack off. This was the longest I had ever gone without an orgasm and the horniness was overtaking me. I had started looking at porn after work and all that did was make me leak more and strain in my cage. I tried playing video games, but my mind kept getting distracted by the overwhelming urge to fuck or get fucked.

By Saturday morning, I was about to go insane. I needed stimulation and I needed it now. The first person I thought about was Kenny, so I texted him to ask what he was doing.

"Hey, bud," he replied. "Not much here. My cousin moved out last night, so thanks again for that. I just woke up here. Figured I'd wank out a few loads now that I got the place to myself again. What about you?"

"I'll be honest," I said, "this chastity cage has me fucking horny as hell and I can barely stand it. Do you think you can fuck those loads into me? I need it bad."

"Say no more," Kenny said. "Come on over and I can pound you till you're walking funny."

He followed that with a devil emoji.

"I'll be there shortly," I said.

"I'll leave the door open, just knock first and then come in."

I jumped up and went into the shower to clean out quickly and I found I was pretty well ready to go anyway. Kenny only lived a few buildings over from me, so it would be a short walk. I threw on some shorts and my sandals and grabbed a t-shirt that was on top of the laundry hamper and headed out the door. It was a little brisk that morning, but I didn't care.

When I got to Kenny's apartment door, I knocked on the door and then entered.

"That you Matt?" Kenny asked.

"Yup!" I said as I dropped my pants and took my shirt and sandals off by the door.

"Come on back to the bedroom," He said.

Kenny's apartment was identical to mine, so I walked back to his bedroom area and found him sitting on the top of the covers. The drapes on the window were parted letting some light in and I saw the fuzzy redhead laying back with one hand behind his head. The other hand was stroking his erect and engorged uncut cock and his legs were slightly bent and spread.

"Come over here chastity boy," Kenny said with a grin. "Suck this cock before I breed that ass."

I grinned back and laid on the edge of the bed and got between his legs. I started to suck on his cock, and he used his feet to rub my sides and he played with my hair a bit with his hand as well.

I love a nice uncut cock. It is very rare to find them in America since most babies are circumcised at birth. His foreskin was not tight either, which allowed me to roll it back and lick and suck on his sensitive head, which made him groan and shutter.

I licked his shaft down to his balls and took them each into my mouth in turn as well. He had that nice musk built up from a day and a night without a shower and it was causing my nub to swell to fill my cage and push forward as much as it could. I made sure to bend my leg just enough to leave room for my nub not to be crushed by the bed to avoid too much pain.

Kenny had his eyes closed and was grabbing the pillow behind him and moaning. I reached up and rubbed his fuzzy belly and brought my hands around to his hips to help give me better leverage to take his cock into my mouth fully.

"Slow down boy," Kenny said, reaching down and pushing me off his cock. "That's not where this load is going. Turn around here and show me that ass."

I moved around and put my ass and nub in his face and put my face on the bed between his legs. Normally I would have tried to suck on him in this position, but being as he was shorter than I was, it would not have worked.

Kenny used his fingers to play with my ass and then reached down and squeezed my swollen nub.

"Damn, boy!" he said. "Those balls look nice and full!"

"Yes, Sir," I replied. "I haven't cum in six days."

"And you aren't today either," he said devilishly as he rubbed them with his thumb.

Precum started dripping off the head of my nub and he collected it and started to rub it into my asshole with his finger. He then brought my ass down and used his tongue to explore my ass as well. The sensation was just what I needed.

"Ohh, fuck!" I groaned as a wave of energy passed through my body.

"You like that, boy?" Kenny asked.

"Yes, Sir," I replied.

Kenny spat on my ass and then collected more of my precum and started to lube and finger my hole. I bit my lip and was moaning as he did so, enjoying the feeling.

"Flip over boy and put those legs on my shoulders," Kenny said.

I got on my back and we maneuvered around with Kenny on his knees so he could line his cock up on my ass. He bent my legs forward and placed the head of his cock on my hole and looked at me with those pale blue eyes and grinned as he slowly entered me.

"Fuck!" I said as his shaft entered me.

"That's a good chastity boy," Kenny said. "Open up and give me that ass."

Kenny got balls deep in one stroke and then adjusted a bit and pushed forward and started to move back and forth letting his cock use the spit and precum that I had produced for him as lube. It was exactly what I needed, and I wanted him to use my ass for all it was worth.

He grabbed my feet and put them near his furry chest and squeezed as he picked up the pace. The bed was creaking with every thrust and my swollen nub was bouncing back and forth sending waves of slight pain but a ton more pleasure through me.

"I need your cum so bad," I said. "Fuck me harder, Sir."

Kenny was starting to work up a sweat. Beads of water were building upon his chest and starting to soak his chest hair. They dribbled down his chest and I could feel them hit my legs and ass. His thick, but powerful legs were giving energy to his thrusts as he entered me.

"Are you ready for a breeding, boy?" he asked.

"Fuck yes," I replied. "Fill me up with your seed, Sir. I need it bad!"

Kenny picked up the pace and was pounding me so hard my head was bobbing back and forth. He threw his head back and squeezed my legs hard as he shoved his cock deep into my ass and coated my insides with his cum.

"FUCK!" Kenny yelled as the wave of his orgasm overtook him. His cock pulsed for a good ten to fifteen seconds before he opened his eyes and pushed my feet together to place his forehead there to rest.

He was drenched in sweat. His fur was glistening, and I could start to smell his musk in the room. The smell of sweat and sex. I was a little moist myself, a combination of some of his sweat that fell on my body and my own.

Kenny pulled out and fell back to lay down. I got up and felt my ass and noticed I was well-bred. There was cum leaking out a bit and I collected it and licked my fingers clean. I then leaned over Kenny and gently took his softening cock in my hands and licked him clean, tasting the remnants of a real man's seed.

Kenny reached down and rubbed my back. "Damn, I needed that," he said.

"I needed that too!" I replied with a grin. "You fuck like an animal!"

Kenny laughed. "Yeah, that boy I have been seeing likes it rough. That's normally how I rut."

"Hey," I said, "I think it's hot!"

"I also sweat like a pig," he said. "Sorry about that."

"Don't be sorry," I said. "I love scents and sweat. You smell amazing."

"Yeah," Kenny replied with a grin. "I have noticed that about you."

He lifted his arms and put his hands behind his head to present his wet and musky pits and I dove in and started to lick and rub my face in them. His scent penetrated the hair of my beard and would be with me for a good long time today.

My nub at this point was still swollen and my balls started to ache from the pressure of the base ring as it was shoved forward. I reached between my legs and tried to adjust, but I could not get a good grip, so I sat up and used both hands to pull my scrotum forward and give more room for my balls to move.

Kenny noticed that precum was still dripping from my nub and he reached over and grabbed it and started to rub it over my balls and swollen head behind the rungs of the cage.

"So, when do you get that off?" he asked, looking up at me as he continued to rub my balls.

"Tomorrow," I said. "This session was a week. The next one after that will be two weeks, and it builds from there."

"Damn!" Kenny replied. "I couldn't do it. I like jacking and fucking too much."

"I'm still learning to cope," I said. "As you can tell, it makes me horny as hell."

"I noticed this!" Kenny said with a smile as he reached under my ass and started playing with my bred hole.

He felt his cum and started to finger my ass again, first with one finger and then with a second. I reached down and started to stroke his cock at the same time which was already starting to get hard again.

"You think you are ready to ride me?" Kenny said. "I have a quick recharge period as you can see, and I can fill you up more."

"You don't have to ask me twice," I said as I moved over to straddle his hips and face him.

He straightened his legs out and kept his hands behind his head. He was looking up at me intently as I guided his hard cock back into my well-lubed ass.

"Damn," Kenny said. "That ass is amazing."

I grinned as I started to move up and down on him and ride him. He reached down and grabbed my hips as he rocked forward and back to my movements ensuring his cock got deep inside me with each thrust. More sweat was building on his chest and his fur was completely soaked, which I reached down and played with as he fucked me.

After several minutes, he moved his legs up and got the leverage to start to jackhammer my ass a bit more. Sweat was bouncing and flying as well as he closed his eyes and bit his bottom lip.

"FUUUUUCK!" Kenny yelled as he pounded his second load into me. The pounding hit my prostate as well and forced more and more precum out to the point that it was flying around in ropes and streams on my belly and his.

Kenny's legs and arms dropped, and he was panting hard. His chest was moving up and down quickly and I'm sure his heart was pounding as well.

"Now you are a well-bred boy," he said as he slapped my ass.

I grinned and rose off him and rolled over beside him.

"Ugh, I needed that so bad," Kenny said. "Thanks for messaging me."

"Hey, thanks for fucking me!" I replied.

Kenny rolled out of bed and steadied himself on the table next to his bed. His legs were a bit weak from the activities. Once he was balanced, he went into the bathroom to grab a towel to wipe down.

"I'm a fucking mess," he said laughing.

"You might need to wash these sheets as well," I replied, joining him in the laugh. "They are soaked with sweat."

"Yeah," he said. "Good thing today is laundry day."

I got up from the bed and stretched and rubbed my ass and collected the last of his cum leaking out and licked it clean from my hands. My nub was still swollen, but not as bad and although I didn't get to orgasm, I felt like I got to burn off some of the horny energy I had.

"I guess I better head back," I said. "Thanks again, bud."

Kenny came over and hugged me and squeezed my ass. "Anytime you need to burn off energy, you let me know. I'll be glad to fuck you silly again."

I grinned and went back over to the door and put my shorts, sandals, and shirt on, and headed back out the door. The cool morning air hit the sweat on my chest and sent a shiver down me, but I felt a ton better.

Saturday afternoon was mostly me in the living room playing video games. I had nowhere to be and I didn't even take a shower when I got back to my apartment so I could enjoy Kenny's musk on me and the cum in my ass as long as possible.

About 3 pm, I texted Bo and Jay to see if they were up to going out to the Eagle later in the evening. Bo told me he was game, but Jay said he needed to catch up on his sleep and would join us another time. I asked Bo if he wanted to meet here or at his place and carpool and he said he could come to my place. I told him to come on over and we could play some video games and grab dinner before and he said he would be over shortly.

Bo was knocking on the door about 30 minutes later and I told him the door was open and he could come in. He had brought some bar clothes to change into later and put those down and then stripped and joined me on the couch. He noticed I was sitting on a towel and my hair was a bit of a mess. He leaned over and took a sniff.

"You smell like sex," he said with a laugh.

"Yeah," I said laughing back as I played my video game, "I have been so fucking horny lately being in the chastity cage, so I texted a buddy this morning and he fucked two loads into me."

"Well, that's hot," Bo said. "Looks like you got his scent all over you too."

"Yup!" I grinned. "I had my face buried in his pits and groin as much as I could."

"I like the scent of a man as well," Bo said. "I'm glad to find someone that's piggy like that as well."

"Oh yeah," I replied. "Do you want a soda? There are some cokes in the fridge. There is also beer in there if you want that too. Help yourself."

"Thanks," Bo said.

He got up and grabbed a beer and asked if I wanted anything and I told him no. When he came back, we booted up some games and played for a while together till it was dinner time. We ordered some takeout and continued to goof off and chill. By 9 pm, it was getting about time to get ready for the night out. Not that I had to, but I wanted to take a shower and get cleaned up. My ass was still a mess from the fucking I had got earlier in the day anyway.

Once I got showered and dried off, I laid out what I planned to wear. My harness and black cap, of course, as well as my boots and tight jeans. I grabbed a shirt as well to wear over the harness till we got to the bar. I brought that into the living room where Bo was playing a game on his own.

"Are you ready?" I asked.

"Sure," Bo said, turning the game and TV off.

Bo reached down to pick up the clothes he brought for the bar. He had a bulldog harness that he put on that was black with green trim.

"Hey," I said. "I like that, and it is color-coordinated to your collar."

Bo laughed, "that's because I had it made specifically for that reason."

He put on some jeans and a black shirt over his harness and bent down to put his shoes on while I finished dressing. Once we were ready, we headed out to his car and he drove downtown.

When we finally got to the Eagle, it was about 10:30 pm. It was pretty quiet in the neighborhood behind where we parked, and we decided to just leave the shirts in the car and walk the two blocks to the bar in our bare chests and harnesses. It was not too cold out anyway.

We walked up to the back of the bar and climbed up the steps to the back deck. There were some people there, but it was still early. We went in and got some beers from the bar and then headed out and chilled on the upper back deck.

About 30 minutes later, the crowd was starting to build a bit and Bo let out a little squeal and ran over to someone to hug him. Curious, I followed him over. The guy he was hugging was about my height and build and was bare-chested showing off some fur on his upper body. He had a chainmail collar on that was colored just like mine: black and yellow.

"Matt!" Bo said, putting his hand behind my back and bringing me in closer. "This is Johnny, my sub brother I told you about. He is the one that recently graduated leaving the spot for you to fill."

Now the collar color all made sense. Sure enough, attached to the lock on the collar was a gold tag that said, 'Sub Johnny / CHASTITY SUB / Collared by Sir Jack'.

"Nice to meet you brother!" Johnny said as he came over to hug me. "Yellow is the best color anyway," he said with a wink.

"Are you here by yourself?" Bo asked Johnny.

"Oh, no," Johnny replied. "Sir Jack, my master, is in the bar somewhere and my sub brother Ryan will be back in a sec. He went to grab a drink."

"So is Ryan also a graduate of Sir?" I asked Johnny.

"Yup," Johnny replied. "He is also a yellow collar. He graduated right before me and Sir Jack collared him. When I graduated, he collared me too."

"Oh, nice!" I replied.

"Here he is now," Johnny said pointing to a thinner guy in a pup hood, harness, and jockstrap. He too had a black and yellow chainmail collar with a gold tag that said, 'Sub Ryan / CHASTITY SUB / Collared by Sir Jack', and the outline of his chastity cage was visible in his jock.

"Ryan," Johnny said as he put his hand around my shoulders. "This is Matt. He is one of Sir's subs that came in after I graduated."

Ryan took his pup hood off to reveal a cute round face with a goatee. He extended his hand to shake mine and said, "Hey! Nice to meet you, Matt! It's a yellow collar reunion!"

We all laughed, and Bo leaned in to ask me if I wanted another beer. I said yes and handed him some money and told him to grab another one for himself as well.

"So, how long since you got your training collar, Matt?" Ryan asked me.

"It will be a week tomorrow," I said.

"Well duh," Ryan said, mimicking hitting his head with his fist. "Of course, it is. Johnny just graduated on Saturday and you took his place."

"That's usually how it works," Johnny said sarcastically with a grin.

"And this Sir Jack collared you right after graduation?" I asked.

"Yup!" Johnny said. "He participated in my ceremony."

"Well," Ryan said as he put his pup hood back on. "I am glad to have you as part of the extended family Matt, but I want to mingle. Barooo!"

Ryan shook the pup tail in his ass as he gave his puppy call and then walked off.

"He seems fun," I said to Johnny.

"Oh, he's a great guy," Johnny said. "I am still getting used to the new dynamics of having a permanent master and fellow sub in one house. I moved in with Sir Jack this week after I graduated, and Ryan and I share a room."

"But everything is ok?" I asked.

"Oh, hell yeah!" Johnny said. "Sir Jack is a huge horn ball and keeps both of us busy and well used. But he is also really laid back as a dominant and affectionate. We are more of a triad. I have a lot more freedom than I did with Sir John, but I am still grateful for all the training he gave me."

"I understand. So, you must have known Dan as well," I said.

"Oh yeah!" Johnny said. "He started when Jack was training and graduated while I was training. He's a close friend and brother. How did you meet him?"

"His master Sir Greg is a friend of one of my friends and I met Greg and Dan at Woofs a few days before I signed the contract with Sir. I had some questions and Dan helped put me at ease."

"Ahh, ok," Johnny said. "Dan was the elder sub when I started, and I leaned on him a lot. I have never met his master though."

"I had my interview with them both this past Tuesday," I said. "It was great to hear about their perspective on the training and the lifestyle. It was also nice to drain Sir Greg's balls too!"

Johnny laughed, "well that is all part of the full service of a sub, right?"

Bo returned with our beers and we started to drink and chat with Johnny until Johnny looked over my shoulder and beckoned to someone. I turned around and walking towards us was a nice-looking daddy bear. He was about six-foot-tall (1.82 m) with hazel eyes and a full beard that was mostly gray and white with some remaining darker browns here and there. His chest was broad and covered in white and gray fur, and it looked like he worked out, but he had a bit of a beer belly as well. His arms were thick and covered in tattoos from his elbows to his shoulders. He had leather suspenders on that attached to tight-fitting jeans that showed off a huge bulge and nice and shiny boots as well.

"This is my master, Sir Jack," Johnny said as he introduced him to me.

Jack extended his hand and I met it. The grip was strong, and he replied with a deep voice, "nice to meet you."

"I'm Matt, Sir," I replied.

My voice shook a bit as I stared at him. The man was hot as hell. Jack released his grip and pointed at my collar.

"Are you training under John?" he asked.

"Yes, Sir," I replied. "I just started this past Sunday."

"Ahh, so you took the place of my boy, Johnny, here," Jack said as he put his big arms around Johnny.

"Yes, Sir," I replied.

"John has got a good program going on," Jack said. "I'm quite fond of my chastity boys."

Jack leaned over and kissed Johnny deeply and reached down and twisted his nipples at the same time.

"You got my cigars boy?" Jack asked Johnny.

"Yes, Sir," Johnny said.

He reached in his back pocket and pulled out a fat one and then handed Jack a cutter he had in the other pocket. Jack then unwrapped the cigar and cut and lit it using the lighter of a guy next to us. He sucked and then blew out a few puffs and then turned to me.

"What do you think of the program so far?" Jack asked.

"I'm just getting started, but so far so good," I replied. I've been a bit horny lately since this is the longest I have been in chastity so far, but I'm managing. I have my first one-on-one with Sir tomorrow."

Jack blew out another puff of smoke and said, "learn all you can boy. It will broaden your horizons and make you attractive to a wide range of doms."

"I will, Sir," I said.

"Well, I will let you boys talk," Jack said as he walked off and down the staircase to the lower back deck.

"Damn, Johnny," I said. "Jack is hot."

Johnny grinned, "Right? I felt like I hit the jackpot when he collared me. And you should see what he's packing in his pants. It is like a baby's arm!"

"I could kinda tell," I said with a grin.

"It's gonna take me a while to get used to it, but I'll be able to be fisted easily once I do!"

We all laughed, and I offered to grab us all another round.

I was waiting in line at the bar when a cubby guy came up and tapped me on the shoulder. It was the same guy I saw last weekend at the bar who sucked me off on the back porch.

"Oh, hey," I said. I could not remember what his name was.

"Good to see you out again!" he replied. "It's a good crowd out tonight. Lots of hot-looking guys that have me turned on."

I grinned. "Hear ya," I replied. "It's usually a good place to find them."

The cubby dude was a little drunk and he came up and groped me. I didn't mind, I mean he did suck me off last weekend, but when he felt the hard cage on my nub he was totally confused.

"What is that?" he asked.

"Chastity cage," I replied.

"Well, that sucks," he said.

"Sorry about that," I replied. "But I am sure you will be able to find someone to play around with around here somewhere."

The guy looked a little embarrassed and said, "OK, maybe I'll see ya around," and he walked off.

I felt a little bad about disappointing him, but it was also a bit awkward for me.

Once I got the beers, I returned to the back porch and continued drinking with the guys. A new person had shown up while I was away, though. He was built similar to me with a thick black wavy beard and a darker skin tone. He looked to be part Hispanic and was quite sexy.

"Matt," Bo said, "This is Carlos."

"Nice to meet you, Carlos," I said, extending my hand to shake his.

"You as well, sexy boy," Carlos replied. "I see you are a chastity boy too."

"Yes, I am," I said.

"Bo was telling me about you all," Carlos said. "I was admiring your collars and noticed what they said. Are you exclusive to a guy?"

"No, we aren't," Bo said. "Well, at least Matt and I are not. Johnny here is collared by a man named Jack who is downstairs."

"Ahh, I see," Carlos said.

For the next hour or so, we hung out on the back porch as the crowd grew. Carlos took a position between Bo and me and would periodically put his arms around us and play with our asses. I got the feeling he was turned on and interested in us.

When Johnny went to go get another beer, Carlos took the opportunity to talk to us both.

"So, are you two interested in possibly playing around a bit tonight?" Carlos asked.

"I could do that," Bo said and looked at me for a response.

"Sure, I am game," I replied.

"My apartment is just four blocks from here," Carlos said. "Why don't we go there now."

Johnny came back and we told him we were heading out and we all hugged. We followed Carlos down the staircase and out into the parking lot and down the street a few blocks and then to the left a few blocks. We eventually came to what looked like a house, but it was subdivided into two sections. Carlos showed us through the door of the left side of the home and into a living room.

"This is my place," he said. "It is just me, so there is no one to bother us."

Bo and I looked at each other and started removing our harnesses and stripping our clothes off.

"You are eager boys!" Carlos said.

"It's a protocol of our Sir's," I said. We are not allowed to have clothes on indoors unless it is inappropriate to be naked.

"I am liking this," Carlos said as he stared at our naked bodies.

He came over and squeezed both our cages and gave me a deep kiss and then moved to Bo and did the same. He then reached into his pants and started to grope himself. I took the opportunity to drop to my knees as he continued to make out with Bo and undid Carlos's pants and pulled them down to reveal a hardening uncut cock that was very thick and suspended over large hairy balls.

Carlos kicked his shoes off and moved his legs up and down to remove the pants completely and pulled his shirt off and threw it on the floor as he continued to make out with Bo. I then took his cock into my hand and started to lick and suck on the head. His foreskin was pretty tight, so I did not pull much on it, but I took as much of the thick shaft in my mouth as I could.

"Come over here big boy," Carlos said to Bo as he moved him over to a couch.

He had Bo get up on one side of the couch and put his chest on the back of it, so his ass was in the air. Carlos bent down and spread Bo's ass and started to tongue his hole and play with his chastity cage.

"Fuck," Bo said as he put his head down on the back of the couch and his arms.

"Come over here Matt," Carlos said. "I want you right next to Bo."

I moved around and got in the same position next to Bo and Carlos moved over and started to tongue my hole as well. He reached down and grabbed my nub in its cage and squeezed and pulled on it a bit.

"Umph," I grunted as my nub swelled from the stimulation.

Carlos stood and went into another room and then came back with some lube and poppers. He offered Bo a hit, but Bo said he was fine. I gladly accepted them, though, after seeing how thick Carlos was. I was going to need to be relaxed as hell to take him.

Carlos lubed his fingers up and worked them into Bo and me. First one, then two, and then three. I took a hit of the poppers and let it hit my brain and relax me a bit. My ass gave a bit and accepted his fingers easier as well.

Carlos lubed his cock and then placed it on my hole and then slowly started to push in. I took another deep hit and he felt me open up for him and he slid the rest of the way in with one movement.

"Fuck!" I replied.

He was thick and it was just on the verge of too much for me.

"Give me a second," I said.

I adjusted a bit to get a better angle for him and then I took a few deep breaths.

"Ok, Sir," I said. "I'm ready."

Carlos grinned and started to move back and forth in my ass. His heavy balls were starting to swing and would occasionally hit the back of my ass.

"Damn, you have a tight ass boy!" he said.

Bo looked over at me and grinned and reached over and held my hand. "That's it, bro." I grinned back and then closed my eyes as Carlos continued to fuck.

After a few minutes, Carlos pulled out and then moved over to Bo. He pushed his cock into him a bit faster than he did me and I saw Bo's eyes widen and he squeezed my hand.

"Fuck you are thick!" Bo said.

Carlos slapped Bo's ass and said, "you can take it, big boy."

Carlos picked up the pace and fucked Bo's ass a bit harder and faster than he had done mine. Bo's larger frame was being forced forward and back and the couch was creaking a bit. I have to admit it was hot watching him pound my sub brother.

Carlos pulled out and switched back to me for a few minutes and then back to Bo. While he was pounding Bo the second time he leaned forward and started riding him harder and faster. Bo reached up and braced himself on the back of the couch and had his eyes closed and was biting his bottom lip.

It was obvious Carlos was close and I looked back to see him pounding furiously until he threw his body forward and yelled, dumping his seed into Bo. Bo grabbed my hand again and winced as the full thickness of Carlos was deep in him all the way to the balls.

When Carlos was done delivering his cum, he pulled out and I got off the back of the couch and moved over to lick his cock clean, tasting the remnants of his seed and our asses. Carlos reached down and forced my head on him a few times making me choke on his cock.

"That's a boy," Carlos said. "Clean me up good."

Carlos grabbed a small washcloth to wipe Bo's ass down and thanked us for the fun time. We told him we were happy to help and we got dressed and walked outside holding our harnesses.

As we walked back down the street, Bo turned to me, "he just about ripped me in two."

"I know what you mean," I said. "But it was hot watching him fuck you."

"Likewise," Bo said. "You must have been a bit tighter than me because he seemed to go a little slower with you."

"Or maybe he just found your ass a lot more pleasurable," I said with a grin.

"Do you want to go back to the bar or head home?" Bo asked.

"Let's head home," I said. "I think we both need to let our asses recover."

Bo smiled and put his arm around my neck. Once we got back to the car, he drove me home and dropped me off and I told him I would see him Monday for cleaning day. I then headed back inside to clean up and get some rest.

CHAPTER THIRTEEN

My First Session

I woke up Sunday morning to the light streaming in between the curtains. I didn't want to roll out of bed, but I needed to gather up all my laundry and get that done before lunch. I had to be at John's house by 2 pm, so I had planned my chores out ahead of time. By noon, I was sitting down to have an Asian chicken salad I got from a local restaurant down the street, and by 12:30 pm I was in the bathroom getting cleaned up and cleaned out to be prepared for whatever John had in store for me.

I stared at myself in the mirror after my shower. So much has changed in the past couple of weeks. I was collared and caged and on my way to becoming a trained sub boy. I had met two new friends that I had quickly bonded with and I felt like I had more of a purpose in my life. I looked down at my phone at the picture I had taken last weekend before my cage was installed. It was true that I missed jacking off all the time, but now that I thought about it, the past week wasn't too bad. I got to service some pretty hot guys as well.

I returned to my bedroom to grab some jeans and shirt and a fresh pair of socks and put them out next to the door and then I went and sat on the couch and pulled out my laptop to check my email before I left.

While I was sitting there, my phone beeped, and I looked down to see a message from Bo.

"Had a lot of fun last night, brother," he said. "Good luck at your session today and enjoy that orgasm!"

He followed that with a big smiling emoji.

He was right. It was the end of my weekly session in chastity, so while I would be training under John today, I would also be getting my cage off and a nice orgasm. That should help the ache in my balls these days I thought.

"Thanks, bubba," I replied.

I pulled into John's driveway about five minutes early. Better early than late I thought. I walked around to the side door and placed my clothes in my bin and latched it shut and then entered the dungeon area. The lights were off, but there was some light coming in from the back glass doors which reflected off the mirrored wall, so you could still see. I took my place on my yellow square on the floor and knelt with my head bowed and waited.

About ten minutes later, I heard John coming down the staircase. The door opened and he turned on the lights to the room. I saw his bare feet pass by me and go into the room and heard some things moving about. A few minutes later he returned and stood in front of me.

"Rise boy and face me," he said.

I got on my feet and saw that he was in his black and blue leather jock again with a pair of leather gloves on and a black cap on backward, but otherwise, he was naked. He told me to recite the creed, which I did so and then he reached down and grabbed my cage and moved it from side to side.

"How was your week in chastity, boy?" he asked.

"It was ok, Sir," I replied. "I have had a pretty bad case of the blue balls the past few days, but I have been managing."

"That is normal," he said. "You will find this next session likely more challenging. Most of my boys say the two-week session is the one they struggle the most with. I will milk you next week in our one-on-one session; however, so that should help you cope some."

"Thank you, Sir," I replied.

"How many men have you serviced this week?" he asked.

"Three, Sir," I replied. "Sir Greg had me swallow his load at my interview on Tuesday. I sucked a friend off on Wednesday and that same friend fucked and loaded me twice on Saturday morning. Saturday evening Bo and I allowed a dom at a bar to take us home and fuck us and Bo got the load. I got to clean his cock off."

"Very well," Sir said. "It sounds like you have a healthy sex life. I will ask that from now on whenever you service a man that you send me an email with what happened preferably at the end of the day, but the next morning will do if it is a late night. I want to be aware of what you are doing, what acts you are performing, and how well you please the men you are with. Is that understood?"

"Yes, Sir," I replied.

"Do you have a regular doctor and are you on Prep?" he asked.

"Yes, Sir," I replied. "I have a gay doctor that I see, and I am on Prep and get tested every three months."

"That is good to hear," John said. "Who is your doctor?"

"I see Dr. Jim Cole downtown," I said.

"Oh, I know him well," he replied. "Several of my friends and my boys have used him in the past. He is very good. He also knows about my program, so you are not to hide your device when you have visits there. Be open and honest about your chastity and let him know what you have been doing."

"I will, Sir," I said.

"Very well," John said. "Today we are going to work on a few things. The first is flogging. I know you do not like extreme pain, but we are going to work on your tolerance a bit today. Many dominants like flogging their subs and you need to learn to work through some pain. As always, you have your safe word and I want you to use it if the session becomes too intense. However, I want you to work with me today. Push your limits as far as you can go and communicate with me. Is that understood?"

"Yes, Sir," I said with a little nervousness in my voice.

"Very well," he said. "Follow me over to the cross."

John brought me over to the Saint Andrews Cross, which is an X of wood mounted on the wall with rings that you can restrain arms and legs to at the four ends. He attached restraints to my wrists and ankles and then attached them to the cross so that I was stretched on it with my back to him.

He reached over and rubbed my back with his gloved hands before reaching over and grabbing his black leather flogger. He moved one hand down its length completely before swinging it gently and the ends hit the small of my back. The next swing was stronger and made an audible smack when it connected with my upper butt. I jumped a bit as well.

The next eleven strokes were of the same low intensity. Enough to make a smacking sound, but not hard. They were delivered for a minute, but even though it was not too hard, the cumulative effect was causing my lower back and ass to feel some heat and hurt a bit. I was jumping a bit forward by the time he got to the tenth and eleventh hit.

John paused for a moment and let me sit there for about ten seconds before lightly brushing the flogger across the same area again. He then proceeded to deliver eleven strokes over thirty seconds this time concentrating on both cheeks of my ass and the lower portion of my back. I was starting to jump more at this point.

Then came ten lashes at medium intensity for thirty seconds. These started to hurt, and I was groaning a bit and moving around as well.

After the last lash, I cried out a bit and he reached down and rubbed my back.

"Boy, I want you to breathe in deeply," he said. "Make the pain work for you. Embrace it and concentrate on where you are and the pleasure you are providing for me. You can do this."

John then took the flogger and moved it gently from my ass and up my back letting it lightly run against my skin. He then proceeded to deliver eleven strokes of low intensity to my upper and middle back for a minute. This was followed by a pause and then eleven strokes over thirty seconds and then ten lashes at medium intensity over the next thirty seconds.

The heat was building across my entire back and the pain was coming as well. John picked up a different flogger that had thinner ends and started to deliver lashes to my back spaced by 1-2 seconds. I started to cry out a bit as the flogger hit my back and sent waves of energy through me. It was an intense experience and I tried to focus my mind and watch my breathing.

John then delivered long, strong strokes to my back. These hurt. I winced and cried out and struggled against the restraints and debated yelling my safeword. At one particular hit, I twisted and yelled, and he stopped and gently rubbed my back with his gloved hand.

"Breathe for me, boy," John said. "How are you doing?"

"I'm ok, Sir," I said as I caught my breath. "It just hurts."

"We will do this for two more minutes," John said. "Focus hard on your breathing. You can do this. I have faith in you."

John then took the larger flogger and delivered ten strokes of medium intensity to my butt and lower back and then the same over my upper back. Then over the next minute, he brought the flogger down with a medium to hard intensity on my ass.

The first stroke made me gutturally yell and I twisted to the side a bit. The pain shot through me and I felt the sting and burning sensation after.

"I can do this," I thought to myself.

But, as the lashes continued, I began to doubt my conviction. I was crying out after each hit and struggling against my restraints. I wanted this to end. I could not take it anymore. Just as I was about to yell my safe word, John stopped.

"And that is it, boy," John said, reaching over to rub my back.

John came behind me and embraced me. He put his head behind mine and hugged me for several seconds. He then gently used his gloved hands to rub over my back very lightly. The redness of my skin was apparent and there was a gentle heat flowing as well.

"A good dominant always incorporates aftercare for his sub," John said. "You have taken the flogging well and I am very pleased. How do you feel?"

"It was intense, Sir," I said as a few tears ran down my cheek. "I almost reached my limit."

"But you stuck through it," he said. "That is what is important. Feel the burn and heat in your skin and feed off it. Breathe in and out and focus your mind."

As he spoke to me calmly, I started to feel better. I still felt the heat and tingling in my back and ass, but a new sensation, almost a wave of energy ran over me as he continued to lightly rub his gloved hands over me. It was not something I had experienced before.

John reached up and released my restraints from the cross but left the cuffs on my wrists and ankles.

He had me get up on the leather table face down and my nub was placed in the open slot in the middle so I could lay flat. He told me to put my arms by my side. He put a leather blindfold on me and then put a small soft pillow on my forehead for my head to rest on. He then put headphones on me and told me to relax.

I could hear nothing at first. The headphones were noise-canceling so it was dead quiet. I then heard John's voice coming through from a recording.

"I am a sub," it began. "I am an instrument of pleasure for men. I will open my mind to exploring new experiences that please men. Pain can be a pleasure. I can endure it. I can transform it. I can overcome it."

This was repeated over and over. It was gentle and soothing. As I sat there listening, I started to zone out a bit. I have no idea how long I was there, but at some point, I felt my arms being moved and secured to the corners of the top of the table past my head and my legs were spread and secured to the corners as well.

The recording continued. A light sound in the background was playing as well. I could not make out what it was. It was a series of tones that I did not recognize. I zoned out again until I felt the first hit of the flogger again.

John had brought down the larger one against my ass. He delivered low-intensity hits to my ass for a minute and the same sequence to my upper back. I winced and jerked a bit.

"I am a sub. I am an instrument of pleasure for men. I will open my mind to exploring new experiences that please men. Pain can be a pleasure. I can endure it. I can transform it. I can overcome it."

Ten more strokes came down on my ass for 30 seconds and the same sequence to my upper back. I twisted and cried out, though I could barely hear my voice.

"I am a sub. I am an instrument of pleasure for men. I will open my mind to exploring new experiences that please men. Pain can be a pleasure. I can endure it. I can transform it. I can overcome it."

Three strong hits came on my ass and I cried out and screamed after the last one. The tears were flowing out of my blindfold and down my face and landing on the padding of the table below. It was then that John stopped the flogging.

I felt him gently rub my back. He moved slowly around my ass and up to my head and back again. He blew against my skin and the sensation sent a shiver up my spine.

"I am a sub. I am an instrument of pleasure for men. I will open my mind to exploring new experiences that please men. Pain can be a pleasure. I can endure it. I can transform it. I can overcome it."

I took a deep breath in and then out again. I repeated this for about thirty seconds as the recording continued to play. I then felt the headphones come off.

"How do you feel boy?" John asked.

"Sore, Sir," I replied. "But I am ok."

"I am proud of you," he said.

John undid the restraints and told me to flip over. The heat on my back and ass were very present and it stung a bit when my bare skin hit the leather table. He reattached my restraints again and then I felt him grab my chastity device and he removed the cage and base ring.

"Stay right there, boy," he said. "I am going to go wash this and give it a good cleaning."

I sat there on the table blindfolded and bound and felt the stinging sensation on my back and ass. I also felt the cool air on my nub. It was free of its confines and I felt myself getting slightly hard. My balls were lifting and shifting a bit as well. It was a pleasant feeling for once after a week of lockdown.

I heard John return to the room. He released my legs and had me pull them up. He lifted my balls and checked under and around them for any sores or irritation. He inspected my half-hard nub for the same as well. I then heard a clipper turn on and felt him run it over my groin and trim up some of the hair that had grown over the past week. I was not trimmed smooth, just enough so that it would not catch in the cage. When he was done, I felt him rub some lotion over my balls and nub and I enjoyed the sensation.

John then grabbed my nub with his gloved hand and started to move up and down my shaft. While he was doing this, I felt him insert something into my ass. It was not thick, but it felt like it was curved. It came to rest on my prostate, and I felt him rub it back and forth as he moved up and down on my shaft. It got me fully hard immediately and I groaned a bit.

He moved up and down with a steady motion on my fully hard nub and continued to rub my prostate with the device. About a minute into this, I felt my balls lift and an intense orgasm flowed over my body as my nub convulsed and streams of cum came gushing out.

"Oh fuck," I yelled as I writhed and pulled against the arm restraints.

"Quiet, boy," John said. "You are not to speak during your end-of-session emissions."

John pulled the device from my ass and pulled his hand off my nub. As I breathed in and out savoring the post-orgasmic glow that was quickly leaving my body, I felt him use a cold washcloth to wipe down my nub and surrounding area. The coolness made me jump and my nub quickly shrank. I felt him put the cage back on again and reinstall the locking screw. I was in my cage again for my two-week session.

John removed my arm restraints and my blindfold and helped me to the edge of the table.

"How are you feeling boy?" he asked.

"I am good, Sir," I said. "That felt great."

"We are not quite done," he replied.

John got me off the table and led me over to the fuck bench. He had me get on it and restrained my arms and legs using its attached straps. I then felt him stick a lubed finger up my ass and he started to open me up before moving to two then three fingers.

I heard the snaps of his jock click as he removed the front portion and released his engorged cock. He placed it on the entrance to my ass and gently started to push forward, its girth filling my insides.

"Remember, boy," he said, "remain quiet. This is for my pleasure."

Once he had reached the point that his balls were at my ass, he pulled back and started to fuck me slowly and then faster and faster. He built up a rhythm quickly and I grabbed onto the bench and gritted my teeth as his fat cock pummeled my ass.

He reached up and grabbed my side and arched his back so he could get the full length in me. I could not struggle if I wanted to. I was tied down firmly enough that my ass was going to take whatever he wanted to give it. The flogging earlier had left my skin red and warm and the smacking of his groin and occasional slaps from his hands brought the stinging sensation out again. I was doing my best not to groan or cry out, but it was taking every ounce of my concentration.

This was not going to be a short ride. John sped up and slowed down. He would pull out and then slam his fat cock deep into me causing me to involuntarily grunt. He would jackhammer me and let his balls slap against my ass at each thrust. My head was spinning.

Finally, I felt him grab my waist firmly and pound hard a few times and then stop. His cock was pulsing and filling me deeply with his seed. I felt his balls move a few times and he slowly pulled back and cum started falling in drips from my well-bred ass.

John came to the front of the bench and presented his cock to me to clean completely of the remaining cum from it and then he undid the straps and let me stand up, catching me a bit when I lost my balance at first.

"You did well, boy," he said. "Clean the dungeon and you may go. I will see you again tomorrow for cleaning day."

John then turned and went across the room and went back up the staircase closing the door behind him.

I went and got the cleaning supplies from the isolation room closet and wiped down the leather table, the fuck bench, and the cross. I wiped up the remaining cum and lube from the floor and did a quick wet mop of the areas as well. Once I had gone to the bathroom to wipe my ass clean, I returned to the hallway to get dressed and headed home.

CHAPTER FOURTEEN

Getting Into the Routine

Monday started a new routine for me that would carry through the rest of the year. I had a busy day at work followed by a quick dinner and then cleaning day at John's. On Tuesday I would get an email in my inbox with a reflective exercise to talk about what happened in the Sunday session, how I felt, what I thought were opportunities for growth for me as a sub, and any feedback I had. Wednesday would be another cleaning day and then the following day would be a 'task day' as John called it.

My first task came in my email after work Thursday.

> Boy:
>
> As part of your training, you need to keep track of what you are doing, where you have to grow, and what successes and failures you experience. To that end, I want you to set up a Tumblr account and to start posting daily pictures. You do not have to show your face, but your nub should always be visible. Along with the pictures, I want you to chronicle what you have done in the past 24 hours prior with emphasis on any training you have done, what your thoughts are, and where you see growth opportunities. If you provide any

sexual services or favors for others, they should be documented as well.

If any follower of your blog asks you questions, I want you to post them and be detailed in your answers. You should also strive to seek out other subs and doms as well to build a community where you can learn what subs are expected to do and what other doms expect of subs.

I want you to have this set up tonight and have your first picture posted by 10 pm. You should document your training last Sunday and anything that has happened of note since then. Send me the link and I will be monitoring this as you continue your training.

Sir

Keeping a blog was something I had done in the past, but an erotic blog that included naked pictures of myself, let alone pictures of myself in chastity, was not something I had ever done or had thought about. But I did go through the process of getting things set up and posted my first picture and recount of my previous training night as well.

I started to look for others in chastity and found a ton of blogs of both subs and doms in the lifestyle. I had added about 100 blogs to my account by the time I signed off that evening and got ready for bed. By Friday morning, I had equally as many follower requests and started to get messages and questions in my inbox.

When I got off work Friday, I opened up my blog and had a private message waiting for me. It was from a guy that was visiting Atlanta for the weekend for work and he liked the picture and recap that I posted. We got to talking for over an hour while I ate my dinner at home. He was a dom from Minneapolis that was in the leather community and had been interested in chastity for one of his sub boys but wanted to know more about my experiences and how I got started, so I gave him the full rundown of the past few weeks.

As we talked, he eventually sent me a picture of himself and I sent him mine. He was a hot-looking man. In his picture, he was sitting on a bench in what looked to be a bar of some sort. He was barechested, and his dark skin was glistening from sweat. He had black chaps on over tight jeans that showed what looked to be a pretty massive package from the looks of the bulge. He had a boy on his knees polishing his boots and he held a flogger on one hand that was draped over the boy's back. My nub was straining pretty quickly.

The picture I sent him was one where I was completely naked and kneeling with my hands behind my back and my head faced forward. My caged nub and collar were on full display. He was impressed immediately and asked if I would be interested in helping him drain his balls tonight. I told him I would be honored to service him, and he gave me directions to his hotel.

It was actually only about 15 minutes away, so I jumped in the shower to clean up a bit and then headed out. When I got close, he told me the room number and asked that I knock three times quickly and then wait. When the door finally opened, I saw him at the threshold in just his boxers.

"Strip boy," he said.

I went to walk in and do so, and he held his hand out on my chest and stopped me from entering.

"Did you hear me?" he said. "I said strip! Right there."

I was a little bit nervous. There was no one in the hall, but the idea of stripping down in a public area was not something I had intended to do. He sat there and looked at me, though, so I started to pull my shirt off and slipped my shoes and socks off and then stripped off my pants and underwear till I was completely naked in the hallway. He held out a bag and told me to put my clothes in it, so I placed them inside and he put the bag next to the door just inside the threshold. My shoes were still in the hallway, though.

"You may come in now," he said.

As he shut the door and turned toward me and told me to go over to the window and kneel facing him in front of it. I did what he asked. The blinds to the floor-to-ceiling window were completely open, and it was nearly dark outside. If anyone wanted to watch, they would have seen my bare ass kneeling quite easily from the third floor with the light in the room as a contrast.

He walked over to me and dropped his boxers as he passed the bed. His dick was impressive. It had to be at least 8 inches long (20.32 cm) and had a slight curve to the left. He had a nice set of balls as well. He walked over until his package was eye level with me and he was stroking it. He let it fall and slap my face a few times and he looked down at me.

"Let's see how well you can suck a man's cock," he said.

I reached out with one hand to grab his root and started to lick and suck on his head. I would have no hope of deep throating this monster, but I did do my best to suck what I could and lick its entire length. I also paid attention to his balls and took one and then the other in my mouth.

He had a musk that got me straining in my cage. I could tell he was a little sweaty and he later told me he had been working out in the hotel gym earlier. I took his cock into my mouth again and started to move up and down on it and used my hands to work the lower shaft. He reached down and grabbed my head and forced me down more than I was wanting to go, causing me to choke on several occasions.

He moved a bit and had me shift as well so that my side was facing the outside window. From the parking lot, you could have seen it all. Me on my knees taking his large cock in my mouth and his hands on my head guiding him. I think he had a bit of an exhibition streak.

After a few minutes, he pulled me off and grabbed a chair, and moved it right next to the window. He told me to get up on the chair and hang my ass off. I knew what was coming next. He went over to the bedside table and grabbed some lube and started to rub it on his long and thick member. I was trying to prepare myself for the onslaught that was coming.

He got behind me and started fingering my ass. When he got to the point that he was fucking me with three fingers, he pushed my ass down a bit with the palm of his hand and pointed his cock at my hole, and moved in, and I let out an audible gasp as his long black cock moved inside me.

"Damn, boy," he said. "This ass is just what I needed."

"Thank you, Sir," I said. "I'm here to serve."

As he continued to enter me, I started to realize just how big his cock was and I clinched up a bit, which caused him to slap my ass in response.

"Breathe, boy," he said. "Don't clinch. Relax and take this cock!"

I groaned as he finally got all the way in and he slowly started to fuck my ass as he held tightly to my waist. It was honestly a bit painful, but I was determined to pleasure him well.

As he started to speed up his thrusts, he reached down and grabbed my shoulders and pulled me up some so my back arched a bit. This gave him a bit more access to fuck me deeply and I was starting to cry out a bit as he pounded till his balls hit my ass.

"How does that feel, boy?"

"Your cock is massive, Sir," I said. "It's a privilege to take it."

"Good boy," he replied.

He pushed me back down onto the back of the chair again and started to pound me with a medium thrust and speed and smacked my ass while he was at it. First one cheek and then the other. At first, it was not too bad, but as he continued, the pain increased, and I could feel the heat building on my ass as they reddened.

"That ass is warming up nicely," he said.

I just grunted and tried to hold back crying out as he continued.

Once my ass had a light red glow, he reached back up to my shoulders to pull me up again and arch my back. He then started to pound me hard and I heard the smack of his low-hanging balls as they hit me.

"It's a good thing you caged that pathetic thing between your legs boy," he said. "This ass is made for a man's pleasure."

"Thank you, Sir," I replied in between a grunt and a cry.

He then pushed my head down with one hand and grabbed my waist with the other and shoved his cock deep into my ass as his cum erupted from his balls and flooded my insides.

"Fuck!" he yelled. "Take that cum boy!"

I was biting the back of the chair and doing all I could not to scream out. His cock was pulsing so hard that I felt it as it moved inside me. He sat there for a moment and caught his breath and then pulled back and then stopped just before he was completely out. He then waited a further few seconds to make sure his cum was well planted before his cock slid completely out.

"Clean me, boy," he said.

I got off the chair and down on my knees and grabbed his cock in one hand and licked him completely clean of my ass and his remaining cum. He ran his hand through my hair and was groaning while I was doing it.

"Thank you, Sir," I said as I finished and looked up at him.

He grinned and told me to get up. He led me over to the door and opened it and picked up my bag of clothes.

"I'll be sure to let you know next time I am in town, boy," he said. He then tossed the bag into the hall and pushed me out and closed the door behind me.

I was in a state of shock for a moment. Cum was running down my leg from my overfilled ass and I was completely naked in the hotel hall. I bent down and grabbed the bag and quickly put my clothes on. As I bent down to put my shoes on, I felt the cum leak out and start to soak my underwear.

By the time I got home, a wet spot had soaked through to the back of my pants. I was happy to get inside my apartment and strip down and clean up a bit. I went to my computer after and typed up a rundown of the evening's adventures and posted it to my Tumblr account and then I emailed John to let him know how things went and that the details were posted.

Saturday morning, I spent the morning cleaning my apartment and after lunch got my laundry done. I dumped it all on my bed after and was starting to fold it all when my phone went off. It was from Jay.

"Hey bro," he said. "Are you busy today?"

"I am just folding laundry," I replied. "What's going on?"

"Can you meet me at my apartment at 3 pm?" he asked. "Bo will be here. We need to discuss a few things."

"Sure, I can be there," I replied.

"Great," Jay said. "I'm on the first floor. I'll send you the address."

As the address came in by text, I was a bit curious as to what was going on. But, as it was 2 pm at the moment, I needed to hurry up and finish getting things put away so I could head over.

Jay lived about 30 minutes away on the north side of the city. When I pulled into his complex, I drove around the side of one of the buildings and found his apartment. Bo was still in his car when I pulled up and parked next to him.

"Hey, Bo," I said.

"Wassup, Matt," he replied and came around to hug me.

"You know what this is all about?" I asked.

"Sir wants us to prepare for something at his house," Bo replied. "But Jay said he would give us more details when we arrived. As the senior sub, it's his job to coordinate for parties and special events and gatherings at Sir's."

"Ahh, ok," I replied.

We knocked on the door and Jay greeted us in just his cage and collar. We entered the room and stripped down to ours as well and folded our clothes next to the door.

"Thanks for coming over guys," he said. "Feel free to sit at the table here and I will grab y'all some drinks."

The kitchen table was to the left of the door and the living area was to the right. The kitchen was in the back left of the room and in the back right it led off to his bedroom and bathroom. Bo sat in the chair next to the door and I sat opposite of him. Jay joined us and sat in the chair on the side of the kitchen area and handed us some cokes.

"Sir has informed me that he will be having two old friends from New York staying with him next Friday and Saturday," Jay said. "They are a couple and have a collared sub of their own that was one of Sir's first graduates. He has informed me that he wants us to be available to cater to their needs while they are here."

"What all will this entail?" I asked.

"One or more of us will need to be around as long as they are here," Jay responded. "We will be expected to respond to any requests including any maid or sexual services they may desire. Additionally, Sir wants all three of us at his house on Saturday from 12 pm to 1 pm to provide sexual services in the dungeon area."

"This happens from time to time," said Bo. "Sir likes to treat his guests like royalty. We get them food and drink, provide massages, provide blowjobs, or let them have use of our ass and things like that. But we also have to stay overnight and be available as well."

"Correct," said Jay. "This means we need to coordinate who will be there, and when one of us has to be awake and available from the time they get to Sir's to the time they leave."

"Ok," I said.

"I have already requested a day off from work so I can get to Sir's house at 9 am to prepare for their arrival at 10 am on Friday. Ideally, I would like to have one of you come over to relieve me at 7 pm that Friday evening. That second shift will be 7 pm to 5 am on Saturday morning and the third shift will be 5 am to 3 pm and will include the time we will be in the dungeon area. They will be leaving at 2 pm, so the one of you that takes the third shift will go with them and tend to any last-minute needs while the second shift person works with me on clean-up duties in the dungeon area. After they leave, the third shift person will have to strip the beds, put the sheets in the wash, and then clean the room thoroughly before leaving."

"I understand," I said.

"Bo is next in seniority among us, so which shift do you want?" Jay said.

"I'll take the second shift," he said. "I'm a night owl anyway and I can take a nap after in Sir's pool house and then join you at noon in the dungeon."

"Very well," Jay said. "That means you are on the third shift, Matt."

"Sounds good," I said.

"I figured Bo here would take the night shift," Jay replied to me. "I talked to Sir about you taking the morning shift and he let me know there are some things that his guests like in the morning, so he will be letting you know what those are and training you on a few things tomorrow during your one-on-one with him."

"Ok?" I asked curiously.

"You will have to wait to talk to Sir about that," Jay said. "He did not let me know any more than that."

For the next couple of hours, we hashed out how things had gone in the past when people visited so I knew what to expect. I would be kneeling in any room they were in and had to respond to any request they asked of me. We also discussed what areas needed to be cleaned afterward and who was to do what. I almost wish I had taken notes, but Bo assured me he would make sure I was up to speed.

After we were done talking, Jay told us he had to get ready to meet some folks. I asked Bo if he wanted to go to Woofs, the bear sports bar, for some drinks and dinner. He said that would be great, so we both got dressed and headed out there.

We arrived at the bar at about 6:30 pm. It was a decent crowd for a Saturday evening, and we got a table in the back and ordered a pitcher of beer to share between the two of us.

"So, Bo, how often does Sir host guests?" I asked.

"Well," he replied. I have only been in training since December. He had some guests at the end of January, but nothing since then."

"Ok," I said. "So, not too common."

"No," Bo said, "But, just be prepared to be on your toes as we said. Sir expects an immediate response to any request and if we do not meet the high standards he places on us, we can be punished after they leave."

"Well, this should be interesting," I said.

Bo poured a glass of beer from the pitcher that arrived at the table and took a drink. He then took the second glass and poured one for me and handed it to me.

"You'll be ok," he said.

As I grabbed the glass and started to drink, I noticed Dan come into the bar and he saw and waved at us and came over to the table.

"How are you, boys?" Dan asked.

I stood up and hugged him as did Bo.

"We are good," I replied.

"Is this seat taken?" he asked.

"No, feel free," Bo replied. "Is your master not with you?"

"No," Dan said. "Greg had to go out of town for the weekend. So, I decided to get out of the house for a bit."

Dan ordered a whiskey sour from our waiter and then asked us, "so, what is knew with y'all?"

"We were just discussing some guests Sir will have over next weekend," I said.

"Oh yeah?" Dan replied. "Where are they from?"

"Jay told us that they were from New York and had a sub that graduated from the program a while back," Bo said.

"That sounds like Wes and Bart," Dan said.

"Did they visit while you were in the training program?" I asked.

"Yes," Dan said. "They have known Sir John for a long time. They collared a sub named Drew and he went with them when they moved to New York several years ago."

"Anything we should know about them?" Bo asked.

"Just that they are very demanding with a sub," Dan said. "Be sure you are ready for anything and don't make them wait."

"Ok," I said. "That is good to know."

"Also," Dan said, "Bart loves to have his balls tugged on when he is getting a blowjob, so if you are asked to service him, keep that in mind. But Wes does not like his balls messed with, so you will need to remember who you are servicing and not mix it up."

"I am glad we talked to you then," Bo said.

"Which one of you will be around in the morning?" Dan asked.

"That would be me," I said.

"Humm," Dan replied with a concerned look. "How experienced are you at watersports?"

"Like drinking piss?" I asked.

"Exactly," Dan said.

"Well," I replied, "I mean I have played with people that have pissed on me before and I have had them piss in my mouth a bit, but not much experience."

"That might be an issue, then," Dan replied. "Bart expects the sub to take his morning piss when he wakes. You will be expected to be on your knees next to the bed and drink it all from the tap."

"Oh," I said with some concern. "I wonder if that is what Jay was referring to earlier. He told me Sir was going to have to work with me on some things specific to his guest's morning needs."

"It's possible," Dan said. "As the morning sub, you will also be preparing breakfast for them."

"What will I be preparing?" I asked.

"I was the morning sub when they visited during my training," Dan said. "I prepared scrambled eggs, bacon, sausage, hash browns, and biscuits."

"Oh, that is not too bad," I said.

"No, you will just need to plan your time accordingly and be prepared to drop everything at a moment's notice if they call for you," Dan said.

"I guess I need to start flagging yellow quickly," I said.

"Just like your collar color!" Bo said with a laugh which Dan joined in with.

"You can train on your own," Dan said with a smile. "Just collect your piss in the morning in a glass and learn to drink it all. It is usually stronger in taste in the morning and the warm temperature was something I had to get used to as well."

"That is good advice," I said.

"Sounds like you got homework to do Matt," Bo said as he took a drink and winked at me.

We all ordered some pub food and hung out for a few hours before Dan said he was getting tired and wanted to head home. Bo and I agreed to do the same, so we paid our tab and I ended up getting home about 10:30 pm.

I walked into my apartment and stripped down and started to head to the bathroom to drain my bladder as a result of the beer I had been drinking but stopped myself when I remembered what Dan had suggested I do.

As I needed to piss bad and knew it would be a lot, I got a large water bottle from the kitchen and held it under my caged nub. I let the piss flow and it started to fill the bottle up. Sure enough, it was pretty much full to the brim by the time I was done.

I lifted the container to look at it and brought it to my lips.

"Well," I said to myself, "here goes nothing."

I tipped the container back and the warm beer piss filled my mouth. It did not have a strong taste and was saltier, more than anything else. The warm temperature was something that was making me gag a bit. I paused for a moment to swallow and then continued to drink till I had recycled it all.

"Ugh," I replied out loud. "That is going to take practice. Especially if I won't have the ability to pause and swallow."

I rinsed out the container and went to sit down and play some video games before heading to bed for the evening.

CHAPTER FIFTEEN

Flagging Yellow

I woke up Sunday and went about cleaning up the apartment and doing my laundry. The night before I had woken myself up a few times from attempted erections in the cage. Overall, I had got better about sleeping through the night, but it was not consistent. I was only a week into a two-week lock-up session and I know this was going to only get worse, not better, so I needed to find ways to distract myself.

I watched the clock and made sure I left myself plenty of time to get cleaned up and cleaned out for my visit with John in the afternoon. I got over to his place a few minutes early and stripped and went into the dungeon and knelt in my square waiting for his arrival.

I heard John come down the staircase and enter the room. He stood before me and paused for a moment. I did not know what was going on as all I could see was his feet in front of me. I heard the click of a lighter and smelt the aroma of a cigar in the air and when he told me to rise and face him, I saw he was in his regular gear, but had a fat Gordo in his mouth.

"How are you doing, boy?" he asked as he blew some smoke at my face.

"I am good, Sir," I replied with a slight cough.

John looked me up and down and drew on his cigar and pulled it away from his face with his hands and blew the smoke into the air. It rose like a cloud and lingered giving the air an acrid smell, but I could also note a hint of some unidentified spices as well.

"As you are aware of by now," he said, "I have visitors coming over this coming weekend. Jay has informed me that you will be taking the morning shift and will be responsible for breakfast as well. Do you have any questions, boy?"

"Not at this time, Sir," I replied. "I have discussed this with my sub brothers and I also met with Dan and he let me know a little about what to expect."

"Ahh," John said as he blew more smoke in my direction. "That is good. Dan did a very good job when they were here last. So, he told you about acting as a urinal for my friend Bart then?"

"He did, Sir," I replied.

"And what are your thoughts on this?" John asked. "I want you to be honest with me."

"I was a little nervous, Sir," I replied. "I do not have a lot of experience in this area, but Dan suggested I start trying to drink my piss this week to get used to it."

"And have you?" John asked.

"Yes, Sir," I replied. "I have. I drank my piss last night after the bar and I did it again this morning."

"How did that go?" he asked me as he continued to puff out clouds of smoke.

"The warm temperature is something I am trying to get used to," I replied. "I noticed the taste was saltier, more than anything else, though it was acrid this morning."

"That is normal," John said. "But, getting used to the taste is one thing, taking it from the tap is another. We will practice that today."

"Yes, Sir," I replied.

"I encourage you to find someone to practice with this week as well," John said. "Your goal should be not to spill a drop. This is not something I normally expect of a sub so early in training, but you will need to rise to the occasion."

"I will do my best, Sir," I replied.

"Very well," John said as he took the cigar out of his mouth and held it in-between his fingers and scratched his forehead above his right eye.

"Tell me, boy," he then said, "how is the chastity cage doing?"

"It is ok, Sir," I replied. "I'm horny and I woke myself up a few times last night. I also have a bad case of the blue balls, but I am managing."

"These feelings are normal," he said. "You will find that over time, as your sessions increase in length, that the urges you will encounter and this blue balls feeling you mention will get worse. You will have to find ways to overcome this on your own. Everyone is different but serving men and finding ways to burn off that energy will help."

"Yes, Sir," I replied.

"I will do a milking session on you today to help with that," John said. "But this is not something we will do every week. I usually perform this every two weeks when you are in longer sessions."

"I understand, Sir," I replied.

"Good," John said. "Follow me."

He led me across the room and then opened the door to the isolation room. He then went to the left and opened up the bathroom. I had never been past this door as Jay had told me this would be shown to me at a later time.

The entrance area had a white tiled floor with a typical sink to the right in a countertop with a cabinet below it. Past this, the room widened a bit. Where a toilet would be, the hole in the floor was sealed shut. There was a small barrier on the floor that ran the length of the room perpendicular to where you entered and beyond this was a square-shaped tiled area that had a drain in the center. I assumed this is where a shower would be, but there were no shower heads on the walls, just a short pipe where you would attach one.

"Kneel over the drain and face me, boy," John said.

I stepped into the square area and knelt on my knees and faced him. He removed the front part of his jock that was attached by snaps and his soft cock fell out. He came over to me and placed it in front of my mouth.

"You are now going to practice taking piss, boy," he said. "Without touching my cock, I want you to open your mouth and take the head in. You will need to make a seal around it and leave room for the piss to flood your mouth. When it starts to flow, you need to concentrate on swallowing and not letting anything escape."

"I understand, Sir," I replied.

"I know you are inexperienced," he said," so if you fail this time you will not be punished, but I want you to concentrate."

"Yes, Sir," I said.

I was very nervous doing this for the first time. I opened my mouth and brought it forward and sealed my lips around the head of his cock. John took a drag off his cigar and blew the smoke down on me as he relaxed, and the piss started to flood my mouth.

He was not controlling the stream in any way. It came at full force and I immediately tried my best to swallow it, but I choked a bit, and it came out of my mouth and dribbled down my beard and my chest.

"You better recover quickly, boy," he said. "I got plenty more in me."

I opened my throat up some and adjusted my mouth to try to take in more and got into a rhythm of letting it fill my mouth and swallow. The taste was slightly acrid and was different than what mine had been like. I initially tried to hold my breath to limit the taste but found I needed to regulate my breathing to avoid choking on the stream.

I had one more incident where I choked a bit and more piss went down over my beard and chest, but I mostly got it all. As the stream started to slow, he reached down and pushed my head back and parted my mouth and dribbled the last bit into me before telling me to swallow.

"For a first attempt," he said, "that was not bad. But you will need to get much better at that by Saturday morning."

"Yes, Sir," I said.

The piss was starting to dry on me and left me smelling like a bit of a urinal. I was hoping John would be letting me clean off, but he told me to rise and follow him back into the dungeon area.

He strung me up on the cross and worked my back over with the flogger like last week. It still stung and he pushed my limits of pain control, but I did concentrate and felt like I did a better job at focusing my mind and making it through the session without yelling out as much. However, as my back and ass took on a shade of red, I could not help but call out near the end in pain.

John rubbed me down and hugged me again as part of the aftercare and then we went to the bench again and he had me lie down on it on my stomach with my nub dangling through the slit in the middle. John put a stool underneath the table and placed a jar that had some clear liquid in it already on this, so it was right under my nub. He then took an instrument out of a drawer and started to lube it up.

"I will now milk you, boy," he said. "This toy will allow me to reach your prostate. Most of my boys tell me that this process will make them feel like they have to pee. The motion of the device will cause your prostate to start to drain its stored fluids. This might take about five minutes or so, but eventually, it will be emptied, and you will find this might help with the slight pain you have been feeling from being caged so long."

"I understand, Sir," I said as I turned my head to the side to watch him.

He placed the device in my ass, and it had a handle that allowed him to angle it right towards the area where my prostate could be found in my ass. He started to move it back and forth and the stimulation was interesting. Not unpleasant, but it was not long until I did feel as though I had to pee, and cloudy fluids started to slowly drip and flow out of my nub. There was no orgasm attached and it took quite a few minutes for him to completely drain me.

When he was done, he removed the device from my ass, and I did feel as though the blue balls feeling had abated. I felt as though I was less horny. He reached under the table and grabbed the jar and told me to sit up on the side of the table. He swirled the contents and let my prostate juices start to mix with what was already in it.

"Drink your fluids, boy," he said as he handed me the jar. "It has a little vodka in it to help it go down."

I swallowed the concoction in one gulp and then handed the jar back to him and he put it to the side. He then had me stand and he went across the room and grabbed the chair and brought it over to the center of the room and he sat in it.

"Boy, I want you on your hands and knees in front of me," he said. "You are to act as a footstool."

"Yes, Sir," I said as I got down in front of him and he propped his feet up on my back.

I stayed like that for a good ten minutes while he relit and continued to smoke his cigar. My knees were starting to get sore and I was doing all I could not to readjust, but it was getting to be too much.

"May I speak, Sir?" I asked.

"You may," he replied.

"I need to readjust to take the weight off my knees, Sir," I said. "Is this allowed?"

"Yes," he said.

I then adjusted a bit and hunched a little lower causing his legs to fall a bit.

"You need to learn what position works best for you," he said. "You might also want to invest in knee pads for this coming weekend as my guests might be using you in this manner."

"Yes, Sir," I replied.

After a few more minutes, he told me to spin around and sit cross-legged in front of him. He then placed one foot in my lap and instructed me on the best way to give a foot massage. He showed me where to apply pressure, how to use my thumbs and fingers, and some basic techniques. He then placed the other foot in my lap and had me practice again.

"Very good, boy," he said when I was done. "This is something else you need to practice before next weekend too. Now, get on your knees and suck me off."

As I got up and started to give him a blow job, he put one hand behind his head and used the other to finish off his cigar. He would occasionally blow smoke over me as I went down on him and when he finally blew and flooded my mouth with his cum, he growled and yelled out and the echo bounced around the room.

John then stood up and looked down at me. I still smelled of piss, cigar smoke, and my beard had some remnants of his cum in it. He smiled.

"You've been well marked today, boy," he said. "Be prepared for a lot more this Saturday. You can clean up the room and go when you are done."

"Yes, Sir," I replied as he crossed the room and went back upstairs.

I got back to my apartment about 5 pm after cleaning up the dungeon and running by to grab some food on the way home. I was a bit of a mess and smelt and looked like I had been used. I saw Kenny as I was heading to my building and he flagged me down and came over to speak to me. When he got close, he noticed the aroma of my session with John as well.

"Damn, Matt," Kenny said with a laugh. "You must be getting back from your Sir's place. What all did he do to you?"

I could not help but grin. "Well, I started to learn to drink piss, and it got all over me a bit. That was followed by a flogging session and giving him a blowjob while he smoked a fat cigar. Unfortunately, I was not able to swallow his entire load, so my beard is a bit of a mess."

"Sounds like you are getting trained well," Kenny said with a smirk. "I need to get my boy Max to take some lessons from you."

"So, he's your boy now?" I asked.

"Well, we have been seeing each other for about a month," He said. "He's subby minded and I am digging it. I am trying to get him out of the place he is staying so we can see each other more. The roommates have put a damper on things."

"I hear ya," I said.

"You need to work on that piss drinking, though," he said. "Otherwise, you are going to start to smell like a urinal if that is going to be more common."

"Well," I said, "he has some visitors coming over next weekend and it's something I will be expected to do for them. I don't have a lot of experience, though."

"Damn," Kenny said, "you don't have long to learn then."

"Not at all," I replied.

"Well, we can fix that," Kenny said as he pushed me over to the wall between two of the buildings. "Get down on your knees boy," he said.

"Umm, right here?" I asked, a bit shocked.

"You are the one saying you needed more practice, right?" Kenny said as he unzipped his pants and pulled his cock out. "You better put your mouth on this dick and drink it all down soon before someone sees."

I was still a little shocked by Kenny's boldness. I was seeing a new side to him. But I put my mouth on the head of his cock and prepared.

"Here it comes boy," Kenny said. "Don't spill anything or it's going to end up on my pants and I will not be happy."

I relaxed my throat just as the stream started to flow and fill my mouth up. I concentrated on swallowing and fortunately, Kenny did not have as forceful a stream as John did earlier. The taste was not as acrid as well, so I was able to manage. A few times I missed my coordination of swallowing and letting my mouth fill and it started to dribble out my mouth and down my beard and onto my shirt, fortunately, though, none of it ended up on Kenny's pants.

As his stream slowed to a trickle, I sucked the last few drops off and opened my mouth so he could use his hands to wiggle the last bit from the head. I swallowed one last time and looked down to see that my shirt was a bit wet from the overflow, but I did a better job than before.

"Not bad there, Matt," Kenny said as he put his cock away. "How about you see me after work a few days this week and we will work on that?"

"Yes, Sir!" I said with a grin.

Kenny patted my head and I got up. He continued to head to his car to run an errand and I headed up to my apartment to take a shower.

Monday and Wednesday during my cleaning days at John's house, he brought me back to the isolation room bathroom to practice taking his piss. On Tuesday and Thursday, I knocked on Kenny's door after work and dinner and he would bring me into the living room and have me kneel and take his as well. By Friday, I was feeling more confident about my ability to take it all without spilling anything.

I had been texting with Dan throughout the week and asking him about his experiences when they visited when he was a sub and updating him on my progress. After lunch, on Friday my phone went off with a message chime.

"Are you ready for tomorrow?" Dan asked.

"I think so," I replied. "When I was with my neighbor yesterday, I was able to get it all down without spilling anything, but I'm still crossing my fingers it goes well."

"I got ya," Dan said. "Well, if you are up for it, my master Greg said to come over on your way home from work and he can give you a final test."

"That would be great!" I replied. "Any particular time?"

"No," Dan said. "He is working from home and said to stop by whenever you are done. I will be working late tonight, so you will have to knock, and he will let you in."

"Perfect," I responded. "Thanks a bunch!"

"No problem," he said. "And good luck!"

I got over to Greg and Dan's condo about 6:30 pm and I parked and walked up the steps to the door and knocked. Greg opened the door and let me in. He was in some jogging shorts but nothing else.

"Good to see you again, boy," he said.

"Thank you, Sir," I replied. "Good to see you as well."

I proceeded to strip all my clothes off and fold them by the door while he watched.

"How has your training been going?" he asked me.

"It has been going well," I said as I finished folding my shirt and standing to face him.

"My boy told me you will be taking care of some visiting guests this weekend," he said. "He said you have been practicing to drink piss."

"Yes Sir," I replied. "I'll admit I did not have much experience before this week, but I have been practicing drinking my own and have taken it from Sir and a neighbor of mine. I was told one of the guests likes to use the sub as a urinal in the morning when he wakes up."

"Ahh," Greg said. "Well, how about we make this as real as possible. Follow me upstairs."

I followed him up to the landing and into their bedroom. He dropped his sweatpants to reveal his hairy ass to me and then he turned and sat on the edge of the bed.

"On your knees, boy," he said. "I've got a full bladder for you."

"Yes, Sir," I responded.

I got down on my knees and leaned forward and put his cock in my mouth. Greg was sitting on the side of the bed with his arms on either side and looked down at me as he let go and the stream started to flood my mouth. It was a powerful blast and I nearly choked, but I recovered and closed my eyes and concentrated on my breathing when it was filling my mouth and swallowing as soon as my mouth was full.

Greg kept pissing and I kept up my concentration. Only a small dribble escaped my mouth and ran through my beard. It was taking all the focus I had to make sure I did not make a mess of myself or the floor. It seemed like he was going to pee forever when at last the flow started to subside.

Greg reached down and pushed my face back and pulled my jaw down with his thumb and let the last few squirts and drops land on the back of my throat before he spat in my mouth and told me to swallow.

"Very good, boy," he said. "I think you are ready. Now, suck me hard and pleasure my cock in gratitude."

"Yes, Sir," I replied.

I reached up and grabbed the root of his shaft and started to move up and down it as his cock started to engorge with blood and lengthen. I put my face in his crotch and took in his intoxicating scent and then proceeded to suck on his balls one by one. I then moved around and went back to his cock again and started to bob up and down on the shaft.

He grabbed my head and guided it onto him. "That's a boy, take that dick."

He face-fucked me for a while and then pulled me off to let him slap his dick on my face. He shoved it deep until his balls were on my chin and I was about to choke. He had me play with his balls and stroke his shaft. Greg was enjoying using my mouth in any way he could.

I saw his legs twitch and prepared for his cum which came shortly after. He grunted loudly and grabbed my face and stuffed his cock right into my throat and added his semen to the piss he gave me earlier.

"Very good, boy," he said as he let go of my face and I backed off his softening cock. "I'll be sure to text John that you are prepared."

"Thank you so much, Sir," I replied.

"You can let yourself out," he told me.

I went back downstairs and dressed and got back into my car and headed home. Between the piss and cum, my belly was pretty full, so I just grabbed a light salad to eat for dinner and then tried to go to bed a bit early as I needed to get up early to get cleaned up and ready for my shift at John's.

CHAPTER SIXTEEN

The Visitors

My alarm went off at 4 am and I groggily turned it off and pulled my CPAP mask off my face. It was still pitch-black outside, and I turned on the side lamp and got up and sat on the edge of the bed and rubbed my eyes. I had thirty minutes to be cleaned up, cleaned out, and dressed to head out the door to make it to John's house. He was only about 15 minutes away, but Bo had asked me to get there a little early so we could properly hand off our shift duties.

I went into the bathroom and turned the shower on and got in and scrubbed down well. I also got my attachment out for the shower and made sure I was well cleaned out for any butt play as well. Satisfied I was ready to go, I stepped out and dried off, and looked at my naked, caged, and collared body in the mirror. Bo and Jay told me not to wear any deodorant and to make sure my hair, beard, and groin area were trimmed according to John's rules. My hair looked ok, but I did do some light trimming on the sides of my beard and ran the trimmer over my groin area to get it all down to a short length.

I walked out into the kitchen and grabbed a granola bar just to have something in my belly and a glass of orange juice to wash it down and then I put on some sweatpants and a t-shirt and headed out the door to the car.

I got to John's house right at 4:45 am and parked and went inside the side door. It was quiet when I entered. I undressed and put my things in my bin and then locked it and quietly went upstairs to the first floor. Bo was coming down the stairs from the second floor and met me right as I closed the door to the basement staircase.

"How was your shift?" I whispered.

"Not bad," Bo replied. "I am really tired, though."

"I can imagine," I said.

"Let me give you the rundown of what to do," Bo said. "I will show you upstairs to the guest room in a moment. You will need to kneel where I tell you and just wait there quietly. Master Wes and Master Bart are sound asleep at the moment, but you need to be ready to attend to them at a moment's notice."

"I understand," I replied.

"They will expect breakfast promptly at 8 am," Bo said. "You will be given leave to come downstairs at 7 am to start preparing it; however, if they need you for anything, you need to be ready to stop what you are doing and immediately come upstairs."

Bo took a chain off from around his neck that had a small black box attached to it and handed it to me.

"This device is connected to a remote they have," he said. "It will buzz and flash if they need you."

I hung the device around my neck and told him I understood.

"Once I leave you, I will go out back to the pool house to sleep in the bed that is out there," Bo said. "I will come back before noon and join you and Jay in the dungeon."

"Sounds good," I told him.

"Ok, follow me, then," Bo said as he turned to go up the staircase.

The staircase went up half a flight, turned 180 degrees at a landing, and went up the other half flight to the next level. At this landing area was a large window in the front of the house and the moonlight was streaming in and lit the area with a cool glow. As we got to this landing and turned to proceed the rest of the way up, I noticed that on Bo's ass there were black marks. Two lines were on one ass cheek and one line was on the other. I poked Bo in the back.

"What are those black marks?" I asked him in a whisper.

"Breeding hash marks," Bo said. "Master Bart marks you on your left cheek for every load he gives you and Master Wes marks you on your right. They like to keep track of who they have bred and how much."

"Ahh, ok," I said.

"Be prepared," Bo said as he turned to head the rest of the way up the stairs. "They have high sex drives."

When we got to the top of the staircase, Bo turned to me. "This door to your right leads to the guest room. When you enter, there will be a long wall to your left with a dresser and a TV on this that faces the bed. You will want to get against the wall between the dresser and the door and kneel there. Don't fall asleep and be ready for anything."

"I understand," I said putting my hand on Bo's shoulder. "Go get some rest and I will see you later."

Bo turned to go back downstairs, and I turned the knob to the door, and it opened. It was very dark in the room. I could not see anything, but I entered and closed the door behind me. I felt for the wall on the left side of the room and followed it to the dresser and then knelt on the floor beside it.

I could hear the two men in the bed in front of me sleeping. As I sat there and my eyes adjusted to the darkness, I started to notice more features in the room. There was a tiny bit of moonlight coming in from above two of the three windows in the room and the illuminated clock on one side of the bed also brought some definition to the room as well.

The room was a nice size, almost the size I would expect a master bedroom to be. There was a large king-sized bed in front of me with two nightstands on either side. The man on the left side of the bed was covered up and all I could see was the outline of his torso under the covers and some dark hair on the pillow. The man on the right was sleeping on top of the covers, though. He was naked and sleeping on his side with one leg bent covering his genitals from view. One arm was under the pillow and the other stretched under his bent leg. He had a nicely built chest and muscular legs. Dark hair ran down his legs and on his arms. His head was shaved, and he had a medium-length, dark beard.

I sat there, motionless watching them sleep and the time on the bedside clock tick by. Just before 6 am, the naked man on top of the covers stirred. He sat up and turned to sit on the side of the bed.

"You there, boy?" the man whispered into the darkness.

"I am here, Sir," I replied, and I got up and came over and knelt before him.

"Did the other boy leave?" he asked me.

"Yes, Sir," I replied. "He will return at noon. I will be serving you this morning."

He rubbed his face and scratched his head a bit. "Ok, sounds good. Get your mouth over here; I need to piss."

I leaned over and took the head of his cock into my mouth and prepared myself. The stream started immediately, and it was stale and acrid tasting. I used the experience I had built up over the week though and took the entire amount without spilling a drop. When the stream slowed down, I sucked the last bits out and he pushed my forehead away and without saying a word. He turned away from me and laid back down to sleep.

I wiped my lips a bit with my fingers to make sure there was nothing left that was missed and then returned to kneel where I had been next to the wall after. I figured that this man was Bart since Dan told me he liked to piss early in the morning, but I was not sure.

About thirty minutes later the other man started to stir. The morning light was starting to creep in a bit, and it made it easier to see. He pulled the covers down and wiped his eyes. He was built similar to the one that had been sleeping on top of the covers. His hair and beard were cropped short, but he had a nice chest of fur that was going gray near the top and matched the salt and pepper in his beard as well.

The man I had serviced earlier reached over and rubbed the waking man's chest.

"You sleep ok, Wes?" he asked him.

"Eh, I guess," Wes replied. "I drank too much beer last night, though."

"We got a sub for that you know," Bart said.

"Yeah, I know," Wes said.

He pulled the covers down to reveal his soft cock that was lying in a tuft of dark hair.

"Boy?" Wes announced.

I came over to his side of the bed and he opened one eye to look at me.

"Oh," he said with a half-grin. "You're cute. Put your face in my crotch and drain me."

I leaned over and lifted his cock into my mouth, and he started to piss. I had not tried doing this from this angle and it was a little more difficult than when I was kneeling, but I managed to drink it all down.

When I was done, I moved away, and he turned and buried himself in the covers again. I went and knelt by the wall again as Bart moved over to cuddle him. He got under the covers and I saw him move close and his legs move under the sheets as he wrapped himself around Wes. He put his face in the back of Wes's neck and started to nibble a bit and moved around to do the same on his ear as well.

Wes reached up and put his hand on Bart's face. "Babe, I know you are horny, but I am tired. Why don't you wear out the boy and let me rest a bit?"

Bart rolled his eyes and scooted out under the covers and looked over at me.

"Get your ass over here, boy," he said.

I got up and walked over to him and he had me get up and lie on my stomach with my head near the foot of the bed. He spread my legs a bit and then put his face in my ass and started to lick my hole. The sensation shot a little electricity through me and I buried my face in the covers to try to prevent myself from moaning.

Bart used his tongue expertly and teased my hole open and spat on it several times as well. He used his thumb to work his way in and then with some more spit and tongue work, he managed to get to the point where he had three fingers in me.

Bart pushed my legs together and then straddled them. He put his hands on either side of my torso and I felt a long, thick cock rest on my ass cheeks. He reached down and positioned the head at the entrance of my ass, and I felt him push forward and it started to enter. His cock was thick and even though he had been working on opening me up a bit, I gasped a bit as he moved completely in with one movement.

Once he was balls deep in me, he adjusted a bit and brought his legs up more towards my waist so he could get in a better position to pound. He put his hands on my waist and grabbed me tight as he started to jackhammer my ass without warning.

A tinge of pain shot through me and I tensed a bit, which caused my ass to grip down on his cock as he was fucking me. Bart leaned down a bit so that he could whisper in my ear.

"You better loosen that ass up, boy," he said. "You got a lot of fucking in store today."

I took in a deep breath and concentrated on relaxing my body as best I could as he returned to his original position and pounded my ass furiously. The bed was bouncing, and Wes grabbed the covers a bit and initially covered his face, but then he put them down again to watch Bart assault my ass.

As I heard the squeaks from the springs in the bed start to sound in unison to the movement, Bart tensed up and slammed his cock deep into me and loaded me up.

"Ummph," he groaned trying his best not to be too loud, though Wes was already fully awake at this point and was secretly stroking his cock under the covers.

He lifted his body off mine and then grabbed a marker from the side table and put a hash mark on my left cheek.

"That's one, boy," he said trying to catch his breath.

Wes pulled the covers off revealing his hard cock underneath.

"Well, I'm awake now," he said. "I guess I'll get in on that since he's pre-lubed."

Bart got off the bed and Wes moved over to take the same position he had been in. He straddled my ass and rubbed the cum that was at the entrance of my hole around with the head of his cock. He then pushed his in and in one thrust was balls deep into me.

I let out another muffled moan as Wes started to move his hips and thrust his cock into me as well. Bart moved around to the foot of the bed and pulled my head up and stuck his cock in my mouth and told me to clean him. As my ass was assaulted from the back, I licked the remains of his cum from his cock.

Wes did not take long. He pounded me furiously for about two minutes and then dumped his load in me as well. He threw his head back and groaned and then slapped my back with the palms of his hands leaving brief red marks behind. As he pulled out, he sat back on the bed with his back against the wall.

"Turn around and clean my cock off boy," he said.

I got up on my hands and knees and turned around and took his dripping cock into my mouth to clean him off and suck the remnants of his load away. When I was done, I got off the bed and Bart came back and sat next to him. Wes called me over and had me turn around. He then took the marker from Bart and put a hashmark on my right butt cheek. I then looked over at the clock and noticed it was almost 7 am.

"Sirs," I said. "Do I have your permission to go down and start your breakfast?"

"You may, boy," Bart said. "I like my eggs over easy and Wes likes his scrambled."

"Yes, Sir," I said.

I felt my ass and used my fingers to collect the remnants of cum that was there and licked them clean as I headed for the door and walked into the hall. The morning light was streaming in as I went down the staircase to the first floor and then walked around to the kitchen. As I entered, I saw John at the breakfast table near the back windows to the house drinking some coffee.

"Good morning, Sir," I said.

"Good morning, boy," he replied with a smile. "Turn around for me."

I turned around and he saw the hash marks on my ass.

"So, the guys started on you early today?" he asked as he took a sip from his cup.

I turned to face him again and smiled. "Yes, Sir."

"That is good," he said. "You will be preparing made from scratch biscuits, sausage, white gravy, eggs, and bacon. The recipes are there on the counter if you need them."

"Thank you, Sir," I replied.

"I like my eggs scrambled," he said.

"I'm on it, Sir," I replied.

John left the room and went back upstairs, and I started to preheat the oven first and read the recipe for the biscuits. I had made them before, but it had been a long time ago. By the time I got the batter ready, the oven was alerting me it was ready, and I got them started. I figured I could keep them warm once they were done and that would leave the rest of the food to make after.

It was about 7:30 am when I was pulling the biscuits out of the oven. I was going to start on the meats next when the box around my neck started to flash and buzz. I covered the biscuits with a towel and put them below the oven to keep warm and headed upstairs to determine what I was needed for.

When I entered the bedroom, the two men were laying on the bed naked.

"Bring us both coffees, boy," Bart said. "I like mine black and Wes likes his with two sugars."

"Yes, Sir," I replied, and I headed back downstairs to fulfill their request.

After I delivered their cups, I returned downstairs to the kitchen and started on the sausage next. I needed the grease to mix with flour and milk to make the white gravy. I worked on the bacon at the same time and I did the eggs last, cracking two eggs and scrambling them for John, scrambling two for Wes, and doing my best to make two over-easy eggs. My dad always liked them that way growing up, so I had some experience, but it was a tricky thing to get right if you have not done it in a while.

I looked at the clock and noticed it was nearly 8 am, so I plated everything and brought it into the dining area and set up the silverware and brought out the coffee pot as well. I placed a jar of orange juice on the table as well and was just turning to leave when Wes and Bart came in the room with John behind them.

"This smells good," Wes said as he sat down.

"Indeed, boy," John said as he also sat down, "I am looking forward to seeing how well you did."

"Under the table, boy," Bart said as he sat down. "I want a foot massage while I eat."

I checked to make sure I was not oozing any more cum from my ass and I crawled under the table and put Bart's foot in my lap and started to rub it. The men were enjoying their breakfast and I heard no complaints, so I felt relieved on that note. Bart lifted his foot out of my lap and replaced it with the other later and I worked on that one next.

After I had worked his feet over for a while, I heard Bart say, "Boy, come up here."

I crawled back out from under the table and stood next to him.

"Very well done, boy," Bart said. "You may take my plate now."

I took his plate and utensils and left to return to the kitchen to start to clean up. When I returned to the table, John and Wes had finished and I took their plates as well. They lingered to talk over coffee while I finished cleaning up and then John called for me to come back into the room.

"Get down on your knees boy," he said. "I need a blowjob."

John had turned the chair and moved it out some, so I got down on my knees and took his cock into my mouth and started to work it till it was fully erect. I cupped his balls and used the other hand to steady his shaft as I worked on his head and before long, he was blowing a load down my throat.

John patted my head after. "Thank you, boy. Gentleman, I will be going upstairs to get cleaned up. He is all yours."

He got up from the table and left me on my knees as he left the room. Wes and Bart ignored me at first and finished off their coffee, but when they both got up, they told me to follow them.

They returned to the room and collapsed on the bed and directed me to my corner to wait. Wes grabbed a tablet to look at something online and Bart was on his phone. After about thirty minutes, Bart had me come to the side of the bed and take his piss again and then he sent me back to my position kneeling at the wall.

It was about 10 am when Wes put his tablet down and rolled over putting his upper torso and arm around Bart, who was stretched out on his back and propped up on a pillow with his arm over his head. Bart looked down at him and took the hand from behind his head and started to rub the back of Wes's head. Wes turned so that he was lying on Bart's belly and he reached up to play with Bart's chest hair. It was an intimate moment and they cared for each other deeply. It was weird kneeling at the wall quietly and watching. I almost felt like a voyeur.

"Boy," Wes said, breaking my thoughts. "Come over here and eat my ass."

I got up and walked over to the other side of the bed and crawled on the bed on my hands and knees straddling Wes's body. I had his ass in front of my face, and I stuck my face in and licked his crack. I used my hands to part his cheeks and I got in deeper. My tongue flicked his hole and circled it. I licked it with gentle strokes and Wes moaned in response.

"Get in there deep, boy," Wes said.

I started to push my tongue into his hole and move it back and forth. I pulled his hairy ass apart more with my hands so that my entire face was pushed into him. I held my breath as my nose dived into his crack giving me better access to tongue him deeply. My beard rubbed on the hair and skin of his ass adding to the sensations that were making Wes start to moan more.

"That's a boy," Wes said.

Bart was rock hard, and Wes had moved down to start to take his cock into his mouth. Wes moved up and down on him while I continued to push my tongue as deep as I could into Wes's ass and continue to lick around as well. Bart had both of his hands behind his head and his eyes were closed and he was groaning softly.

"Now this is relaxing," Bart said. "But, I'd rather have you up here making out with me."

Wes pulled off his cock pushed me off his ass with his hand and moved around so he could start to make out with Bart a bit. Before he started, though, Bart looked over at me.

Come over here and face the foot of the bed and lower your ass on my cock, boy," he said.

I crawled over and turned to face away from them. Bart's legs were bent and spread apart, and I got between them and put my legs under them and got into position to sit down on his cock. I spat on my hand and used my fingers to rub my hole a bit to get it wet and then I positioned his cock and brought my ass down on it till he was deep inside me.

"Fuck that load out of me, boy," he said as he and Wes had their tongues in each other's mouths.

I reached forward and steadied myself on the bed and lifted my ass up and then back down again. I rocked back and forth and reached down at one point to grab my cage and noticed I was starting to precum, which I collected as fast as I could and swallowed, to avoid a mess on the bed.

Bart was moaning as they continued to make out. Wes was rubbing Bart's nipples and I saw Bart's feet in front of me start to move back and forth as he stretched them. His toes spread out and then came into a curl and the joints cracked a little bit as he did so. I reached under my cage and felt the large hairy sack of Bart and his massive balls as they moved slightly inside building up the seed that would be in my ass soon.

Bart started to moan more, and I started to rock back and forth and move up and down on his cock faster. He reached up and grabbed my side and took Wes into his mouth deeper as he tensed and then his cock exploded cum deep in me.

"Fuck!" Bart yelled as he broke the embrace of Wes.

I brought my ass completely down on him, so his cock was embedded in me. I felt him pulse and I squeezed my ass in between the pulses to milk every drop.

"Damn, boy," he said. "You do know how to work a cock."

I grinned and continued my ass work until he was spent and started to slowly slide out of me.

"Are you good, Wes?" Bart asked.

"I am babe," Wes replied. "I'll save myself for later."

"You know I've got the Viagra to pop later," Bart said.

"I know," Wes said. "But I am ok for now."

He grinned and kissed him again while I lifted myself off the bed and reached behind me to clean the remaining cum off my ass with my hand. I turned around and went down on Bart with my mouth to clean his cock as well.

"Grab me the marker boy," Bart said.

I handed it to him and turned around and he added a second hashmark to my left ass cheek.

At 11 am, John knocked on the door and stuck his head in to tell Bart and Wes that I was needed. I got up from where I was kneeling at the wall and came into the hall.

"Boy, please go into the kitchen and finish cleaning up there and in the dining room," he said to me. "Then I want you to collect Bo from the guest house and start to get the dungeon area set up. Jay should be over shortly to help you. I have given you instructions on what to do on the whiteboard in the isolation room."

"Yes, Sir," I replied, and I went back downstairs.

After I had all the dishes and pans that had been used washed and put away, I wiped down all the surfaces with some disinfectant and made sure everything was spotless as it had been when I came in. It was about 11:30 am when I went downstairs into the dungeon and turned the lights on down there.

I walked over to the back sliding door and opened it to go outside. It felt pretty nice out and I walked around the pool and over to the pool house and knocked on the door. I didn't hear anyone, so I opened it and Bo was still passed out on the bed. He had just collapsed on the top of the covers and some drool was running out the side of his mouth onto the pillow.

I reached down and put my hand around his left foot which was hanging off the bed and shook him a bit.

"Bo," I said. "Hey, Bo. It is time to wake up."

Bo pulled his leg back from me and started to roll over. His cage appeared from under him and there was a stream of precum coming from it and a wet spot on the covers. He was filling his cage and I assumed it was an attempted morning erection. That was just something you got used to in chastity.

Bo reached down and adjusted his cage a bit and tugged on his balls to allow a bit more room. He opened one eye slightly and looked at me.

"Already?" he groaned.

"Yeah," I replied as I sat on the bed next to him. "I hope you got a few hours rest."

Bo closed his eyes again and completely rolled on his back. He stretched his legs and arms out fully and then brought his hands back to his face and rubbed it and then starched his beard. One hand went back to his straining cage and balls again.

"Fucking nub doesn't know when to give up trying to get hard," he said with a laugh.

"I noticed," I said with a grin.

"How did breakfast go?" Bo asked.

"It went well," I replied. "No issues and Masters Bart and Wes seemed to be in a good mood."

"Well, that is a good thing," Bo replied.

He sat up and sniffed under his arms.

"Well, I stink," Bo said.

I laughed. "I don't think they will care."

Bo laughed as well.

"Sir told me that he wants us to get the dungeon area set up," I said. "The instructions are in the isolation room."

"Ok," Bo said. "But, let me take a piss first."

"I'll do the same when you are done," I replied.

After we were done in the bathroom, we walked back around the pool and into the dungeon area again. Jay was just coming into the room from the entrance hall when we closed the sliding door behind us.

"Hey guys," Jay said. "How did y'alls shifts go?"

"Ok," Bo said, still stretching. He turned around and smacked his ass a bit and showed off his three hash marks.

"As you can see, they had a good evening," Bo said.

"Well, I have three as well, so the morning was just as good," I said with a laugh.

Jay smiled and turned around and shook his ass a bit at us. He had two hash marks on each cheek.

"Well, I beat you both then," he said as he turned to face us.

"You were not kidding when you said they had high sex drives," I said to Bo. "And they brought Viagra for this afternoon."

Bo rolled his eyes and Jay walked over. We headed to the side of the room and went into the isolation room. When we turned on the light, we saw some instructions typed and taped to the whiteboard.

> Boys:
>
> You three will be required to be in the dungeon area from noon to 1 pm. Jay, as the senior sub, will be in charge of the setup.
>
> Please set out the hand towels, lube, and wet wipes on the side table like normal. The plugs should be set out as well. Please have the music playing at a volume of three and the lights set at setting four.
>
> I want Matt blindfolded and strapped to the fuck bench. Please be sure the number three black gag is secure on his mouth.
>
> I want Bo restrained to the cross with his ass facing the room.
>
> Jay should be in the sling but will be expected to be used in other ways as well.
>
> Sir

"I am assuming this makes perfect sense to you, Jay?" I asked.

"Yeah," Jay said. "Grab four or five hand towels from the closet over there Matt. Bo, you go back into the dungeon and get the plugs set out."

"Will do," Bo said as he left the room.

Jay bent down and opened a door on the cabinet to the right of the door and turned on the switch on a panel. Dials began to glow, and he set it to start playing electronic music through speakers in the ceiling. He set the volume at three. He then flipped a switch labeled 'four' on another panel and in the dungeon area, red lights came on and the main lights dimmed by fifty percent.

I returned with the towels and we went back into the dungeon closing the door behind us. I set them on the side table where Bo had set out a series of butt plugs that ran from small to absolutely huge.

"Umm," I said, a bit scared at the look of the biggest plug, "I hope they don't plan on using that on me."

Jay laughed. "Don't worry. Sir won't break you."

Once we were satisfied that things were all set up as John wanted, Jay told me to come over to the fuck bench.

"Go ahead and climb on," he said. "Bo and I will help get you strapped in."

I got on the device and Bo strapped my arms down and Jay strapped my legs down. Jay then brought a black gag over to me. It was square leather with straps to go around the head, but it had a rubber piece that stuck out of the middle of the square.

"This part goes in your mouth and you can bite down on this," Jay said. "Be sure to try to muffle any sounds you make as best as you can."

Jay placed the rubber piece in my mouth and then brought the gag flush with my face. He secured it around my head and made sure it was nice and tight.

"How are you doing?" Bo asked me.

I gave him a thumbs up with my hand.

"Good," he replied. "I'm going to put the blindfold on you now."

Bo secured the leather blindfold over my eyes and also strapped this tight around my head. Once I was ready, Jay helped to secure Bo's arms and legs in the restraints on the cross and then he climbed into the sling and we waited for John and his guests to arrive.

The room was a little cool as usual. I felt the air come on and a slight breeze blow past my exposed ass and dangling caged nub. The pulsing beat of the music was on a medium level and with the gag and the blindfold on, it would have been easy to zone out. However, just as I was relaxing, I heard the sounds of the three men coming downstairs.

The door opened and I heard Bart first. "Now, this is what I have been waiting for."

I heard them come over and stand somewhere behind where I was. Cigar smoke started to waft through the room, and I felt a gloved hand run over my ass. It hit my left ass cheek and then my right and then rubbed my lower back.

"There's my chubby sub," I heard Bart say from the direction of the cross.

The sound of the music drowned out anything else I could hear for a while until I heard the sound of a smack of leather against skin and a low groan coming from Bo. I then heard the chains of the sling clanging as it started to move back and forth as Jay was getting fucked by someone. Another smack of the flogger echoed through the room and then I felt the spit of someone as they got my ass wet. A finger soon followed. It moved back and forth and then was replaced by two and then three.

I felt a hand on my back and then someone leaned over near my ear. "I wanted that cute furry ass first."

It was Wes. That meant that John must have been fucking Jay as Bart worked Bo's back over. I took a deep breath as Wes moved back to my ass and I felt his cock slap against my crack. He pointed it towards my hole and shoved it in.

I bit down on the gag as I felt his cock move into me. I felt him move back and forth pulling almost out and then slamming home. The loads from earlier were mostly absorbed, but what was left merged with the spit and acted as lube as he picked up the pace and started to pound me furiously. I gripped the wooden bench as it groaned slightly from the momentum of his thrusts.

The sound of the flogger hitting Bo's back and ass was starting to pick up and I heard him groan and cry out on occasion. The chains of the sling were bouncing back and forth as Jay was getting railed by John. The smell of cigars was filling the room and the scent of sex, sweat, and musk was soon to follow.

My mind was racing as I focused on the sense of sound, which was my only clue to what was going on around me. I heard Wes start to breathe heavily and a puff of smoke came drifting down over me.

"Take it boy!" he growled as he thrust forward and dumped his load in my ass. He thrusted three more times in quick sensation and then held his cock in me to make sure it was delivered deep.

I felt a marker add the second hashmark to my right ass cheek and then the cool air blew by me again and the cum dripping out of my hole sent a small shiver down my spine and my balls contracted a slight bit behind the base ring of my cage.

I felt Wes's hand on my ass again and then a plug was inserted into me. It felt like it was about a medium size and it was filling, but not painful. He then left and I was left with the sounds of the flogger and the clink of the chains of the sling.

I don't know how long I sat there. I heard muffled sounds and the smack of a paddle on ass, which I assumed was Bo. Eventually, I felt another hand run across my ass and the plug was pulled out. The cock that replaced it felt a lot like Bart's.

"That's a boy," Bart said as he slid into me. "Wes left you nice and creamed I see."

He started to fuck me, and I heard the sound of Wes's cum being churned and dribbling out as Bart's cock moved back and forth. I felt it run over my caged balls and drip off as my nub bounced back and forth from the thrusts of Bart.

From the area of the cross, I heard a cracking sound almost like electricity and Bo cried and jumped. It scared me to think about what was going on. Another cracking sound and Bo cried out a second time. The sounds of the chains across the room had stopped, but I did hear John talking to Jay, though I could not make out exactly what he was saying.

Bart broke my concentration as he reached down and grabbed my waist firmly and started to pound my hole furiously. I bit down on the gag and used it to muffle my groans. The smacking sounds of his cock and balls against my hole merged with the slosh of cum dribbling out. He kept up his pace and then I heard him growl and shove his cock deep and his cock exploded cum into my ass. I felt like I was about to break my jaw as I bit down on the gag and made a muffled cry.

I had the sense to squeeze down on Bart's dick as much as my loose asshole could do. I knew he enjoyed that last time.

"That's a boy," Bart said. "Milk my cock."

When he pulled out, I felt a slightly larger plug go back in and a third hash mark was added to my right ass cheek.

Again, I sat there for quite some time. I listened to the sounds of the room and tried to determine what was going on. It sounded like Bo had been taken down from the cross and was sucking someone off. I did not know where Jay was at first, but then I heard a paddle hit bare skin and he cried out. More smacks and cries followed, and I heard someone groan as they dumped a load into Bo's mouth.

Finally, I felt the plug being pulled from my ass again and the voice of John followed.

"Looks like you are lubed and loose, boy," he said as he mounted my ass with one thrust.

I was so used that it did not even register with me at first, but then a few tinges of pain came shooting up my spine to remind me of his thick cock. I groaned as he rode my ass and the sloppy sound of the cum dribbling out amplified the smack of his cock against my hole. He rode me for a good five minutes straight before dumping another load up my ass. But he pulled out quickly and I felt it start to dribble out.

I was used and exhausted. I had built up a sweat even with the cool nature of the room. I was concentrating on the feeling of my sore ass when I felt a furry face and tongue run up my crack.

"That's it, boy," I heard Bart say. "Clean that ass up."

I did not know which of my brothers was down there at first, but from the feeling of the beard that was rubbing on my cheeks as they licked and swallowed the remnants of the latest three loads I received, I figured it was Jay. He moved down and licked my balls clean near the end and I felt them jump a bit in their metal prison.

"All clean, Sir," I heard Jay say.

I sat there strapped to the bench for a while longer. The sounds of sucking and someone getting pounded in the sling followed before things quieted down and I felt my blindfold being removed. I blinked my eyes a few times to get accustomed to the light again and looked up to see Bo. He looked exhausted as well and he had some red marks that crept over his shoulders. He unbuckled my gag as I felt Jay undoing the bindings on my legs and arms.

Bo helped me get off the fuck bench and I was weak on my legs at first and Jay caught me before I fell.

"Holy hell that was intense," I said, rubbing my ass.

"Tell me about it," Bo said as he turned to take the gag and blindfold to the table at the side of the room.

As he turned, I saw his back and ass were bright red from flogging and paddling.

"Are you ok?" I asked slightly concerned.

Bo laughed as he turned back to me after placing the items down. "I'm fine bro. I am a bit of a pain pig. Believe me, it is no big deal."

"Well, you made it," Jay said, grabbing my shoulder. "Now just wait till one of Sir's big parties that lasts several hours."

"Ugh," I replied as I started to walk around a bit.

"It's not over yet," Bo said. "Sir said to report upstairs to their room as soon as you are able."

I groaned a bit but nodded.

"We will clean up here. Just be sure to clean up the bedroom and start the sheets in the wash after they leave," Jay said. "The laundry room is right across the hall from their room."

"Understood," I said. "Thanks, guys."

"We will see you soon," Bo said with a wink.

I headed back up the staircase to the main floor and then up to the second floor and entered the guest room. Wes had a towel around his waist from the shower and was bending over to pack a few things up and get out what clothes he was going to wear home. Bart was still naked, and his body hair was matted from sweat. He was laying down on the bed with his head propped up by two pillows and one arm.

"Hello boy," Bart said as I entered.

"Hello, Sir," I said as I went to kneel by the wall.

"Come over here," he replied.

I turned and went over to the bed and he got up and sat on the side of the bed.

"Time for a piss break, boy," he said.

I put my mouth around his cock and took his piss. After he was done, he pulled me in closer and let his soft cock move to fill my mouth and my nose and face came to rest in his crotch. The smell of sweat, cum, and musk filtered through my nose and I breathed in deeply.

"Looks like you like my scent," he said.

I groaned in response. He pulled me off his cock and laid back and told me to lick his balls. I dove in and the scent was even more intense as I licked and rolled my tongue around his large sack and felt the balls that had delivered so many loads in the past 48 hours.

He pushed me off and sat up again and told me to go to the wall. I got up and knelt there while he started to gather his things and then went to take a shower. Wes finished packing while he was gone, and he told me to grab his suitcase and follow him downstairs. Once we got down to the main floor, we made our way over and into the garage and he opened the back door for me to place it on the seat.

As we came back inside, I saw John at the kitchen table and Wes joined him. I returned upstairs and knelt by the wall in their bedroom again. Soon after, Bart returned to the room. A towel was around his neck and his soft cock was swaying between his legs as he walked. He tossed the towel on the bed and got dressed and finished packing his suitcase.

"Take this downstairs for me boy," he told me.

After I had his bag in the car, I returned inside and the two of them were talking to John.

"I will take it from here, boy," John said. "Please go up and start cleaning the room."

"Yes, Sir," I replied. "I hope you have a good trip home Master Bart and Master Wes. I feel privileged to have served you."

Wes grinned and winked at me and Bart replied, "Thank you, boy."

I returned upstairs again and stripped the sheets and put them in the wash. I then got the vacuum and ran it over the floor and then wiped down all the surfaces and threw away the trash. By the time I got down to dress and leave, it was a little after 3 pm and I was mentally and physically exhausted. I put my sweatpants on and pulled them up over my sore ass, threw my shirt and shoes on, and then I headed home.

When I got inside and stripped down, the first thing I did was to go take another piss. I turned on the light in the bathroom and looked at myself. I looked like I had been well used. My beard was matted and smelled of ass and musk. I turned around to see the three hash marks on my right butt cheek and the two on my left. I relieved myself and then thought about taking a shower but opted to just collapse on the top of the covers and put my CPAP mask on and drifted off to sleep.

CHAPTER SEVENTEEN

Bear Pride Atlanta

It was Friday, the 24th of April and it had been three weeks since Masters Bart and Wes stayed at John's house. John bound me to the table in the dungeon the next day after they left during my one-on-one visit and blindfolded me to take my cage off and give me a manual release. Once reinstalled, I had started my month session in chastity. In that time, he had milked my prostate once, on Sunday, the 12th of April. The milking helped with my horniess level at first, but in the intervening week and a half, it had built back up again.

My situation was not helped in that I had not had a chance to direct the pent-up energy in any direction as much as I had previously. I saw John on Sundays and he continued to work on my pain thresholds while flogging. We also worked on my bootblacking skills as well before he loaded my ass up. But, outside of those encounters, I had only had the occasion to service another man once, which was last week.

That encounter had happened the previous Thursday. I had been chatting with some guys on the Growlr hook-up app on my phone after work when I got a message from a hot daddy bear that lived only a few miles away. He was horny and wanted to drop a load, so I was able to drive over and suck one out of him before grabbing dinner and heading back to the house.

While it was a hot session, I needed to expend more energy, and I was hoping I would get a chance later. This evening was the start of a new event in the city called 'Bear Pride Atlanta'. In the past, the main event for the hirsute crowd was Atlanta Bear Fest that was held in July, but this year, local organizers wanted to add another event to the schedule. Rather than centered around any specific hotel or location, the event was split over several days and included parties at the local clubs.

I had read about it in the local gay magazine a few weeks ago and Chris and Rick made plans with me to attend a few of the parties, the first of which was to be held at the club Heretic in the city. We agreed to meet at their place after I got done with work for dinner and I had put a change of clothes in my car for the evening.

After I got off work, I drove over to their apartment and when I entered, I saw Rick was playing games in his underwear as usual and Chris was busy folding clothes in the bedroom.

"Don't forget to strip after you enter subby boy," Rick announced, not even looking back at me.

"Uh-huh," I said as I was taking my shoes and socks off and dropping my pants.

I had been to their place a few times since I started training under John and Rick was well aware of the rules that John had put in place. We had not played around since last month, but I got the feeling Rick did enjoy seeing me walk around in just my cage and collar.

After I had taken all my clothes off and folded and put them next to the front door and then adjusted my balls a bit in the cage, I walked over to the couch and sat next to him. Rick paused his game and put his hand on my leg.

"You do look cute in that," he said with a grin.

"Yes, well," I said, "this is all partially due to you since you introduced me to Sir."

Rick laughed and slapped my leg. "Eh, I think you just found your true calling."

He got up and went into the kitchen and called out, "you want anything to drink there, boy?"

I rolled my eyes and looked back at him. "Sure, Sir."

Rick had a huge grin on his face. He was enjoying teasing me a bit. He brought me a beer to drink and sat down and went back to his game. Chris came into the room soon after.

"Hey, Matt," he said.

I turned around to look at him and said, "hey bubba. You all done in there?"

"Yeah," he replied. "I just needed to finish putting away the laundry. You ready for tonight?"

"I am," I replied. "Sounds like it will be a fun time."

"Well, I need to sit down here and finish up a few emails, and then we can determine what we want to do for dinner. You got anything else you need done before we head out babe?" Chris said, directing the last question to Rick.

"I'm just about ready," Rick said, pausing his game again. "As soon as the chastity boy gets on his knees and sucks me off, that is."

Chris rolled his eyes and went to the kitchen table to his computer and I turned to look at Rick. Rick looked at me and raised an eyebrow. "Well?" he said. "I don't think John would want me asking twice."

I grinned and got down on the floor between his legs and pulled on his boxers as Rick lifted his butt. They slid down to reveal his half-hard cock that was rapidly starting to rise now that it was completely free.

I reached up and grabbed the root of his shaft and pointed his head towards my mouth and took it in and swirled my tongue around.

"Umph," Rick said as he put his hand on the back of my head. "That's a good boy."

He pulled his hand towards him which forced my head down on his cock till it hit the back of my throat and I choked a bit.

"You still need to work on that I see," Rick said.

He took his other hand and placed it on my head as well and used them to force my head back and forth, fucking me on his thick cock. My spit was starting to dribble down his shaft and it mixed with his precum making his dick glisten as I came up and went down.

I reached under and fondled his balls as he continued to use my mouth. They were hanging low in his sack and the size of large eggs. I felt one and then the other and rolled them around and gave them a slight tug.

Rick adjusted a bit moving his hips down slightly and arching his back a bit more as he continued his thrusting motion. He then removed his hands, and I came off his cock and licked down the entire shaft and then sucked on his balls one at a time. Rick had his hands behind his head now and his eyes were closed, and he was groaning.

I grabbed his shaft again and started to move my hands up and down on it while I sucked on the head and the upper portion. Rick responded by groaning more and he lifted his legs a bit and arched his feet. I started to suck faster, then, and quickened the pace of my strokes on his shaft.

Rick stretched his arms out on either side of the sofa and grabbed on the back and I felt him tense up. I sucked deeply on his cock, taking it fully into my mouth as he erupted cum and it filled me and went down my throat. His legs shuttered and he threw his head back and moaned loudly.

"Fuck, yes!" Rick exclaimed.

I backed off and watched the last few pulses of cum come from the head of his cock and dribble down the shaft, which I immediately licked clean and swallowed. I then looked up as Rick raised his head and opened his eyes.

"Thanks a lot for that," he said with a grin.

I grinned back and said, "I'm here to serve!"

Chris had a huge grin on his face as he finished the last email and heard Rick come down off his orgasm high.

"Well, if you are now well-drained, you horn ball, let's figure out dinner," Chris said.

As I was watching Rick's face, he smiled and patted my head. "I'm good now!"

I got up and went to grab the clothes I brought to wear to the club. I had my black neoprene jock that I put on first. Over that, I wore some tight-fitting jeans to show off my ass and chastity bulge and I had a nice fitting black shirt to go over it. I put my socks and boots on last and then adjusted my collar.

Chris and Rick came in as I was finishing getting dressed by the door. Rick had a tank top on with his jeans and Chris had a V-neck on with his.

"Y'all look good!" I said.

Chris smiled and groped my cage through my pants. "You are looking good too, subby boy!"

We went and grabbed some dinner at the sandwich place down the road from their house. I opted for a salad as I wanted to make sure I didn't have anything heavy in case I got to find someone for some ass play later.

We drove downtown and got to the club just as the party was starting. The parking lot was full as usual, so we used the lot a few blocks down and walked across a bridge to get back to the entrance.

The interior of the place is a bit of a maze. I maneuvered around to the bar to grab a beer for Chris and me while Rick went to go dance. It took me a minute to find out where Chris ended up, but he waved me down from the side of one wall and we got to drinking.

About an hour into the event, I felt someone grope my ass from behind me. I figured it was Rick or Chris, so I turned and was face-to-face with a really hot guy. He was very much my type, so I did not mind at all. He stood about 6 ft (1.8 m) tall and was a little chunky but had a nice amount of fur over his bare chest that was matted a bit from sweat. He had a full beard and deep blue eyes.

"How are you?" he asked.

"Doing well," I said. "My name is Matt."

"Kyle," he said with a nod. "I'm here from out of town with my buddy Cody."

"Oh, nice!" I said. "Are you here for the event or just visiting?"

"We drove over for the event," he said. "We live in Birmingham, Alabama."

"Oh, that is not far," I replied.

"Naa," he said. "We got a nice hotel room in Midtown."

"Nice!" I said. "I live on the west side of the city."

Kyle looked down and saw the tag on my collar and cocked his head a bit.

"Chastity sub, huh?" he said.

"Yeah," I replied. "Been in my cage now for almost four weeks. Horny as fucking hell."

An evil grin appeared on Kyle's face and he reached down and felt my crotch and the metal prison encasing it. He was sipping the last bits of some sort of colored drink out of a plastic cup and was swaying side to side a bit to the beat of the music.

"Would you like to go out on the dancefloor for a bit?" I asked.

"For sure!" he said as he put his cup down and followed me over to where everyone was dancing.

It was starting to get warm inside and most people had their shirts off. I took mine off on the way out to the floor and stuck the end of it in my back pocket and let the rest dangle out. As I started to dance with Kyle he reached over and started to rub his hands through my chest hair.

"You're cute," he said, leaning in so I could hear over the electronic beat of the music.

I grinned and said, "thanks, you are damn hot!"

Eventually, at some point, he ended up behind me and I felt his hands on my hips. He groped my ass a bit more and then reached around and felt my crotch and the metal cage underneath.

"I hope you don't mind my roaming hands," he said leaning over beside my ear.

"Not at all," I said with a grin. "Feel free to explore."

As the night wore on, we drank a bit more and Kyle continued to grope me as well. On several occasions, he put his hand down the back of my pants and fingered my ass. I got a distinct impression that he wanted more.

At one point I was grabbing another beer for me and a drink for him and ran across Chris.

"Hey bud," I said to him.

"Hey!" Chris exclaimed, waving his hands in the air. He was tipsy. "Are you having fun?"

"I am," I said. "I think I might be going to play with someone in a bit, so I will find my way home."

"Sexy sub," he said, putting his finger on my sweaty chest. "Just be sure you treat him right."

I laughed. "I will bubba."

I kissed him and then returned to find Kyle.

It was a little after midnight when Kyle leaned over to my ear. "So, you up for some fun in my hotel room?"

I grinned and looked back at him. "I'd love to!"

"The buddy I came with is at the bathhouse and I don't know how long he will be there. So, there is a chance he might be back early or come in while we are in the room. Is that a problem?" he asked.

"Not at all!" I said. "I'd be happy to play with him too!"

Kyle grinned again. His southern drawl was much more evident now that he had been drinking. I found it pretty hot.

"I am sure he would like that!" he replied.

We left the club and got a car to take us over to his hotel room. He was putting his hand down the back of my pants and rubbing my belly periodically on the way there and in the elevator ride up, I returned the favor and groped his crotch, and we kissed a bit as well.

When we got to his room, he kicked off his shoes and tossed his socks and shirt on the floor. He undid the button on his pants and sat down on the bed. I took my shirt, shoes, and socks off at the side of the door and dropped my pants to reveal my jock.

"Now you look sexy in that," he said with a smile.

I grinned and then took my jock off and adjusted my balls in my cage.

"That is so hot," he said. "Come over here and let me play with that."

I walked over to him and he held my cage in his hands. He licked the front of the cage and then noticed that I was starting to precum a bit and collected it with his tongue.

"You look to be a bit of a leaker," he said.

I grinned. "That's for sure."

I kneeled in front of him as he slid his pants and boxer briefs off. He had a nice set of balls and a cock that was starting to harden now that it was free. It grew to about 7 in (17.8 cm) long and had a nice girth and a slight curve to it. He was also starting to precum a bit too and I licked his head and then started to go down on him.

"Dayam, boy!" he said with a thick southern accent.

His toes curled and he leaned back a bit on the bed and his head fell back as I started to work his cock up and down and fondle his balls. He looked back down at me and then moved one of his feet, so his toes started to play with my cage. A bit of precum got over his big toe in the process.

"Such a hot subby boy," he said. "You're making a mess of my foot!"

I pulled off and looked down and saw several streams of precum over his toes. I pulled his foot up and started to lick it off and he groaned a bit. His foot was sweaty and musky, and the scent got me straining in my cage even more.

I put his foot back down and started to suck on his cock again and he was fingering his nipples when the door latch clicked, and his friend came in the room.

"Well, hell yeah!" his friend Cody exclaimed with what had to be a Texas accent. "Now this looks like a party!"

I grinned at him and then went back to bobbing up and down on Kyle's cock.

"This here is a chastity boy, Cody," Kyle said.

"Chastity boy?" Cody said inquisitively as he kicked his shoes off and pulled off his shirt and socks.

"Yup," Kyle said. "Check out the leaky caged cock on him."

"Nub," I corrected with a smile before going back to sucking on him.

"Sorry, nub," Kyle said with a grin.

Cody was taking his pants off and bent down to see my cage swinging between my legs as I moved to start to suck on Kyle's balls.

"Dayam," Cody said. "Well, I am glad I came back when I did!"

Cody dropped the jock he had on and sat on the other bed to watch and jack off a bit.

"Why don't you help him out there, Matt?" Kyle said to me.

I got up and walked between the two beds and got between Cody's legs and knelt. Kyle moved around so he was sitting behind me on his bed at the same time.

Cody had a nice cock as well. Uncut and about the same size as Kyle's. He had a nice brown bush of hair framing his balls as well. I took him into my mouth and started to go down on him.

"Fuck," Cody said. "Now this is nice."

Kyle smiled at him and watched as I sucked on his cock and balls.

I alternated between them for a while. Sucking one while the other jacked off. Eventually, Kyle moved to lay down in the bed and told me to get up on all fours and suck him that way, with my ass near the end of the bed. This gave Cody the ability to get behind me and he started to stick his face in my hairy ass and tongue my hole.

I was starting to moan as his tongue moved in and out of me and got to loosen my hole up and get it wet as well. I felt Cody start to play with my cage and the precum started to flow out and he collected it and started to lube my hole with it.

I felt him push my ass down and I crouched a bit on the bed. He pointed his hard dick at my hole and started to push in. I gasped a bit and then took Kyle deeply into my mouth at the same time.

They both growled.

Cody started to fuck my ass and my cage started to swing. My head moved forward and back, and I used the momentum to suck Kyle deeply at the same time and use my hands to jack his shaft. Kyle was fingering his nipples and his feet were curling. It was not long till I started to feel shoots of cum go into my mouth and down my throat.

"Fuck yeah boy!" Kyle said as he grabbed my face and fucked his load into me.

Cody grinned and started to pound me harder till his balls started to lift and he dumped his load into my ass.

"Yeahhhh!" Cody growled as he bit his lip and rode the wave of his orgasm.

He pulled out and put his face into my ass and licked the remnants of his load and then slapped my ass and went and sat down on his bed. I was sucking down the last bits of Kyle's load at the same time and then I backed off.

"Come up here and make out with me a bit sexy," Kyle said.

I crawled up on him and started to kiss him and explore his mouth with my tongue. I moved down and licked his shoulders and chest and moved over and stuck my face in his armpit which he raised for me. He had such a nice manly musk. My cage was straining the whole time. I then looked down and he was still hard and stroking.

"I'm ready for round two," Kyle said with a grin.

I looked back at him and grinned and swung my legs over his torso and used my hands to put his cock in my ass using Cody's load for lube. I sat down on him and reached out and played with his nipples while his eyes rolled back in his head and he groaned. He was right, he was still as hard as before.

I bounced up and down on him till I started to hear the sloshing sound as Cody's load was being churned in my ass. Kyle then grabbed my waist and moved his hips up and started to take over and thrust his cock into me faster. I groaned from the sensation and looked down to see fluids starting to come out of my cage. He was milking me with his cock.

"Damn Kyle!" Cody exclaimed as he watched. "Your fucking a load out of his nub!"

Kyle continued to jackhammer my ass and I felt him tense up and he finally dumped his second load up into me.

"Fucking hell!" Kyle said as he threw his head back and his body collapsed on the bed.

I moved up and down to ride the last bits out of him and then got off and fingered my ass and licked the remnants of their two loads.

His belly had a puddle of my prostate juices on it and I leaned over to lick those up as well.

"Thanks for that," I said. "I needed my balls emptied."

Kyle laughed. "You weren't the only one!"

We all chatted a bit after. They had some questions about chastity and John and such. But eventually, Cody wanted to go out and smoke some weed, and Kyle offered to join him. I took the cue to get dressed and leave and I thanked them again for a great time.

Saturday, the weekend event moved to the club called the Jungle with the theme of "Bear Invasion". I had asked Chris and Rick if they were going out, but they said they had decided to stay home. I felt a lot better since I got my prostate drained the night before but was still up for any fun I could find, so I went out on my own.

I grabbed a drink when I entered and was chatting with another friend of mine that was there when a bigger guy that was hot started flirting with me. He started to grope me and noticed my cage and then saw what my collar said. The look on his face was priceless.

"How long have you been locked up boy?" he asked.

"Almost four weeks in my current session," I said. "My Sir is working me up to longer and longer periods locked up."

He had a devious grin on his face, and I could tell he was getting turned on. We talked a bit about my chastity and some of my experiences while I had been training under John. He was amazed I had gone as long as I had without an orgasm but was impressed as well.

"I probably jack off two to three times a day myself," he said, putting his arm around me and getting in close. "I'd love to give you a few loads tonight if you are interested."

I grinned back. "That sounds hot."

He took his hand and grabbed mine and put it in his crotch. I could feel his hard cock underneath and it felt large.

"I got a room nearby if you want to go now," he said. "Just be prepared, when I fuck, I go until I am shooting blanks."

"I'm game," I said with a grin.

I finished my drink off and followed him out into the night air. He put his hand down the back of my pants and felt my ass and rubbed his middle finger over my hole.

"My car is over here," he said.

We got in and drove ten minutes down the road to where he was staying. While we were in the car, he was telling me how much he was going to enjoy using my ass and how much I was going to like his cock. His voice was deep and sensual, and he pulled up his shirt and let me rub his fuzzy belly. I was making a precum mess in my pants.

Once we got to his room, I stripped down and folded my clothes, and placed them neatly on the floor on my shoes. While I was doing this, he was pulling his clothes off and went and sat in the chair in the corner.

For a larger guy, he was pretty damn hung. A nice set of balls swung under a cock that looked well above average and he had a nice covering of hair over his body. As he sat in the chair, he admired my cage as it popped out of my jock as I lowered it.

"That is so hot boy," he said. "Come over here and kneel before me."

I went over to the chair and got down on my knees and reached up and took his cock in my hands and started to rub it. A bead of precum formed at the tip, which I swallowed, and then I went down on him slowly and used my tongue to move around his shaft.

"Fuck yeah, boy!" he exclaimed as he reached down and grabbed my head and guided it down on his hard dick.

I blew him for a while and then he wanted to lay back on the bed. I followed him over and got down on my belly in between his legs and started to go down on his cock. He took my head and guided me down on him again as I worked his hot cock over and rubbed and groped his balls. He was precumming and it was so tasty. Several times he pulled me down on his cock till my face was buried in his belly and he grunted and groaned.

He stretched his legs out and put his hands behind his head and looked down at me.

"You're good at that you know?" he said with a growl.

"Thank you, Sir!" I replied as I lifted off his cock and then went down on him again.

After a bit, he got up and had me get up on all fours and he dove his tongue in my ass. He was groping my cheeks and pulling them apart and had his tongue so far in my ass I thought he would hit my prostate and milk me just like that.

"Fuck!" I groaned as he continued to move in as deep as he could.

He eventually pushed on me enough to make me collapse on my belly and he started slapping my ass while he continued to eat me out.

"Damn I love a good furry ass," he said.

He pulled my ass cheeks apart with one hand and started fingering me with his other hand. He had thick fingers and the sensations felt so good. I was groaning and precumming all over the top sheets. He collected some of my emissions and added his spit and added his second finger to get me all worked loose for what was to come.

"I think you are about ready," he said.

He came around and laid on his back again and told me to sit on his cock with my back to his head. I used my hand to position his fully engorged cock and pointed it towards my lubed hole and started to move down on it.

"That's a boy," he said with a groan. "Take that dick."

Once he was balls deep in me, I moved up and down and took his dick slow. He let me set this rhythm at first, but eventually, he took over and started to thrust his hips and pound me pretty good.

I had spread my legs pretty wide to accommodate his hips and legs and my legs started to get sore; however, so he got me on my back near the edge of the bed and put my legs on his shoulders and entered me that way next.

Looking up at him from that angle was hot. He had a nice beard and belly, and I rubbed his chest hair as he thrusted his cock into my ass deeply. He reached down and played with my cage as well.

"It's really hot knowing I'm the only one that is going to cum tonight," he said with a grin.

I grinned back at him. "Just make sure you drain those balls good, Sir!"

He grabbed my legs and continued to fuck me slow and methodically. I think he was wanting to take his time. He pushed my legs back toward me into a V formation and looked down to see his fat cock slide in and out of his hole and he occasionally spat down on his cock to add a bit more lube. He moved my feet back on his shoulders again and then pinned my legs till my knees were on my chest and held my feet together and fucked me some more.

"You have some great stamina, Sir!" I said.

"It usually takes me about 20 minutes of fucking to nut, so you best be ready for some more!" he exclaimed.

My eyes widened and I grinned and put my hands behind my head and watched him pleasure himself. He was having a good time playing with my cage while he pounded me as well. The more precum I made the more he smeared on his dick, so I was making my own lube for his extended assault on me.

The sweat was building upon his body and he was starting to pant more. His chest hair was starting to collect droplets which fell on the bed and me. This was a workout for him as well. Eventually, though, I felt him start to tense up and he grabbed my ankles tightly and started to pound a bit harder.

At the backswing of one final thrust, I heard him grunt and then stick it back in as I felt him pulse and fill me with his first load.

"Take it slut!" he shouted.

He held his cock deep in me and his big balls filled me up. He pushed my feet together and rested his sweaty forehead on them and caught his breath.

After a few minutes, he told me to hold my legs back and when he pulled out he slapped my ass a few times and took a picture of my dripping used hole.

He then came around and collapsed on the bed again. I had gotten up and was feeling my sore ass when he looked at me.

"We are not done, boy," he said pointing at his still rock-hard cock. "I told you, we are going till my balls are dry."

This man was a machine. I crawled between his legs and sucked on him pulling out the remains of his load. He started to face fuck me after a bit. I started to massage his large balls and began to wonder how much more he had to give.

"Put that hole back on this cock, boy," he said.

I got up and pointed his cock at my still dripping hole and sat down on it facing him. I took it slow and bounced up and down on him and he grabbed my waist and pushed me down to make sure his cock was fully embedded in my ass in each thrust. After about ten minutes, I was starting to get sore, but I felt him tense and yanked my ass down on him again just as he popped his second load deep in me.

"Fuck yeah!" he growled loudly.

He was covered in sweat at this point and his chest was heaving up and down. His legs went flat against the bed and I felt his cock continue to pulse as his load went deep in me. I reached down and rubbed his belly and felt his wet chest hair as I moved back and forth over him.

"Go grab me a towel out of the bathroom boy," he said to me.

I lifted off his cock and when I went to stand, my legs wobbled a bit and I had to catch myself.

"You are already walking funny I see," he said with a grin.

I grinned back and made my way to the bathroom and grabbed him a towel and brought it back to him. He wiped his forehead and chest off as I stood and watched him. I felt his loads leaking out and dripping down over my balls and legs. He must have flooded me.

"Get down here and clean my dick off boy," he said.

I laid down between his legs again and took his now softening cock into my mouth and sucked the last remnants of his load away.

Afterward, we talked for a bit and he had me grab him some water out of his fridge as he rested a bit.

About thirty minutes passed and he started to get hard again. I was just amazed at this point. My poor ass was aching from the fucking and the two loads he had already put in me.

"You think you can handle another load, boy?" he asked.

"I'm here to serve, Sir!" I said, with a little trepidation in my voice.

He had me get on the end of the bed again and put my legs on his shoulders. My ass was still a sloppy mess with his previous loads, and they churned and made a sloppy smacking sound as he started to fuck me again. He was deep in me and started slow but built up his speed. My ass just hurt, and I closed my eyes and gritted my teeth a bit.

"Stay with me, boy," he said as he squeezed my feet and looked down at me.

"Yes, Sir," I said as I opened my eyes and bit my lip a bit.

He continued to fuck me for another five minutes and then I felt him speed up a bit and he pulled my legs apart into a wide V and then started slamming me till I got his third load.

"Fuck yeah, fucker... that ass is filled!" he yelled.

I winced as he pushed his cock in the last time and it began to pulse. Taking a deep breath and letting it out slowly, I tried to squeeze down to milk him, but I was just too worn out.

"That was amazing, Sir," I said looking up at him as he held my feet and pulled his cock from me.

A glob of cum fell out and I heard it hit the floor.

"Damn, that's a messy hole," he said.

I put my legs down and tried to catch my breath and he wiped himself down with his towel.

"You want a shower boy?" he asked.

"I'd love that," I replied, and he helped me up to my feet and steadied me till I could walk over to the bathroom.

He turned on the hot water and helped me inside and then got in behind me. I leaned forward and the water ran down my back. He took the soap and lathered his hands up and started to rub my ass and finger me a bit.

"Go ahead and let that cum out, boy," he said rubbing my red and raw hole with his fingers. "It is ok."

I relaxed and the cum started to run out and mix with the water and soap.

"That's a boy," he said as he rubbed my ass and pulled my ass cheeks apart. "So fucking hot."

He reached up and rubbed down my back and started to massage it a bit and then ran his hands up and down my thighs and over my ass again. It felt so good. He brought his hands under me and felt my cage and squeezed it. A bit of precum shot out and mixed with the water in his fingers.

"Well, your balls are still full," he said with a chuckle.

"Yeah," I said. "But I hope yours are drained."

"Oh, believe me, boy," he said. "You did a really good job. You'll have to give me the email of your Sir. I'll be happy to give you a good review."

I turned around and helped to wash his body and spent some time rubbing his belly and thighs which he seemed to enjoy. We made out a bit as well until the room was filled with steam and it was getting hard to see.

"Time to get out, I think," he said with a laugh.

We stepped out and dried off and I thanked him for a great time. We also exchanged numbers for the next time he was in town and I got dressed and got a car back home.

All in all, it was not a bad Bear Pride.

CHAPTER EIGHTEEN

Memorial Day Weekend

It was Wednesday, May 20th, and Jay, Bo, and I were over to clean John's house as usual. We had just arrived and stripped down and were kneeling in our spots when John came downstairs to greet us as he normally did.

"Rise boys," he said.

We got to our feet to face him and he smiled.

"As you all know, I work for a law office downtown. One of my colleagues that I used to work with at another firm will be coming over on Monday to hang out at the pool for the Memorial Day holiday. He is a fellow dom and has been wanting to come to visit and see some of my subs for some time now. I would like to have you all there if possible."

"Sir," Jay spoke up.

"Yes Jay," John replied.

"Unfortunately, I was asked to work that day as we have a major contract we are trying to close at the office," he replied and bowed his head. "I am sorry for the inconvenience."

John reached his hand out and brought it gently under Jay's head and pushed it up facing him.

"Do not feel ashamed, Jay," he said. "This is short notice and I understand. What about you two?"

"I am off of work and can be here for as long as you need me," Bo said.

"I can be here as well," I replied.

"Good," John said. "I will need you both here at 10 am, then. I will have you set up to serve us lunch on the back patio and then you will be available for any requests that are made of you that afternoon."

"Yes, Sir," we both replied.

"Please have the pool house door open and the bed stripped of the top sheets," John continued. "It may be used in addition to the dungeon area. Set out the lube and toys, as usual, Bo."

"I understand, Sir," Bo replied.

"Jay," John said, turning to him. "I will expect you to clean up on your own when you get off of work. That will include washing the pool house sheets and cleaning up the main floor and the second floor. Is that understood?"

"Yes, Sir," he replied.

"Very well," John said, folding his hands over his chest. "Recite the creed for me boys."

We chanted in unison, "I am a sub in training under the supervision of Sir John. My goal is to serve men in the best way I can and derive pleasure from that service. My chastity cage and collar are a symbol of that service and I desire one day to be in permanent chastity and receive my formal graduation collar as proof of my commitment."

"Excellent," he replied. "I'm heading back upstairs to work on a few things."

"Thank you, Sir!" we all said.

After he had left, we headed back to get our supplies from the isolation room closet and get to work cleaning the house.

The rest of the week was pretty mundane. I cleaned my apartment on Saturday and got the laundry done and I decided to stay in and play video games that evening instead of going out. Sunday, I got up and cleaned myself up and out and trimmed my beard, hair, and groin in preparation to visit John for my one-on-one.

When I arrived at his house and knelt in my spot, as usual, I noticed that the lights were on and some equipment had been set out near the fuck table. John came down the steps after a few minutes and was in some gym shorts and a tank top.

"Rise boy," he said to me and I stood to face him.

"Today we are going to explore electro-play," he said. "Have you ever had this done to you before?"

"No Sir," I replied.

I had seen videos of people tied down and probes and pads applied to their body and electricity applied through them, but I had never been with anyone that had ever tried to do that with me before.

"We will start slow, then," he replied. "Come over and get on the table."

I walked across the room and laid down on my back. He secured a blindfold over my eyes and then bound my arms and wrists to the table. He then told me to pull my feet back and push against the table to lift my ass. As I did, I felt a metal butt plug go in with some wires coming out of it, and then he told me to put my legs down and then he secured them.

"There are many forms of electro-play, boy," John said. "The plug that I put in you is bipolar and will deliver a mild charge to your sphincter. Prepare yourself."

After a second, I felt the plug send a charge through my nerve endings and my ass muscles contracted, and the plug was forced in a bit. I gasped at the new feeling that was powerful and also stimulating. When the charge ended, my muscles relaxed, and the plug moved out some. The pulses came in waves. I felt a contraction and movement of the plug, as well as a firing of my nerve endings in my anal area, and the plug also hit my prostate gland as well. After only a few pulses, my nub was starting to dribble precum out of it.

"I think we are getting the desired effect," John said with a grin.

He took a hand towel and wiped my nub off and let me sit there a minute while the plug pulsed at various rates. I was groaning and moaning after only a few minutes of the stimulation.

John turned off the current and my body went back to rest on the table. I then heard a buzzing sound and a crackle.

I felt the tip of a wand pass over my belly and felt the tingle of electricity. It moved across and over to my shoulders and then back near my nipples and then I felt a sharp charge and a crackle as he passed over my right nipple.

"Fuck!" I yelled and I strained against the restraints.

John grinned. "This is what we call a violet wand. I can control the charge it sends as it moves over your body."

I felt him move the wand over to my arm and it gave me a shock causing me to jump again. He then passed it over my side and hit me with a few more shocks and then I felt the plug start up again. It pulsed in my ass and then I felt more shocks to my side and arms. I was straining against the restraints and it was getting intense.

John pulled the wand off and I was catching my breath when I felt it hit my caged balls with a short jolt.

"FUCK!" I screamed as I forced myself up on the table as much as I could as the plug continued to pulse inside my ass.

The buzzing sound stopped, and the plug turned off and I felt his hands run over my body and rub in slow circles over my chest.

"Breathe deeply for me, boy," I heard his voice say with a soft tone. "Stay with me."

"Yes, Sir," I replied.

He moved away for a moment and then came back, and the buzzing sound started again. This time a globe moved just over my body, but not touching it. The hairs on my skin reacted to the very light charge as it moved near my skin and as it came down on my upper arm a jolt went through me and I jumped.

It moved downward again and away from my body and then I felt it make contact with my balls again and I cried out.

"Breathe boy," John said. "You will be ok."

The session continued as he moved the wand around and delivered shocks on various parts of my body. The plug would go through a pulsing routine and then stop as well. I noticed a warming sensation in my ass at the same time from the repeated pulses.

As I started to build confidence and control my movements more, he started to deliver stronger jolts to my nipples, arms, and lower legs. The effect led to my entire body becoming almost hyper-charged and even the touch of his hands would give me a shiver.

The next instrument he used almost felt like a collection of small metal rods all joined near the base and spread out at the top. As they moved over my skin, the electric sensation built and when they made contact, I felt the jolt.

After fifteen minutes, I was reaching my limit. I heard the buzzing stop and felt his hands rub over my body. The sensation was pleasurable and almost electric on its own. He rubbed my balls which were a little sore at this point and then he took my blindfold off.

"How are you feeling, boy?" John asked.

"I'm ok Sir," I said. "That was pretty intense."

"You handled yourself well," he said. "Though the plug has led to a bit of a mess around your nub."

He undid my arm restraints and let me sit up and I noticed not only a pool of precum on my belly but also a large amount of prostate juices.

"Looks like you got your milking today," he said with a grin.

"Yes, Sir!" I replied as I reached down and collected the fluids with my hands and started to swallow them.

He handed me a hand towel to wipe down with and then helped me off the table.

"On your knees, boy," he said. "Time to drain a load out of my balls."

"Yes, Sir," I replied, and I got down and worked his cock till I had a mouthful of his cum.

He rubbed his hands through my hair and had me stand and hugged me after.

"After-care is very important when it comes to intense play like electro and impact play," he said. "I want you to be honest with me if you ever feel as though things have gone too far."

"Yes, Sir," I replied. "I will."

"Very well," he said. "Clean the room and you may go for the evening. I will see you and Bo tomorrow at 10 am sharp."

"Yes, Sir," I replied.

John turned and left the room and I wiped down the table and put the dirty towels in the hamper. I looked at the wand that he was using and the attachments as well since I was unable to see them before. It was a strange sensation, but one I would not be opposed to experiencing again.

On the way home, I grabbed some late dinner and ate it while I was watching TV. I was wound up from the play session earlier and decided to play some video games after. It was after 2 am when I finally put things away and started to get ready for bed. I knew I would be tired tomorrow, but I tried to get as much sleep as I could.

Monday morning, I arrived at John's house about five minutes before 10 am and saw that Bo was pulling up behind me.

"Hey bro!" Bo said, waving to me as he closed his car door. "Are you ready for today?"

"Yeah, I think so," I said. "I was up a little late last night, so I am a little behind on sleep, but I drank some coffee before heading over."

"I hear ya," Bo replied. "I had a cup myself this morning."

We walked around to the side door and got undressed in the entrance hall and put our clothes in our respective bins. After adjusting our cages and collars a bit, we entered the dungeon area. It was still dark in there, so I went and turned the lights on, and Bo opened the back door to let some fresh air in.

"I am going to go out back and get the pool house ready," Bo said. "Why don't you start getting the dungeon set up and then I will join you and we can turn to the pool next."

"Will do!" I replied.

Bo walked outside and I went back into the isolation room and grabbed some clean hand towels to set out near the sling and fuck bench. I also put out the lube and toys as well. I was just wiping down the fuck bench when Bo came in.

"Ok, the bed is ready to be used if needed and the bathroom looks nice and clean out there," he said. "How are we doing in here?"

"I'm just about done," I replied. "Shall we go and pull the solar blanket off the pool?"

"You got it!" Bo replied.

We pulled the plastic cover off and rolled it up and then tested the water to make sure the pH was right, and the temperature was comfortable. I grabbed the skimmer to catch a few stray leaves that had got in and Bo wiped down the chairs and table on the patio.

"I think we are ready!" Bo said.

We walked back inside the dungeon and John was walking around in his boxers with a coffee cup and inspecting everything. We stood at attention next to each other with our hands behind our backs.

"Looking good boys!" John said.

"Thank you, Sir," we both replied.

"Todd will be here in an hour at about 11:30 am," he said. "Please run the vacuum once in the living room and straighten the kitchen."

"Understood, Sir," we replied.

"After you are done with that, the refrigerator upstairs is stocked with alcohol and beer and there are containers that are labeled in there that contain the cheese and crackers, meats, and other foodstuffs," John continued. "I want you to bring the food down and set it out here on the counter on the side wall. Grab a cooler from the garage and ice from the deep freezer out there and put the beer and alcohol in this and bring this down as well."

"Yes, Sir," we replied.

"After everything is ready, please kneel in your spots and wait quietly."

"You got it, Sir!" Bo replied.

"I want to emphasize that I want you two on your best behavior," John said. "Todd has been interested in my training program for a while and may look into collaring one of you or one of my future subs at some point. I want him to see how disciplined, respectful, and trained you are."

"Yes, Sir," we replied.

"Ok boys," John said as he snapped his fingers. "Jump to it."

Once we got the upstairs straighten up and the food and coolers set out it was about 11:15 am. So, we washed our hands and then went and knelt in our colored spots on the floor near the wall and waited.

We were there about 20 minutes before we heard footsteps on the staircase. When the door to the dungeon opened, John walked out first, and his friend Todd was behind him. They were both naked. I was struck by how attractive Todd was.

He was about 5'11" (1.8 m) tall and a chubby build. He had a nice tummy and thick arms and legs that showed a little muscle as well. He was quite furry, and his chest had turned white which blended to a salt and pepper below his nipples and then to a deep brown from there on down. He was bald and had a medium-length beard that was shades of brown and gray with some white near his chin. He had deep blue eyes as well. Tattoos of flowers and small animals were on his shoulders and upper thighs and he had a nice set of low hanging balls and his soft cock was swinging as he walked.

"Rise, boys," John said. "This is my friend Todd. Todd, the boy in the yellow collar here is Matt. He has been training with me for almost three months now. The boy in the green collar is Bo. He has been in the training program for about six months."

"Hello, Master Todd!" I replied followed by Bo.

Todd came over and rubbed Bo's belly and then felt my ass after.

"Very nice John," he replied. "I'm looking forward to seeing how well they do!"

"Come over here and grab you a plate, Todd," John said as he directed him over to the wall where the food was set.

Once the two men had their plates full, they grabbed a few beers and went out on the porch beside the pool to eat. Bo and I followed them and stood at attention with our arms behind our backs near the back wall of the house until we were called to get another drink, refill a plate, or throw trash away.

Once they were done eating, John had Bo get down in front of Todd and massage his feet and legs while they drank and relaxed. I cleaned the table at that point and once I was done, returned to my stance near the wall.

"Do you mind if I take Bo here into the dungeon for a while?" Todd asked.

"Feel free," John replied. "I will take a dip in the pool while you are entertaining yourself."

Todd got Bo up from the floor and he followed the man into the dungeon area and Todd closed the sliding door behind them. John, meanwhile, went to sit on the edge of the pool and put his feet in.

"Ahh," John said. "This is the perfect temperature."

John looked over at me and snapped his fingers.

"Boy!" he announced. "Come get in the pool and put your face on my cock."

"Yes, Sir!" I replied.

I waded into the pool. It was a little cool at first and my nub shrunk a bit, but it was not too bad. I came over and put my head between his legs and reached up to grab his cock.

"Put your hands down boy," John said. "I need to piss."

He placed his cock in my mouth and I closed my lips around him, and I felt his stream hit the back of my mouth almost immediately. I concentrated on my breathing and swallowing and drank down his beer piss without spilling any of it. As he finished, I added some suction and licked the last few drops from his head.

"Good boy," he said looking down at me. "You may now touch my cock and start to suck it."

I smiled and reached up and grabbed the base of his cock and started to suck it into my mouth. It began to harden, and I used my hands to move up and down on it till it was engorged fully. John leaned back on his hands and let his head fall back a bit and he closed his eyes while I worked on his shaft.

I reached up and felt his balls and let them roll around in one hand as I used the other to work the root and my mouth to work the head. He was starting to precum and I sucked out the tasty juices from his cock as he groaned a bit.

He sat back up and grabbed my head with his hands and started to face fuck me for a bit. Some of my spit and his precum dribbled out my mouth a bit and down my beard. I gagged a few times when he went in deep and hit the back of my throat, but I was getting a lot better at controlling my gag reflex. One skill I was very grateful he was teaching me.

He started to force me down on him faster and I knew he was getting close. He threw his head back just as his cock erupted and shoved me deep on him, so it went right down my throat. Pulse after pulse filled my belly to join his piss and when he was done, he let me nurse his softening member to get the last bits out.

"Thank you boy," he said. "You can get out and return to where you were."

As I went to get out of the pool and towel off, John slid into the water and started to wade around. I returned to attention with my hands behind my back near the wall of the house after I was dry and was there for about ten minutes till the door to the dungeon area slid open.

Todd walked out and his chest was sweaty, and his fur was matted a bit. He walked over to the showerhead that was positioned on the wall near the pool and turned on the water and rinsed off a bit before stepping in the pool to join John. Bo came out a few minutes later and was equally as sweaty. I figured he must have gotten a workout by Todd.

As he came over to stand next to me, John called out. "Matt! Please get Todd and me another beer."

"Yes, Sir," I replied, and I entered into the dungeon.

As I was walking through the room, the smell of sex and musk was still lingering in the air. A flogger was lying on the floor next to the fuck bench and a bottle of lube next to it. My nub started to swell a bit thinking about what must have been going on in here earlier before I turned my attention to the cooler and the beers and then headed back outside.

For the next hour and a half, John and Todd swam, waded around, talked, and drank. We were brought over to get them snacks or another beer and Bo took Todd's piss at one point as well. If we were not being used, though, we stood at attention near the wall. My legs were getting a bit stiff and sore, but I concentrated on trying not to lock them.

At one point, Todd went over to John and they leaned in to have a private conversation. When they finished, he put his beer down on the side of the pool and looked back at Bo and me.

"Matt!" Todd announced.

"Yes, Sir!" I replied.

"Grab my towel for me," he said as he moved to the stairs out of the pool and walked up to the patio.

I handed him his towel and as he dried off, he said, "go wait for me in the pool house."

"Yes, Sir!" I replied and I walked over to the building behind the pool and entered through the door and knelt on the floor next to the bed.

Todd came in a few minutes after me and closed the door behind him. He had his beer in one hand and his towel over his other. He turned to the chair next to the door and placed his towel over the cushion and sat down in it facing me. He leaned back and spread his legs. His hardening cock was lifting and starting to point towards the ceiling.

"Come over here between my legs, boy," he said. "Suck my cock."

I crawled over and put my hands on either side of his spread legs and took his dick fully into my mouth. He looked down at me and grinned and took another drink from his beer while he enjoyed the sensation.

Down I went on him and up. I moved side to side and savored the precum that I started to milk from his raw cock. I took him in fully till my nose was in his belly and his cock hit the back of my throat causing me to cough a bit. I rubbed his large balls and my nub started to strain in its cage.

"Good boy," he said as he continued to drink his beer and watch me.

I used my right hand to grab the base of his cock and hold it steady as I licked and sucked on his head. I moved in circles with my tongue and bobbed to the right and the left, feeling his cock move around my mouth.

His belly lifted and fell as he breathed in and out and groaned a bit, his head moving back slightly and his mouth parting as he bit his bottom lip.

"On the bed boy, face down one leg extended, and one leg bent," he said.

I got up and went over to the bed and as I got into position, he put the beer down on the side table and then climbed up on the bed behind me, straddling my extended left leg. His cock was fully hard and engorged. He had it grasped with his right hand at the root and he slapped it on my furry ass.

He rubbed the end a bit and then stuck it in my hole and guided it in with his hand. The shaft moved forward, and my ass accepted his man dick.

"Uhhh," I grunted as the full length entered me.

I twisted slightly putting my weight on my left arm and my right arm raised and bent with my palm grasping at the bedsheet. I forced my head into the bed to muffle more groans as he got completely inside me down to his balls.

"Aww, yeah," he sighed with a growl in his voice.

My right arm slid down and my upper torso went flat on the bed with my arms on either side of my face.

As he started to pull out, he grabbed my ass with his right hand and spread my cheeks to see his thick shaft as it slid out and then back in. He then pulled completely out and spread my ass wide to expose my hole to enter again.

Deeply he penetrated me, and he brought his thumb near my hole to feel as his dick entered and left me. He played with the entrance to my ass and the sensation had my nub completely strained in its cage and leaking precum into the sheets below me.

Back and forth he went. He was taking his time and enjoying every moment. He groaned and then groped my ass cheeks as he moved it back and forth. He pulled out again and stuck his thumb in my ass and explored the entrance before guiding his dick back in again.

"Daaaghh," I grunted loudly as his dick reached the deepest parts of my ass.

I twisted again, putting my weight on my left side, and turned to look back at him.

"Ohh, fuck," I continued to exclaim as he started to pick up the pace and fuck me deeply from nearly out to completely in.

"You like that dick, don't you boy?" he asked, looking into my eyes.

"Yes, Sir," I replied as I twisted back, and my face fell forward and embedded in the sheets again.

My body was being forced forward as he thrusted, and I felt my belly move back and forth. I grabbed the bedsheet to steady myself and allow him to get as deep as he wanted.

He slowed down again and spread my ass with his right hand. He spat on my hole and watched as it became lube for his shaft as he entered. His hand moved up to the small of my back and he applied a firm pressure to slightly arch my ass upward as he moved forward. The effect allowed him to fill my ass with his cock to the fullest extent possible.

My eyes were rolling back in my head from the sensation. His cock felt wonderful. I grabbed a pillow in front of me and put my face into it and continued to grunt and groan as he continued his fuck.

He stopped for a moment to adjust. He moved forward and pushed my bent leg up on the bed some. I turned my head to the right, and he used his left hand to push my head into the pillow and he steadied himself on my bent leg with his right hand. He had the position now to start to lift his ass backward and slam forward, letting his cock enter my ass in one motion.

"FUCK!" I yelled as his thumb moved and entered the side of my mouth.

"That's a boy, take that dick!" he growled as he started to jackhammer my ass.

"Aww, fuck!" was my only reply as I tried to steady myself on the bed, my body moving forward and backward into the sheets.

He adjusted again and brought both arms to my shoulder blades and pushed hard. His ass flew back and forth, and the momentum brought his cock deeply into me time and time again. His large balls were slapping my ass and bouncing with each thrust.

He slowed and brought his cock deeply into me and held it there and he moved his arms back and used his hands to completely spread my ass and watch as his shaft slowly pulled out. He grabbed it at the root and slapped it a few times on my ass and I heard the smack and plop as it bounced on my hole.

"Lay back," he said.

I moved and turned around and he got me on my back with my legs propped on his shoulders. Precum was running out of my nub and had soaked the bed and my groin area. He reached down and grabbed some and leaned forward to feed it to me.

He pointed his cock at my hole and started to enter again. My feet jerked a bit due to the sensation and I threw my head back as I arched them, and the joints in my toes popped. I then looked back up at him as his cock fully entered me and I reached up and felt the thick gray fur on his chest and went for his nipples.

He put both hands on the underside of my knees and forced my legs and back down into the bed, keeping my feet on his shoulders. He arched his back some and then started to fuck hard and fast again as I continued to play with his nipples.

He looked down at me with a serious face. His mouth was parted, and his tongue was at the entrance. He licked his lips and then cracked a wicked smile.

"Your ass was made for fucking and breeding, boy," he said to me.

"It's all for your pleasure, Sir," I replied.

He continued to grin and then I saw his eyes close and his head move backward as he started to fuck harder. The sound in the room was of the smack of his groin as it made contact with my ass and his cock entered fully. It echoed off the walls as did his growing growls and groans.

He moved his hands to my waist and grasped it firmly. He pulled me into him as he thrust forward. He started to pound hard with a medium speed and I knew he was getting close.

He sped up; the smacks were coming three to four a second. His belly was bouncing as his cock was furiously pounding my hole. I felt him tense up as his face distorted and he started to yell.

"FUCK!" he exclaimed as his cock erupted deep inside me. He pushed forward in one last thrust and held it there as it pulsed and delivered its load. His body bent and he grabbed under my knees again and forced my legs flat against the bed and he bent forward as much as my body would allow him to. My feet were pinned as he bit his lip and then groaned again.

"UUGHH!" he replied as the orgasm swept over his body and the cum continued to pulse out.

His head fell and he sat there with his eyes closed as I watched him breathe deeply and his whole body move as his racing heart started to slow again.

"Damn that was good," he replied as he opened his eyes and moved his weight off me.

He grabbed my feet and pushed them forward as he started to move his cock back out. He noticed some cum dribbling out as the head popped out and he brought one hand down and used his thumb to push it back in again.

"That's a real man's seed boy," he said. "It is staying right there inside you."

"Thank you, Sir," I replied looking back up at him with a smile.

Todd got off the bed and grabbed his towel and beer and opened the door. I got up and sat on the edge of the bed and looked out to see Bo in between John's legs acting as a urinal again. I stood up and felt some cum dripping down my leg, so I grabbed a washcloth out of the bathroom and cleaned myself up a bit before heading back out to the pool.

Around 4 pm, the two men got out of the pool for a while and sat in some lounge chairs, and Bo and I massaged their feet and legs. John told us to go grab the cheese and crackers after and they snacked and chatted some more as well. It was a lazy afternoon from that point and we mostly just took the trash away as needed and refilled drinks as they swam some more.

Todd said he needed to head home around 5:30 pm and he got out and dried off followed by John.

"Boys," John said, "go ahead and start cleaning up the dungeon area. Come to the living room when you are done."

"Yes, Sir," we replied, and we headed in to collect the used towels and put away things. We wiped down the equipment with sanitizer and threw away the remains of the food that was left and cleaned the cooler out and replaced what drinks were still left in the refrigerator.

When we were done, we came into the living room and stood at attention with our hands behind our backs. Todd was dressed and John was sitting with a towel wrapped around him.

"Thank you for a lovely time, boys," Todd said. "I look forward to visiting again."

"You are always welcome," John said.

Todd turned and walked by us and as he did he reached around and squeezed Bo's ass and winked at him. He then went out the front door and John closed it behind him.

"Excellent job, boys," he said. "You can go."

"Thank you, Sir!"

As we walked down the staircase, Bo let out a sigh.

"Whew," he said. "My legs are killing me."

"I know the feeling," I said as we entered the dungeon area and closed the door to the staircase behind us. "Looks like Todd took a liking to you."

Bo grinned. "Yeah, we had a good time. He flogged me a bit on the fuck bench and then dumped a load in me. But he took the time to rub my back and ass and after he was done fucking me he brought me over and let me hug him and feel his fur and put my face in his pits. He seemed like a nice guy."

"Yeah," I replied with a grin. "I had a pretty hot time with him on the bed as well. He knows how to hit all the good spots if you know what I mean."

"Well, maybe we will see him again soon," Bo said as we entered the hallway to get our clothes and dress.

"I think he will be a return visitor for sure," I replied.

CHAPTER NINETEEN

The Cabin in the Woods

I was tied down to the fuck bench and I had just been bred by John. The scent of sex, sweat, musk, and cigar smoke mixed and lingered in the room. It had been an intense session. He started with some flogging on my back and ass and then he put me on the fuck bench for a while and tied me up to practice his knot and rope work. While I was tied on the table, he had me blindfolded, gagged, and put the headphones on me with the familiar mantra playing in the background.

"I am a sub. I am an instrument of pleasure for men. I will open my mind to exploring new experiences that please men. Pain can be a pleasure. I can endure it. I can transform it. I can overcome it."

I felt the jolt of electricity hit my shoulder first and in my bound state, all I could do was wiggle a bit and groan into the gag. After he was done with the electro-play, he smoked his cigar for a while as I sat there bound and zoned out to the hypno track. When he finally untied me, he removed the headphones, but left the blindfold and gag in, and led me over to the fuck bench for my breeding.

As I sat there, my ass well used and dripping with his load, I felt him reach down and grab my nub and release it from its cage. I had momentarily forgotten that it was June 7. I had just completed 42 days in chastity, and it was time for my manual release.

John had brought a chair over and sat down so my ass and dangling nub were accessible. He twisted my shaft and inspected it to make sure there were no sores or cuts, and he felt my balls to make sure things were healthy as well. I felt my nub starting to fill with blood from the stimulation and I got hard pretty quickly. Satisfied that I was in good shape, he placed a jar beneath my nub to catch any fluids, and then he put some lube in his hands and rubbed them together.

I felt him grab my balls and squeeze them a bit and he pulled his hand back till his thumb was starting to enter my used hole. As he pushed in, my balls were pulled back more and at the same time, he used his other hand to stroke my shaft in a downwards motion, applying pressure like you would do if you were milking a cow.

"Ummph," I groaned as my balls felt the pressure from his hand and his thumb entered my hole.

I was fully hard, and he continued to stroke downward with his other hand and when he got to the end he would grab the root of the shaft again and start down again. I started to precum almost immediately, and a thread of liquid started to hang down and fall into the glass jar below. His thumb started to move in and out of my asshole and the sensation put me over the edge. It only took about two minutes and I was shooting ropes of cum into the jar below and I got a headrush as the orgasm moved through my body.

He stroked me a few more times to get the remnants out and then wiped his hands down on a towel.

"I'll be right back, boy," I heard him say.

I sat there for a few minutes and breathed deeply. My nub shrank down to his flaccid state and I felt a dribble of cum hanging from my head as well as the remnants of John's load roll down my balls.

When John returned, he had a damp washcloth in his hand. He ran it over my ass, balls, and nub and then dried them with a clean towel. He sat the jar to the side for a moment and then I heard him move across the room. Drawers were opening and closing, and I heard some metal clanging a bit.

"I will be installing a smaller cage length on you, boy," he said as he came back and sat behind me. "I have been noticing that your cage has had some extra room in it lately. That is pretty normal. When you are caged for longer periods, you will notice some reduction in flaccid length."

I felt him place the new cage on me and he guided it down till it locked into place on the post of the metal base ring. I immediately noticed the difference. It felt as though my shaft was a bit more compressed, but it was not painful. He adjusted the skin a bit and pulled on my balls till he was satisfied it was a good fit, then he reinstalled the security screw and started to undo my restraints.

As he helped me up, he removed my blindfold and I looked down to see that my cage was now about half the length it had been. The head of my nub and just a bit of the shaft appeared under the bars and my balls hung low beneath.

"That looks much better," John said as he poured a shot of vodka into the glass and swirled it around with the cum in the jar.

He handed me the glass and I swallowed it completely and then he told me to kneel. I got down and looked up at him and he crossed his hands across his chest.

"You are now ready for your three-month session," he said. "We will probably move to your final, smaller cage length before you start your six-month one. How are you feeling?"

"I am good, Sir," I replied. "Thank you for letting me serve you."

"You are welcome, boy," he said. "Now, I have some news for you. Next Sunday we will not be having a one-on-one session. I have to go out of town on Thursday and I will not return till late Sunday night."

"I understand, Sir," I replied.

"You are free to do what you wish, just be sure to keep your blog updated so I know what you have been up to," he said reaching down to run his hand through my hair. "For now, go ahead and clean up down here and you may go. I will see you and your fellow subs tomorrow."

"Yes, Sir," I replied as he left and went back upstairs.

I reached down and felt my new cage and began to wonder how small it would eventually be. Jay's cage was big enough just for the head of his nub. The shaft was barely visible. Bo's looked to be about the same length as I had now, so I figured it might eventually end up like Jay's in the end.

I turned and started to clean up the room and wipe the surfaces down and then got dressed to leave. I was texting Chris on the way out to my car and he asked if I wanted to come over for dinner. I told him I would head over shortly and after getting some gas, I drove over to their apartment.

When I entered, Rick was in the kitchen mixing a drink and Chris was sitting on the couch watching TV.

"Hey Matt," Chris said, turning to look at me as I was getting undressed and folding my clothes beside the door. "How was your session with your trainer?"

"It was good," I said, dropping my underwear and then adjusting my cage a bit. "It was the end of my chastity session and he gave me an orgasm before locking me up again."

"You must be feeling better then," Chris replied.

"Very," I said with a grin.

Rick was coming back over into the living room and reached around to grab my ass as he leaned over to give me a quick kiss. He looked down at my cage and then grabbed it and ran his hands over it.

"Looks like you got a smaller length cage now," Rick said with a smile and wink.

"Yeah," I said with a bit of a blush in my cheeks. "He said I had too much room in the other one."

"Yeah," Rick said, walking over to sit next to Chris. "You don't want too much room for growth there."

I walked over and sat on a chair next to them and Rick put his hands in Chris's lap and started to grope him.

"Chris just put his cage on this morning as well," Rick said with a bit of an evil grin. "He's going to stay in it till next Sunday.

Chris looked over at me and gave me a wink. "So, you are not the only one caged now."

I laughed a bit and I got up and went and grabbed a soda from the refrigerator.

"Sir told me he will be out of town next weekend, so no session with him next Sunday," I said as I came back over and opened the can and sat down.

"Oh, nice!" Chris said.

"We are planning on driving up to the North Georgia Mountains to stay at a cabin my family owns next weekend," Rick said.

"Yup!" Chris said. "If you are going to be free, you are welcome to join. The place is huge. You can even bring a friend with you if you want."

"Indeed!" Rick said. "Maybe some of your fellow subs would like to come."

Chris laughed. "What he is saying is he would love for you to bring a bunch of caged boys up so that this one can get all the attention."

"Well, duh!" Rick laughed and he reached over and put his arm around Chris.

"That might be fun," I replied. "I will see the boys tomorrow during my normal cleaning day at Sir's, so I will ask them then."

"Sounds like a plan!" Rick said as he picked up a controller. "Let's play some games before dinner."

The next day, after we had got done cleaning the house, Jay and Chris were coming into the dungeon area as I was finishing my dusting.

"Hey guys," I said to them as they were getting ready to leave, "you got a moment?"

"Sure," Bo said.

"What's up?" Jay replied.

"So, my friends are going up to stay at a cabin this weekend," I said. "They are heading up Friday morning and coming back Sunday afternoon. With Sir out of town, I was planning on taking off work for the day and going with them for an extended weekend. They said they have plenty of room and you were welcome to come if you wanted."

"That sounds like fun," Jay said.

"Yeah," Bo replied. "I'm in."

"Are they ok with us being in chastity?" Jay asked.

I laughed out loud. "Well, my friend Chris is in chastity for the week himself and his boyfriend is the dom friend I told you about that introduced me to Sir."

"Oh!" Jay said laughing. "So, four caged boys and a dom in a cabin in the woods, eh?"

"Pretty much," I replied with a grin.

"I hope he has a lot of stamina!" Bo said.

"Well, why don't you confirm you can get the time off and if so, then we can meet at my apartment Friday morning and we can take my car to meet and then follow them up," I said.

"Perfect!" Jay said.

By the end of the week, the plans had been set and everyone had the time off to go on the trip. It was a typical summer Friday morning in the South as I was packing some things into the back of my SUV. The sun was just rising on the horizon and it was humid and sticky. I wiped a bit of sweat off my brow and put my hat back on. I had packed a few changes of clothes in case we went out anywhere, but I figured we would be naked most of the time. I put a cooler in the back with some drinks and food and some towels as well. I had just got things situated when Jay and Bo came in and parked across from me.

"Hey, guys!" I said as they walked over with some things.

"Perfect timing," Bo said with a smile.

We had arranged ahead of time for me to buy the food and drinks we needed between us. Rick told me there was a store near the cabin, so we had packed enough for the first day and would restock later. My sub brothers put their things in the back with mine and I closed the hatch and then they climbed in and we headed over to meet up with Chris and Rick.

As I pulled into their parking lot, I saw Rick closing the trunk on their car. I pulled in beside him and he gave me a wave as we parked and got out.

"How is it going, guys?" Rick said.

"Not bad!" I said. "I am looking forward to a little time out of town. Rick, these are my sub brothers. The bigger guy is Bo and the thinner, fuzzy one here is Jay."

"Well, John sure knows how to pick attractive subs!" Rick grinned as he shook their hands.

"Nice to meet you!" Bo and Jay said.

"Looks like everyone is here!" came a voice from behind us. I turned to see Chris walking towards us with a bag in one hand.

"This is my boyfriend, Chris," Rick said to Bo and Jay.

"Hello!" the guys replied, and Chris gave them each a hug.

"Are we all set?" Rick asked.

"Yup," Chris said. "We are ready to go!"

"Sweet!" Rick said.

Rick gave me the address to the place we were going in case we got lost, but the plan was to follow them up in my car. Jay and Bo got back in with me and we pulled out and headed out onto the road.

We had a little traffic we ran into getting around town, but once we started heading north, it was not a big issue. The surrounding landscape became more rugged as we went, and we started to enter the southern Appalachian Mountains. After about two and a half hours, we pulled into the cabin that Rick's family owned.

The house was on the top of a ridge and surrounded by trees. I didn't see any other homes or cabins in the vicinity. Rick pulled in the gravel driveway to the home and I parked behind him. We got out and saw that the cabin was raised off the ground. The lower area was for storage and the main living areas were above. We followed Rick as he led us up a staircase on our left and to the main door which he opened.

We entered a large living room that was paneled in cedar and had high ceilings with two fans that hung down to circulate air. To our right, as we entered, there was a doorway that led to the kitchen and a side door off this led to one bedroom. Along the right wall of the living room, there was another small hallway that led to another bedroom and the bathroom. In the back of the living room that was in front of us, there were windows and another door that led to an enclosed porch that had more windows that looked out over the back of the property and there was also a third bedroom off to the side.

Bo, Jay, and I walked over and through the porch area and opened the back glass doors to reveal a deck that looked out on the sloping hill below us. It dropped down to a small river that was winding its way through the mountains and the sun filtered down through the trees as a light wind hit us.

"Now this looks relaxing," Jay said.

"For sure!" Bo added. "This is gorgeous!"

"I am glad you like it!" Rick said, coming from behind me and putting his hands around my waist.

"You can swim in the river there and we have some tubes that you can float in as well," Rick said. "It is very secluded, so no swimming trunks necessary. My family owns the surrounding forty acres."

"This is so cool," I replied.

"Speaking of clothes, though," Rick said, turning me around and grinning. "You boys are not allowed those in a home right?"

"Point taken," Jay said as he took his flip flops off and began to undress on the deck. Bo and I followed and got completely undressed as Chris was walking out back.

"What's going on out here?" Chris said.

"They are following protocols," Rick said. "As a locked boy you should be too!"

Chris rolled his eyes and started stripping off as well. Once we were all naked and had adjusted our cages a bit, Rick smiled. He looked at Jay and Bo approvingly and grabbed his crotch a bit.

"I am going to enjoy this," he said with a smirk.

"Ok, let's get the rooming situation settled," Chris said.

"Good deal," Rick replied. "Chris and I have the bedroom in the back here off the porch. There is a middle bedroom with a queen bed by the bathroom and the bedroom in the front off of the kitchen has a full bed. It might be better for two of you to share the middle room and one use the front room, or one of you can sleep out here on the porch. The couch has a pull-out. It is your choice."

"I'd like to take the front bedroom if that is ok," Jay said.

"I'm fine with that," I replied. "Bo, do you want to share the middle one with me?"

"I'm game with that!" Bo replied with a smile.

"Ok, boys," Rick said, clapping his hands. "Go get your gear and get unpacked."

It was a little stuffy in our room and we opened the windows and turned the ceiling fan on to circulate the air a bit. Once Bo and I had got our things put in the room, we went to sit out in the living room where everyone eventually gathered.

Rick was the last to come in. He had taken his shirt off to reveal his broad, furry chest and had changed into some gym shorts that showed off the fact that he had no underwear on as the outline of his huge, but soft cock was visible. He came over and sat on a couch between Bo and Jay.

"So, you two are John's other boys, eh?" he said, putting his hands behind each of them on the back of the sofa.

I looked at Chris who was sitting next to me in a chair across from them and we both grinned.

"Yes, Sir!" Bo said looking up at his massive frame. "I've been in training for six months."

"I've been in training for nine months, Sir," Jay replied looking up and then down at Rick's bulge in his pants that was starting to grow.

"I do love subs with experience," Rick said as he reached around Bo's head and brought his face into his armpit.

Bo breathed in his scent and started to move his face around in his pit and lick it. As he did so, Rick turned to his right.

"Get down on your knees, boy," he said to Jay. "Let's see if you are as talented a cock sucker as John says you are."

"Yes, Sir!" Jay said with a grin as he got down in front of Rick and pulled his shorts off to reveal his hardening cock.

"That did not take long," Chris said in a low voice leaning over to me.

"Are you surprised?" I said with a slight chuckle back to him.

We watched as Jay went down on Rick, taking his cock fully into his mouth. It was obvious he had little to no gag reflex and was deep throating his massive cock very well. Rick had one leg stretched out and was flexing his toes and was moaning as Bo continued to roll his head in his armpit and then moved down to his chest and started to nibble on his nipple.

Rick grabbed the back of Bo's head with one hand and pushed him into his chest a bit and with the other forced Jay down on his cock as well. He leaned back and was groaning loudly.

"God damn you are good, boy!" Rick yelled as he shook, and his cock erupted down Jay's throat.

Jay coughed a bit at the massive volume of cum that he was rapidly trying to swallow, but nothing leaked out. Bo began to rub Rick's fur on his chest as he had his eyes closed and was breathing deeply coming down from the orgasm high.

"That was hot, Sir!" Bo said.

"Was a fucking huge load too!" Jay said with a chuckle as he came off Rick's cock.

Bo got down on his hands and knees to lick the remnants off Rick's cock and licked his lips.

"Tasty too!" he said.

Rick opened his eyes and brought his hands down to rub their heads as they knelt beside his legs.

"You both will be getting a good review when I see John next week at the gym," Rick said.

"Thanks, Sir!" the boys replied.

"Well, I know you two got some protein," Chris said, standing up. "But do you mind if we all take a break and grab some lunch?"

Rick laughed and got up and we all went to the kitchen to make some sandwiches.

Later in the afternoon, Jay, Bo, and I went down to the river and got in and waded around some. It was rather shallow and only came up to your waist at the deepest point. The water was a little cool and caused our balls to contract against our cages, but it was refreshing in the heat of the day.

"I could get used to this," Bo said as he was floating beside me holding on to a rock.

"Indeed," Jay said. "Do you think Chris and Rick will be coming down?"

I looked up at the cabin on the hill above us and saw Rick laying on a lounge chair with Chris sitting in his lap moving up and down. The sun was glinting off his cage as it bounced as Rick fucked him.

"I think they are otherwise engaged," I laughed and pointed up at the deck.

The boys looked up and joined me in a chuckle and we continued to wade around and talk.

As we came back up to the deck a few hours later, Rick was naked and getting some sun in his lounge chair and Chris was on his stomach and getting some sun on his well-used, but very white ass.

"You three have a good time?" Rick asked as we sat down on some chairs.

"We did!" Jay said. "The water is nice!"

"Yeah," Rick said. "I used to love coming here as a kid with my brothers. It's a good way to spend the summer in the South. I hope you opened your windows to air out the bedrooms."

"We did," Bo replied.

"Good," Rick said. "Not having air conditioning is a bit of a pain, but you will find that in the evening there is a mountain breeze that comes through that makes it pleasant to sleep, though you might be sleeping on top of the covers."

"I'm sure it will be fine," I replied.

I went and grabbed everyone some beers and we sat out and relaxed in the afternoon sun and chatted a bit more. As the evening started to fall, we grilled some hotdogs and had a nice dinner as well.

We moved into the screened-in porch after dinner to avoid the mosquitoes that were ravenous at dusk and broke out some cards and played penny poker for a while. Rick smoked a cigar and shared it with Jay. The rest of us got drunk and lost everything we had to Rick, who was a bit of a card shark.

Eventually, Rick and Chris went off to get some sleep and Jay went back to his room after. Bo and I sat up for a little while longer, but we eventually decided to hit the hay as well. As we walked back to the bedroom and closed the door, I noticed that a slight breeze was moving through the room and it felt a bit better in there.

"I'll need to sleep on the right side if you don't mind Bo," I said. "I need to plug my CPAP in."

"No worries, bro!" Bo said as he flopped down on the bed.

I came around and laid down beside him with my mask in my hand. He reached over and rubbed my belly.

"Thanks for inviting us," Bo said with a smile.

I grinned back and put my mask on, turned on the machine and we drifted off to sleep.

The morning sun came through the window and woke me up the next day. Bo was snoring beside me and I decided to get up and go take a shower and have a little breakfast. When I got one and dried off, I opened the bathroom door and turned to our bedroom and noticed the door was shut and some grunting and creaking sounds were coming from behind it.

As I opened the door, I saw Rick had Bo bent over the bed and was pounding his cock into his ass. I stood there for a moment and watched as his balls slapped against Bo's ass with a 'smack'. Bo had his eyes closed and was clenching the bedsheets and moaning.

"That's a boy!" Rick growled.

My nub was instantly swelling and filling its prison and I had to adjust my balls a bit to accommodate the cage being pushed forward a bit.

"You like that dick?" Rick asked.

"Yes, Sir!" Bo groaned. "Breed my pussy, Sir!"

Rick grinned and grabbed Bo's waist and started pounding him harder. Bo bit down on the sheets to avoid screaming as he was forced forward and back on the bed and the frame started to creak more.

Rick threw himself forward in one final thrust, burying his cock deep in Bo's ass as he came.

"Oh fuck, Sir!" Bo yelled, unable to hold it back any further.

"That's a boy," Rick said softly as he ran his hand over Bo's back and down to his waist.

As his cock's pulsing slowed, he slid out and some cum dribbled out and down on Bo's caged balls.

Rick turned and smiled at me. "Morning Matt!"

"Good morning!" I replied, smiling just as much.

I dropped my towel and bent down to take Rick's softening cock in my mouth and sucked the remaining cum away. I then turned to Bo and put my face in his ass and licked up it from his balls to the top of his crack and then used my tongue to clean away the seed that remained.

"Oh my!" Bo grunted with a sigh. "Fuck bro, that feels good."

I gave him a few more licks and then got up and patted his ass a bit.

"I told you he was thick," I said to Bo as he turned to look at me and Rick.

"That was awesome, Sir," he said, looking at Rick who was scratching his chest. "Thank you again."

"Ok you two," he said. "I am going to go take a shower."

"You ready for some breakfast, Bo?" I asked.

"Yes!" Bo replied standing and wiggling his ass a bit like a happy pig.

After breakfast, Chris, Rick, and Bo went down to swim for a while, and Jay and I sat out on the porch and had a drink and relaxed.

"It's been great hanging out with you, Jay," I said. "We don't get to do that often."

"I know," Jay replied. "I feel like you and Bo are a bit closer because of that and I am sorry."

"It's no problem," I said. "Just know we are there for you."

"I have been meaning to tell you something," Jay said turning to me.

"What's up?" I asked.

"I've been seeing someone recently," Jay said. "His name is Master Jeff, and he lives down in Savannah. I met him at Sir's Christmas party back in December and we started chatting. On work trips, he would have me come over and service him in his hotel and every other weekend for the past couple of months he has had me drive down and stay with him."

"That is awesome!" I exclaimed. "Do you think he might be interested in collaring you?"

"It's a distinct probability," Jay replied. "He has known Sir for a few years, and I think they have been talking about it."

"Well, congrats!" I replied. "Will you move down there if he does?"

"Yeah," Jay replied. "He has a nice house and is an accountant there. I like him."

"Nice!" I replied. "Well, Bo and I will be very sorry to see you go, but I do hope it works out."

"Thanks, bro," Jay said as he reached over and clinked my beer bottle. "I have to say you have come a long way. When we first met you, I was a bit unsure. You seemed a little green and nervous, but you fell into the sub role quickly. It's been great having you as a brother."

"Aww, thanks," I replied with a blush. "It was all Rick's doing. I think he saw the potential in me and figured John would be a good influence."

"Well, I hope you find a good dom to collar you one day too," he replied. "You deserve it."

The guys came up from the river for lunch and then Rick drove into town to stock up the supplies for us. When he returned, he had a case of beer that we put in the cooler and started to get into later in the afternoon. We grilled burgers that evening and played some more cards before going into the living room to sit down and relax.

"Well, I know this has been a short trip," Rick said, "but I am glad you boys came with us. I have enjoyed it."

"I know you have," Chris said, looking at Rick with a huge smile.

"Don't you worry babe," Rick said grinning back. "When we get back that cage is coming off and I'll be draining you dry all evening."

"Damn right you will," Chris replied groping his cage.

"In the meantime," Rick said looking at Jay with a bit of a devilish grin, "I got to sample Bo's ass this morning, how about you come over here and sit down in my lap and let me see how tight yours is."

"You got it, Sir!" Jay said as he came over and Rick slid forward a bit so Jay could straddle his legs and bring his ass down on Rick's stiffening cock.

"Bo," Chris said. "Why don't you come over here and lean over the chair. I can't fuck you, but I'd love to rim that ass."

Bo grinned. "Say no more!"

He came over near Chris and leaned over the chair and Chris spread Bo's ass cheeks and started to dive in with his tongue, which elicited a huge moan from Bo. At the same time, Jay was starting to move up and down on Rick's cock as he was moaning.

My nub was swelling again, and I felt precum coming out of it as well. I licked it off my fingers and started to rub it over my balls as I watched my sub brothers' asses getting used.

Jay reached down and grabbed his cage to hold it still as he started to bounce up and down and force Rick's cock deep into him. He leaned his head back and closed his eyes as he felt the full thickness of Rick's dick spread him wide.

"Fuck!" Jay said as his legs trembled a bit.

I looked and saw that he was having a caged orgasm and cum started to form at the head of his nub and began to spurt and flow out and onto the floor. Bo looked up and saw this as well and grinned.

"Damn, bro," he said between a moan from the rim job he was getting, "he fucked a load out of you! I'm jealous!"

"Me too!" I replied as I rubbed my full balls.

Rick looked back at me and grinned and then closed his eyes and grunted. His balls jumped as he too started to shoot his load deep into Jay's ass. Jay stopped moving and started to flex his ass muscles and Rick groaned with approval.

As Jay lifted himself off Rick, he got down on his hands and knees and licked the load off the floor that had come from his caged nub. Chris licked Bo's ass a few last times and then sat back and Bo went over and sucked Rick's cock clean.

"Well, that was fucking hot!" I said.

"Another round of beers before bedtime I think boys!" Rick said as he got up and grabbed us all some cans.

After we were done, we all headed off to our rooms and as I sat in bed with Bo I looked over at him.

"Have you had hands-free orgasms like what Jay had?" I asked.

"Only a few times," Bo said. "It depends on the cock that is fucking me and how it hits my prostate."

"Ahh," I replied. "I have not had one yet. I have had plenty of guys milk my prostate fluids out, but no orgasms."

"Well," Bo said. "Orgasms are great, and if you can get one from getting fucked by a good dom, that is even better, but as a sub, the most important thing is that the dom is pleasured."

"Oh, I know," I said. "I think it is just the prospect of being in this cage for three months straight now. As I work towards longer times and the prospect of permanent chastity, I think my mind is just panicking a bit."

"It's all good bro," Bo said, rubbing my chest. "You'll be ok."

"Thanks, bubba," I replied, and we nodded off to sleep.

The next morning, I was awoken by a knock on the door. I opened it to see Rick in the hallway.

"You two up yet?" Rick asked.

Bo turned to look up at him and was wiping his eyes. I took my CPAP mask off and stretched as well.

"Up now," I replied groggily.

Rick smiled and crawled in between us and laid on his back with his hands behind his head. His frame made us have to move to the edges of the bed and turn on our sides to avoid falling off.

"Your turn to get the morning load, Matt," he said.

I rolled my eyes and grinned and said, "how do you want me?"

"You can climb on facing me," Rick replied.

I moved around and got to where I could suck on Rick's dick a bit to get it wet. He started to precum as well and I used that to lube my hole and then I straddled his legs and brought myself down and let his cock enter me. As I was doing so, Bo moved to the side a bit and buried his face in Rick's armpit like the good little pig he was.

I arched my back a bit so that Rick's cock got as deep as it could, and I reached back and felt his balls a bit.

"Feels like they are full again," I said with a smirk.

"You are about to find out," Rick said, grinning back.

I started to move up and down on him and Rick closed his eyes and lifted his arm a bit more as Bo started to rub his face and beard in it, covering himself in his musk. Bo's nub was swollen and dripping precum which ran in a long dribble down until it landed on his leg.

"Good boys," Rick said as we pleasured him.

He started to rock his hips a bit to push his cock deeper in me and I reached down to play with one nipple as Bo played with Rick's other one. Rick stretched his legs out and his toes curled as he moaned in approval. More precum was flowing out of his cock and it coated my insides to the point that I started to hear the smack of his cock as it slid in and out of my ass.

Rick began to breathe more heavily, and his chest was heaving up and down as he started to thrust faster, and his cock began to pound my hole. Bo and I squeezed his nipples hard and he growled loudly as his cock immediately reacted by dumping its load deep inside me.

"That's it, Sir," I replied, "fill my ass up good."

Rick opened his eyes and smiled at me and then he reached over and started to make out with Bo and put his tongue deep into his mouth. I was so caught up watching them that I had not noticed that my nub was covered in prostate fluids. When I reached down to adjust my cage, I noticed how wet my hand was.

"Damn, Rick!" I replied. "I think you milked my prostate dry!"

Rick broke his embrace with Bo and looked down at my messy caged nub.

"Good boy!" he exclaimed.

After we got off the bed and got cleaned up, we had breakfast as a group in the kitchen and then went out on the back deck to have a cup of coffee before preparing to leave. Rick had one hand around Chris and the other around Bo and I was standing next to Jay.

"Hopefully we can do this again sometime," Rick said.

Jay put his hand around my waist and hugged me a bit. "Indeed, this was fun."

After we finished, we got dressed and packed up, and headed back to Atlanta. It was a fun trip, and I was happy to have had time to get to know Jay a little bit better. I was also looking forward to giving John the recap of what happened.

CHAPTER TWENTY

The Pool Party

It was Wednesday, July 1st and I was just getting home after my cleaning duties at John's house. He had told us that we would be hosting his annual 4th of July pool party this coming Saturday and we three subs had stayed a little later to figure out who would be doing what as far as set up and preparation. We knew that ten doms would be there for sure, but John told us to let him know if we knew of anyone to add to the list.

As I pulled into my apartment complex, there was still some light left in the sky due to the later sunset at this time of year. When I parked, I noticed that Kenny was just getting out of his car next to me.

"Hey, Kenny," I said as I closed the door to my car.

"Hey, Matt," he replied. "How have you been?"

"Doing well," I said. "Still training under Sir. Just getting back from my cleaning duties at his place."

"Very nice!" he said with a smile. "I need to get my boy to start cleaning my apartment up regularly."

I smiled back and walked over to him.

"How is that going by the way?" I asked. "The last time I think you told me he was living with roommates."

"Yeah, that is still the case," he replied. "But I am hoping to move him in with me at some point if things continue to go well."

"Nice!" I replied.

"Do you have any 4th of July plans?" he asked.

"Well, I am planning on going to the Eagle on Friday night for the Atlanta Bear Fest event," I said. "Sir is having a pool party at his house on Saturday as well."

"That sounds like fun," Kenny said. "Is your Master going to have a lot of people there?"

"He will be having some local doms over," I replied. "It is one of the bigger events he throws. It also allows us to meet other doms and possibly find ones that might collar us after our training."

"Well, that is convenient," he replied.

"Yeah. Plus, they all get to use us as party favors," I said with a grin.

"You think I might be able to get an invite?" Kenny asked. "I've been interested in your training program. It might be something I might want to get my boy to enroll in."

"Sure thing! I can talk to Sir tonight," I replied.

"Thanks!" Kenny said.

He gave me a wave and went back to his apartment and I entered mine and stripped down to relax a bit. I pulled out my phone and texted John about Kenny's interest.

"I would be happy to have him over," John replied to me a few minutes later. "Please send him my phone number and I will arrange it."

"Thanks, Sir," I replied and then I sent Kenny John's number for them to connect.

I had Friday off since the Independence Day holiday was on a Saturday. I had slept in and didn't get around to stepping into the shower until close to lunch. When I got out, I had a text from Chris. I had asked him earlier if he was planning on going out to the Eagle tonight.

"Can't tonight, bubba," Chris had replied. "Have fun out there for me!"

"Will do!" I replied and then I went and grabbed some lunch and sat on the sofa and played games most of the afternoon.

After dinner, I grabbed some bar clothes. I put on a black jock I had that showed off my ass a bit. Over that, I put on some tight jeans and my boots, of course. I went back and forth on wearing my harness but decided to throw it on as well and a black shirt over that. After throwing on a red Nasty Pig ball cap, I headed downtown to the club.

After I parked, I took my shirt off and left it in the car and walked up to the back deck. It was already pretty crowded and there were lots of hot guys around. Some were in town for the yearly bear event at a local hotel, but most were locals. I grabbed a beer and then walked out onto the upper back deck to drink.

Next to me was an older man who was graying at the temples and had a nice chest of white, gray, and brown fur. He had on a black leather cap and leather suspenders that were attached to his shorts. He had a pipe in his hands and had just finished lighting it and sent out a few puffs of smoke when he turned to me.

"How are you?" he asked.

"Not too bad," I replied with a smile. "My name is Matt."

"I can see that!" he grinned as I noticed he was reading my collar. "My name is Owen. Is your master around?"

"No, Sir," I replied. "I have been training under him for about four months now. I don't live with him and am not exclusive to him."

"Interesting," he said as he blew out some smoke and leaned against the railing.

"He trains boys like me to be good subs," I continued. "We learn about things that doms like and the intent is that after a year we can be collared."

"How is your training going?" he asked.

"Very well," I replied. "He has taught me so much. I didn't know what it meant to be a real sub at first, but I've embraced it over the past few months. I like challenging myself to always learn and do better."

"I had a boy for about fifteen years," he said. "It started plutonic and eventually became romantic, but I did enjoy having him around and using him when I needed him."

"That's nice!" I replied. "What happened? If you do not mind me asking."

"We had a falling out," he replied. "As he got older, he became less subordinate and more switch and eventually wanted to be more dom. We are still friends, but we parted ways about four years ago."

"I'm sorry," I said.

"No worries, boy!" he said with a puff of smoke. "As I said, we are still friends, but I do miss having a boy around."

We sat there and chatted a bit about the city and random topics. He moved over closer to me at one point and put his hand around my back.

"The pipe does not bother you, does it, boy?" he asked me.

"No, Sir," I replied. "I love the smell of a pipe. The tobacco you have in there smells great."

"It has some cherry notes in it," he replied. "It's quite good."

He blew some smoke between us and then pulled me in closer. He had been sweating a bit in the evening heat and humidity and there were some beads of sweat on his chest. His armpits were moist, and his musk was starting to waft by my nose, and it had an intoxicating smell. I eventually turned and put my face under his arm, and he raised it so I could breathe in his scent deeply.

"You like that, boy?" he asked me.

"Yes, Sir," I replied.

I reached down and rubbed his belly and felt the sweat run down and moisten his fur. I noticed his nipples were sticking out a bit and I moved to take one in my mouth and as I nibbled a bit, I heard him groan.

"Those are directly connected to my cock, boy," he said, taking my hand and placing it on his crotch.

I felt his cock stir under his pants and I continued to nibble and run my tongue around his nipples. He put his hand on my back and reached down and I felt his finger run down my crack and rub my hole.

"I love a boy with a nice furry ass," he said.

We made out for a bit and had a few more beers while he smoked. After about an hour, he asked if I wanted to go back to his hotel room. I told him I would love to, so we got a car to take us over to where he was staying in town.

As we were riding up in the elevator, he grabbed my bare chest and played with my nipples a bit and then put his hand down my pants and felt my cage.

"Your nub seems to be pretty swollen there boy," he said with a smile.

"It's reacting to the hot daddy I am with," I replied.

When we got to the room, I took off my boots, socks, pants, and jock and he watched while sitting on the bed. I was about to take my harness off when he stopped me.

"Leave it on, boy," he replied. "It looks good on you."

I walked over and then knelt in front of him. I ran my hands over his thighs and up to his waist and undid the button on his shorts and unzipped them. There was a white jock underneath that was holding his semi-hard cock and it was a little moist. I put my head in his lap and gave him a good sniff. It was a stronger smell than from his arms and I opened my mouth and let my tongue run across the sweaty fabric tasting him.

"Good boy," he groaned.

As I continued to lick and take his jock into my mouth, he took his hat off and kicked his shoes to the wall. He reached down and pulled his shorts down and then leaned back. I could see the outline of his hardening cock underneath and he had a metal cock ring on as well.

I pulled the fabric down and let his cock spring free and placed it in my mouth and sucked on it down to the root. He groaned with pleasure and reached down and rubbed my shoulders.

"Back off for a moment, boy," he told me.

I pulled back and he took his jock off and placed it on the side of the bed. He then took his socks off and placed them next to it and then reached down to grab my head and he brought me back onto his hard cock and started to slowly face fuck me. He was dribbling precum and the additional spit I produced had him slick and sliding in and out of my face quickly.

After several minutes, he stopped and got up from the bed. He reached over and grabbed his jock and he wadded up.

"Open your mouth, boy," he said staring into my eyes.

When I opened, he stuffed his sweaty jock into my mouth and then spun me around and bent me over the bed. He reached under my balls and felt my nub and noticed the amount of precum I was producing, and he collected it and rubbed it over my hole. He pushed one finger in, then two, then three. I was moaning into the jock and could taste him as the sweat mixed with my spit and I swallowed.

Once I was good and lubed, he took his socks and wadded them together, and put them in my outstretched hand.

"Bring these up to your nose chastity boy," he said with a firm voice. "I want you to smell and taste the essence of a real man as he fucks you."

"Yes, Sir!" I replied and I brought his socks to my face and put them over my nose.

The aroma was strong and between the socks and the moistened, sweaty jock in my mouth, I was feeling marked by his musk. I breathed in deeply and my head started to spin a bit just as I felt his cock enter my ass.

I grunted as he pushed forward. He grabbed my waist and started to fuck me with long, slow strokes. His cock was a nice size and it fit me perfectly and I was in pig heaven. I heard the smack as he hit my ass with his abdomen and the squishing sound of his cock as it slid in and out as well. I breathed in and smelt him, I swallowed, and I tasted him.

"That's a boy," he growled as he started to fuck harder. "It's a good thing you locked that thing between your legs away. Your ass was made to please real men."

I grunted in response and I heard him start to breathe harder and pant. He tensed up and slammed his cock deep into me.

"Take that cum, boy," he growled. "Take it deep inside you where it belongs."

I bit down on his jock and sucked more of his sweat out as I breathed in his scent again. I was in a daze and lost track of time. Eventually, I felt him pull off me and he fingered my ass a bit, making sure that any leaking cum was put back in me. When he was done, he helped me up and took the jock out of my mouth.

"Thank you, boy," he said as he gave me a quick kiss. "It has been a long time since I have been able to rut with a good sub."

"Thank you, Sir!" I replied with a smile.

I gathered my clothes and put them on and then went down to get a car back to where I had parked to get home. While I was waiting, I noticed I could still smell him and taste him.

The next morning, I was up early. I needed to be over at John's house by 8 am to start the setup for the party. It had rained a bit in the morning but was looking to be clearing off. It was supposed to be rather mild today at about 88 °F (31.1 °C), so it was looking to be a good day for a pool party.

When I opened the side door to John's house, Bo was just taking his underwear off.

"Heya Matt," he said, as he adjusted his cage and then closed the door to his bin. "You ready for today?"

"Yup," I replied as I pushed in the code to open my bin and started to undress. "Have you seen Jay yet?"

"He's inside," Bo said. "He got here just before me. You do anything last night?"

"I did," I said with a grin as I put my shirt and shoes in the bin and started to drop my pants. "Ended up going over to the Eagle last night for Atlanta Bear Fest. Hooked up with a hot older daddy."

"Oooo," Bo said wide-eyed. "Details!"

"Let's just say you would have been in heaven," I said as I took my underwear off and put them in my bin and closed it. "I had his jock in my mouth, his sweaty socks under my nose, and a butt full of cum at the end of the night."

"Piggy fun," Bo said with a grin.

I adjusted my cage a bit and then we headed into the dungeon area. Jay was already in there getting things set out. He had turned some electronic music on low and dimmed the lights a bit for the afternoon festivities.

"Hey bros!" Jay said with a smile. "I'm just about set up in here. Can y'all go out and start getting the pool ready?"

"You got it!" I replied.

Bo and I headed out to take the solar cover off and put it away. While Bo cleaned out the filter, I used the skimmer to remove a few leaves that had fallen in around the cover, and then we tested the water to make sure it was good to go. It felt refreshing and was crystal clear, so there was not much else to do.

After the pool was set, Jay came out and helped to wipe down the furniture and set out enough chairs for everyone. We put out some lounge chairs near the back of the pool where there would be full sun and we opened up the pool house and took off the top sheets so that the bed could be used if needed.

John had some folding tables in storage that we brought out and set up to put food on later and we swept the patio one last time before heading back inside.

"Well, that checks off the dungeon and the pool area," Bo said. "What is next Jay?"

"Sir asked us to thoroughly clean the first floor of the house, so Bo, why don't you come up and get started on that with me," Jay said. "Matt, there are some large garbage cans in the storage shed out back. We need those set around the pool and one in the dungeon area and a liner needs to be put in it."

"Will do!" I replied.

By 10 am, we had everything spotless on the first floor and the dungeon level and pool area were ready to go as well. John came down to the dungeon area about the time we were putting things away. He was in a tank top and gym shorts and was sipping a mimosa.

"Looking good boys," he said. "The first guests will start getting here in about an hour."

"Are we allowed to know who is coming?" I asked.

"Well, I believe you know Greg, who collared Dan, and Jack who collared Ryan and Johnny. Todd will be coming as well, and your friend Kenny will also be here. My friend Jeff is coming in from Savannah and the others, Hugo, Joe, Khavan, and Dusty, I don't think you know. However, Jay and Bo will remember them from the Christmas party."

"Oh, I remember Hugo," Bo said rubbing his ass instinctively. "That man is thick!"

John chuckled. "Well, just be sure you all tend to their every need. I have some last-minute things to do upstairs. When you are done putting things away, go to your spots and you can sit cross-legged till the first guests get here."

"Yes, Sir!" we replied, and John went back upstairs.

"So, Hugo was the one that you were talking about that wore your ass out in December," I said with a laugh to Bo.

"Fuck, yes," Bo said. "He's got a huge, thick, uncut churro, and big balls to boot."

"I thought he was pretty damn hot," Jay replied. "But of course, I have a thing for Hispanic men too. His beard was so thick. I wish I had a chance to service him, but he was mostly interested in Bo here."

"Well, you are welcome to share with me this time!" Bo laughed.

"I suspect Jay might be otherwise engaged since Jeff is coming," I said with a wink to Jay.

"Yeah," Jay said. "I'm excited for you two to meet him."

Once we had things put away we went over to the side wall and sat in our colored squares on the floor. We chit-chatted a bit about various topics till we heard John on the staircase. He opened the door and told us that the first guest was arriving and to get in our kneeling stances. So, we sat up on our knees with our hands behind our backs and our heads bowed and waited.

More footsteps on the staircase could be heard about ten minutes later and when the door opened, we heard a couple of men come in. I recognized the voice of Kenny, but the other man I did not recognize.

"Wow!" Kenny said. "This is an amazing space, and I see you have your subs trained well."

I had no idea how Kenny would react when he saw me in my space kneeling. We had talked about my training and John's house, but this was the first time I was going to be serving someone I knew before John.

"Rise boys," John said. "This is Kenny and Jeff."

All three of them were naked already. Kenny was smiling as he stared at me and I got my first look at Jeff as well. If I had to describe him, I would say muscle bear for sure. He had a huge chest with bulging pecs and thick arms and legs. He looked to be mixed race and he had a wonderfully medium-colored skin and dark hair over his chest and arms. He sported a medium-length dark beard, and his head was shaved, but you could see a few weeks growth of dark hair on top that looked to be receding.

"Nice to meet you Sirs!" we replied.

"Gentleman, would you like some mimosas?" John asked. "I have some mixed up."

"That would be awesome," Kenny said.

"Sounds perfect," Jeff replied.

"Well, make yourself comfortable out on the patio," John said. "Jay, please get these two men some drinks, and Matt and Bo, please see to their needs."

"Yes, Sir!" we replied.

Kenny took a seat under an umbrella near the pool and had Bo massage his feet and legs and Jeff sat across from him. I waited by the side wall till called.

The next men to arrive were Greg, Jack, and Todd. While we were getting them drinks, Hugo showed up as well, and I could tell from what was swinging between his legs that Bo was not exaggerating in the slightest.

Joe, Khavan, and Dusty were the last to arrive. Joe had very dark skin and little chest hair, but a nice tummy and a sexy smile. He was a hugger and very congenial. Khavan was a thin man that had a small tuft of hair on his chest. I later found out that he was born in Japan but had grown up in Los Angeles. He worked with John at the law office and had a very stern appearance. Finally, Dusty was pure country. He had a thick Alabama accent and a well-proportioned chubby appearance. He had short, sandy-blond hair, deep blue eyes, and a long beard. At first glance, you would think he was rather below average endowed, but he was a grower and not a show-er and had a massive set of hairy balls on him.

After John got finished greeting Dusty, he turned to everyone around the pool.

"Well, gentleman, everyone has now arrived," he announced. "Boys, please come and stand next to me."

We walked over to him and stood beside him with our hands behind our backs. John walked around and stood behind Jay and put his hands on his shoulders first.

"You all met the boys when you arrived, but I wanted to give you a more formal introduction," John said. "The senior sub in training is Jay here. He completes his service in two months and Jeff here has expressed interest in collaring him should he continue to impress him."

"Next to him is Bo," John said moving over to place his hands on Bo's shoulders." He has been in service for seven months now and is the pain pig among the group. So, Khavan, this is your sub."

John gave a wink to Khavan and he had a wicked smile on his face in response. Finally, John moved over and put his hands on my shoulders.

"Finally, we have Matt. He has been in service since March and has been a quick learner. I would ask that you refrain from any paddling or hard floggings on this one, but he has a great ass."

John smacked my ass with his hands and then moved to the side of us.

"We will be serving lunch first and afterward, the boys are yours to do with what you want," John continued. "We have discussed the safe words and please respect those if they are used. Otherwise, please enjoy yourselves!"

The guests all cheered, and we went to work bringing down the food from the kitchen and setting it out on the tables near the pool. Jay was on grilling duty and wore an apron as he grilled up hotdogs and hamburgers. I handled the sides and Bo took the drink orders.

I noticed that Jeff spent a lot of time around Jay and playfully smacked his ass and nibbled on his neck while he was grilling. I could tell they had a connection, and I was happy that Jay had found someone he liked.

After lunch was over, we got things cleaned up and put away to avoid attracting flies and then prepared for anything that was about to come. Most of the men were content to wade around the pool and request drinks from us. Bo and I took the piss of a few of them and Jay was on his knees sucking a load out of Jeff early on in the afternoon.

I had to go upstairs to grab more bottles of liquor at one point and as I was coming back down through the dungeon area, I noticed Hugo had Bo on the fuck bench and was fucking him deeply which was eliciting groans and yelps from Bo. Dusty was beside him waiting for a turn and was stroking his cock, which had grown from just the head poking out soft to close to 7 in (17.78 cm).

As I walked out into the pool area, I saw Jay bouncing up and down on Kenny's cock as Kenny laid down in the lounge chair and Joe was feeding Jay his monster cock, which was challenging even his deep-throating skills.

"Matt!" Todd announced. "Come here please."

"Yes, Sir!" I replied.

Todd had just got out of the pool and was drying off. I walked over to him and he smiled.

"How about you get that hot ass over in the pool house again," he said with a smirk. "I've been looking forward to pounding it again."

"Happy to, Sir!" I replied as I walked over to the building.

"Mind if I join you Todd?" asked Jack as he stood from where he was sitting.

"Not at all," Todd replied.

We walked into the pool house and Todd had me kneeling on the floor and sucking on him quickly after. Jack started stroking his cock as he watched and eventually I moved over to suck him too and alternated between the two older, chubby, daddy bears.

Jack went and sat on the bed with his back on the wall next and had me lay on my belly. Todd spread my legs apart and laid down between them and buried his face in my ass and started to tongue my hole, which got me moaning.

"You like getting your ass eaten, boy?" Jack asked.

"Yes, Sir!" I replied as I took a break from deep throating him.

"My boy Ryan loves that too," he replied with a grin.

Todd started to spit in my ass and finger it and then he pushed my stretched-out legs together and straddled them and began to slide his cock in.

"Oh fuck, Sir!" I groaned as he impaled me.

Jack reached down and used his hands to force me deeper on his cock.

"You focus on me, boy," Jack said. "That will keep you quiet."

Todd reached down and grabbed my waist and started to thrust into me deeply while I went down on Jack. Jack put his hands on my shoulders and started to rub them and then leaned back a bit and closed his eyes to enjoy the blow job.

As Todd picked up the pace and the bed started to bounce and squeak a bit, Jack took to holding my head again and face fucking me more. I was being impaled on both ends and trying to watch my breathing and gagging reflex so I did not choke on his cock.

"FUCK!" yelled Todd as he went over the edge and flooded my hole with his cum.

"Fill him up good," Jack said. "That will make good lube for me."

Todd grinned at Jack as he pushed himself deeper into me till his cock stopped pulsing. He pulled out and they switched places and as I cleaned off Todd's cock, I felt Jack slide right in.

"Damn," Jack said. "You loaded this boy up Todd!"

Todd was still grinning, and he put his hands on my head and moved them through my hair as I moved around his crotch licking his softening cock and balls. Jack started to pound me quickly. He was already pretty close to the edge from the blowjob, so it did not take long for him to add a second load to my ass.

"There you go sub boy!" he growled as he filled me.

Jack spread my ass apart as he withdrew and watched as his cock pulled out of my hole. The froth of two cum loads had been churned and surrounded the outside and as his head popped out, a dribble of cum ran out and down over my caged balls.

"Such a nice sight," Jack said.

"I wondered where you two went to," came a voice from the door.

It was Greg and he came over behind me as Jack got off the bed. He spread my ass and stuck his finger in my hole which caused me to groan in Todd's lap.

"You know I have only had this boy swallow my loads up till now," Greg said.

"Well, mount up!" Jack said as he grinned and turned to leave.

Greg got up behind me and placed his thick cock on my ass. I felt him slide it in and even after getting fucked twice, his girth made me tense up. Todd reached down and massaged my shoulders and ran his hand over my face.

"Breathe boy," Todd said. "Try to focus."

Greg pushed his cock in, and I felt him hit bottom and then he started to move back and forth in me slowly. The squishing sounds of the loads I had already received combined with the smack of his skin against mine as he fucked. I was being forced into the bed a bit and I reached up and grabbed Todd's thighs and buried my face in his crotch to take in his scent as a distraction.

Greg arched his back and pushed his cock deeply with each thrust. He pulled out just to the point his head was about to pop out and then went back in again. His cock was stretching me, and the loads were starting to dribble out more as they slid down my caged balls and onto the bed. He picked up his pace and I forced my face into the bed to avoid screaming.

"Umph!" Greg yelled as the orgasm came over him.

His cock let loose a torrent of cum and my overfilled ass could take no more and it started to come out even though he was deep in me. Once he had caught his breath, he pulled out and fingered my ass some more.

"I have to say that that was just as good as the head you give, boy," Greg said. "Well done."

Greg smacked my ass and winked at Todd and then grabbed his towel and walked out.

"You ok, boy?" Todd asked looking down at me.

I turned my head and looked into his deep blue eyes. He seemed genuinely concerned that I was not in any pain and I smiled back.

"I'm good, Sir!" I replied. "Just had to catch my breath."

"Good deal," he said as he tussled my hair and got up. "You've done a good job so far."

After Todd left the room, I got up and grabbed a washcloth from the bathroom and wiped down my ass, balls, and legs where the cum had run down. I then headed back out into the pool area.

Jay was in Jeff's crotch again and I heard a smack from the dungeon area and saw that Bo was tied to the cross and was getting flogged by Khavan.

"Matt," Kenny said, getting my attention. "Can you get me another beer?"

"Sure thing!" I replied.

I took his old can away and brought a new one to where he was now laying down and lounging by the pool.

"Are you enjoying yourself?" I asked as I knelt next to him.

"Very much so," Kenny said. "I have already talked to John and I am going to have my boy meet with him to discuss taking over Jay's spot when he graduates.

"Oh, nice!" I replied.

"Yeah," Kenny said. "John explained all the things he has been training you to do and the experiences you have had. I think that Max would greatly benefit from a more structured program under a dom and I know I would love to have a well-trained boy."

"Well, I look forward to possibly meeting him then," I said.

Kenny reached over and smacked my ass and gave me a wink and then I stood up and went to bring some drinks to a few men in the pool next.

"Hey, boy!" I heard a deep, southern voice call me.

I turned to see Dusty coming over to the side of the pool and climbing the steps to get out and I walked over to him.

"Get on your knees," he said. "I need to take a piss."

I got down in front of him and had to move forward to get his soft cock in my mouth. I pushed my face into his crotch to get a good hold of his head and when the stream started he reached down and held my head in place. His large balls sat nestled in my beard and I felt them move a bit as he drained his bladder. When he was done, he pulled back and lightly slapped my face, and then returned to the pool.

As the day wore on, I sucked off Jeff and Dusty as they lounged, and Bo spent a lot of time on the cross getting flogged or ass up in the fuck bench getting railed by Hugo. Jay did mostly light serving duties but was getting fucked in the pool house by Joe at one point.

By 5 pm, the party was winding down and the guests started to go upstairs to get dressed and leave. The last few to be left in the pool were John, Todd, and Jeff.

"Jay," John shouted out. "Please go grab three cigars from my humidor in the office and Bo, get three whiskeys ready."

I was standing next to the wall as they went to carry out John's request and John then looked over to me.

"Matt, you can start cleaning up the pool house and dungeon area," he said as he started to get out of the pool. "We are going to relax out here for a bit."

"Yes, Sir!" I replied.

The three men were sitting around smoking and drinking while we cleaned up everything and put the food away. We were inside doing a final wipe down of the equipment when they came into the dungeon area. We all stood at attention with our hands behind our backs when they got in.

"Boys, you did very well," John said. "Everyone told me they had a great time."

"Indeed," Todd said with a smile looking and me and Bo. "I'm looking forward to coming back again."

"Jeff here has requested some alone time with Jay in the dungeon," John said. "So, you two can go ahead and leave. I will see you again on Monday."

"Thank you, Sir!" Bo and I replied, and we headed over to the door to the entrance hall to dress to leave.

"Well, how is your ass?" I asked Bo after he closed the door and turned to get his things out of the bin.

Bo laughed. "Let's just say that I'm full of Mexican cum."

I chuckled and turned to get dressed.

"Khavan was interesting," he said as he put his pants on.

"How so?" I replied, putting on my shirt first.

"He's quiet, but when he's flogging you, he gets pretty verbal," Bo said as his head popped through his shirt.

"But, good?" I asked as I buckled the belt on my pants.

"Oh yeah," Bo said as he put his flip-flops on. "He knows what he is doing and spends time after to rub you down as part of aftercare. He also fed me a nice load after."

"Nice!" I said as I put my last shoe on and closed the door to my bin. "Well, I know I will be walking funny for a bit after the fucking that I got today as well."

Bo smiled and hugged me. "You have a good weekend bro."

"You as well," I replied, and we headed out to go home.

CHAPTER TWENTY-ONE

Kenny's Boy

I got off of work Thursday and headed out into the parking lot to find my car. It was the height of the summer in August, and while the temperature was not extreme, the humidity was making it oppressive. I got inside the oven that was my vehicle and turned on the air conditioning and sat there a bit till things cooled off. My phone buzzed at me and broke my train of thought and I looked down and it was a message from my brother.

"Are you all done with work?" he asked.

"Yeah," I replied. "Just about to head home now."

"Swing by my apartment if you can," he said. "I need to talk to you about a few things and I have a package for you from mom."

"Sounds good," I replied, and I headed over to his apartment.

Since I started my training with John five months ago, I had been over to my brother's house a few times. I had explained what was going on and he understood the protocols of no clothes in a home and such, but it was still awkward being naked in front of him. We are twins, so it's not like we had not seen each other naked growing up, and as gay men, we were both comfortable with our bodies, but still, it was my brother.

I got to his apartment and walked in to find him in his hospital scrub bottoms and crocs. He was standing in the kitchen stirring a pot that had some noodles in it.

"Hey bro!" Steve said.

"Heya," I replied, closing the door behind me. "Ok to strip, yes?"

"You are fine," he replied. "No one here but us two."

I took off my clothes and folded them next to the door and walked over to the kitchen. Steve glanced my way and noticed the smaller cage I was in.

"That's shorter than the last time you were here," he replied.

"Yeah," I said, instinctively grabbing my cage. "Sir swapped it out back in June. I guess I have not been by here since then."

"Well, to be honest," Steve said, "it's been crazy busy with work, so don't worry about it. Would you like some spaghetti?"

"Sounds good!" I replied as I sat down at his kitchen table. "What did you need to talk to me about?"

"Oh," Steve replied, turning to put a tray in the oven that had garlic bread on it. "It is nothing serious. Uncle Bill is heading out of town for the weekend and needs someone to take care of the dogs and watch the house. I can probably swing it, but I wanted to see if you were free."

"Yeah, that's no problem," I replied.

Our Uncle lived in Marietta, not far from where we lived. He was a bachelor and had two older yellow labs that lived with him at his house. It was a nice place and had a big backyard with a nice pool. We usually house sit for him when he had to go somewhere and made sure the dogs were fed.

"Cool," Steve said as he grabbed a beer and turned to me. "I'm going to stop by Friday night and feed the dogs, but if you can handle their morning and evening meals on Saturday and the morning on Sunday, that would be helpful. Bill gets back in the afternoon Sunday."

"I'll take care of it," I replied.

"He said we are welcome to have a friend over if we want, but nothing crazy," Steve said.

"I don't plan on having an orgy there," I said with a laugh. "Don't worry."

Steve smiled and grabbed me a beer and then plated the food and sat down to eat with me.

When I got back to the apartment, I saw Kenny sitting in his car on the phone. As I got out, he hung up and waved at me.

"Hey, Matt!" he replied.

"How are you doing bubba?" I asked.

"Not bad," Kenny said with a smile as he walked over to me. "Listen, I have been talking to John a few times over the past week. I want to set up some time for my boy to meet up with you and some of your sub brothers if that is ok. Max seems interested but a bit nervous and I want him to go into this willingly as his decision."

"Oh, no worries at all!" I replied. "Let me talk to the boys and see what we can figure out. Is it ok if I call you later this evening?"

"Yeah," Kenny said. "I will just be sitting at home."

"Cool," I replied. "Talk to you soon."

Kenny smiled and waved to me and we parted ways. When I got back to my apartment and had stripped down, I texted Bo and Jay to see if they might be free to meet Max.

"I'm around all weekend," Bo replied first.

"I'm going to be in Savannah this weekend," Jay said, "but if it is later in the month we can figure something out."

"Sounds good guys," I replied. "Let me talk to Kenny and figure out the details."

I called Kenny next to see how soon he wanted things set up. Jay would be graduating in three weeks, so there was not much time left if we wanted to include him.

"Hey bud," Kenny replied as the line connected.

"Hey," I said. "So, I messaged Bo and Jay. Bo will be around this weekend, but Jay is out of town. He said we can do something later in the week or next week if you wanted him to be there."

"Well, Max is free this weekend," Kenny replied. "But we could push it off. What do you think?"

"Well, Jay is graduating soon, so if Max is considering taking his spot, sooner is probably better than later," I said.

"That is true," Kenny replied.

"Plus, we will be his brothers if he starts training under Sir, so it might not be a bad idea to meet informally to determine if this is right for him and we can work as a team."

"That is true," Kenny said. "So, this weekend then?"

"Yeah," I replied. "I will be at my Uncles watching his house, but he did say I could have friends over. Why don't you see if Max would be willing to drive over Saturday and spend an afternoon with us? There is a pool, and we can relax at a neutral spot and talk, and he can leave whenever he wants."

"Yeah, I like that idea," Kenny said. "I'll talk to him tonight and get back to you."

"Sounds good!" I replied. "Talk to you later."

Saturday morning, I was up early so I could head over to feed Bill's dogs. When I got to his place, it was about 9 am, and walking in the two dogs lumbered over wagging their tails in anticipation of their morning meal. I stripped down and put my clothes on the washing machine near the garage door and then walked into the kitchen and bent down to grab their bowls. As I was grabbing the second one, I felt a cold nose on my balls, and I jumped up.

"None of that Coop!" I replied, turning around.

I filled their bowls and then opened the back door. The storm door inside the frame had a flap on it to allow the dogs to go in and out, but you had to open the main door for them to access it. I went out through the second storm door and walked around the back patio.

It was a humid morning, but nice and sunny. The birds were chirping, and I heard a crow cawing in the distance as well. Bill's backyard was surrounded by trees and was completely private. I knelt by the pool and stuck my hands in, and the water felt nice and refreshing.

As I stood up, I heard the flap to the door make a sound and Alex and Coop came running out to do their business in the yard. After they were done, they came over to me and licked my legs and I picked up their ball from the yard and played catch with them for a bit before heading inside to grab a drink.

I had arranged for Bo to stop by in the morning. I figured we could hang out and chill for a while before Max arrived. He was due after lunch and Kenny said that he could be a bit shy at first and to be prepared.

It was about 10 am when I heard the doorbell ring, and I went and opened the door to let Bo in.

"Hey!" Bo exclaimed as he hugged me and came inside. "This is a nice house!"

"Yeah," I replied. "My Uncle does a lot of entertaining with his friends here, so it's a bit of a bachelor pad."

Alex and Coop heard someone at the door and bounded through the doggie door and hurried over with their tails wagging to greet Bo. He reached down and petted them both.

"Well, they are friendly," Bo said with a grin.

"They mostly lounge outside and sleep," I said with a chuckle. "But they love new people."

"Where should I put my clothes?" Bo asked.

"Come over here by the garage door," I said. "I undressed in the laundry room and put my clothes on top of the washer away from the dogs."

"Sounds good!" Bo replied.

After he got stripped down, we grabbed some drinks and went and laid out by the pool for a while to enjoy the morning sun. It was not too hot out yet, and there was a slight breeze from the east. The dogs sprawled out and napped in the grass and apart from the sound of the birds in the area and the tones of a wind chime Bill had on the back of the house, it was quiet and pleasant.

"I could get used to this," Bo said as he stretched out on the lounge chair on his back.

I had gotten up to turn some music on low and grab a refill. As I went to lay down next to Bo in another chair, I tossed him a washcloth.

"Put that over your nub," I said with a grin. "That metal will heat up in this sun and you don't want to burn your nether regions."

"Ha!" Bo said with a smile as he laid it over his nub. "Good point."

After we soaked up some rays for a bit, it was starting to get warm, so we headed inside, and I pulled out some sandwiches I had brought with me.

"Can you believe that Jay will be leaving in a few weeks?" I asked, opening a small bag of potato chips and eating one.

"Time flies," Bo said as he bit into his sandwich and washed it down with a soda. "I am going to miss him, but it seems like he has found his new master."

"I like Jeff," I said. "He seems like a caring dom and let me tell you, he had a pretty big load that I swallowed from him at the pool party."

Bo chuckled. "I never got to service him, but I agree he seemed nice. What do you think of Master Todd?"

"I like him!" I replied. "That white fur on his chest and those deep blue eyes are a nice combo. Well, that and his cock and balls too."

Bo grinned. "Yeah, he is attractive. I was glad to get a chance to service him again at the party last month. He also messaged me a few times after and I got a chance to go to his house last night."

"Oh?" I said with a raised eye. "How did that go?"

"His place is gorgeous," Bo said, putting down his sandwich and leaning back to gesture with his hands. "He must be rather wealthy. I felt a little nervous walking inside."

"Nice!" I replied.

"He had a dungeon area in his basement as well," Bo continued. "Not as big and elaborate as Sir's but it was well-equipped. He had a cross painted on the wall and eye hooks were secured to the studs where they would be if they were attached to a real one. There was a leather-covered fuck table, a cage on the floor, eye hooks in the ceiling for suspension play, and a wide variety of toys and bondage equipment on shelves."

"What all did you do?" I asked.

"Well," Bo said, "he first had me get on the floor and massage his feet. I got the impression he loves to have his legs and feet rubbed. He suspended my arms above my head to a ceiling hook and put some nipple clamps on me and then did some light flogging. That was followed by giving him some head for a while. He then blindfolded me and put me in the cage with some hypno tracks on some headphones over my ears and after I zoned out a bit, he came back and bent me over the fuck table and loaded me up."

"Sounds like a really hot time!" I replied.

"Yeah," Bo said. "Afterwards, he got me up and just hugged on me for a while and rubbed my belly and shoulders. It was very erotic. My nub was straining the whole time."

"Sounds like you might have caught his eye," I replied with a grin.

"Maybe," Bo said, returning the smile. "I would not be upset if he did want to go further."

After we finished lunch and chatted a bit more, I cleaned up and threw away our trash and we headed back outside again. I helped Bo reapply some sunscreen and he did the same for me and we lounged a bit more and then swam a bit as well.

Around 1:30 pm, I heard the front doorbell chime. I grabbed my towel and dried off some and then hurried over to the front door. As I opened it, a younger man in his early twenties looked up at me and smiled.

"Hey, I am Max!" he said.

"Hey, Max!" I replied, opening the door fully. "I'm Matt."

Max was extending his hand to shake mine and he looked down and saw I was naked and in just my cage. Bo showed up behind me at the same time naked as well.

"Umm, wow," Max said with a stutter. "I did not expect everyone to be naked."

"Ha!" Bo laughed from behind me. "We don't bite. I promise. My name is Bo!"

Max came in and shook his hand as well and I shut the door behind him. He was about my height, 5' 10" (1.8 m), and looked to be about 195 lbs (88.5 kg) or so. He had dark hair on his head that was buzzed very short and dark green eyes. His beard had some red in it in addition to dark brown and was a medium length. He had on a t-shirt and you could see some tufts of chest hair sticking out and his legs were pretty hairy as well below his shorts. It even extended to his feet where there were tufts of dark hair showing on his toes poking out of his sandals.

"Umm," Max stuttered. "I'm a little nervous here, to be honest."

"Oh, please do not be," I said putting my hand around his shoulders and leading him into the living room. "You are among friends. Kenny has spoken very highly of you and was wanting us to meet you."

Max grinned. "Sir has been telling me a bit about you and Sir John. He thinks it would be a good experience for me to train like you have been, but I am a little unsure."

"Well, that is why you are here!" Bo said.

"We were going to go back out to the pool," I said. "Is that ok?"

"Yeah!" Max said. "Sir told me you had a pool here. I brought some swimming trunks."

"Well, feel free to wear them or go naked like us," I replied. "You do what makes you feel comfortable."

"Yeah," Bo said. "We want you to relax and have a good time."

"I'm fine being naked," Max said with a grin. "Where should I put my things?"

I showed him where the laundry room was, and we headed back outside. After Max had undressed, he came outside, and the dogs noticed him and ran up wagging their tails to get petted before returning to their shady spot under a tree to sleep.

Max was a furball. He had dark hair all down his chest and back and a furry ass, which Kenny had mentioned before. He had put on a ball cap to keep the sun out of his eyes and we helped him rub some sunblock on, though it took a while to get all absorbed with his hair in the way. He had a nice set of hairy balls and his cock started to swell a bit as we rubbed his skin.

"Sorry about the erection," Max said as he covered himself slightly embarrassed.

"No worries!" Bo laughed. "I almost have forgotten what it is like to randomly sport wood."

Max smiled and after all the lotion was applied he sat down with us in some chairs around a table.

"Well, I guess we better introduce ourselves," Bo said. "As I said earlier, my name is Bo, I am 30 years old and I have been training under Sir since December of last year. I am from Texas originally, but I have lived here in Atlanta for about five years now."

"And I am Matt," I replied. "I am 39 years old and originally from Tennessee, though I have lived all over the south. I have been here in Atlanta for eight years. I started training back in March."

"Nice to meet you both in person," Max said. "Sir has been telling me about you. I'm Max, as you know. I just turned 23 and I was born and raised here in Georgia in a little town south of Atlanta. I moved up here after college to get away from home and I am rooming with some friends. I've been seeing Sir Kenny since the end of February and have been interested in learning more about what being a good sub is all about."

"Well, you ended up with a hot boyfriend," I said with a grin.

"I do like him," Max beamed. "But he has been wanting to explore kinks with me that I don't have a lot of experience with, so I am hoping to learn more. We hope to move in together in the next year as well."

"Would you consider yourself top, bottom, or switch?" Bo asked. "Just out of curiosity."

"Oh, very much bottom," Max said. "I'm kind of an insatiable one. I love getting fucked and sucking loads out of guys."

"Well, that is a good skill to have!" I said with a laugh.

"What about chastity play?" Bo asked.

"That would be new to me," Max said. I have never done it, though Kenny and I have talked about getting me started wearing one."

"I was a newbie like you when I first met Sir John," I replied. "If you decide to train with him, chastity is a requirement, but you will be given time to adjust. It's not easy, but you adapt."

"I can see that!" Max said as he grinned and looked at our cages.

"Are they painful at all?" Max asked. "They look so small!"

"It's not bad," Bo said. "There is an adjustment period, but over time you will learn to live in it and sometimes forget it is there. Assuming that it is fitting well that is."

"Yeah," I added. "Sir makes sure that it's a good fit so that you don't have issues and he checks you periodically to make sure you are not developing any irritation or sores or anything."

"I'm in my final six-month session before going permanent now," Bo said.

"Permanent?" Max said wide-eyed.

"That is one thing that Sir works you up to," I replied. "You will start at a week and over time he will build you up to longer and longer periods locked up. The last session is six months and at the end, you will be permanently locked in your cage."

"Well," Bo said, "That is unless the man who collars you wants it otherwise, but the intent is that you could be permanent if your master wants."

"I haven't discussed that with Sir," Max said.

"Don't let it scare you, though," I said. "This is all consensual. If it's too much for you, you can leave the training program. The idea is that you push your limits, learn new skills and techniques, and find your true self in the process."

"Yeah," Bo said. "Believe me I was nervous going in, but I have not regretted one day since I started my training. I've also bonded with some great sub brothers like Matt here."

Bo and I grinned at each other and held up our drinks as a toast.

"Well, I am looking forward to learning more, but I'd like to take a dip in the pool if that is ok," Max said. "It's hot out here!"

"Let's jump in!" I said with a laugh and we all jumped in the water and cooled off a bit.

Throughout the next couple of hours, Max started to relax a bit and was more comfortable around Bo and me. We talked more about the program, the different kinks we have been exposed to, and the parties as well. Max seemed most wide-eyed about the most recent party over the fourth of July. We had started to discuss that after we got out of the water and were sitting down having a beer. Max started to pop an erection as he was sitting in his chair as we told him about the men we serviced and what went on.

"Damn!" Max said not even trying to hide his hard cock. "That sounds so fucking hot. I would have loved to have been there with those hot guys."

"I can see that!" Bo said with a big grin looking at Max's dick.

"Sorry, guys," Max said. "My hormones are raging."

I laughed. "You in a chastity cage will be an interesting thing to see with as much wood as you sport."

Max chuckled back. Bo got up and knelt in front of him. "You mind if I take care of that for you?"

"Umm, sure!" Max said as he moved forward in the chair a bit.

Bo reached up and put his hands under Max's balls and guided his hard cock into his mouth. As Bo moved down his shaft, Max let out a groan and leaned back a bit. I smiled and sat back and watched as my nub swelled in its cage.

It was well known between my sub brothers that Bo gave the best head. He had given me tips over the past few months but watching him in action was hot. He had just about lost his gag reflex and he could work up a nice amount of spit to help a man's dick slide in and out of his mouth with ease. The way he could wrap his tongue around the shaft helped as well. He had a lot of skills all around.

As Bo started bobbing up and down on Max's cock, he started to move his finger under his ass and play with his hole.

"Oh, fuck!" Max said as he leaned back some more and put one leg on Bo's back to give him better access to his furry ass.

Bo got his finger in deeper and found his prostate gland and started to rub it gently as he picked up the pace and used his other hand to assist his mouth in working Max's shaft.

I saw Max's toes curl as they laid on Bo's back and he closed his eyes and bit his bottom lip. Bo started going hard at it and stimulating Max's prostate and it was not long before he lifted his ass a bit and yelled.

"Fuck!" he screamed as he came. Max grabbed the sides of the chair hard to steady himself and Bo lifted off and watched a few spurts of cum fly into the air and land back on his face and beard. He then went back on Max and swallowed the rest.

After he caught his breath, Max looked down at Bo who was smiling back at him licking the cum covering his mustache and cheeks.

"That was amazing!" Max said. "You need to teach me how to do that to Sir!"

I laughed. "I am quite sure Kenny would love for you to do that Bo."

Bo sat up and returned to his chair and used his fingers to collect the remaining cum and swallow it.

"You shoot a pretty big load there," Bo said with a grin.

"You defiantly know what you are doing," Max said with a grin. "Well, this has been great guy. I have enjoyed getting to know you both and I will talk things over with Sir some more. He said I am probably going to meet with Sir John next week."

"That will be good," I said.

"Just be prepared," Bo said. "He will size you up at that first meeting. If he thinks you are a good candidate, he will give you some tasks to carry out. Just be honest with him and see how things go. But, we would love to have you as a brother as well."

"For sure," I added. "Maybe this time next month you will be part of the chastity club."

Max grinned. "I guess I better shoot a bunch of loads over the next few weeks then."

We all laughed and got in the pool and swam around a bit more before Max said he needed to leave, and we got out and went inside. After he was dressed, we all hugged, and I saw him out the front door.

"He seems like a nice guy," Bo said.

"Yeah," I replied. "Kenny likes him and thinks he would be a great fit as one of Sir's subs. But we will have to see what Sir thinks."

"He's tasty too!" Bo grinned.

I put my arm around Bo and pulled him close and rubbed his belly. "You are a little piggy."

"Oink, oink!" Bo replied with a snort.

CHAPTER TWENTY-TWO

Summer in the City

I awoke early the following Tuesday morning. The longer days meant even at 6:30 am there was some light coming in through the curtains already. I pulled off my CPAP mask and pulled off the top sheet that was over me and stretched. My nub had been leaking overnight and I noticed some crust on the sheets.

I was about ten weeks into my three-month chastity session. I was due to be released on September 6, the day after Jay graduated, which was still a few weeks away and I was feeling it deep in my balls. Rick said I was 'in heat' when I mentioned it to him a few days prior and I wasn't going to argue with him.

I was walking to the bathroom to piss when my phone buzzed. I looked down to see that it was a direct message from a follower on my Tumblr page.

"Big fan of your blog!" it read.

I had been keeping an almost daily journal of how my lockup was going and the different experiences I had encountered along the way. Although John got me started, I had gotten into it and had been offering advice to others that were looking at chastity or sub space as well.

"Thanks!" I replied.

I had posted the night before about how horny I had been lately and that it had been a few days since I had the opportunity to service any doms other than John.

"Do you provide morning blowjobs?" he asked.

"I do," I replied. "It just depends on if I am running late to work. Are you interested?"

"Yes. My wife has not been in the mood lately and I need my balls drained," he replied. "Do you live anywhere near Smyrna?"

"Yes," I said. "Not far at all."

"Can you be here at 7:15 am?" he asked.

He provided me an address and I noticed it was only about ten minutes away.

"Sure," I replied. "Let me get cleaned up quick and I will be there."

"Perfect," he said. "Park in the street."

I put my phone down and jumped in the shower and washed down well. My nub was straining in my cage at the thought of getting to blow off some horny energy. After drying off and grabbing a quick breakfast, I put my clothes on and headed out the door.

The address he gave me was in an older neighborhood and there were a lot of trees that blocked the view of the houses. I finally found the correct address and parked in the street. I was sitting there for about a minute when I saw someone appear behind a tree where the driveway to his house bent down a hill into a secluded lot.

He was an older man, clean-shaven with light brown hair that was graying at the temples. He waved at me and walked over to my side door and I rolled down the window.

"Thanks for coming over," he said as he leaned on the window frame. "My wife is still asleep. Do you think you can just blow me here beside the car?"

"Sure," I said.

I got out and came around and opened the back door and sat down on the floorboard and he came in front of me.

"You think I can see your cage?" he said. "I've been a big fan."

"Sure," I said with a smile.

I undid my belt and pulled my pants and underwear down and then sat down in front of him again. He unzipped his pants and pulled out his hardening cock and then reached down and felt my cage.

"I love it," he said.

His cock was at full mast pretty quickly and I grabbed it with one hand near the root and started to slowly take it into my mouth. He groaned and put his hands on the door frame and looked down to watch.

As I started to move up and down his shaft, I ran my fingers over his balls lightly and then started to grope them a bit. His cock responded by producing precum which I lapped up quickly. He adjusted his stance a bit and reached down with one hand to put it behind my head and guide me back and forth on him.

"I needed this so bad," he whispered to me.

I started using my hand to work his cock and started to suck on him harder. He began to move his hips and force his cock deeper and deeper into my mouth. I was proud that I was able to take him as well as I was doing. My deep-throating skills were improving.

My nub was straining again, and I felt some precum start to leak out and drip down my balls and land on the street below. He looked down and saw this.

"You were not kidding when you said you were horny," he said with a grin.

I smiled and then started to work his shaft. He grabbed onto the frame again tightly and started to groan more. I felt his balls jump in my hand just as his cock started to pulse and streams of cum hit the back of my throat.

"Fuck," he groaned as he put his face over his arm.

His legs started to shake, and his ass clenched as his balls finished emptying in my mouth. When he was done, he looked down again and I pulled off him and licked the head of his dick a few times and then smiled at him. He reached down and pulled his pants up after.

"Thanks again," he said, and he turned to leave.

I watched him return around the tree and down the driveway and I reached down and went to pull my pants up. My nub was covered in precum, but fortunately, I had some extra napkins in the car from a meal I had brought home a few days ago, so I wiped myself down before dressing and returning to the front of the car.

I was checking my face in the mirror to make sure I did not have any cum in my beard when a car drove by on the street.

"Well, they missed seeing a show by minutes," I said to myself with a nervous laugh.

On Wednesday I was cleaning with my sub brothers as usual at John's house. When we had finished, we went downstairs to put the cleaning supplies away and when we came back into the dungeon, John was standing there.

"Well done with the house as usual boys," he said. "I have a treat for y'all. Once a year in the summer, I set aside a day for my boys to use the pool and backyard and bond a little bit. With Jay's upcoming graduation, I have decided that this Saturday will be set aside for you three. I will be out of town for the day, so you can use the grounds as you see fit. My only request is that you clean up after yourself."

"Thanks, Sir!" Bo said with a big smile.

"That sounds awesome," Jay said.

"Agreed," I replied with a grin.

"Very well," John continued. "Bo, I will see you for your one-on-one visit tomorrow and the rest of you have a good evening and drive safe."

"Thank you, Sir!" we replied.

"Please tell me you both are coming," Bo exclaimed after John left.

Jay laughed and put his hand on Bo's shoulder. "I'll be here brother."

"I'll be here as well," I said.

"Cool," Bo said. "I'll bring some things to grill out if someone can bring some drinks and sides."

"I can get the drinks," I said.

"I'll handle the side foods then," Jay said.

"Ok, so we meet here by noon Saturday then?" Bo asked.

"Sure," Jay said. "I might even get here a bit before that. It depends on how late I stay up the night before and when I roll out of bed."

"Sounds good to me," I said with a laugh.

Saturday was another hot day in the South. There was not a cloud in the sky but at least the humidity level was not as oppressive as it usually was. I pulled up to John's house at about 11:45 am and came through the side door with the drinks and put them down to strip and put my clothes away before continuing into the dungeon. Jay was already inside and had the music going and set out some coolers.

"Well, you did get here early!" I replied.

"Yeah," Jay said. "Decided to get things set up."

"Hey bro!" Bo said as he walked in from the pool area. "I have the grill all set up and ready to go."

"Well, here are the drinks," I said. "I brought some beer and soda, so you have your pick."

We put the cans in the coolers and Jay opened some bags of chips to snack on while Bo put on an apron to grill up some hamburgers and hotdogs. After everything was plated, we sat at a table under an umbrella and ate.

"Are you excited about your upcoming graduation Jay?" Bo asked.

"Very much so," Jay replied. "Hard to believe it's already been a year. My sub brothers Johnny and Nick both messaged me this week to check in on me."

"How's Nick doing out in Seattle?" Bo asked.

"He loves it," Jay replied. "He told me his master, Adam, is dating another hot daddy bear, and it is looking like he will be moving in with them."

"Sounds like he will be busy!" I chuckled.

"For sure," Jay replied with a smile. "I'm hoping I get a chance to go out and see him again at some point."

"And how are Johnny and Ryan?" I asked. "I have not seen them out at the Eagle lately."

"Johnny said they have been busy," Jay replied. "They have some sort of business they are running. I don't know the details, but I do know that it's been taking up most of their time lately."

"I was going to say that I will be sad to see you go, but I guess change is part of the program," I replied.

"Oh, I will miss you both a lot, but we will still keep in touch and I am sure I'll see you around," Jay said. "But you are right. First Nick and Johnny leave, and then you two come in, and then I leave y'all behind. It goes by way too quickly."

"How's Master Jeff doing?" I asked.

Jay smiled. "He's great. We talked about him collaring me and moving me down to Savannah. Still working out the details, but it's looking good. So, fingers crossed, I might have his name on my collar."

"From the sound of it, Bo might have one come December as well," I said with a wink.

"Oh?" Johnny questioned with an eyebrow raised. "Is this Master Todd?"

"Yeah," Bo said. "Could work out. I have seen him a few times and he has been showing interest in me."

"Nice!" Jay said. "He's a hot daddy bear."

"For sure," Bo said, turning to look at me. "But, he has been eyeing Matt here as well."

"Well," I said with a laugh, "I think you might have a leg up on me since you are graduating first."

"Well boys," Jay said, "shall we take a dip in the pool for a while?"

"Right behind you," Bo said.

Jay got up and dived in the pool and Bo was right behind him jumping in cannonball-style and making a huge splash. I opened to walk in on the shallow side and work my way in.

"What is the matter," asked Jay jokingly, "afraid to get your hair wet?"

"No," I replied with a grin, "I just wanted to wade in."

"Whatever," I heard Bo say before he dove under the water and in-between my legs to knock me off balance and send me under.

"Bo!" I exclaimed as I stood back up and blew out some water I swallowed.

"Be careful there Bo," Jay said. "It is better to do it this way."

Jay grabbed me sideways and pulled me over and under again and I came up and pulled him under immediately after.

"Now he's moving!" Jay said with a laugh.

I grinned back and ran my hands through my wet hair. "It's a good thing I like both of you."

Bo was still laughing and came behind me and hugged my waist and put his head on my shoulder.

"I'm just glad we have some time to blow off steam," Bo said. "I've been horny as fuck lately."

"Oh, me too," I replied.

"I don't know Matt," Jay said with a grin as he swam over in front of me. "I've been reading your blog. You seem to be getting some opportunities to burn energy off."

I blushed a bit and Bo playfully bit my shoulder.

"Hey!" I exclaimed, looking back at him.

"So, when was the last time you got to service anyone?" Bo asked.

I told him about my encounter with the older man on the way to work on Tuesday and followed up with how close I had come to getting caught.

"Oh, that's nothing," Bo said. "I remember back last fall when a guy wanted me to come over and let him use my ass. When I got there, it turned out he was nineteen years old and living with his parents. He made me lay down behind a hill near their house while he fucked me. After he loaded my ass up, he went back inside, and as I was walking around to get back to my car his father showed up."

"Oh shit!" Jay said.

"What happened?" I asked.

"He said he watched his son fuck me from the second-floor window of their house and asked me if I would be willing to take his load too," Bo continued. "So, we walked over in the woods a bit and he bent me over a log and fucked a load in me as well."

"Ok, that is fucking hot," Jay replied.

"You're a mess Bo," I replied as I reached back and tousled his hair.

Bo wrapped his legs around me and I felt his cage push into my ass crack. He then squeezed his arms around me tighter and put his head next to mine.

"You know your nub is caged right?" I asked jokingly. "It isn't going in my ass."

"Oh, hush you," Bo said. "I just like hugging you."

Jay smiled and came in front of me and wrapped his arms around my waist as well and put his legs around Bo. He squeezed as well, and I was stuck in the middle.

"It's a Matt sandwich now!" Jay said and gave me a peck on the lips.

"Ugh, you two are a handful," I said rolling my eyes and laughing.

We waded around a bit and then grabbed some beers and drank and talked. It reminded me a lot of our trip with Chris and Rick up to the mountains. We were able to let our guards down and just talk and grow closer.

As the shadows started to creep over the pool in the late afternoon, Jay started to move towards the stairs to get out.

"Well guys, I think I am going to get out and dry off," he said.

"Oh boo!" Bo replied. "Damn this day has flown by."

We followed Jay out and dried off and then sat for a few minutes to finish off the rest of our drinks.

"You don't have to stay and help clean up Jay," I said.

"Yeah, Matt and I agreed to take care of it if you want to head out," Bo said. "It's not much to do anyway."

"Thanks, guys!" Jay said getting up.

He came behind us and gave us each hugs around our necks and then headed into the dungeon to get dressed and leave.

"You up for going out to the bar tonight Matt?" Bo asked.

"Sure!" I replied. "You want to follow me over to my place and we can get a car to take us in from there?"

"Deal," Bo said with a wink.

So, we threw away our trash, cleaned up the pool area, replaced the solar cover, and then cleaned out the coolers. After everything was put away, we got dressed and headed over to my place, and got a car to take us into town.

Bo and I got to Woofs, the bear sports bar, about 6 pm. It was a little early, but the crowd was still decent. We ordered a pitcher of beer to split and headed back to the back tables to sit down for a while. After about thirty minutes, I felt a tap on my shoulder, and I turned around to see Max standing behind me.

"Hey, bud!" I said. "How have you been?"

"Not bad," Max replied. "You got an extra seat?"

"Feel free to pull up a chair!" Bo said with a smile.

"Sir Kenny is meeting me here, but I got here early," Max said.

"Nice!" I replied.

"Have you made a decision yet on joining the program?" Bo asked.

"Well, I had dinner with him and Sir Kenny on Thursday," Max said. "It gave me a chance to meet him informally. He had me wear a chastity cage overnight and I had to freeze the keys in the freezer. It was maddening!"

I grinned, "I remember doing that the first time with him."

"Me too!" Bo replied with a grin as well.

"Well, he said that since I made it overnight that I could meet with him tomorrow evening for dinner and we would talk more," Max said. "He gave me an assignment to work on today to think about what I would be interested in exploring and how this might help me grow closer to Sir Kenny."

"It sounds like he is interested," I replied. "I had to do something similar when I was going through my initial interviews with him and thinking about it."

"Yeah," Bo said. "He usually has some tasks for you to do that allows him to size you up and determine if you will be a good fit."

"Ok," Max said. "He told me to bring my chastity cage with me in the car to dinner tomorrow, so I am assuming that more sessions are in store."

"Yeah," I replied. "Just be sure to be open and honest with him."

"Hey boys!" came a voice from behind me. I turned around and saw Kenny smiling and moving to stand behind Max.

"Hello, Sir!" Max replied and he bowed his head and Kenny kissed his forehead and hugged him.

"Nice to see you out and about," I replied with a smile.

"Yeah," Kenny said. "The boy and I haven't had a chance to get out much, so we figured we would have a few drinks here before dinner. What have you all been up to?"

"Not much," I replied. "Bo and Jay and I had some bonding time at Sir's house but other than that it's been pretty uneventful as far as the week goes."

"Has the boy told you he and I met with John this week?"

"He did!" Bo said. "Sounds like he might be our sub brother soon!"

"I hope so," Bo said, gripping Max's shoulders. "I would love for him to be as well-trained as you two are."

"Thank you, Sir!" Max said with a smile looking back at Kenny.

"I don't want to be rude boys, but I have a friend here that I met on the way in and I wanted to introduce Max to him," Kenny said.

"No worries!" I replied. "It was good to see you!"

"You ready, boy?" Kenny asked Max.

"Right behind you, Sir!" Max replied as he got up and followed Kenny over to another table.

"I still remember freezing my key for Sir that first time," I said to Bo. "It seems like a lifetime ago."

Bo smiled and tapped his glass of beer against mine. "You made the right choice."

CHAPTER TWENTY-THREE

Jay's Graduation

Saturday, September 5 was Jay's graduation day. John had told Bo and me to be at his house by 1 pm to help set up and that the ceremony would begin promptly at 2 pm. When I arrived, Bo's car was already in the street and I found him undressing and putting his clothes in his bin when I walked in the side door.

"Hey," I replied with a wave. "I can't believe it's time for Jay to move on."

"Yeah," Bo said as he locked his bin. "I'm a bit sad, but I am also happy for him."

"So, you went through this before when Johnny graduated," I said. "Is there anything I need to know?"

"Just follow my lead," Bo said. "The ceremony will mostly revolve around Sir and Jay. We will watch from our spots, but there will be a few places where we will participate. I will leave that as a surprise though."

"Ok," I said.

"I think you will enjoy it," Bo said with a grin.

After I was undressed and my clothes were put away in my bin, we entered the dungeon area. John was already downstairs and setting things out. He was in some sweatpants and a tank top and glanced our way as we closed the door behind us.

"Good to see you boys," he said. "I was just refilling some of the lube containers and bringing down some paperwork. Bo, since you have been through this before, why don't you take charge and help Matt get the room set up. I need to go upstairs to take a shower and get dressed."

"Yes, Sir," Bo said.

"You do remember everything that happened when Johnny graduated, right?" John asked.

"Yes, Sir," Bo said. I will make sure the room is ready to go."

"Good boy," John said, and he patted Bo's shoulder as he passed by to go back upstairs.

"Ok, Matt," Bo said. "Let's get started."

Bo walked back to the isolation room and as we entered, there were three bags on the counter next to the door.

"Those are for us," Bo said, "but, we will get back to that. Go ahead and grab some hand towels and set them out at the table and bench."

I went and did as he said as he grabbed some folding chairs and brought them back out to the dungeon area. He set them out next to one another near the fuck table and then helped me as we wiped down all the equipment and made sure everything was clean and sanitized.

After we were done, he brought out a box and opened it. Inside were some banners that were folded up. One was black with silver trim and said, 'Graduation Day'. We hung this on one wall horizontally. The other four were vertical banners that were red, yellow, green, and black and trimmed in silver as well. These were hung on the wall next to the door we used to enter beside where our portraits hung. As the banners unrolled, I noticed that they had names on them in black marker.

"Part of the graduation is adding your name to your colored banner," Bo said as he helped me to hang the red one. "If a master is here to collar you, they will add their name to the black banner with a silver pen."

"Pretty cool!" I said as we finished hanging the rest of the banners.

There were five names listed on the red banner, ending in Dan. The yellow banner also had five names with Ryan and Johnny the most recent ones added. The green banner had four names listed ending with Nick. Nine names were listed on the black banner.

"Sir has had quite a lot of graduates," I said as I looked over the names.

"Indeed," Bo said as he reached out and touched the green banner. "It won't be long till I will be up here as well."

"Anything else we need to do?" I asked.

"The bags!" Bo said with a smile.

He led me back into the isolation room and we opened the bags that had our names on them. Inside mine was a nice black leather jock with yellow trim and stripes on the front. It had five snaps along the top, two down the side, and one at the bottom that held a detachable cover piece. Beneath this was a flat piece with an opening that I would be able to put my nub through and it had two small straps on either side of the hole that could attach to the base ring of my cage. Along the back of the waist, it said 'Boy Matt', and the detachable cover said 'Chastity Boy' near the top. Bo had a similar one that was green with his name. Also in the bag were two colored leather armbands and ankle bands.

"You will be able to keep everything in the bag once you graduate," Bo said. "Until then, it's your uniform for the graduation of your brothers and you will return it to Sir at the end of the ceremony."

"Nice!" I said.

We put on our jocks and arm and ankle bands and then we headed back into the dungeon area.

"Now, we wait," Bo said.

We walked over to our colored squares near the side of the wall and sat cross-legged on the floor and talked for a while. About 1:40 pm, the door beside us opened and Jay walked in.

"Hey, bro," Bo said looking up at him.

"Are you ready for your big day?" I asked.

Jay smiled back. "Yes! I am so nervous."

Jay walked past us and went into the isolation room and put on his jock and bands and then came out and sat next to us in his square.

"I barely slept last night," Jay said. "Master Jeff will be here to collar me!"

"That's awesome!" I said with a huge grin.

Bo reached over and gave him a big hug and had a tear fall down his face. "I am so happy for you bro!"

"So, are you moving down to Savannah?" I asked.

"Yup!" Jay said. Moving out later this month when my lease expires. Master Jeff has already arranged for the moving plans."

"Too cool," I said.

About five minutes to 2 pm, the sound of a bell could be heard coming from a speaker near the ceiling of the room.

"That's our cue boys," Jay said.

He got up on his knees and bowed his head and put his hands behind his back and we did the same. We sat there for several minutes and then heard footsteps coming downstairs. When the door opened, I saw two sets of bare feet come and stand in front of us.

"Rise," I heard the voice of John say.

When I got to my feet, I saw John to my left and Jeff was next to him. John was in his leather chaps and black leather jock and Jeff was in a similar jock as well. They both wore leather vests that said Master down one side and had a leather flag on the other. We stood there at attention with our hands behind our backs for about a minute before John spoke again.

"Boy Jay," he said. "You have completed a year in my service. In that time, you have grown to become a well-trained and experienced sub. Are you ready to proceed to the next step in your journey?"

"Yes, Sir I am," Jay said.

"Step forward," John said.

Jay took a step forward and John went over to the table and grabbed a blindfold which he placed over Jay's eyes. He then led Jay over to the side of the room where the cross was and bound his arms and legs to the X-shaped structure. Jeff walked over to the folding chairs and sat down while he was doing so.

"As part of your service agreement, you have agreed to be in chastity," John said. "You have done so of your own free will as a way to show your status as a sub. You have embraced your new role as the instrument of pleasure for dominant men and your cage is a symbol of this commitment. You have now completed your six-month lock-up session and earned a release."

John reached down and removed the detachable portion of Jay's jock and then handed the piece to Jeff. He then walked over and got the key to the security screw and removed it from Jay's device and took the cage and base ring off his nub and balls which he also handed to Jeff.

"Your brothers have been your support base through your journey, and they will now be called upon," John said. "Boys Bo and Matt, please come forward."

We both stepped out of our spots and walked over to the bound and blindfolded Jay and stood in front of him.

"What is the service creed boys?" John asked.

We all spoke up as one in answer. "I am a sub in training under the supervision of Sir John. My goal is to serve men in the best way I can and derive pleasure from that service. My chastity cage and collar are a symbol of that service and I desire one day to be in permanent chastity and receive my formal graduation collar as proof of my commitment."

"Do you, Boy Jay, now wish to take the next step in your journey and enter into permanent chastity and receive your formal collar?" John asked.

"Yes, Sir," Jay said.

"Do you understand the commitment this will entail, and do you do this of your own free will?"

"Yes, Sir."

"Boy Bo," John said. "As Jay's sub brother, I will task you with providing Jay with the last manual release he will receive before his permanent cage is installed. Are you willing to do this?"

"Yes, Sir," Bo replied.

"Boy Jay," John said. "I will ask one final time. Do you agree to submit to one last manual release from your sub brother before your permanent cage is installed?

"I do, Sir," Jay replied.

"Boy Bo, please step forward," John said.

Bo got down in front of Jay and reached out and took his balls in his hand. Jay's legs shook a bit and his nub started to stir and began to grow in front of him. He placed the head into his mouth and Jay gasped a bit as Bo started to use his hands to manipulate his swelling shaft.

Bo was careful not to give him a blow job like he would give a dom. He was just jacking his shaft and placing the head in his mouth to catch anything that came out. Jay was starting to squirm from the sensation and it only took a minute before his balls released their stored seed.

"Oh Fuck!" Jay gasped as his body shook.

Standing there watching him, I could only imagine the thoughts going through his mind and the sensations he was feeling. I looked down and saw that Bo had his mouth closed and looked to be holding Jay's load in his mouth.

"Boy Matt, step forward," John said.

I walked over to where Bo was, and he reached out and pulled me close and brought his lips to mine, and shared Jay's cum with me. It was a pretty large load and a bit of it slipped out and dribbled on my beard which Bo licked clean. I was surprised and found it a very sensual experience and felt my nub swell in its cage as I tasted Jay's load for the first time and swallowed it. Bo then pointed to Jay's nub and I used my mouth to clean it of some lingering dribbles of cum.

After we were done, we stepped back, and John directed us back over to the wall to our colored squares where we stood at attention with our hands behind our backs. While we did so, Jeff stood and walked over to stand next to John.

"Boy Jay," John said. "Master Jeff has expressed interest in collaring you and taking you into his home as his sub. Do you accept his offer?"

"Yes, Sir," Jay replied.

"Master Jeff, please install his permanent cage," John said.

Jeff walked over and bent down and reinstalled the base ring on Jay and then slid the cage portion over his nub and installed the security screw. He then reattached the front portion of his jock and removed Jay's blindfold and stepped back. Jay blinked a few times and then looked at the two men.

"You will now receive your formal collar," John said.

Jeff reached up and unlocked Jay's collar and removed the silver tag. He then grabbed a small jar and brought it over to John.

"Inside this jar is your formal tag showing your status as a collared, chastity sub," John said. "It sits within five collected loads of Master Jeff which have marked it."

John held the jar and Jeff reached in and pulled a gold tag from the milky white fluids. On the tag, it read 'Boy Jay / CHASTITY SUB / Collared by Sir Jeff'. Jeff put the tag on Jay's collar and reinstalled his lock.

John grabbed a shot glass from the table and poured the vodka that was in it and swirled the jar till it was mixed. He then handed it to Jeff who brought it over to the bound Jay and tipped it into Jay's mouth until he had swallowed it all completely. He then gave Jay a long kiss and then stepped away.

"Boy Jay," John said. "With the acceptance of your collar, you have completed your service to me and are no longer my sub. You are now under the service of Master Jeff. Master Jeff will now consummate the relationship."

John stepped back and turned to sit down in one of the folding chairs. As he did so, Jeff reached up and released Jay's restraints and brought him over to the fuck bench. Jay got on it and Jeff got behind him and brought his face down into Jay's ass and began to tongue his hole.

I could see Jay closing his eyes and gripping the side of the bench from across the room and watched as Jeff lubed up his fingers and started to open Jay up. Jeff took off his jock and his cock was hard as a rock and he lubed it next and then pointed it at Jay's ass.

As Jeff mounted Jay from behind, Jay opened his eyes and gasped a bit. Jeff started to move slowly at first and then picked up the pace and was fucking him hard soon after. The bench was groaning a bit and moving slightly back and forth with the thrusts and Jay started to moan. I have to admit, I was swelled completely in my cage and dripping precum a bit as I watched, and Bo was as well.

After several minutes, Jeff started to pant and he shoved his cock into Jay. His load followed, shooting out to fill him deeply.

"That's my boy!" Jeff said loudly as Jay closed his eyes and bit his lip.

When Jeff came off his orgasm high, he slid out of Jay and grabbed a towel to wipe Jay's ass down a bit. He then got Jay off the bench and embraced him, and they kissed and made out a bit.

When they were done, Jay came over to where John was sitting, and John stood.

"Thank you Sir John for taking the time to train me," he said.

"You are welcome, boy," John said as he extended his hand with a smile to shake with Jay and then followed it with a hug.

Jay then came over to stand before us.

"I could not have done this without your support brothers," Jay said with a tear in his eye. "I love you both!"

He gave us hugs and a kiss and both Bo and I had a few tears of our own.

"The final task is to add your names to the banners of honor," John said to Jeff and Jay.

Jay signed his name at the bottom of the red banner and Jeff added his to the black banner.

"Jeff and Jay, please follow me upstairs for a meal that has been prepared in your honor," John said. "Boys, please stay to clean up the room and you may leave."

"Yes, Sir," Bo and I replied, and we watched the three of them pass by and head up the stairs.

Once they were gone, I relaxed and wiped my eyes.

"Well, that was amazing," I said.

"Yes, indeed," Bo said with a smile.

We went around the room and gathered up the materials that were set out and wiped down the cross and bench. We then took down the banners and put them away and took off our jocks and arm and ankle bands and put them back in the bags with our names on them.

"Well, that is it," Bo said. "You want to go out for a drink?"

"That sounds like a wonderful idea bubba," I said, and we headed for the side door to dress and leave.

The next day, Sunday afternoon, I was at John's house kneeling in my spot as usual for my one-on-one. When he came down, he stood in front of me and told me to stand at attention.

"How are you today, boy?" he asked.

"I'm ok, Sir," I said.

"You did well at Jay's graduation," John said as he crossed his hands over his chest. "I will be having the new boy that will replace him come over on Tuesday for his initiation ceremony. That means that when you come tomorrow for cleaning, you will be doing some different duties and doubling up."

"I understand, Sir," I replied.

"Bo will be moving up to cleaning the second floor of the house and I will be busy showing him specific things he will need to do," John said. "You will need to clean the first floor and then move down here, and I will have him come down to help you after."

"I understand," I said.

"You have now completed three months in chastity and are about to start your final six-month session before you decide to move into permanent chastity," John said. "Have you had any issues I need to be aware of with the device?"

"No, Sir," I replied.

"Good," John said.

He reached down and grabbed my caged nub and inspected it, putting his fingers through the bars and feeling my balls.

"We have the right base ring size still," he said, "but I think you are now ready for the smallest cage size. I will install that after your manual release."

"Thank you, Sir," I replied.

"Unfortunately, I am very busy with work today, so this will not be a long session," John said.

He turned and walked over to the counter to grab the key to remove the security screw to my device and then grabbed a blindfold as well. He put the blindfold on me and then brought a chair over and sat in front of me. I felt him removing the screw and the cage came away after. He pulled on my nub and twisted it in his hand as he inspected it to see if there were any sores. I then heard the sound of lube squishing between his fingers and hand and I felt him grab my nub.

I instantly got hard after three months in the cage and gasped a bit. My legs shook a little as he started to stroke back and forth with his hand, and I felt the lid of a glass briefly touch my head. I assumed he was holding that with his other hand to catch any emissions.

It only took about sixty seconds for the feeling of an orgasm to start to build in my balls. I bit my lip and tried to maintain my stance as my nub soon exploded cum. I felt the head of my nub being forced into the glass and heard the 'plop' sound as a few streams of cum hit the side and ran down to the bottom of it. I squeezed my ass a bit as

I felt him milk the last bots out of my nub and then he let go and it hung there going soft above the glass.

After a few minutes, I felt a cold washcloth run over my nub and clean it up, and then the new smaller cage went on and I felt him secure it in place with a screw. When he removed my blindfold, I saw him standing in front of me and I looked down at my new cage. It was small enough that only my head was barely showing. I had no hint of a shaft anymore. It was as small as Bo's cage was.

"Thank you, Sir!" I replied after taking a deep breath.

"You are welcome, boy," John said as he poured a shot of vodka in the glass and swirled it around with the cum load before feeding it to me. "This will be your final cage that you will wear under my service. You may keep it after you graduate."

"Thank you, Sir," I replied.

"Now, get on your knees and take my load," he said.

I got down before him and sucked on his cock until it was exploding in my mouth. He then patted my head and told me that I could leave, and he would see me tomorrow for our cleaning day.

CHAPTER TWENTY-FOUR

Max's Initiation

John had told us to be at his house at 7 pm on the Tuesday evening after Jay's graduation to prepare to meet the sub that would replace him. I figured this might be Max, but I was not one hundred percent sure. When I arrived and started to undress in the hall, though, I noticed that Jay's name had been removed from the red bin and Max's was there in its place. Bo walked in the door as I was finishing stripping and putting my clothes away.

"Looks like Max will be the new sub," I replied, pointing at the bin name tag.

"Nice!" Bo replied. "I think he will be a good fit."

"So, how does it feel to be senior sub now?" I asked with a smile.

"Well," Bo said as he took his shoes and socks off, "the biggest thing is that it reminds me I am only three months from graduating myself. It is kinda scary."

"Do you want to try to meet up with Max after his initiation into the program tonight?" I asked.

Bo had taken his shirt off and was unbuckling his pants. "Yeah, I would like to, but didn't you say he is living with roommates?"

"Last I heard, yes," I replied. "Maybe we should leave him a note in his bin after we have to leave and ask him to text us when he is done. I don't mind having him over at my place if he's up for that."

"Yeah, that sounds like a plan," Bo said as he took his underwear off and adjusted his balls a bit in the cage.

After we both had our bins closed and locked, we walked into the dungeon. John was already inside getting the room set up and had put the contract for Max to sign out on the table as well. He was in his black leather chaps and black and blue leather-trimmed jock and looked to be almost ready.

"Hello boys," John said, looking over at us.

"Hello Sir!" we replied.

"I know you have been through this once before Bo, but do you have any questions, Matt?" he asked me.

"No Sir," I replied. "I remember my ceremony well. I'm ready."

"Good deal," John said. "I told Max to arrive at precisely 7:15 pm. I will have him wait in the hall for fifteen minutes before I go in to greet him to allow time for him to prepare himself. I will have you two kneeling in your spots when he comes in and we will go from there."

"That sounds good, Sir," Bo said. "We were interested in maybe meeting up with him after he was done to talk and get him up to speed. Do you think you could pass along my phone number Sir?"

"I would be happy to boy," John said. "I'll be sure he texts you before he leaves."

"Thank you, Sir!" Bo said.

"Please go ahead and sit and wait quietly," John said. "When I snap my fingers, please assume a kneeling position with your heads bowed and hands behind your backs."

"Yes, Sir," we replied as we sat down on the floor in our spots.

John opened the door to the hall and placed a piece of paper on top of Max's bin with the code to open it and then returned to the dungeon, closing the door behind him. He then set out a pen next to the paperwork on the table and went to a drawer and pulled out a red and black chainmail collar and a small lock, which he placed in a box and also set on the table.

Once he glanced around and felt like things were set, he sat down in the chair next to the table. A few minutes later, we heard the outside door open and close and someone in the hall. John snapped his fingers, and we assumed our kneeling position. He then got up quietly and stood in the room near the door.

We heard the rustling of someone undressing and then the door to a bin opening and closing a short time later, then it was silent. For fifteen minutes, we knelt on the floor in our spots, without saying a word. John stood motionless with his arms crossed over his chest as well, until the clock on the wall showed 7:30 pm. He then moved forward and opened the door to the hall beside us.

"You may look up, boy," we heard him say. "Follow me into the dungeon and stand at attention with your hands behind your back after we enter."

"Yes, Sir," was the response.

I saw John's bare feet walk by and then the furry feet of Max appeared next to me.

"I have the cameras on in here boy to record your first day under my service, so please act accordingly," John said, closing the door.

"Yes, Sir," was the reply from Max.

"Please step to your right and kneel in front of the table," John said.

I saw Max's feet turn and move off and then heard him kneel on the floor. I then heard the chair drag along the floor a bit as John moved it back to sit down. John asked Max to review the contract on the table and after he gave him some time to read it all, he asked if there were any additional questions. When he heard none, John had Max sign the service contract and the addendum.

We heard John move around and place the collar around Max's neck next and then he told him to stand up and walk over to the far side of the room. John then found a good fitting chastity device and locked it around Max's nub. I could still picture everything that went on when I went through my initiation and wondered how Max was feeling at this point.

"And with that, you are now officially one of my boys," John said to Max. "Please go over to the wall and kneel in the red square with your hands behind your back and your head bowed like your sub brothers."

Max came over to us and knelt in his spot and I heard John closing drawers and putting some things away. He then came over and I saw his feet standing in front of us.

"Boys, please rise and face me," John said.

We all stood and then John said, "Bo, come forward and introduce yourself."

Bo stepped forward and turned to face Max and said, "My name is boy Bo. I am your sub brother and have been in training under Sir for nine months." He then returned to where he was standing before.

John then looked at me. "Matt, please come forward and introduce yourself."

I stepped forward and turned to face Max and said, "My name is boy Matt. I am your sub brother and have been in training under Sir for six months." I then returned to where I was standing before.

"Finally, Max, please come forward and introduce yourself," John said.

Max stepped forward and turned to face us and smiled a bit. "My name is boy Max. I am your sub brother, and this is my first day training under Sir." He then returned to his original position.

"Well done Max," John replied. "Bo and Matt here will indeed be your sub brothers. Think of them as your family. I will give you their contact information before you leave tonight. Bo here is your elder brother. He has asked that you text him as soon as you are finished here. Is that understood?"

"Yes, Sir," came the reply from Max.

"You will find them an excellent source of information on what I expect and how to behave. You will have tasks that you will perform with them and I expect you to support them as they support you," John added.

"Yes, Sir," Max replied.

"Bo and Matt," John said. "Please recite the creed for Max."

Bo and I immediately responded. "I am a sub in training under the supervision of Sir John. My goal is to serve men in the best way I can and derive pleasure from that service. My chastity cage and collar are a symbol of that service and I desire one day to be in permanent chastity and receive my formal graduation collar as proof of my commitment."

"Well done as usual boys," John replied. "You may both leave now."

I turned and gave Max a quick wink as I passed by and went into the hall. Bo followed me and closed the door behind us.

"Do you just want to follow me over to my place Bo?" I whispered.

"Yeah," Bo replied quietly as he grabbed his clothes out of his bin, "that sounds like a plan."

After we got back to my apartment and stripped down, I grabbed us both drinks and we sat down in the living room to play video games for a while. We had just got into playing one game when Bo's phone dinged.

"It's Max," Bo replied. "I'll give him your address and tell him to come over."

"Good deal!" I replied.

About fifteen minutes later we heard a knock on the door. I opened it to find Max staring back at me with a smile and his shiny new collar and tag around his neck.

"Good to see you brother!" I said with a smile and I let him in.

Bo and I hugged him and I asked if he wanted a drink.

"I'm ok," Max replied.

"Go ahead and strip down," Bo said. "You need to get used to doing that."

"Oh right!" Max said as he pulled his clothes off and put them beside the door.

When he bent over to take his pants off, I noticed that the hair on his ass was crusted and matted and he had a large butt plug inserted in him.

"How was your first breeding by Sir?" I asked with a grin.

"It was so hot," Max said, reaching back to feel the plug in his ass. "I will say that this cage is well made, though. It fits a lot better than the one Kenny had got for me."

"Yeah, I have never had an issue with mine," Bo said.

"I noticed you both have smaller cage lengths than I do, though," Max replied. "Do you always start with a larger one?"

"Yes," I replied. "Sir will move you down to smaller cages over time. I just got my new, smaller cage Sunday when I started my six-month chastity session."

"That seems like such a long time to be locked up," Max said, grabbing his cage.

"You will work your way up to it," Bo said. "Don't be too freaked out."

"Yeah," I said. "Besides, that cage looks great on you!"

"Thanks," Max said with a blush. "I can't wait to show Sir Kenny."

"You do need to trim a bit," Bo said as he pointed at Max's crotch.

"Come with me, Max," I said. "I'll take you back to my bathroom and I'll get you fixed up."

Max followed me back into my bathroom and I got my trimmer out and went to work knocking back some of Max's thick hair around his crotch and then trimmed his beard back a bit as well. I then gave him some pointers on lubricating the base ring and how to deal with night erection attempts and any pain he might encounter. I also showed him the support strap that Bo had told me about that I wore a lot to help support the cage and we ordered one for him as well. After we were done, I walked back into the living room and Max waddled behind with his plug moving a bit in his ass.

Max sat down next to Bo and he and I gave him the rundown on the cleaning days and what to expect. We talked about some of the parties John had in the past and the basic expectations he had of us. Max was very inquisitive and asked a lot of questions and took notes on his phone as well.

"This has been all a whirlwind of an evening," Max said after there was a break in the conversation. "I am trying to keep everything straight."

"It's ok, Max," Bo said, reaching over to put his arm around Max's shoulders. "We are here to help you. If you ever have questions, just text one of us or call us to ask."

"Be sure to monitor your email as well," I said. "Sir will keep in pretty much daily contact with you at first."

"Yeah, he already emailed me on the way to your apartment," Max said. "I am supposed to meet with Master Jack who collared some boys he trained."

"Jack is awesome," Bo replied. "He collared Johnny, who was my sub brother before Matt here. He also collared Ryan, who preceded Johnny."

"He's a pretty hot guy," I replied with a wink to Max. "He's a tall, older daddy bear with a nice belly and an impressive package as well."

"You'll have a good time," Bo said with a smile. "But be sure that you prepare for your interview. You will probably be interviewing both Ryan and Johnny in addition to Jack."

"I will," Max said with a grin. "But, if it's ok with you two, I want to go see Sir Kenny before it gets too late. I promised I would let him know how the initiation went."

"Absolutely!" I replied as we all stood up.

I gave Max a hug and Bo did as well and then Max got dressed and left.

"I think I better hit the road as well, bubba," Bo said as he turned and gave me a quick kiss and a big hug. "See ya, tomorrow bro."

"Drive safe," I replied.

Wednesday evening after work, I was over at John's house as usual. Bo and I had arrived a little early and we were waiting on our knees in our spots when we heard John come down the staircase. As he walked into the dungeon area, we heard the door open in the entrance hall and the sound of Max rapidly trying to undress and put his things in his bin. He opened the door shortly after and John was staring at him when he came in. He was not pleased.

"You are late, Max," John said with a scowl.

"I am sorry, Sir," Max said as he stood and bowed his head. "I lost track of time."

"I don't want to hear excuses, boy," John replied. "Kneel in your spot."

Max hurriedly came over and knelt in his square on the floor.

"I know you are a new boy, but there are certain rules that are more important to me than others and punctuality is one of them," John said with a stern tone.

"I am sorry, Sir," Max said, with some hesitation in his voice. "I have no excuse."

"And I did not ask for any excuses, boy," John replied. "All three of you stand now!"

I was a bit concerned at this point, as I had never seen John upset before. Up to this point, I had done my best to follow all the rules and had never found myself afoul of him. We all stood and Bo and I put our hands behind our backs and Max followed suit.

"Come with me, Max," John replied.

Max left the spot where he was standing and followed John over to the fuck bench. John had him get on it and he strapped his legs and arms down. We then watched John cross the room and grab a large paddle from the wall. Max had turned his head to see where John was going, and you could see the concern in his face. John returned and stood behind Max's exposed ass.

"As punishment for being late, you will receive three swings from the paddle," John replied. "An additional swing will be added for trying to offer an excuse. When a swing has been delivered, I expect you to loudly thank me for your punishment. Is this understood boy?"

"Yes," Max said timidly.

"What was that boy?" John asked Max.

"Yes, Sir!" Max replied louder.

"I am adding another swing for not addressing me properly and not speaking up," John said. "Prepare yourself, boy."

Bo and I watched as John's arm arched back and the paddle came swinging down and hit Max's ass with a loud smack. Max yelped in response but immediately spoke up loudly.

"Thank you, Sir!" he replied.

The remaining four swings followed in the same way. When the final swing of the paddle was administered, we heard Max reply "thank you, Sir" once more and then a slight sob. John ran his hand over Max's ass. We could see it was slightly red from across the room. He then undid the restraints and had Max stand up and face him.

"Kenny has told me that you can be forgetful, and your punctuality is not the best," John said. "This is not a good start to your service to me. This is something you need to work on. When you are late, you are disrespecting the time of others."

"I understand, Sir," Max said, with tears running down his cheeks.

John reached up and wiped his face and put his hand on Max's shoulder.

"The punishment was delivered, and I consider the matter closed," John said. "Take a deep breath and go and stand next to your sub brothers."

Max bowed his head a bit and then turned and came back over to where we were and stood in his spot.

"Bo," John said after coming over and standing in front of us. "Please show Max the areas he will be responsible for cleaning today and how things work at the house. When you are done, you can come upstairs to my office so I can discuss a few things with you before you start your duties."

"Yes, Sir," Bo replied.

John then turned and left the room and went back upstairs. When the door closed behind him, we relaxed a bit and Bo turned to Max and hugged him.

"Are you ok, bro?" Bo asked.

Max hugged Bo back and then wiped his eyes.

"I'm ok," Max replied. "I'm just upset with myself more than anything. He is right. Sir Kenny has been on me about my forgetfulness and time management."

"We can help with that," I replied, going over to hug Max as well. "You just need to make a conscious effort to be early and set yourself alarms."

"You are right," Max said as he rubbed his sore ass. "It is a learning experience."

"Well, let's get started," Bo said to Max. "We have a lot to show you before we get started cleaning."

Max followed Bo and me over to the isolation room and we showed him where the duties were posted, where to find the cleaning supplies, and a basic rundown of what John expected of his subs. Max took over my duties that I had previously, and I started cleaning different rooms. Bo, as senior sub, was now responsible for the cleaning on the second floor.

"You're moving on up!" I grinned at Bo.

"I'm finally getting a piece of that pie!" Bo replied, with a laugh.

Max looked so confused at both of us and I rolled my eyes and explained the reference before we headed out to start our duties.

After I was done, I came downstairs to help Max finish wiping down the surfaces in the dungeon area. We were just finishing when Bo came down the staircase.

"You all done, Bo?" I asked.

"Yes, indeed," Bo replied. "That was the first time I have ever been in his office upstairs."

"I haven't been in there myself," I replied.

"Well, you will be up there soon enough," Bo said. "But I need to get going as I have some things to do before bed tonight. Are you ok closing up, or should I stay?"

"Max and I can handle it, bro," I replied. "Have a good evening."

Bo waved his hand and then left through the hallway door. I went back into the isolation room where Max was putting his cleaning supplies away. His furry ass had returned to a normal color and his cage was dangling between his legs as he bent down to put some rags away.

"How is the cage working out?" I asked him as he stood and turned towards me.

"So far, so good," Max said. "I'm still having trouble with night erections, though."

"Those will get better over time," I replied. "Your body just needs to adjust. The main thing is that you don't have any pain in the ring or any sores developing."

"Nothing like that," Max replied.

"That's good," I said, with a smile. "When do you go to see Sir Jack and his subs?"

"Tomorrow," Max replied.

"Be sure to set yourself an alarm on your phone and get there early!" I said.

"Oh, I plan on setting one as soon as we are done here," Max said.

I came over and gave him a big bear hug one more time and then put my arm around him.

"You'll get there, bro," I said.

Max laid his head on my chest and rubbed my belly.

"Thanks," Max said.

CHAPTER TWENTY-FIVE

My Work Trip

The week after Max was initiated, I was called into my boss's office. I was a little nervous as I did not talk to Richard a lot and he had a pretty stern demeanor.

"Come in, Matt," Richard said as I knocked on the side of his open door.

"What did you want to see me about?" I asked.

"We have a bit of an issue I am hoping you can help me with," he replied. "Jim was supposed to be flying to Denver this week to present the proposal you worked on for X Corp."

I knew Jim well. He and I worked on a team of individuals that had drafted a technology proposal for the start-up. We were bidding to handle their IT needs and support and we had been working on an analysis of their needs and how we could step in to help.

"Did something happen?" I asked.

"His wife just called me and told me that he had to be rushed in for an emergency appendectomy earlier today," Richard replied.

"Yikes!" I said. "Is he ok?"

"Well, they found out it had burst, and it was touch-and-go for a while there, but they think he will be ok," Richard replied. "The big issue is that he will not be able to present the proposal. Would you be able to step in and do it for us?"

"I'd be happy to," I replied.

"Good," Richard said. "You'll be flying out Thursday morning and coming back Saturday afternoon. They will expect you to have dinner Thursday night with a few of the X Corp team members and you will present on Friday. I'll have Betty arrange the travel for you. Please talk to your team and get up to speed on anything you might have questions about."

"Thanks, Sir!" I replied as I turned to leave.

As I was walking down the hall back to my office, I was going through a myriad of questions that I wanted to address to prepare. I reached down to scratch my leg and my hand hit my cage under my pants and then I panicked. How was I going to get on a plane with this metal cage?

When I got back to my office, I texted John and let him know what was going on. He told me not to worry and that we could discuss it when I was over for cleaning. He assured me that this was not something new for his subs and he had a solution.

So, on Wednesday, after I was done with my duties and my sub brothers had left, John came downstairs to the dungeon area to talk to me.

"So, where will you be going, boy?" he asked as he went over to a cabinet against the wall.

"Denver, Sir," I replied. "I'll be taking over for a colleague of mine that got sick."

"And I am assuming you have never flown with a chastity cage on," he said as he rummaged through some drawers.

"No, Sir," I said. "I was not aware you would be able to wear one, given security."

John found the item that he was looking for and turned around to look at me. "You will be fine. Chastity devices are considered 'religious and cultural wear' and the TSA should allow you through. However, you should be aware that you will likely set off the metal detector or show up on a scanner."

In his hand, John had a small plastic box. He took the key that would remove my security screw and placed it in the box. When the lid closed, there was a small opening that he put a plastic lock through that was numbered and he closed and locked it. He then handed it to me.

"This plastic lock is numbered and cannot be relocked if removed," John said. "In this way, I will know if you have tried to access the key within. You should pack this in your carry-on bag. If they require you to remove your device for any reason, break the plastic lock and remove the key to do so. However, you should immediately text me if this occurs."

"I understand," I replied.

"You may be required to have a pat-down and in rare instances, they may move you to a private room, but I have never had one of my subs told they needed to remove it," John said.

"Ok, Sir," I said.

"Text me when you land tomorrow and let me know if you ran into any issues," John added.

The next morning, I was rushing to get ready for my flight. I had packed the night before, but I still had some last-minute things to do. When I finally put my clothes on and headed out the door, I didn't have much time to spare.

The trip to the airport on the south side of the city took about thirty minutes to reach. I parked in the parking deck and headed into the airport a little nervous about how this was going to go with my cage. I got my luggage checked and then headed to the security checkpoint.

When it was my turn, I walked up to the TSA agent and he checked my ID and my ticket and then I went to the table to put my CPAP device through the x-ray machine as well as my carry-on bag. They were putting people through the body scanners, so after I removed my shoes and belt, I walked into the booth and raised my hands and the device scanned me.

When I walked through to the other side, the image on the screen showed my body and two large yellow squares over my crotch. A large man in a TSA uniform looked at me.

"Do you have any metal objects in your pockets or jewelry on, Sir?" he asked.

"I do have something on down there," I said quietly and pointed to my crotch.

"Come over here, Sir," he replied, and he got another man to come over.

"What are you wearing, Sir," the second man asked me as we moved off to the side.

"It's a chastity device," I said nervously.

"Very well," he said. "Stand and spread your legs."

I felt him pat down each leg and then he used the back of his hand to move up and it bumped the metal in the cage. He then stood up.

"You can move on through," he replied.

I took a giant breath in and let it out and then grabbed my things to head for the plane.

I landed in the early afternoon and after I got my things, I picked up my rental car and drove over to my hotel. It was a nice day out and the mountains were beautiful in the background. We have mountains in Georgia, but they would be little more than hills compared to the Rockies. After checking in, I put my things down and collapsed on the bed, and texted John to let him know that everything went well.

"Are you checked into your room?" he texted me back.

"Yes, Sir," I replied.

"No clothes allowed if you are there by yourself," he said.

"Understood, Sir," I texted back, and I got undressed and then sat back on the bed.

I had several hours to kill before I had to meet up with the potential clients for dinner, so I opened up a couple of cruising apps and browsed to see who was around. Anytime you are new in an area, you get a lot of attention. I was the 'new meat' as it were. Most of the guys that messaged me did not keep the conversation going or were not interested when they found out I was not a top. However, one man did catch my eye.

His profile picture was just his chest and I normally do not respond to headless profiles, but he quickly added a picture of himself after he initially messaged me. He was clean-shaven and slightly overweight. He had a receding hairline and ash-colored hair. But, what got my attention was his private pictures. His cock was massive. It looked to be as thick as a beer can and there was proof in a later picture where he had it next to a can of Coors.

"What brings you to town, boy?" he asked me.

"Work trip, Sir," I replied. "I am just in town tonight and tomorrow."

"Show me that ass," he said.

I sent him a picture of me kneeling on the floor with my ass up in the air. My cage was dangling prominently beneath me as well.

"I love a hairy ass, boy," he said. "How long have you been in chastity?"

"Since March," I replied. "I have been training under a dom and he has been working me up to longer and longer periods in the device."

"Are you wearing it now?" he asked.

"Yes Sir," I replied. "I flew with it on."

"That's hot," he said. "I would love for you to service me."

"When are you free," I asked.

"I am right now," he replied. "Are you in a hotel?"

"Yes Sir," I replied. "I would be honored to service you today if you want to come over."

"Send me the address, boy," he replied. "I'll be right over."

After texting the location of the hotel to him and my room number, I got into the shower and cleaned myself out with the travel douche that I had with me and then cleaned the rest of my body of the sweat I had built up from travel. I was just walking to the bed again when I heard a knock on the door.

I walked over and looked through the peephole and saw that it was him. When I opened the door, he looked me over from head to toe and then reached over and felt my cage.

"You've got some full balls there, boy," he replied in a deep voice as he closed the door behind him.

His eyes were dark blue, and he stared at me intensely for a moment before using his hands to push me to my knees. He then unbuckled his belt and his pants fell, revealing his stiffening cock under his belly. I reached out and took it in one hand and tried to get it into my mouth, but it was so thick that I could only get partway down it.

He reached around and grabbed my head and tried to force me down farther, but I could not take it and I started to choke. He pulled me off a bit, but then forced me down again till I gagged.

"You better get used to this cock, boy," he replied, looking down at me. "You got me over here, so I'm using you as I see fit."

He then continued to force his cock down my throat and the constant gagging and coughing were making me a bit nauseous. Spit was flowing out of my mouth and down my beard and was dripping on the floor as well.

He pulled his shirt off and rubbed his belly and then moved me over to the bed and bent me over it. He knelt and put his face in my ass, and I felt his tongue start to explore my hole. I was groaning in pleasure and my nub started to leak and it ran down the side of the bed sheets.

He pulled his face out and replaced it with his large finger and I felt him move in and out of my hole. My legs wobbled a bit as he forced it in and out and then moved to put two then three fingers in me. As he was doing so, he was stroking his fat cock with his other hand and preparing for his assault.

I felt him move up and start to mount me next. He placed both legs on either side of my body and pointed his cock towards my hole. When the head started to go in, I gasped loudly and clenched my ass shut. He smacked my ass hard with one hand in response.

"Open up, boy!" he replied forcefully.

I took a deep breath in and tried to relax, but as he started to enter me, it was taking all I could muster not to cry out. It felt like he was ripping me in two.

When he finally got all the way in, I felt like I was impaled by a tree trunk. I felt his belly on my ass and he leaned down a bit and rocked his cock back and forth a bit to let me try to adjust as much as I could.

"Here it comes, boy," he replied as he started to pull out and then push back in again.

As he started to fuck me, I grabbed the pillow in front of me and bit down hard on it. He reached down and grabbed my waist to hold me still and started to pick up the pace and use me for all I was worth.

I am not going to lie, it was painful. I was doing everything I could to not cry out and tell him to stop. I concentrated on my breathing and tried to think of anything other than the massive dick that was testing my limits.

He started to fuck faster, and the sensation overload kicked into me and the pain lessened. I started to feel his belly slide around on me as he began to sweat a bit and he gripped my waist hard and started to grunt louder and louder. The bed started to move and creek and he pounded away.

"Fuck, boy," he said as he breathed hard. "Are you ready for my load?"

"Fill me up, Sir!" I yelled.

He grunted loudly and shoved his cock deep inside me. I felt every pulse of his cock as it moved within me and he laid down on top of me and I felt his chest move up and down as he caught his breath. He nibbled my neck a bit and then lifted himself off me and slid out.

I felt like my hole was gaping. I felt his cum run down my leg and he smacked my ass a few times as he caught his footing.

"That's a well-fucked ass," he said, reaching down to put his thumb in my hole and feel his load.

He reached down and felt my cage and noticed that cum was running out of my nub as well.

"Looks like I fucked a load out of those full balls too!" he said with a laugh.

I was trying to move and get up and was concentrating on how sore my ass was and had not even noticed. When I got to my feet, I noticed the cum running out of my nub and it was all over the side of the bed.

"That you did, Sir!" I said with a smile.

He grabbed a towel from my bathroom and wiped his sweat away and then tossed it on the bed. He had me get down on my knees and clean the cum and ass off his cock as well before he got dressed.

"Thanks for that, boy," he replied as he slid his shoes on to go. "Enjoy your trip here."

He waved at me as the door closed behind him and I smiled back. After he was gone, I reached around and felt my ass. Cum was still running down my leg and there was a little red in it as well. I decided to go take another shower and clean up again and then take a quick nap before dinner. I knew for sure I would be walking funny the rest of the night, though.

The dinner that evening went, well as did the presentation the next day. The clients were impressed with our services and cost analysis and I ended up securing the contract with them. I was exhausted after a long day and ended up going to bed early that night. The next day, I packed up and headed back to the airport to drop the car off and catch my flight home.

After I got my luggage checked, I headed back to the security checkpoint. As in Atlanta, I showed them my identification and ticket and then headed back to take my shoes and belt off before screening. This time, they were using a metal detector. As I went through, the device went off.

"Is there anything in your pockets, Sir?" the TSA agent asked me.

"No, Sir," I replied, and he waved me through again.

The device went off again and before I could explain, he had me move over to the side and another man came over.

"Is there anything in your pockets, Sir?" he asked me.

"No," I replied. "Though I am sure I know what is setting it off."

"What is that?" he asked.

"My chastity device," I replied.

"Your what?" he asked with an inquisitive look.

"I'm wearing a metal cage on my genitals," I replied, as my cheeks started to redden from embarrassment.

"Come with me," he replied.

He led me around to a private area and then told me to drop my pants. He patted around my socks and moved up and then let the back of his hand move around my crotch area.

"I'm afraid you will have to pull your waistband back and let me see the device," he said.

I was mortified at this point with my pants around my ankles, but I pulled the waistband to my underwear forward and he took a quick look at my cage.

"Are you wearing that of your own free will?" he asked.

"Yes, Sir," I replied.

He gave me a weird look and then waved his hands.

"You can dress and leave," he said.

I pulled my pants off and went back to the screening area to grab my things and then headed off to my gate. I was sure to text John when I had the chance to let him know how things went.

CHAPTER TWENTY-SIX

The Gay Pride Festival

In the United States, pride month is in June, but in Atlanta, it is held in October. There are several reasons for this. The main one was due to a drought one year that forced them to move the event to later to secure the space they needed from the city, but it was also linked to National Coming Out Day in October as well. In 2015, the event was held Saturday and Sunday, October 10 and 11.

The weekend before it occurred, I was down in the laundry washing clothes when Kenny appeared in the doorway in his shorts, t-shirt, and flip-flops. He looked a little sweaty and the front of his shirt and the area around the armpits were wet.

"Heya, Sir!" I said with a wave.

"Hey," Kenny replied with a smile. He then turned behind him and shouted out the door, "hurry it up, Max!"

As Kenny came in and sat down on the bench next to me, Max came running in with a large basket of clothes.

"Don't forget to separate the whites, boy!" Kenny said as Max put the basket in front of the washers.

"Hey bro," Max said with a smile as he caught his breath and wiped his forehead.

"Good to see you, Max," I replied.

Kenny turned slightly toward me and lifted and bent his leg and rested it on the bench. He took out a washcloth from his back pocket and wiped his forehead as well. I could smell the musk coming off him and it was obvious he had yet to shower today. I always loved the way he smelled, and the aroma sent my nub into swelling mode instantly.

"The boy here has been helping me do some cleaning around the house while I worked on my car," Kenny said.

"Anything wrong with it?" I asked as I adjusted my crotch to accommodate my shifting cage.

Kenny grinned as he saw me adjust, knowing the reason. "No, I just needed to change a worn belt. It did not take long, but the humidity is a bit of a bitch today. Got me all sweaty."

Kenny took the washcloth and ran it under his shirt to wipe down his chest and then he put it under his armpits to soak up the sweat. After he was done, he brought the cloth over to my face and held it over my nose and used his other hand to reach behind my head and force my face forward into it.

"Breathe it in, boy," Kenny said with a low voice. "I know you have been missing my scent."

I closed my eyes and inhaled deeply. It was slightly pungent but sent signals directly to my brain that had my nub leaking quickly. I reached up and replaced Kenny's hands with my own and held the cloth over my face and continued to take it in. Kenny brought one hand behind me and down the back of my pants and rubbed my ass and with the other, he started to feel my caged nub. The precum was flowing so much that it was starting to wet my pants and show through to the front.

"You got a nice little wet spot forming there, boy," Kenny said.

I pulled the cloth away from my face and looked down to see.

"Ugh, you know how to turn me on," I replied with a smile.

Kenny moved his hand up and rubbed my back and I leaned over and made out with him a bit.

"All done, Sir!" Max said as he turned on the machines that had Kenny's clothes in them.

Kenny broke away from me and turned to face Max.

"Come over here, boy," he said.

Max walked over and stood in front of Kenny and he pulled the front of Max's pants down to expose his nub and adjusted his balls a bit to get them to hang a little lower in the cage. He then brought his face forward and licked the bars and the head of Max's nub a bit, making Max's legs shutter and causing a drop of precum to form at the tip, which Kenny licked clean.

"Max here is about a week into his month-long chastity session and has been very horny," Kenny said with a smile as he pulled Max's pants back up over his cage. "He's been fun to tease."

"I know how it is," I replied, looking up at Max and winking. "You just have to exercise self-control."

"He's learning," Kenny said as he patted the side of Max's thigh. "He stayed with me last night so he could service me as a distraction. Working on getting him to cum from me fucking him. Not got there yet, but we will."

"Yes, Sir!" Max said as he smiled and looked down at Kenny.

He leaned down and kissed Kenny and then turned and then brought a chair over and sat in front of us.

"I want to thank you and Bo for being such good role models for him," Kenny said. "He has learned a lot and I have already noticed a great deal of improvement in his attitude and punctuality."

"He's been a great brother," I replied as I handed the washcloth back to Kenny and he put it back in his pocket.

"Are you going out next weekend for Pride?" Kenny asked me.

"I wanted to, but I have not made plans yet," I replied.

"You should come out with us," Kenny said. "I'm taking the boy out with me Saturday to the vendor fair in the park."

"That sounds like fun," I replied with a smile.

"See if Bo wants to come out as well," Kenny replied. "Would love to have all three of you over for a little fun before we go out."

"I can ask for sure!" I replied.

Max was smiling and pulled his shirt up to wipe his forehead. His furry belly was all matted from sweat and he looked tired.

"Have you ever been to pride here in Atlanta, Max?" I asked.

Max dropped the front of his shirt back down and looked at me. "Nope, this will be my first time."

"Oh, nice!" I said. "Well, this should be a good time, for sure. Are you going to try to brave the Eagle after?"

"Maybe," Kenny said. "It is always a freaking nightmare of people, but we might swing by. I love to show off my boy."

Kenny reached over and squeezed Max's knee and Max leaned over to kiss him again. The bell on my machine went off after and I got up and put my clean clothes in my basket. After I was done, I turned to face Kenny.

"I'll talk to Bo and get back to you later today, Sir," I said.

"Sounds good, boy," Kenny said with a smile and he lightly spanked my ass as I walked past.

I had texted Bo to see if he might be interested in going out with us next weekend, but I did not hear back from him till later in the afternoon when my phone rang.

"Hey Matt," Bo said. "I got your message. Do you mind if I swing by your place? We can discuss that, and I have some things I wanted to talk to you about."

"Sure bro!" I replied. "I'm just cleaning up a bit. Just come on in when you get here."

"Ok," he replied. "See you soon."

I had just turned off the vacuum and was putting it away when there was a knock on the door and Bo entered.

"It smells nice in here!" Bo said as he started to undress next to the door.

"I got a diffuser," I replied. "Pumpkin spice for October."

Bo laughed as he dropped his pants and underwear and folded them and placed them on top of his shirt and shoes. He adjusted his cage a bit and walked over to the kitchen, where I was grabbing a drink.

"You want a coke?" I asked.

"Sure!" Bo replied.

I grabbed one for him too and handed it to him and then opened the can and leaned on the counter.

"So, what is up?" I asked.

Bo opened his can up and took a drink and then swallowed.

"Well, first off, I would love to join you all at pride next weekend," he said. "We can work out the details later. But I needed to ask you about something first."

"Sure, go ahead," I said.

"As you know, I have started to see Todd a bit more," Bo said as he paused to take another sip. "I was over there yesterday evening after work and he invited me to stay the night and I just left there a bit ago."

"Your first sleepover!" I replied with a laugh.

"So many good things to tell you about that later," Bo said, smiling. "But Todd told me he has a place down in the Florida Keys that he goes to regularly and invited me to come with him."

"Nice!" I replied. "You should have fun."

"Well, we got to talking," Bo continued, "and Todd asked if you might be willing to come as well."

"He asked for me specifically?" I asked.

"Yes," Bo replied.

"What about Max?" I asked.

"No, he didn't ask about him," Bo said. "He likes you and would like to get to know you better. He also picked up from the way I talked about you that you and I were a little closer than just sub brothers."

I smiled a bit. I wondered if Bo had noticed that our relationship had grown a lot since we first met in March. I supported him as a sub brother, but I also liked him a lot. We got along really well, and I had to admit that I was attracted to him. But, I had never discussed my feelings, as I felt it was a bit awkward given our situation.

"I hope I was not out of line in saying so, but I've been picking up on things the past few months," Bo said.

"Well, I'm glad he is interested in getting to know me more," I replied. "I think he is very attractive and enjoyed servicing him. I'm also glad to hear you say that about us, though. I didn't want to be the first to say anything, but I do care for you a lot and I admit I might have been flirting a bit at times."

"Oh, I know," Bo said with a grin. "We have our responsibilities and duties to Sir and to each other as sub brothers, but I do really like you. In fact, you'd be someone I would love to explore a deeper relationship with within the confines of our current situation, that is."

"I'd like that," I replied.

"I discussed all this with Todd last night," Bo said. "He thought it might be a good idea for you to come down with us and talk about it more."

"When is he wanting to go?" I asked.

"The weekend after pride," Bo said.

"Ok," I said. "Count me in!"

"Yeah!" Bo exclaimed as he came over and gave me a big hug.

He pushed me into the counter a bit and then looked me in the eyes and then moved in to kiss me. I reached around and ran my hands down the fur on his back and felt my nub start to swell as he moved his tongue into my mouth and reached up to bring my head in closer. We made out for a bit until I started to feel liquid running down my leg. I pulled back and noticed it was a stream of precum from his nub. Bo blushed and I reached down and collected it with my fingers and ran it across his lips, which he licked clean.

"Well, I would say let's have some fun in bed, but that is not going to happen," I said with a grin.

"I know," Bo replied as he grasped his cage. "How about we play some video games instead?"

"Deal," I said as I leaned in to kiss him again.

We went over to the couch and sat down and played games for a few hours till he had to head home to get some chores done. After he left, I sat down and turned the TV off. I was glad we got things out in the open, but this was going to be complicated, for sure.

The following Saturday, Bo had made plans to meet me at my apartment at 10 am in the morning and we would walk over to Kenny's place together. I was surprised, therefore, when a knock came on my door at about 9:20 am. I walked over to the peephole and saw it was Bo and let him in.

"You are early!" I replied.

"Yeah, I am sorry," Bo said as he undressed. "I woke up wired this morning for some reason and I just drove over. I debated waiting in the car but wanted to see if you were up."

"It's ok, bubba," I replied, rubbing my eyes. "I just rolled out of bed, though. I need to take a shower still."

"You think I can join you?" Bo said with a sly grin.

"Sure!" I replied grinning back. "It will be a bit tight in there, but there is room."

He followed me back into the bathroom and I ran the water a bit till it was warm and then we both stepped in and closed the door behind us. I did not have a huge shower, but it was a walk-in and just big enough to accommodate the two of us.

"Hand me the soap," Bo said.

He lathered up his hands and ran them over my chest and arms and rubbed my neck after. He then had me lift one leg and then the other and he lathered them up as well. I smiled and gave him a peck on the lips at one point and the water ran over my head and hit him in the face.

"Hey!" Bo said with a laugh.

"Sorry," I replied, grinning.

"Ok, turn around now," he said.

"Yes, Sir!" I replied.

He ran his hands over my back and massaged my upper shoulders a bit under the warm water that ran over and down my back. He then rubbed my ass and brought the soap up in between my cheeks and fingered my hole a bit making me groan.

"Don't move," Bo said as he reached for the hose attachment I had in my shower to clean my ass out with.

He brought it up to my hole and switched it on to fill my ass with water and had me squat a bit to let it out. After a few times, things were running clear and he had me turn around again.

"Ok, my turn," Bo said, handing me the soap.

We moved around a bit and swapped places and repeated the same process. As I moved my hands over his body, he closed his eyes and bit his lip. I saw his nub swell as I moved down to get his legs and ass. He turned around and I ran my hands over his back and down over his ass, fingering his ass a bit. Bo reacted by backing his ass up a bit to give me more access and I rubbed his hole a bit.

I used the attachment to clean his ass out as well so that we were both ready for Kenny later. After I put it back in its holder, Bo put his arms around my shoulders and leaned into make-out with me a bit. As the water cascaded over his large frame, I felt his tongue enter my mouth and I brought my hands around and rubbed his sides and back. He did the same and we embraced and took in the moment as the steam built up in the room.

"Ok, bubba," I replied, pulling back. "Hand me the shampoo and let me wash my hair so we can get going."

"Boo!" Bo said with a pout and a grin. "You had to kill the moment"

"Hey!" I replied with a laugh. "It's getting to the point where I can barely see you in here."

After we were done, I turned off the water and we both stepped out.

"Fuck!" I exclaimed. "I forgot to get the other towel from the basket."

"It's ok," Bo said. "You dry off first and I'll just use your towel."

I dried off quickly and then handed the towel to Bo, who brought it up to his nose for a moment and then brought it down to dry off. He then wrapped it around his waist and watched as I brushed my teeth.

"At least the weather should be nice today," Bo said.

"Oh yeah?" I asked.

"Yeah, pretty mild and it should be mostly cloudy, so the sun won't be beating down on us," Bo replied.

"Well, that's a plus," I said as I washed my mouth out and put down the toothbrush.

Bo handed me the towel and I hung it over the shower door and then we walked into the bedroom and he watched as I got the clothes out I was going to wear for the day and then we went into the kitchen and I grabbed a glass of orange juice.

"Well, are you ready to head over?" I asked after I finished.

"Whenever you are sexy!" Bo replied with a grin.

We both put our clothes on and then headed out the door to head over a few buildings to Kenny's apartment. When I knocked on the door, I saw it open and Max appeared.

"Hey, guys!" Max said with a grin and he gave us hugs as we walked in and got undressed.

"Kenny's in the bedroom," he said. "Come on back when you are done."

Max walked back into the bedroom and we finished undressing. As Bo and I walked in after him, I noticed that Kenny was laying on top of the covers and stroking his hard cock. Max was kneeling at the foot of the bed and licking his feet.

"Glad to see you, boys!" Kenny said with a smile. "Bo, why don't you come over here and lie down on the bed and put your mouth on my cock. Matt, I didn't take a shower for the past two days, so I'm sure you will enjoy my pits."

Kenny raised his right hand over his head, and I came over and laid next to him and stuck my face under his arm and took a deep breath and started to lick. Meanwhile, Bo came around to his left side and laid down on the bed and took his thick cock in his hand and guided it into his mouth.

"Good boys!" Kenny said as he closed his eyes and let his head fall back.

He wiggled his feet as Max continued to worship them and he reached around and started to rub Bo's back as Bo bobbed up and down on his cock. I was in hog heaven and rubbing his scent all over my beard and face as I licked and nibbled under his arms. I ran my hands through his chest hair and played with his nipples as well. When I gave them a good squeeze, he started precumming more and Bo began to lap it up as he continued to give him head.

"Matt," Kenny said as he opened his eyes, "get down behind my boy and get that tongue of yours to work on his ass. I want it nice and lubed so I can dump my load in it when I am ready."

"Yes, Sir!" I replied.

I got off the bed and got down behind Max and used my hands to spread his furry cheeks and then dove in with my face and got my tongue in his hole. Max started to groan as Kenny put his feet over Max's face and Max grabbed them and ran his beard over them. I worked my tongue back and forth and used my spit and fingers to open Max up. He started to wiggle his ass a bit and his nub started to swing as well.

"Ok, Boy," Kenny said. "Your brother Bo has me close. Jump on my cock and take my load."

"Yes, Sir!" Max replied with a grin and he climbed up on the bed as Bo backed away.

Max faced Kenny and lowered himself down on his thick ginger cock. I watched as it slid into his ass until it disappeared and only his bush and balls were visible. Kenny started to thrust upward into Max, and he began to bounce a bit in rhythm to Kenny's thrusts. This caused Kenny to start to moan and he closed his eyes again and tilted his head back.

"Daddy's about to cum boy!" Kenny growled.

"Breed me, daddy!" Max replied.

I saw Kenny's ass squeeze and his balls jump and then his taint started to pulse as he exploded into Max's ass. He came so much I saw it start to dribble out the sides and down on the sheets below. Max came down on Kenny's fat cock and sat there till it stopped pulsing. He then leaned down and gave Kenny a kiss, causing the deflating dick to pop out of Max's ass in the process. Bo immediately moved in behind Max and licked his ass clean of the cum that was there and then took Kenny's cock into his mouth after to do the same.

Max rolled off to the side and Kenny looked down at Bo and smiled. "Thank you, boy!"

Bo smiled back and then Kenny looked at me. "And thank you as well!"

Kenny sat there a while to catch his breath and then he got up and had Max follow him into the bathroom.

"You two go wait in the living room, we will be there shortly," Kenny said.

After Kenny and Max got cleaned up, we all piled in my SUV and I drove us into town. Kenny's office is not far from Piedmont Park where the vendor fair was being held, so we had the option of free parking there and it was not a long walk over.

Once we got to the vendor area, I heard a voice call my name and turned around to see Chris and Rick.

"Hey, boys!" Chris announced as he and Rick walked over.

"Are you taking the subs on an outing Kenny?" Rick asked as he put his arm around me.

"They did a good job servicing me this morning, so figured it's a nice reward," Kenny said with a smile.

I rolled my eyes and hugged Rick. "How have you been, big fella?"

"Not bad," Rick replied. "Chris wanted to get out of the house for a bit."

"You headed out to the Eagle after?" I asked.

"Oh, hell no!" he replied. "After last year when we spent an hour looking for a place to park only to be squeezed into the parking lot once we got there, we decided to pass this time around."

"Yeah, I am on the fence for the same reason," Kenny replied.

"Why don't you all come over to our apartment later," Chris said. "We can play cards or something."

"Or something," Rick said with a devilish grin as he stuck his hand down my pants and squeezed my ass.

I returned his glance with a smirk. "Uh-huh," I replied.

"That sounds like fun to me," Bo replied.

"Yeah," Kenny said. "The boy and I are game."

"Cool," Chris said. "Shall we wander?"

"Lead on!" Kenny replied.

The vendors were lined up around the curving path through the park. It took quite a while to work our way down through them all. We stopped for some drinks and snacks along the way and Bo bought a few pieces of art he liked and a neat hemp necklace. On several occasions, Bo took my hand as we walked and snuck a kiss here and there. After making the rounds, we grabbed a spot to sit down for a while and catch up before everyone decided it was time to head out.

The game plan was to go our separate ways for the time being and meet back up at Rick and Chris's apartment about 7 pm. So, everyone exchanged hugs and I drove my crew back over to the apartment complex. Kenny and Max went off to run some errands and Bo asked if he could stay with me, which I said was fine.

When we walked into my apartment, Bo and I got undressed and yawned.

"You up for a little cuddle siesta before dinner?" Bo asked.

"Sure thing!" I replied and he followed me back into the bedroom and we laid down.

I was on my back and had my arm propped behind my head and Bo came in beside me on his side and put his arm around my waist and his leg over one of mine. It wasn't long before he was snoozing with his head cradled on my chest and arm.

I was kind of surprised how quickly he had become affectionate after we brought things out into the open about our feelings for each other. It was still weird, though. I thought of him as my sub brother, but also almost like a boyfriend as well. I was hesitant to push too much, though as he was about to graduate from John's service, and I had no idea where the future would lead to for him. I also had no idea where I would end up either. Still, listening to him snore lightly and feeling his warmth on my body was comforting and I relished the moment.

I had dozed off at some point as I woke up to find Bo running his fingers through my chest hair. I stretched my legs a bit and he looked up at me and smiled.

"You have a good nap?" he asked.

"I did!" I replied as I ran my hand over his head. "How about you?"

"Nicely recharged for the evening," he replied as he came up and kissed me.

"Shall we grab some dinner then?" I asked.

"Sounds like a great plan to me," he said as he got up and sat on the bed.

"Ok," I replied. "Let me hit the bathroom quick and we will be off."

When we got to Chris and Rick's and knocked on the door, Chris opened it and let us in. He was in his boxers and Rick was sitting on the sofa in his boxers and socks. Max was next to him playing a game and Kenny was in the kitchen in his shorts.

"Looks like the gang's all here!" I replied as I started to undress.

"Well, now the party can start since the subs have all arrived!" Rick said grinning back at me.

I rolled my eyes and finished undressing as did Bo. We went over to the kitchen and Kenny handed us both a beer and we went into the living room and sat on the floor in front of Rick and Max.

"On the floor next to your brothers Max!" Kenny said as he swapped places with him.

Max got up and sat next to Bo on the ground and Chris sat in the chair across from us.

"I know you might have had dinner, but I've got some pizza on the way as a bit of a snack," Chris said.

"That's cool," Bo replied. "How much do we owe you?"

"You can work that off this evening I am sure," Chris said with a smirk.

"Well, you are not caged today then," I replied.

"Nope!" Chris said. "Just you subs!"

Rick reached down and started to rub my shoulders and I turned to look at him.

"Speaking of that," Rick said. "How about you get started here."

Rick pulled his waistband down over his cock and balls and I watched as it stiffened quickly. I turned around and got on my knees and started to lick the head of his dick and play with his balls a bit. As I did so, Bo turned around in front of Kenny and reached up to expose his ginger cock as well.

"I do love a sub with initiative," Kenny said with a smile.

Max turned to watch us as we sucked on the two men and Kenny frowned a bit.

"Boy, quit watching and turn around and start sucking your host's cock!" he said.

Max spun around and Chris pulled his underwear down to expose his member as well. All three men started to groan as we worked on their dicks. Bo was swirling his tongue around Kenny's uncut cock causing it to precum a ton and I was deep throating Rick, who reached down to put his hand behind my head to guide me back and forth on him. From behind me I heard Max cough and choke a bit.

"Looks like you need more practice," Chris said with a smile.

"Yet another reason I am glad he is training," Kenny said, grinning back at Chris.

"You mind if I borrow your sub?" Rick said, looking at Kenny.

"All yours!" Kenny replied and Rick stood up.

"Follow me back to the bedroom boy," Rick said to Bo.

"Yes, Sir!" Bo said as he stood and followed him.

I moved over and took Kenny's hard cock into my mouth and he put both arms on the back of the sofa and leaned his head back. As he did so, he moved forward a bit and it gave me a bit more access to get him deeper into my mouth.

"Bend over the chair boy," I heard Chris tell Max from behind me.

I took a quick look over at them while I was working Kenny's cock and saw Chris spread Max's ass with one hand to bury his face in his ass and tongue his hole and he started to stroke his dripping cock with his other hand.

Kenny grabbed my head and pointed me back in his crotch and I focused my attention on him. As I felt his head hit the back of my throat, I heard Max moan as Chris started to enter him. From the back of the apartment, I started to hear the creak of the bedframe and Rick start to grunt.

I pushed my head down as far as I could go on Kenny and had my nose in his bush. I could smell his sweat from the day, and I felt his full balls as well. I started to move up and down faster and used my hands to help with the stroking motion. Kenny closed his eyes and groaned loudly as I heard Chris start to pound Max's ass and Bo start to cry out from the back bedroom as well.

Rick's voice soon echoed down the hall as he yelled out as he came in Bo's ass. Just as he did so, I felt Kenny's balls move and he reached down and held my head as he exploded as well.

"Fuck yeah, boy!" Kenny growled.

The cum was still pulsing out of his cock and down my throat when I heard Chris announce he was unloading in Max as well. What followed was a series of grunts and groans and heavy breathing from the men as they came down from their orgasm highs. I pulled off Kenny's cock and watched as a few drops of cum ran down his shaft.

"Why don't you two switch out and clean us off?" Kenny said.

I turned and saw Chris with his tongue in Max's ass licking his load out. Chris backed away and Max got off from the chair and knelt in front of Kenny and cleaned his cock and crotch and I moved over and knelt in front of Chris and cleaned him.

"Well, that was enjoyable," Chris said with a smile, looking down at me.

"You got that right," Rick said as he walked into the living room again, naked with his soft cock flopping side to side.

Bo waddled in after him and was catching some cum coming out of his ass.

"Come over here bro," I said to Bo, as I turned around on my knees.

Bo came over and bent over the chair a bit and I stuck my tongue in his ass and lapped at his hole. I could taste Rick's load as it came out and I made sure to clean him out good before I backed away.

"Damn, Rick," I replied as I rubbed Bo's butt. "You came a lot."

"Boy's got quite an ass and knows how to work a real man's cock," Rick said with a smile.

Once the men were sitting down again, we got back on the floor and after the pizza arrived, we all played some video games, had some beer, and socialized a bit. After a few hours, Kenny told Max to get dressed and they headed out first. Bo and I stayed on for a bit longer, though until Rick started to doze off and we took our leave to head back home as well.

CHAPTER TWENTY-SEVEN

Beach Bums

The following Friday I had taken the day off of work so I could join Bo and Master Todd for the weekend getaway to Florida. Bo had given me the directions to Todd's house and told me to be there by 9 am. As I pulled up to his place, I was impressed. Bo told me he was pretty well off, but the two-story house was gorgeous with a perfectly manicured lawn. I drove up the driveway and parked off to the side. Inside the open garage, I could see Bo putting some luggage in the back of Todd's car.

"Good morning!" I said as I walked up to him.

"Hey, Matt!" Bo replied as he turned and gave me a big hug and kiss. "I just put my things in the back here, go grab your stuff."

"Will do," I replied, and I went and grabbed my bag and put it in the back of the car as well.

"Welcome to my home, Matt," I heard the voice of Todd say.

I turned and saw him come around the car. He had a Hawaiian shirt on, and the top buttons were open showing off his white fur on his chest. He had some cargo shorts on and sandals. He looked like he was ready for vacation.

"Thank you, Sir," I replied. "I also appreciate you inviting me along."

"No problem," Todd said as he put his arm around Bo's shoulders. "The boy and I have been talking and I figured it would be a good chance to get to know you better and discuss some things as well."

"For sure," I replied with a smile.

"Boy, go inside and check my bedroom for anything we missed and then lock up the house and then get in the car," Todd said to Bo.

"Yes, Sir!" Bo replied as he went back inside.

"Matt," Todd said as he looked at me. "I have been talking to John and I have decided to collar Bo at his graduation ceremony in December. I have not told him this formally yet, but I think he has a good idea. I will be telling him of my decision this weekend."

"That's great to hear, Sir!" I replied.

"I picked up on the fact that you two were a bit close and he and I discussed the relationships a sub can have while collared," he continued. "I told him it was ok to spend time with you as long as John is ok with it as well, but we needed to have a more formal discussion in case he came into my home, as he will be soon."

"I understand, Sir," I replied.

"For the duration of this weekend, I want you to continue to follow John's protocols, but I also want you to feel free to speak up and voice your opinions and thoughts as we talk about various things," Todd said.

"Thanks, Sir," I replied. "I appreciate that."

Todd smiled and squeezed my shoulder and then turned as Bo came back into the garage.

"Everything is packed, and the house is locked up, Sir," Bo replied.

"Good deal," Todd said. "You two boys get in the back."

We climbed into the back seat as Todd got in the front and then he pulled the car out and down the driveway and we were off. Todd had a small plane that he was qualified to fly at the local public airport and that's where we headed next. When we pulled up to the hanger, a man came to greet us, and we grabbed our bags and he drove Todd's car off to park it.

We walked over to the small plane and looked inside. It had two seats in the front and four seats in the passenger area. It had two props and was white with some dark blue striping.

"This is my Beechcraft," Todd said. "It's a little older, but it's my baby and a reliable plane as well. Go ahead and stow your bags inside and get settled and I will be in shortly."

"Yes, Sir!" we replied, and Bo and I boarded the plane.

I had never been aboard a private plane before. It wasn't overly large but was comfortable to sit in. We put our bags in the back seats and then sat opposite one another.

Bo smiled at me. "Are you excited?"

"Yes!" I replied. "This is a new experience for me."

"Me too," Bo replied.

Todd came in and then made sure we were buckled in.

"It's about a three-and-a-half-hour flight down to the keys," he said. "It depends on the wind and how we are routed. There are some drinks there in the cooler. Just let me know if you have any issues or questions."

"Yes, Sir!" we replied.

Todd got into the pilot's seat and did his pre-check and start-up procedures and then we started moving and were off not too long after. The flight was pretty smooth. We flew lower than a normal commercial plane does, and you could see more of what was around you. As we neared the Gulf of Mexico, the blue water shined the sun back at us and I watched the coastline as we flew down.

It was a little after 1 pm when we started to make our descent down to the small airport on Marathon Key. After we pulled up to the hanger and the plane came to a stop, someone came over to help with getting the plane stored and brought over a car for us as well.

"You boys put our luggage in the back, and I will join you in a second," Todd replied.

After the car was packed, we got in the back seat and Todd got in the front soon after. He drove us around the island, and we ended up on a road that paralleled the water. As we neared the end of the road, we came upon a gate and Todd stopped the car to punch in a code and it swung open after. As the car pulled in the driveway, I saw a cute bungalow home appear that was surrounded by palm trees and bushes.

"This is my vacation home," Todd said. "It's called 'Point Comfort'. It's surrounded by a fence and my next-door neighbor is a friend of mine. He is not here this weekend, so the property and beach area will be private for us."

"That sounds awesome," I replied.

Todd stopped the car and we all got out and grabbed our things. When we walked up to the front door, he unlocked it and let us in. The living room was surrounded by windows and we could look back and see that at the far side, there was a wall of windows and some doors that led out to the private beach area. The kitchen was off to the side and there were three bedrooms and a bathroom as well.

"Strip down, boys," Todd said. "Unless we go anywhere, you will be naked the whole weekend."

"Yes, Sir," we replied and started to undress.

Todd went around and started to open the windows. The temperature was rather warm and the breeze off the water helped to cool down the place and air it out some.

"On your knees, boys," Todd said to us as he walked back over.

We got down on our knees next to one another and he stood in front of us.

"Here are the rules," Todd said. "First, in my home, wearing clothes and the use of furniture is a privilege for collared boys only. You two are neither. Second, I expect you to keep the house clean while we are here and follow any request I have of you. Finally, you are not allowed to leave the house without permission. There will be designated time for you to enjoy yourselves, but first and foremost, this is a vacation for me, and I will be using you to that end."

"Yes, Sir," we replied.

"Bo, please stand," Todd said.

Bo stood up and put his hands behind his back. Todd came over and stood in front of him and placed his hand on Bo's chest.

"Bo, I have been very impressed by your level of obedience and the skills you have shown me over the past couple of months," Todd said. "As we discussed last weekend, I have given serious consideration to collaring you when you graduate. I have made it clear I am not looking for a romantic partner at this time, though if something develops, that is fine. Have you thought more about this?"

"Yes, Sir," Bo replied. "I would be so honored to be your sub. I enjoy the time we spend together and pleasing you brings me a lot of pleasure."

"I am happy to hear that," Todd said. "I am letting you know, then, barring any issues over the next few weeks, you will be receiving my collar then."

I saw Bo's face beam and a huge smile appear. "Thank you so much, Sir!"

"We will use this weekend to talk more about this, but I want you to start the process of putting in your notice to leave your apartment as well," Todd said. "I expect you to move in with me in December."

"Yes, Sir!" Bo replied.

"Matt, please stand," Todd said.

As I got up, Todd moved over to stand in front of me.

"Matt, I know you and Bo have a close relationship," he said. "How would you describe it?"

I swallowed hard and looked at Bo and then Todd. "Well, Sir, Bo is my sub brother. I look at him first and foremost as my family and someone I want to look after and support as we do our duties. But, we have also discussed our feelings for one another. I am attracted to him and would consider him as a boyfriend if it were not for Sir John's program. I am nervous about exploring a deeper relationship with him until we can figure out where our lives will be headed. But I do care a lot for him."

Bo smiled and reached over and held my hand. Todd grinned back as well.

"Bo has stated similar feelings," Todd said. "I encouraged him to be honest with you and to talk to you about them. Has he done so?"

"Yes Sir, he has," I replied.

"As a collared boy, Bo will be part of my household in December," Todd said. "But, as long as John approves and is ok with it, I want you to feel free to continue to see him and spend time with him after this time. However, he will have dedicated responsibilities to me, and my needs will come first."

"I understand," I replied.

"Bo," Todd said as he turned to him. "What are your thoughts?"

"It's like what Matt said," Bo replied. "I like him a lot. I appreciate you allowing us to explore this more."

"Well, there are other aspects we need to talk about as well," Todd said. "A romantic relationship can be complicated for locked boys. I expect permanent chastity from my subs. That means you two will not be able to experience the intimacy that most males have when dating. However, I will be exploring some things with you this weekend that may offer some help in that regard."

"That sounds interesting, Sir," Bo said with an inquisitive look.

Todd smiled devilishly. "I am looking forward to seeing how it works myself. In the meantime, let's grab a late lunch."

We followed Todd back into the kitchen area and he microwaved some meals for us out of the freezer. We sat on the kitchen floor and ate while he ate at the table. After we were done, he showed us out the back doors. The beach extended from the waterline right up to the back of the house. There was a dock that extended out from the shore into the water and a boat was moored to it. There was a nice breeze blowing off the water and it felt wonderful outside.

Todd stripped naked and grabbed a lounge chair and walked out onto the beach.

"Grab three towels out of that box just inside the door there, Bo, and follow me out here," Todd said.

After grabbing the towels, we stepped out into the sand. It was a bit warm on our bare feet and we walked quickly over to where Todd had placed his chair. He took one of the towels and placed it on the lounge chair. He then placed the other two towels on either side of the chair and then laid down.

"You boys can sit beside me," Todd said as he pointed to the towels.

We sat cross-legged on either side of him and he laid back with his arms behind his head and closed his eyes. I looked out to the water in front of me. It was crystal clear near the shore and there were waves gently moving in that gave a soothing sound, in addition to the calls from seagulls flying around.

Todd started to snore a bit and we realized he had nodded off. Bo got up and came around and sat behind me. I felt his cage poke my ass as he leaned over on my shoulder.

"This is nice," Bo said. "I could get used to this real quick."

I laughed a bit. "It is relaxing. I have not been down to Florida in quite a while."

"Me either," Bo said. "But it reminds me a bit of the beach back in Texas. Just not as hot here."

I laughed again and then brought my hands up over his and leaned my head back and he nibbled on my ear a bit. We sat there for about fifteen minutes and relaxed and I had just started to close my eyes when Todd spoke.

"You like my little hide-a-way, boys?" he said looking over at us.

"Yes, Sir," I replied. "It's very nice."

"How would you two like to join me in a swim?" Todd asked.

"That would be great," Bo replied.

"Come on, then," Todd said as he got up and walked over to the water.

We followed him in and waded out a bit. The ground was a mix of sand and some rock and we saw some fish move around as we moved.

"The boat that is docked there is mine as well," Todd said. "We will probably take that out tomorrow, as long as the weather holds."

"Do you fish much?" I asked.

"Some," Todd replied, "but I just like being out in the water."

After swimming for a bit, we got back out and dried off and Todd had us follow him back inside. Once we closed the door behind us, he directed us back into a bedroom in the corner of the home that also faced the beach. When we entered, we saw it was set up as a mini-dungeon area. There was a sling and fuck bench, as well as a small cross on the wall and various toys in shelving on one side. Todd opened the windows to let some air in and then turned to us.

"Now for some fun boys," Todd said. "Matt, I think it is about time you and Bo bonded a little bit more. Come over here and get on the bench."

"Yes, Sir," I replied, and I walked over and laid down on it. It was virtually identical to the one Sir had and he strapped my arms and legs down in it.

I turned my head and watched as Todd went over to the cabinet to the side and pulled out some items.

"Come over here, Bo," he said.

As Bo walked over, I saw what was in Todd's hand. It was a strap-on dildo harness. I watched as he buckled it around Bo's waist and then he lubed the dildo that was attached to it.

"How long has it been since you have fucked anyone, Bo?" Todd asked.

"Over a year, Sir," Bo replied.

"Well, this dildo is molded after my cock, so in a way, you will be fucking Matt with my dick," Todd said.

He got some lube and started to rub it over the dildo and then he brought Bo over behind me.

"Bend down and put your face in Matt's ass and get him loosened up Bo," Todd said. "Then I want you to fuck him good."

"Yes, Sir!" Bo said with a smile.

I felt him put his face in between my cheeks and his tongue started to dart over my hole. I moaned a bit and my nub started to leak. Bo is an expert rimmer and started to work me over pretty well and used lots of spit to get me lubed up too. When he was about ready to mount me, Todd came over and stood in front of me.

"Open up, boy," Todd said. "You're gonna get my dick in both ends."

As Todd pushed his hard cock into my mouth, I felt Bo slide the replica of Todd's cock in my ass. I groaned as I was penetrated from both ends and Todd reached down and held my head as he started to assault my throat. Bo started fucking me slowly as well and then with a moderate speed once he got used to the strap-on.

"You enjoy fucking Matt, Bo?" Todd asked as he looked over at him.

"Yes, Sir!" Bo replied.

"Good boy," Todd replied.

Todd started to fuck my face harder and was hitting the back of my throat more. I had gotten better, under Sir's training, at deep throating, but I still was gagging a bit, sending more spit out of my mouth and down my beard and onto the floor. He was not slowing down, though, so I concentrated on making sure my teeth did not get in the way. It was not long before he was grunting and breathing heavily.

"You want my load boy?" Todd asked.

I grunted as best I could as a way of saying yes and I felt him tense up and then his cock exploded cum down my throat. He pulled out a bit and it filled my mouth up and started to leak out and down my beard. He then shoved it in again and let me suck him off and swallow his load.

Todd held my head until he was done and then pulled back. Bo was still fucking my ass and he had just the right angle that it was hitting my prostate in a good way. I felt the sensation deep in my groin area and knew it would not be long until he would be fucking an orgasm out of me.

"Sir!" I yelled.

"Yes, boy?" Todd replied, looking down at me.

"May my nub have an orgasm?" I asked.

"Bo must be hitting the right spots," Todd said. "Will you agree to fuck him the same way and give him one too?"

"Yes Sir!" I replied.

"Then you have my permission," Todd replied.

Bo grinned and started to fuck me with Todd's cloned cock harder and the sensation started to build behind my balls. I squeezed my ass a bit and could hold it back no longer and I felt a wave of energy explode through my nub as the internal orgasm hit me. Cum started to dribble out of my cage and I groaned.

"Oh fuck!" I replied as I closed my eyes and gripped the bench. "Thank you, Bo!"

Bo slowed down and then brought the dildo completely inside me and leaned over me and embraced me and kissed my back. He then slid the dildo out and leaned down and licked my cage clean of the cum that was dangling from it.

"Don't forget what's on the floor, boy," Todd said, pointing at the puddle on the floor and Bo got down and licked that clean as well.

"Good boy," Todd replied. "Now it's time for Matt to repay you for that."

Todd came over and undid my restraints and helped me up and then took the harness off Bo and put it on me. He then tied Bo down and I got behind him and bent down and started to rim his ass.

Bo started to groan as I got my tongue deep in him and I used my fingers and some spit to start to open him up as well.

"Fuck me, Matt!" Bo shouted as I started to put three fingers into him.

I smiled and stood up and brought the dildo over to his ass. It was amazing how much it looked like Todd's cock. I watched as it started to enter his ass and Bo clenched the bench as it filled him.

Fucking him with the dildo was a new experience for me. I had never used one before. The last person I had fucked was Chris back in March. Over seven months later, I was trying to get back into the headspace and make sure I was hitting the right spots for Bo as well. As I worked the dildo in and out of his ass, Todd started to stroke his cock and it was getting hard again. He came up behind me and rubbed his cock over my ass.

"Hold still for a moment boy," Todd said as he slid his cock into my loosened ass.

I felt it enter me and I squeezed my ass a bit to grip it. Todd groaned in response and then put his arms around my upper chest.

"Now, use that clone of my cock to fuck a load out of Bo and use your ass to milk my cock dry," Todd said.

I started to move back and forth pushing the dildo into Bo as Todd's cock came out of mine and then as I pulled out, bringing Todd's cock back into me. It took a bit of work to get the rhythm right, but I eventually got to where Bo was getting a good fucking and so was I.

"How are we doing down there, Bo?" Todd asked.

"I'm getting there, Sir!" Bo replied.

"So am I," Todd growled into my ear.

Todd started to fuck me a bit and I slowed down and shoved the dildo deep into Bo. As I held it there, Todd started to piston fuck my ass and the force drove the dildo into Bo's ass a bit deeper as well and started to move it slowly back and forth. The sensation was just what Bo needed, because soon after he spoke up.

"Oh, my nub!" Bo shouted.

"You close, boy?" Todd asked as he continued to fuck me.

"Yes, Sir!" Bo replied.

"You have my permission to cum," Todd replied.

Bo started to groan loudly as his nub started to pulse in its cage and cum began to drop onto the floor. Todd growled as well and shoved his cock into me as it delivered its second load deep into my bowels.

"Fuck, boy!" Todd exclaimed as I felt his cock pulsing inside me.

After a few minutes, he pulled out and I gasped a bit. I then slowly pulled out the dildo from Bo's ass and then got down on my knees to clean his cage and nub off and then lick Bo's load off the floor. When I was done, Todd had me clean his cock off, and then he took the harness off me and let Bo up.

"I think you need to clean him again Bo," Todd said pointing at my cum covered ass.

"Gladly!" Bo smiled and I leaned over the bench so he could tongue me clean.

When he was done, I got up and we hugged each other and kissed and Bo licked some of the dried cum out of my beard.

"See boys?" Todd said as he grabbed a small towel to wipe his hands and forehead. "Chastity sub-boys can still find ways to be intimate. While you must follow John's protocols as his trainees, I believe that life is not all about service. You have to find your pleasure in it as well. But, if you want to do this again, you will have to do so under my supervision or permission."

"Yes, Sir!" we both replied.

"Bo, on your knees," Todd said. "I need to piss now."

After Bo took Todd's piss, we went back into the living room area and Todd laid down on the sofa to take a nap and we cleaned up the playroom before coming in and sitting down on the floor. Bo then laid down and put his head in my lap and rubbed my legs.

"I enjoyed that," Bo said as he looked up at me.

"Me too bubba," I replied, and I rubbed his chest as he started to doze off.

I had been leaning against the wall and had dozed off myself, so I was a bit out of it when I felt Todd's hand on my shoulder, waking me up. I opened my eyes and saw him looking down at me. Bo was nowhere to be found.

"I sent Bo down the road to the corner store for some food," Todd said. "We need to talk."

"Yes, Sir," I replied as I rubbed my eyes.

Todd sat in a chair in front of me and picked up a glass of whiskey he had poured and put it on a table. He took a few sips and then looked at me.

"Bo will be my collared boy very soon," Todd said. "As I have said, I am fine with you continuing a relationship with him; however, we need to talk about some ground rules."

"I understand, Sir," I replied as I brought my legs up and sat cross-legged.

"When do you complete your service with John?" Todd asked me.

"March of next year," I replied.

"So, you will be busy with him and your sub brothers and those responsibilities come first," Todd said. "When you have free time, though, you are welcome to come over to my house to see Bo but as a collared boy, he will have seniority over you in the house. In effect, you will be the beta boy in the house, and he will be the alpha sub when you are visiting."

"That makes sense," I replied.

"I have been seeing someone myself that may turn into something at some point," Todd replied. "If that is the case, then we may have to reevaluate things."

"Yes, Sir," I replied.

"I do not believe in 'owning' boys," Todd replied. "Bo will be my collared sub and will have duties and responsibilities, but I also will respect a certain amount of freedom on his part to develop his own relationships. If you two continue and things get more serious, I am not opposed to possibly collaring you as well. How do you feel about that?"

I was a bit shocked as he took another sip and looked at me. I had not even considered being collared at this point, but the thought of being a sub with Bo under Todd was nice.

"I would be very honored, Sir," I replied. "You are a very kind dom and I have enjoyed being around you."

"I appreciate that boy," Todd said. "I will have to think more about this and see how things work out with Bo once he moves in with me, but I can see where having the two of you around would be nice. Plus, if I do end up in a relationship with Pat, the man I have been seeing, then it would be beneficial to have two subs around as well. We shall see, though."

"Thank you so much for considering it, Sir," I replied.

"Well, why don't you come over here and massage my feet while we wait on Bo to return," Todd said.

I crawled over in front of Todd and put his big feet into my lap and started to rub them. He leaned back and sipped on his drink and relaxed until Bo returned. We then put the food away that he had brought and went back out on the beach and relaxed until the sun started to set. As we watched the glowing orb on the horizon, Bo sat behind me on the towel and hugged me tightly, and lightly kissed my neck.

CHAPTER TWENTY-EIGHT

Visiting Key West

I woke up Saturday in Todd's guest room. He had Bo spend the night with him in the master bedroom. The light was coming in from the window and I heard the sound of the surf out the open frame. I got out of bed to go to the bathroom and after I was done, I walked down the hall and noticed that Todd's door was open. When I started to peek in, I saw a cot at the foot of the bed with a pillow and sheet on it where Bo had been sleeping, but it was empty. Once I got to where I could see the bed itself, I saw Todd laying there with the sheets pulled back and Bo was in between his legs giving him a blowjob. Todd looked up and saw me in the hall.

"You sleep ok, boy?" Todd asked me as Bo continued to work his cock.

"Yes, Sir!" I replied with a smile.

"I'm glad," Todd said. "Why don't you get some breakfast started and I'll be in shortly after the boy drains me."

"Will do, Sir!" I replied and I continued into the living room and around to the kitchen.

I opened the refrigerator and scratched my belly as I determined what I could make. Bo had picked up some fresh eggs and sausage, so I pulled those out and I got out some bread for toast as well. I found an apron hanging on the wall to protect my nub and I started to scramble some eggs and fry up the sausage in a pan.

The smell of the sausage started wafting through the house and it was not long till Todd came around the corner into the kitchen. His balls were a little less heavy.

"Smells good, boy!" he said as he inspected everything and then started some coffee brewing.

"Did you sleep ok, Sir?" I asked as I turned the patties.

"I did," Todd said as he grabbed a coffee cup. "I always do here. I find the sound of the water soothing."

"I agree, Sir," I said as I moved the pan off the heat and finished scrambling the last of the eggs.

The toaster dinged and I pulled the last two slices out and put them on a plate with the others.

"I am almost done here," I replied.

"Good," Todd said as he put his cup down and turned to look at me.

After I had finished the eggs, I put the pan to the side and turned to get some silverware.

"Before you get to plating anything," Todd said, "how about you get on your knees and help me here. I need to piss."

"Absolutely, Sir!" I replied.

I took off the apron and got down in front of him and he placed his soft cock in my mouth. I looked up at him as he placed both hands back on the counter and I felt his warm stale piss start to flow into my mouth. I closed my eyes and concentrated on my breathing and swallowing and managed to get it all down without a drop spilled.

When I felt the stream start to slow, I opened my eyes and saw that Todd was smiling at me.

"Very good job, boy," Todd said as he reached down and wiggled his cock in my mouth to get the last drops out.

Once he was done, I stood back up and he turned to fill his cup with coffee and then went and sat down at the table. I plated his food for him and brought it over just as Bo was coming into the kitchen.

"Morning, Bo," I replied with a smile as I laid the plates down and then turned around.

"Good morning, bro," Bo said as he came behind me and hugged me.

Bo followed me into the kitchen after and I gave him his plate and grabbed mine and we walked over next to Todd and sat on the floor to eat.

"I've decided to take the boat out today, boys," Todd said as he ate some of the eggs. "I can show you some interesting places around here and then after we can drive down to Key West. Have you two ever been there?"

"No, Sir," we replied.

"Good deal," Todd said as he took a drink of his coffee. "I have a friend that has a house just off Duval Street. I think he would like you two."

"That sounds like fun, Sir!" Bo replied as he finished his food.

"In that case, Matt, why don't you clean up the kitchen and I'll go take a shower," Todd said. "Bo, you can come join me as well."

"Will do, Sir!" I replied and I got up and started to take the plates into the kitchen as they left the room.

After I had finished washing all the dishes and drying and putting them away, I wiped down all the surfaces and then walked over to the back door and opened it to let in some fresh air. I was leaning against

413

the threshold, enjoying the morning breeze when Bo came behind me and put his arms around my waist.

"Todd said you could go take a shower now if you wanted," he said as he put his head on my shoulder.

I turned around and kissed him and then said, "sounds good."

After I had got cleaned up, we all put on some clothes and followed Todd out to the boat. He had us get on and threw off the lines and then started it up and drove us around the island. There were several places where the vegetation had overgrown and there were lots of birds nesting and flying about. He also showed us some good fishing spots and gave us a little history of the area as well. He had grown up here as a kid before moving away and the land the house was on had been his grandfather's. He had built the home thereafter he became a partner in the law firm in Atlanta.

We had packed some sandwiches before we left, and we got those out and ate on the boat near the shore as we watched some seagulls compete for some scraps of something on the beach.

"So, what do you boys think?" Todd asked as he took a bite of his sandwich.

"It's a really neat area, Sir!" Bo said.

"I agree," I said. "I can see why you like coming here."

"It's a lot more enjoyable when you can share it," Todd said. "I am glad you could come with us, Matt."

After we had finished our lunch, Todd drove the boat over to a dock area to refill it with fuel and then we headed back to the house. We pulled in about 2 pm and after he tied the boat up, we walked back into the house.

"Keep your clothes on this time, boys," Todd said as he closed the door behind us and locked it. "I'm going to grab my keys and we can head down into the city."

It took us about an hour and a half to get down into the city, as we had to stop for gas along the way. As we got into Key West, I noticed how many people were wandering around.

"This is a tourist city," I said.

"Yeah," Todd replied, "it can be pretty hectic on the weekends. The home we are going to is a bit out of the high population area though."

We drove across Duval to Whitehead Street and he parked next to a corner home that was above a small shop.

"We are here, boys," Todd said as he got out.

He led us up some back stairs and knocked on the door and when it opened, an older man greeted us.

"Hey, Bill!" Todd said loudly as he leaned over and hugged the man. "How have you been?"

"Doing well, Todd!" Bill replied. "Are these the boys you told me about?"

"Yes, indeed," Todd said as he turned to the side and pointed at Bo. "This one here is Bo and the one that I plan on collaring in a few weeks. Next to him is his boyfriend and fellow sub, Matt."

I blushed a bit as Todd introduced us, as this was the first time someone had addressed me as Bo's boyfriend.

"Good to meet you both," Bill said as he extended his arm to us and shook our hands.

Bill was a little shorter than me and was bald, with blue eyes and a bright white beard. He did not have a shirt on, and he was covered in dense white fur. He had a nice belly and a large tattoo of an anchor on one arm. Below his cargo shorts, I saw more white hair running down his legs and on the top of his bare feet.

"Come on in!" Bill said.

Todd walked in and we followed him, and Bo closed the door behind us.

"Go ahead and strip, boys," Todd said, as he followed Bill over to a couch. "You will follow the same protocols as in my home."

"Yes, Sir," we replied, and Bo and I took off our clothes and folded them next to the door.

Todd had us come over and sit in front of them near the couch as the two men talked.

"Would you like a beer, Todd?" Bill asked.

"That would be nice," Todd replied.

"Bo, go into the kitchen there and get your Sir here a drink," Bill replied. "They are on the bottom shelf. If you two are thirsty, there is some bottled water in there as well."

"Yes, Sir!" Bo said as he got up and went into the kitchen.

Bo returned with a beer for Todd and some water for us and then sat down again and we watched quietly as the two men talked about what they had been up to lately and what was new with some of their friends. I got the impression that Bill was an old friend of Todd and that he had lived on the island for some time.

"I've got a guy coming over to give me a massage shortly," Bill said. "Would you like to have one too, Todd?"

"That would be wonderful," Todd said.

"Are you ok with the boys leaving for a while?" Bill asked. "It would be better if it was just the two of us here while the masseuse is doing his work."

"I'm sure they can find something to do," Todd said as he looked down at us. "Why don't you both get dressed and you can head into town and do some sightseeing."

"Thanks, Sir!" Bo replied.

"When should we be back?" I asked.

"Come back at 6 pm," Bill replied.

"Sounds good, Sir," I replied and we both got up and dressed and then headed outside.

As we walked down the stairs to the street, Bo turned to me and said, "where should we go first?"

"Why don't we go up to Duval and hang a left," I said. "That's where we saw everyone coming from."

"Following you!" Bo replied.

We headed down the street and followed the crowds as it started to get busier. After stopping to get a frozen margarita to sip on, we continued down till we got to Mallory Square. There weren't any cruise ships docked there, so there was a perfect view of the water and the sun that was starting to get low on the horizon. Some performers were starting to show up to get set up for the entertainment that they put on before sunset, but it otherwise was low-key.

Bo put his arm around my waist and leaned on my shoulder as he sipped his drink.

"So, did the whole boyfriend thing freak you out a little?" he asked. "You had this look on your face."

"Well, I was not expecting him to introduce me like that, but I didn't mind if that is what you were asking," I replied.

"I get that," Bo said as he moved up and kissed me on my cheek.

I turned and put my arm around him and started to kiss him on his mouth. We both closed our eyes and got lost in the moment as our tongues explored each other and we rubbed each other's backs. My nub started to swell, and I reached down to adjust my cage a bit.

"You know if we keep this up," I said as I backed away for a moment, "I'm going to have a serious wet spot on my pants."

"Me too," Bo said with a grin.

"It's been a while since I have dated anyone," I said. "And I sure have not done it in a cage. So, I suspect it might be a bit awkward at times."

"It's ok," Bo said. "I broke up with my last boyfriend last year and he never understood my interest in chastity. At least we have the same kinks and interests."

"And doms to explore them with," I replied with a smile.

"That felt so good when you were fucking me with that dildo, though," Bo said. "I am glad I got permission to cum. That helped my sore balls."

"Ugh, I know the feeling," I replied. "And I am only just about two months into my six-month lock session."

"Only a little over a month till I'll be given the choice to go permanent and have one last normal orgasm," Bo said.

"Are you nervous at all?" I asked.

"I mean, yeah, I am," Bo said. "But with you to support me and the encouragement of Sir John as well as the prospect of a collaring by Sir Todd, there is a lot to look forward to."

"And I'll be giving you your last blow job," I said with a grin.

Bo grinned back. "I know. Makes me look forward to graduation even more."

We kissed one more time and then decided to start to make our way back. We walked around to see some of the sights and also took a side street by the Hemingway House before getting back to Bill's house just before 6 pm. We knocked on the door and Todd let us in, and we started to undress again.

"Did you boys have a good time?" Todd asked.

Todd was naked but had a towel wrapped around him. Bill was the same way and was in the kitchen grabbing a beer.

"We did, Sir!" Bo replied. "Did you both have a good massage?"

"Indeed," Todd said. "But no happy ending."

"That's what you subs are for," Bill said with a smile as he took a sip of his beer.

Bill pulled open his towel and revealed a large, low-hanging set of balls. They could be door knockers I thought. I watched as he adjusted them a bit and started to grip his cock as it began to grow.

"You better get on that, Matt," Todd said to me. "Don't make him wait."

"Yes, Sir!" I replied and I moved over and knelt in front of him.

I took his cock into my hand and started to go down on him. Bill leaned back a bit and spread his legs more for me to get better access. As I started to work his shaft, Todd snapped his fingers at Bo, who came over and started to work his cock as well.

Bill's cock was a nice average size and fit perfectly into my mouth. I was able to give him some good deepthroating action as well and I fondled his large balls. That got a reaction from him and he stretched his legs out and groaned. I rolled his balls in my fingers gently as I started to swirl my tongue down his shaft, and he looked down at me and grinned.

"Someone has been teaching you well," Bill said.

"My friend John has both of these boys in his training program for subs," Todd said as Bo bobbed up and down on his cock.

"Remind me to thank him," Bill replied.

Bill reached down and put his hand on the back of my head and guided me down on his cock and forced me deeper on him. I moved my tongue from side to side as I went down and when my nose hit his bush, he held me there till I ran out of air and coughed, and he let me up. I went back down on him again and took in his scent from his crotch and my nub started to swell in its cage as a result.

I looked over and saw that Todd had gotten up and bent Bo over the side of the couch and was starting to fuck him. Bo looked up at me and smiled and then put his head down to concentrate on gripping Todd's cock as he pushed in and out.

Bill grabbed my head again and turned me back and forced me down on his cock again and I focused my attention on him as Bo started to grunt from the force of Todd's thrusts. I felt Bill's balls start to move a bit and knew he was close, so I increased my speed a bit and used my hands to jerk the bottom of his shaft as well. Bill stuck his legs out and groaned and I felt his balls lift in my hands as his cock exploded cum into my mouth, which I greedily swallowed. Bill reached down and held me on him till he stopped cumming and then collapsed a bit as I lifted off and licked him clean.

"Fucking hell, that was good," Bill said as he looked down at me.

I was smiling back as I heard Bo start to grunt harder and he started to grip tightly on the couch. Todd was fucking him hard and I could hear the smack of his groin as he made contact with Bo's ass. It was not long till Todd was blasting his load deep in Bo's ass and Bo squeezed down at the same time to milk his cock dry.

Once Todd had recovered from his orgasm, he pulled out of Bo and slapped his ass a few times and then came around and sat next to Bill again and grabbed a beer to take a few sips.

"Thank you, Sir," Bo replied as he fingered his ass.

"You are welcome, boy," Todd replied a bit out of breath.

I crawled around behind Bo and parted his ass with my hands and dove my head in to lick it clean. Cum was running out of his hole and

I licked it up and then dove my tongue in a bit for good measure as well. Bo groaned in response and almost lost his balance.

"Looks like we got some piggy subs," Bill said with a laugh.

"Indeed," Todd replied. "I'm pretty happy with that."

The two men finished their beers and then Bill got up and said that he needed to run some errands, so Todd told him we would head out and we all got dressed and piled back into the car to head back to Todd's house.

"How did you enjoy your afternoon, boys?" Todd asked us from the front seat.

"It was a lot of fun!" Bo replied as he reached over and held my hand. "We toured around the city a bit by foot and went by the water as well. Seems like a neat place."

"Yeah," Todd said. "I'll probably take you down here for New Year's Bo. It's quite an experience and I have some fellow doms that would love to ring in the new year using you."

"Yes, Sir!" Bo said with a smile.

We picked some food up on the way home and ate it at the house, then packed up as we needed to fly back early to make it back to Atlanta by the afternoon. I still had my one-on-one with John and Todd had some things to do as well. After dinner we played some cards for a while and relaxed and then when it was time for bed, Todd brought Bo into his room and closed the door, and I went back into my bedroom and caught some sleep.

The next morning, I made breakfast again, and then after we cleaned up, we were out the door and headed to the airport. Some weather in the area delayed our take off for a bit, and I was nervous about missing my set time with John. I had neglected to tell him I was heading out of town so I texted him to let him know what was going on and I might be late.

"How late will you be, boy?" John replied.

"It looks like maybe thirty minutes, Sir," I said. "We are just about ready to take off."

"Ask Bo to come with you when you come over," John replied. "We need to talk."

"Yes, Sir," I replied.

I had a concerned look on my face and Bo looked over at me.

"What is wrong?" he asked.

"I forgot to tell Sir I was heading down here with you and I was letting him know we would be a little late coming back," I replied.

"Well, I did tell him you were invited," Bo said.

"I know, but I did not," I said.

"Oh," Bo replied with a worried look.

"He asked if you would come over to the house with me when we land," I said.

"I can do that," Bo replied. "I hope you are not in trouble. I would feel bad."

"Don't be," I said as I reached over to hold his hand. "It was my mistake."

Bo squeezed my hand back and then we sat back and prepared for takeoff. The flight back up to Atlanta was pretty smooth and we landed only a little late. Todd drove us back over to his house and then Bo followed me in his car as I drove over to John's.

When we arrived, we took our clothes off and put them in our bins and walked into the dungeon area. It was about 35 minutes later than I normally came. John was inside on a chair waiting for us. I was a little concerned as we moved to the side and knelt in our squares on the floor. After we sat there a moment in silence, John finally spoke.

"Stand up, Matt," he said firmly.

I got to my feet and faced him with my hands behind my back.

"Todd called me a bit ago, before you both arrived, to let me know what went on," John said. "I am glad you both were able to serve and please him, but I have some concerns. Do you know what they are?"

"I neglected to tell you I was going out of town and as a result, I was also late today," I replied.

"Those are transgressions we will address, but I am also concerned about the relationship you two have," John replied. "Bo, please stand."

Bo got to his feet and stood next to me with his hands behind his back as well.

"While I respect the views that Todd has, I would prefer that my subs not be romantically attached," John said. "You have a lot to learn and you will be relying on each other during the process. Relationships can be tricky and volatile at times and I don't want anything to impact your duties as subs under me. Do you understand this?"

"Yes, Sir," we replied.

"What you do on your own time is your business, but while you are a trainee of mine, you will put a halt to any relationship outside of the sub brother aesthetic," John said. "Do you both agree to this?"

"Yes, Sir," we replied.

I felt a pain in the pit of my chest as I said those words. I was worried about the dynamics of exploring a relationship with Bo and while I liked him, I was disappointed that I did not come to John first to discuss it and get his permission.

"Bo," John said as he looked at him. "You will be graduating soon, and should Todd follow through and give you his collar, you will be under his house and rules. If you two wish to pursue something at that time, you can do so as long as it does not infringe on Matt's duties and responsibilities with me. Is that understood?"

"Yes, Sir," Bo said.

I turned my head to where I could see him, and he was visibly a bit upset and a tear ran down his cheek.

"I am not trying to be heartless, boy," John said as he walked over to him and wiped his cheek. "But do you understand why this has to end at least until you graduate?"

"Yes, Sir," Bo replied.

"Matt, step forward," John said.

As I did so, I noticed the leather paddle sitting on the chair that he got up from. He grabbed it in one hand and looked at me.

"Bend over and touch your toes, boy," John said.

I swallowed hard and did as he asked. Bo held his breath as he watched John pull his arm back up into the air. The paddle then swung quickly down at me. The impact was hard and the sound of the smack on my ass echoed through the room. I grimaced at the intense pain as a result, but managed not to make much of a sound.

"That was for not informing me of your trip," John said loudly.

"Thank you, Sir!" I replied loudly.

A second impact hit my ass with the same force shortly after.

"That was for your tardiness today," John said.

"Thank you, Sir!" I replied

Finally, a third swing came down on me and almost made me lose my balance due to the force of the blow.

"And that was for not telling me about your relationship," John said.

"Thank you, Sir!" I replied again.

My ass was on fire and I bit my bottom lip, trying not to cry out.

"Rise, boy," John said as I turned to face him.

I looked over and Bo had tears in his eyes, and I felt horrible. I wanted to rush over to him and hug him and tell him it would be ok, but I knew I had to stay still. John placed the paddle on the chair and told me to return to my spot next to Bo.

"Everyone makes mistakes, boys," John said. "The matter is closed, and we can move forward. Bo, you can leave now. I will see you tomorrow for cleaning day."

"Yes, Sir," Bo said with some cracking in his voice.

He turned and left the room and then John turned to me.

"You understand why that was necessary, right boy?" John asked.

"Yes, Sir," I replied. "I apologize."

"Apology accepted," John replied. "Go over to the cross and prepare yourself. I need to burn some energy off in our session today."

"Yes, Sir!" I said.

John was not kidding when he said he had to burn off some energy. After flogging me on the cross for a while, he pissed down my throat and then bent me over the fuck bench and loaded me up twice before he sent me home. As I walked into the apartment, I felt well-used. I closed the door behind me and was getting dressed when I heard a knock. I turned and opened it and saw Bo standing there.

"Do you mind if I come in for a moment?" Bo asked.

"Sure, bubba," I replied, and I let him in.

I finished pulling my clothes off and he undressed as well and then came over and embraced me.

"I am so sorry you had to get punished," he said as he started to sob a bit. "Right after I left, I drove over here and waited for you to get home so we could talk."

"It's ok bubba," I replied as I held him. "I made a mistake. I should have told him. He was completely correct. I also knew it would be complicated to become closer to you."

"I know," Bo said as he wiped his face.

I pulled him back and looked into his eyes.

"I do care a lot for you Bo," I replied. "But let's just be really good friends and sub brothers for now and in December after you graduate, we can see what happens. You've been a great support and friend to me during my training and I don't want to ruin anything we have. I think we can wait a few weeks."

"I agree," Bo said with a smile.

I gave him a quick kiss and then rubbed his cheeks.

"Would you like to stay awhile and play some video games?" I asked. "I would love the company."

"Yeah," Bo said. "I'd like that a lot."

CHAPTER TWENTY-NINE

Office Service

A few weeks after my trip down to Florida, the cold of November had taken hold of the city. Bo and I had reconciled our relationship to be one of close friends and brothers for the time being and even Max started to grow a lot as a sub and was more attentive and punctual. John even spent some extra time training him to lose his gag reflex and increase his pain threshold, which had pleased Kenny immensely.

I had made plans to go visit family with my brother for the Thanksgiving holidays. Bo was planning on spending the extended weekend with Todd and Max had plans with Kenny. So, the Saturday before, we decided to all get together at my apartment for a little celebration for just us. I was in the kitchen cooking when Max arrived.

"Hey, bro!" Max said as he shook a bit. "It turned off chilly out there!"

"I turned the heat up a bit in here since we will be naked," I replied. "But, let me know if you are uncomfortable."

"Oh, it feels good in here!" he said as he stripped down.

"I would have thought that thick fur all over your body would help keep you warm," I said with a smile.

Max laughed and came over to me and hugged me.

"There are drinks in the fridge," I replied. "Help yourself!"

"Thanks!" Max said as he grabbed a beer out and sat down on a chair in the dining area.

"Did you say you and your brother are going to see your parents?" he asked me.

"Yup," I replied. "This is about the only time of year when we all get together. Plus, I'm looking forward to some good home cooking."

"No doubt," Max replied.

"What do you and Kenny have planned?" I asked.

"Sir and I will be having the holiday to ourselves," Max said. "I'm sure I will be well-stuffed in more ways than one."

I laughed out loud. "Lucky you. Kenny is a hot guy."

"Thanks," Max said with a grin. "I'm lucky he found me."

A knock on the door drew my attention and I looked over to see Bo walk in.

"Hey, Bo!" I replied.

"Hey, guys!" Bo said. "Sorry, I am a bit late. Traffic was a bit of a bitch."

"No worries," I replied. "Come over and grab you a drink. Dinner is almost ready."

Bo got undressed and then walked behind me and gave me a big hug and a kiss before grabbing a beer and sitting next to Max.

"We were just talking about our plans next week," I said. "What have you and Sir Todd got planned?"

"He's having this guy he is seeing over," Bo replied.

"Oh, that Pat fella, right?" I asked.

"That's the one," Bo said as he took a drink. "He's got this big romantic dinner planned and I will be serving them both and acting as part of the 'entertainment' as well."

I laughed. "In other words, you will likely be full of cum before the weekend is over."

"More than likely," Bo replied with a smile. "A piggy's work is never done."

Max rolled his eyes. "I've noticed the doms seem to like your ass."

"What can I say," Bo replied as he pointed his thumbs at himself. "I got mad skills thanks to Sir's training."

"Well," I replied as I pulled the turkey out of the oven, "I think some of that is a natural talent, too."

Bo and Max smiled, and I turned to grab some plates.

"Come and get it, boys," I replied. "I hope you are hungry."

We all filled up our plates and had a great time talking and socializing. After dinner, we played some video games for a while, and then the guys helped me clean up some. It was about 8 pm when Bo said that he needed to get back to his place as he had some things to catch up on. After he left, Max stuck around, and we sat on the sofa and goofed off a bit longer.

Thirty minutes after Bo left, I got a message on my phone. I looked down and it was from John.

"What are you doing, boy?" he said.

"Well, that's interesting," I said to Max.

"What's up?" Max asked.

"I just got a message from Sir," I replied. "He's asking what I am up to."

I told John that I had Max over at my apartment and that we had finished eating dinner and were doing nothing special.

"Ask Max if he can come with you to my office," John replied.

"You up for a little adventure?" I asked Max.

Max smiled. "I'm game!"

I told John that Max was with me and he gave me directions on how to get to his office building downtown and where to park. By the time we got there, it was about 9:15 pm, and other than some light traffic in the street, it was quiet.

"I'm assuming you have never been here before," Max asked me.

"Nope," I replied. "I knew he worked downtown but never been asked to come here."

When we came in, the security guard checked to make sure that we were on the list to be let in and he directed us back to the elevators and pushed the floor button for us. The elevator took us up to the tenth floor and when we exited, it was dead quiet.

"This is a little creepy," Max said.

We looked around for John's office and found it at the end of a hall. We knocked on the door and shortly after he unlocked it and let us in. As we entered, we saw he was in his boxers and that was it.

"Thanks for coming over, boys," John said. "We have a big case coming up and I had to work a bit late today to prepare. I'm a little stressed, so I need you both to help."

"Happy to serve Sir!" I replied.

John showed us down to his private office and let us in. It was a bit messy inside. There was paperwork piled on one side of his desk and he had some other materials on a couch to the side as well. The back wall was all glass windows and the buildings beyond were visible in the dark.

"Go ahead and strip, boys," John said as he crossed over to his desk. He dropped his boxers before sitting down in his chair to complete some work.

We both got undressed and put our clothes next to the door and then stood at attention for a few minutes next to one another. John finished writing some things up and then looked up at us.

"Max, come over here and sit under my desk and rub my feet," John said.

Max walked over to the desk and then crawled under. I saw John close his eyes and groan a bit and then he turned his attention to his computer and typed up some things while Max massaged him.

"You ok standing there, boy?" John replied.

"I'm here when you need me, Sir," I said.

John smiled. "You are a good sub."

It was a little chilly in the room, so my balls were starting to contract up near the base ring of my cage a bit. I started to pay attention to the window behind and saw some movement in the windows of the far office building, but nothing I could make out. I wondered if they could see anything that was going on here as well.

"You have my permission to suck my dick, boy," John said down to Max.

I heard a few bumps from under the desk as Max maneuvered to get in-between John's legs and then heard the sounds of him sucking on his cock soon after. John stopped what he was doing and leaned back in the chair and I saw the top of Max's head as he started to bob up and down on John's cock.

"Come out here, boy," John said to Max as he pushed his chair back. "Get on all fours and I will lower my chair so you can still suck me."

Max had his head in John's lap and was going down on him and his butt was pointed in my direction.

"Time to put yourself to good use, Matt," John said to me. "Get down behind your sub brother and get that ass ready for me."

"Yes, Sir!" I replied.

I got down behind Max and spread his furry ass and put my face in to start to lick his hole. He shivered a bit when I licked across it and when I started to push my tongue in him his legs twitched.

John used both his hands to hold on to Max's head and started to face-fuck him as I continued to eat his ass out. I spat on his hole a few times and started to work my finger in first. I had seen Max take Kenny's fat cock with ease before so I knew he could get loose, but he was tight at the moment. I worked my finger in and started to move it back and forth and then dove my face in some more to tongue him and then moved back to put in two fingers.

By the time I had worked three fingers into him, Max was starting to groan a bit and John smiled.

"You like your brother's fingers in your cunt, don't you, boy?" John asked.

Max backed off his hard cock and looked up at him. "Yes, Sir!"

"You think you are ready to be fucked?" John asked.

"Please, Sir," Max replied. "Please fuck me."

"Stand over by the door boy," John said to me.

I walked over and stood at attention while he bent Max over the desk. He licked Max's ass a few times and then spit on his cock and pointed it at his hole.

"Take a deep breath, boy!" John said as he slid inside him in one motion.

Max gasped and yelped a bit and then gripped the table firmly.

"Such a fucking hot ass," John said as he reached down and rubbed his hands through Max's back fur.

He started to move back and forth and pounded Max forcefully enough that the desk started to wobble and the papers on top started to move. John appeared not to care and gripped Max's waist and held him tightly while he railed his ass. I watched John's chest move up and down as he panted, and he bit his lip as he growled. John's ass flexed as he forced his cock inside Max's ass, and I watched as his balls bounced back and forth as he fucked as well. The scene was enough to get my nub hard and dripping precum.

"How much do you want this load, boy?" John asked Max.

"I want it so bad, Sir," Max replied. "Please breed me with your seed!"

"Here it comes, boy!" John growled as he took a few quick breaths and then shoved his cock inside Max.

"Fuck, boy!" John yelled as he coated Max's insides.

Max had his eyes closed and had placed his head on the table and his face was distorted. I could not tell if he was in pain or pleasure. John slid out a few times and then pushed back in, but once his cock stopped pulsing, he pulled out and stepped back.

"Clean my cock, boy!" John said to me.

I came over and got on my knees and took his cock into my mouth and sucked the remaining cum out of him. Once he was clean, he had me turn around and clean Max's ass off as well. Once Max was allowed to stand, he almost lost his balance and I helped him over and we stood against the wall near the door again.

John grabbed a hand towel off the table behind him and wiped his brow and chest and then put his boxers on again and sat down.

"I do enjoy having obedient subs on call," John said with a smile. "You may go."

"Thanks, Sir!" we replied, and we grabbed our clothes and got dressed, and headed back out.

Once we were back in the elevator, Max looked at me. "You up for heading out to the Eagle? We are already downtown, and I still have energy."

"Sure," I replied. "I'm game."

The bar was only a few blocks away, so when we got there, it was still early, but there were some people around. I headed inside to grab a beer for Max and me while Max hung out on the back porch, where some leather daddies were smoking some cigars. I made my way around the different rooms of the bar once I was inside. The place used to be a private home and over the years was transformed into a bar. It meant that there were a lot of smaller rooms to maneuver around to get to the front bar where they were serving.

Once I got up to the bar, I waited in line behind a cute, younger cub. I felt a tap on my shoulder and turned around to see Dan standing behind me.

"How are you doing, stranger?" Dan asked me.

"Hey, bud!" I replied as I hugged him. "Not too bad. Sir had us come over and service him at his office and we decided to come over here after."

"Ahh, late-night office service," Dan said with a grin. "I did that for him a few times myself. Who is we?"

"Max and I," I said. "He is out on the back deck."

"Red collar like me, right?" Dan asked.

"Yup," I replied. "He was the one that replaced Jay."

"That's right," Dan said.

The cub in front of me moved off and the bartender turned to me, "how can I help ya?"

"Two beers please and whatever he wants," I said, pointing to Dan.

"Well thank you!" Dan said. "I'll have a beer, too."

"Three bottles coming up!" the bartender replied.

"You didn't have to do that," Dan said, scratching my back.

"Anything for a fellow sub brother," I said with a smile.

I paid the bartender and left a nice tip and then handed Dan his beer and grabbed my and Max's beers and headed out to the deck and Dan followed. When we walked out the back door, we saw Max making out with one of the cigar daddy's while another was behind him fingering Max's ass.

"Damn, son!" the younger man behind Max said. "You feel like you been bred recently."

"I have," Max said with a grin, turning to look at him.

"Don't mind him," I said, handing Max his beer. "He's my piggy sub brother. Loves a dick in his ass."

Max grinned and gave me a wink and I winked back and tapped my bottle on his. The older man grinned as well. "Well, that's good to know."

Dan and I walked over to the railing and leaned against it.

"How is Sir Greg?" I asked.

"He is well," Dan replied. "He had to go out of town this weekend, so it's just me for tonight."

"You have Thanksgiving plans?" I asked.

"Yeah, I am going to see my sister," Dan replied. "What about you?"

"My brother and I are headed to my parent's house," I replied. "I had my sub brothers over for a little dinner tonight and then Sir messaged me after Bo left and that's how Max and I ended up over at his office."

"Ahh," Dan said with a smile.

The two cigar daddies and Max walked by us and sat on the benches at the far end of the upper deck and we followed them over. One sat on either side of Max and Max was groping the older one while the younger one continued to finger Max's ass.

"You two got the same type of collar he has," the older one said to me.

"Yes, Sir," I replied. "We all trained under the same dom. Dan here was collared last year, and Max and I are still in training."

"What are you getting trained to do?" the younger one asked.

"Please a dom in any way possible," Max piped up.

I smiled and Max smiled back at me.

"In that case, you two subs come a little closer and block the view a bit," the older one said as he unzipped his pants and pulled out his cock. "Come sit in my lap, Max."

Dan and I moved in and faced the man so that there was a bit more privacy and Max undid his belt and pulled his pants down a bit and then straddled the man's legs. His cock was fully hard and sticking up and Max sat down on it, using John's cum from earlier as lube.

"Damn boy," the older man said as his cock disappeared into Max. "That's a nice ass!"

"Thanks, Sir!" Max replied, as he started to bounce on the man's cock.

The younger man started to grope himself as he watched his friend fuck Max. The older man put his hands back on the railing behind him and watched as Max did all the work. He took him deep and then pulled almost out and then went back again. The older man took a deep draw off his cigar and blew it up into the air.

"Wait till you try this ass, Chad," the older man said. "Fucking great."

"I can see that," Chad replied.

A few other guys saw what was going on and came over to watch. They helped us by standing beside me to keep the view to a minimum. Public sex might be hot, but it's a bit of a risk, even in a gay bar. They started to cheer Max on a bit as he started to work the older man's cock.

"Fuck!" the older man said as he brought his arms down and grabbed Max to hold him down. "You feel that cum, boy?"

"Yes, Sir!" Max said as he felt the man's cock pulse inside him. "You had quite a load saved up there."

"Well, that groping you were giving me had me excited," he said with a grin.

He took another drag from his cigar while his cock finished pulsing and then Max got up from his lap and turned around and licked him clean. Chad undid his belt and pulled out his hard cock next and Max moved over to sit on him next.

"Damn, that ass is sloppy," Chad said.

"You are welcome," the older man said with a smile.

The audience had grown by two more and they all watched as Max rode Chad until he was cumming as well. As with the older man, Max turned around and cleaned his cock after.

"Let me see that cage closer," the older man said to Max.

Max moved over and the older man reached out and felt his balls and his nub behind the bars. Some precum squirted out into his hand while he was doing so.

"Sorry about that," Max said.

"All good, boy," the older man said as he licked his fingers clean. "You got some pent-up balls there."

"Yes, Sir!" Max replied with a smile.

Max pulled his pants up and grabbed his beer and sat down between the two men again. We started talking some more and the crowd started to get pretty thick.

"Well, boys," Dan said. "I am going to head on home. You two have a good night."

"You as well, bud," I said as I hugged him.

"Keep in touch!" Dan said as he waved at us and walked off.

Max and I continued to hang out with the cigar daddies for a while and then we moved around and talked to some friends we saw show up as well. They got me some Jell-O shots and a few tequila shots and before long I was drunk. I lost track of Max after midnight due to the crowd and before long found myself back up at the back deck with the cigar daddies again.

"Where is the furry fella that came with you?" the older man asked me.

"Lost him," I said through a fog of alcohol. "He will show up, though."

"You look like you have had a good time," he said with a smile as he blew some smoke my way.

"My friends got me a little drunk," I replied. "Been slurping down Jell-O shots."

"How about you slurp down this then," he said as he unzipped his pants again.

Without thinking, I dropped to my knees with everyone around me and pulled his cock into my mouth. A guy behind me was hooting in encouragement as I started to deep throat him. I could still taste Max's ass on him, but I didn't care at this point. I fondled his balls and stroked him with my hand and mouth, and he reached down and put his hand behind my head and started to face-fuck me as well.

I have no idea how long I was down on my knees, but I do remember swallowing his load and the load of the guy behind me that was watching before Max showed up and smiled.

"There you are!" Max said. "Having fun down there?"

I grinned and cum leaked out the side of my mouth. "Yup!"

"You are a mess, bro," Max said as he helped me up and leaned over and licked the cum out of my beard. "You are not driving home like this."

I handed Max the keys and replied, "they are all yours!"

Max put his arm around me and said goodbye to everyone and then we made our way down the staircase, with some difficulty, and back out into the street.

"I think we both got our helpings of semen protein today," Max said with a laugh.

"Exactly!" I replied as I hugged him a bit. "But I'm glad you were here to help me. Love ya brother."

Max laughed. "This will make a good story one day."

CHAPTER THIRTY

Bo's Graduation

Saturday, December 5 was Bo's big day. He was set to graduate and had told me a few days before that Todd would be there to collar him. I was excited for him and also glad that it would open the doors for us to continue to pursue our relationship as well. I got there a little bit before 1 pm and once I got undressed, I walked into the dungeon area and found John setting things up for the ceremony.

"How are you doing today, boy?" John asked me.

"Doing well, Sir," I replied. "I'm excited for my sub brother Bo but will be sorry to see him move on."

"It's the way of things," John replied as he set a bottle of lube down next to the fuck bench. "I am closer to some of my sub trainees than others and there are times when it is harder to see them move on. Bo has been a great asset to my program and has impressed several of my friends. Todd is getting a talented boy."

"Yes, Sir he is!" I replied with a smile.

"That means you will be the senior sub starting this afternoon," John said. "Why don't you stop by this afternoon around 5 pm and we can discuss a few things related to that position."

"I'll be happy to Sir," I replied.

Max came through the door behind me and looked up and saw the two of us and smiled. "Hello, Matt. Hello Sir!"

"Good to see you boy," John replied. "Max, please follow Matt's lead on what to do to get set up and prepared for the ceremony today. I need to go upstairs and get a few things done and dress."

"Yes Sir!" Max replied.

John then squeezed my shoulder and walked by me and went upstairs closing the door behind him.

"Follow me," I said to Max as I turned to walk over to the isolation room.

As with Jay's graduation, there were three bags set out labeled with our names that contained our uniforms. I told Max we would look at those in a second and the first thing we did was set out the folding chairs for John and Todd and then we took out some disinfecting wipes and made sure all the surfaces of the equipment were clean and ready to go.

I grabbed the box of banners and Max followed me back into the dungeon area where we hung the 'Graduation Day' banner on one wall and the four vertical banners, one for each color collar and one for the doms, on the other wall. Max was reading all the names that were listed on the banners.

"Dang, I had no idea he had so many subs that have graduated," Max replied.

"Yeah," I said. "That was a surprise for me too when I saw them during my sub brother Jay's graduation. I guess my name will be on here soon enough."

"Goes by quick, huh?" Max remarked.

"Well, yes and no," I replied. "I have to admit there are times that being in chastity makes it feel like forever."

Max laughed out loud. "You got that right."

We laid out some markers for signing the banners and then I had Max follow me back into the isolation room to open his bag. Inside was his custom-made black leather jock with red trim and detachable codpiece. It said 'Boy Max' on the back of the waist and 'Chastity Boy' near the top similar to how mine was made.

"Kenny is going to love this!" Max replied as he put his on.

"Well, you will have to return this after the ceremony, but it will be yours to keep after you graduate. Maybe we can take a picture for him after we are done today," I said.

"That would be awesome!" Max said with a grin.

We put our color-coordinated arm and ankle bands on as well and then headed back into the dungeon area.

"What do we do now?" Max asked.

"Now we just sit around and wait," I replied. "Sir just likes us to get here early so things are all set up and situated with time to spare."

"Makes sense," Max said. "Should we kneel in our spots on the floor?"

"In our spots, yes," I replied. "But we are allowed to just sit and wait since it will be a while."

Max and I sat down next to the wall in our colored squares and passed the time talking about Bo and my recent trip down to Florida. I also told him about Key West and meeting Bill and how I was looking forward to getting to know Todd more, possibly. Around 1:45 pm, the door beside us opened and Bo walked inside.

"Hey, guys!" Bo said with a giant smile on his face.

"You look happy!" I said.

"So freaking happy," Bo replied. "A bit nervous though. I was shaking a bit in the car."

"Anything wrong?" I asked.

"No," Bo replied as he adjusted his cage. "It's just a big day. I get like this."

"I understand," I said with a smile.

"Be right back," Bo said as he went over and entered the isolation room to get in his jock and bands.

When Bo came back in the room, he adjusted his jock a few times and then his collar in one of the mirrors on the wall and then walked over to us and sat down next to me. He took a deep breath and then leaned over and gave me a big hug and then hugged Max as well.

"I am so glad that I've had you both as sub brothers," Bo said as he wiped a tear away. "Sorry, I get emotional."

"It's ok," Max said as he placed his hand on Bo's back. "Thank you for being a great role model. You as well Matt!"

The sound of a bell rang through the room through the speaker system near the ceiling and we knew it was almost time. We each got up on our knees and put our hands behind our backs and bowed our heads. At exactly 2 pm, we heard two sets of footsteps come down the staircase, and then the men crossed and stood in front of us.

"Rise boys," John said.

As I got up, I looked at John and Todd. John was in his usual attire of leather chaps, leather jock, and some leather armbands. Todd was standing next to him in just a jock and it was a tight-fitting one that showed off his package well. I had to admit to myself, he was one hot daddy bear. He smiled at us and his deep blue eyes were mesmerizing.

"Boy Bo," John said. "You have completed a year in my service. In that time, I have watched you grow to become a talented and obedient sub worthy of a master. Are you ready to proceed to the next step in your journey?"

"Yes, Sir," Bo replied after taking a deep breath.

"Step forward, then," John said.

Bo stepped forward and John retrieved a leather blindfold and fastened it over his eyes. He then took Bo by the hand and led him across the room to the Saint Andrews cross and bound his legs and arms to the four points. While he was doing so, Todd walked over and stood in front of the folding chair and then sat down in it once Bo was secured.

"Boy Bo," John said. "As part of your service agreement, you have agreed to be placed in chastity. You have done so of your own free will as a way to show your status and determination to be the best sub you can be. I have watched you embrace your new role as the instrument of pleasure for dominant men and your cage has become a symbol of this commitment. This week you completed your final lock-up session that lasted six months and have earned a release."

John reached down and removed the detachable codpiece from Bo's jock exposing his caged nub. He then passed the codpiece to Todd and walked to the side of the room to grab the key to Bo's cage. He unscrewed the security screw with it and removed the cage and base ring and rubbed Bo's nub a bit before handing the cage parts to Todd. I watched as Bo's nub started to chub up a bit from the stimulation.

"Your brothers have been your support base through your journey Boy Bo, and they will now be called upon to witness your next step," John said. "Boys Matt and Max, please come over next to me."

I looked at Max and gave him a wink and then we walked over and stood next to John in front of the bound Bo. I looked down and got to see Bo's uncaged nub for the first time. He was about half hard and I was amazed at the girth he had. There was a little bit of precum forming at the tip of his head as well.

John turned to us and then said, "What is the service creed boys?"

We all spoke up as one in answer. "I am a sub in training under the supervision of Sir John. My goal is to serve men in the best way I can and derive pleasure from that service. My chastity cage and collar are a symbol of that service and I desire one day to be in permanent chastity and receive my formal graduation collar as proof of my commitment."

"Boy Bo, do you now want to take the next step in your journey as a sub and enter into permanent chastity and receive your formal collar from your new master?" John asked.

"Yes I do, Sir," Bo replied.

"Do you understand the commitment this will entail, and do you do this of your own free will?"

"Yes, Sir," Bo replied.

John smiled and looked at me. I knew what was coming next and I had a pretty good idea that Bo did as well since we had been talking about it just recently.

"Boy Matt," John said. "As his sub brother, I will now task you with providing Bo with the last manual release he will receive before his permanent cage is installed. Are you ready and willing to do this?"

"I am, Sir," I said.

"Boy Bo," John said. "I will ask you for the final time. Do you agree to submit to one last manual release from your sub brother before your permanent cage is installed?"

"Yes, Sir, I do," Bo replied after taking a deep breath.

"You may step forward, Boy Matt, and perform the release," John said.

I walked over and knelt in front of the bound Bo. His legs were shaking a bit much like Jay's did and he was breathing a bit fast. I reached up and grasped his balls and he gasped and flexed his feet a bit in their restraints. His nub reacted instantly and became fully hard.

He was girthy and the precum started to flow freely, which I licked off the head of his nub. I stared at him a bit as this would be likely the first and last time I would see him out of his cage and hard.

"Be careful there," John said. "This is not a blow job, boy. You are to perform a manual release and that's it."

"Yes Sir, I understand," I replied.

I started to move my hands up and down on his shaft and Bo's legs flexed and he moved up a bit as the stimulation sent pulses of energy up and down his nervous system. He gasped again and tried to control his breathing, but I could tell that this was going to be an intense experience even if it was just a manual release.

I continued to jack his nub and Bo started to bite his lower lip and move his hips forward a bit. The precum started to flow heavily and I leaned forward and licked and sucked it off as I continued to jack him. Bo started to groan loudly, and I could tell he was nearing the brink.

"I'm so close, Sir!" Bo shouted.

John reached down and put his hand on my shoulder and whispered to me, "drain him."

I started to jack faster, and I massaged his balls and Bo started to buck his hips.

"This last load is for you Sir!" Bo shouted as he groaned, and his nub started to shoot.

I leaned over just in time and put his hard nub into my mouth and let him shoot his load into it. He filled the back of my throat and I was trying hard not to swallow it and let it just collect. His load was so huge, though, that I was on the brink of not having a choice. Fortunately, after several pulses, his nub started to calm down and deflate and I slowly brought my mouth off it and closed my lips to contain his load. I then stood and faced John and Max.

"Boy Max, step forward and face Boy Matt," John said.

Max came over to me and I put my hand behind his head and brought his lips to mine. I opened my mouth and let some of Bo's load spill into Max's mouth and then we both swallowed it. When I pulled back, Max smiled and winked at me and licked his lips. John then directed us to walk back over to our squares next to the wall and to stand at attention.

Bo was still taking deep breaths and his nub had fully deflated and was hanging free for the moment on his body. John motioned to Todd and he got up and walked over and stood beside him in front of Bo's bound body.

"Boy Bo," John said. "Master Todd is here, and he has expressed to you an interest in collaring you and taking you into his home. Do you accept?"

"I do, Sir," Bo replied, still out of breath.

"Master Todd, you may now install Bo's permanent chastity cage," John said.

Todd walked over and bent down and pulled Bo's nub and balls through the base ring and then started to fit the cage. He noticed a little bit of residual cum on the head of Bo's nub and he licked it clean with a grin before fitting the cage and starting to insert the screw.

"I'm proud of you for taking the step of permanently locking your nub and handing me the key, boy," Todd said, squeezing Bo's balls a bit after the security screw was installed.

Todd stood after he was done and reached around and unfastened the blindfold on Bo and removed it. He then leaned over and kissed Bo before stepping back to stand next to John.

"You will now receive your formal collar," John said.

John handed a key to Todd and he unlocked Bo's collar and removed the silver tag. He then went over to the side of the room and grabbed a small jar of liquid and unscrewed the top.

"As is my custom for collaring ceremonies, Master Todd has collected five loads of his cum in this small jar," John said. "Within these fluids, your new permanent tag rests."

John took the jar from Todd and held it as Todd reached in and pulled out the cum covered gold tag. It read 'Boy Bo / CHASTITY SUB / Collared by Sir Todd'. Todd shook the tag a bit over the jar and then put the tag on Bo's collar and reinstalled the lock.

Once Todd was finished, John walked over to the side of the room and grabbed a shot glass of vodka and poured it into the jar and swirled the cum concoction around. He then handed the jar to Todd who brought it over to Bo. Todd placed the Jar on Bo's lips and he tipped it forward and Bo swallowed it all as he stared into the eyes of Todd. When Todd removed the Jar, he wiped Bo's lips with his finger and licked them and then gave Bo a wink before stepping back to stand next to John.

"Boy Bo," John said. "With the acceptance of your collar, you have completed your service to me and are no longer my sub. You are now under the service of Master Todd. Master Todd will now consummate the relationship."

Bo was smiling as John walked over to the folding chairs and sat down. Todd walked over and unhooked Bo's arms and legs and then led him over to the fuck bench and Bo mounted it. Todd grabbed some lube and started to push his fingers into Bo's hole and Bo grasped the bench and started to moan. When he got up to three fingers, Todd knew that Bo was ready.

I watched as Todd removed his jock and let his hard cock free. It was at full mast and ready to breed. He pointed it at Bo's ass and started to push forward in one motion. Bo gasped as Todd entered him.

"Damn, I do love this ass," Todd said as he slapped Bo's ass cheek.

Once he was fully in, he slid his cock back out and then forward again. He was taking his time and he gripped Bo's waist with one hand and rubbed his back with the other. I saw Bo's feet start to curl and flex as Todd began to pick up the pace some and then reached down to firmly hold Bo's waist with both hands. He began to thrust forward and back more forcefully, and I could hear the slap of his groin against Bo's ass from across the room.

Todd was starting to breathe heavily, and his chest flexed a bit as he fucked Bo hard. Bo, for his part, was gripping the bench with all the strength that he had and closed his eyes and clenched his teeth. I was expecting Todd to start breeding him, but what surprised me was the sound from Bo.

"Oh fuck!" Bo yelled and I saw fluids coming out of Bo's cage and hitting the floor.

Todd had given him a caged orgasm from the fucking. I was impressed as was Max, who was mesmerized watching Todd fuck. As Bo continued to pulse cum, his ass clenched and drove Todd over the edge.

"Here comes my load boy!" Todd shouted as he closed his eyes and lifted back his head and filled Bo's ass with his load.

Todd slowed down a bit and then shoved his cock deep into Bo as it finished pulsing. The force sent one last dribble out of Bo's caged nub and Bo opened his eyes and gasped. Todd smiled and ran his hands through the fur on the small of Bo's back and then slapped his ass a few times.

"You never disappoint boy," Todd said.

"Thank you, Sir!" Bo replied between gasps.

John stood and looked over at Max. "Get over here boy and clean up this sub's mess on the floor!"

Max got up immediately and hurriedly walked over and got down on his hands and knees behind Bo and licked the remains of Bo's caged emission off the floor. When he was done, he came over and knelt by me again and Todd helped Bo off the bench and wiped his chest and forehead before cleaning the remains of the cum off of Bo's cage. When Bo had regained his composure, he turned to John.

"Thank you Sir for all the training you have provided me," he said. "I would not be the sub I am today without your guidance."

"You are most welcome, boy," John replied with a smile.

Bo turned to us and walked over to where we were standing and gave us both hugs.

"Thank you two for being there for me," Bo said with a tear running down his cheek. He then gave me another hug and whispered in my ear. "I loved having your mouth on my bare nub babe and I'm looking forward to our time together."

He pulled back and kissed me and then walked back over to where John and Todd were.

"Your final task is to add your name to your banner of honor," John said.

Bo skipped a bit and then walked over to the green banner and using the marker he added his name. He then handed the marker to Todd who signed his name on the black banner for Masters and then put the pen down on the table.

"Todd and Bo, we now will head upstairs for a meal in your honor," John said. "Matt and Max, please clean up the room and you may leave."

"Yes, Sir," we replied as the three walked past us and went upstairs.

Once they had left, we relaxed.

"Wow!" Max exclaimed. "That was intense!"

"You liked that did you?" I replied with a grin.

"I can't wait to have Kenny collar me like that!" Max said.

"Well, you will have to tell me all about it when it's your time," I replied, putting my hand on his shoulder. "But, for now, we need to clean."

I had Max grab the supplies and clean, wipe down, and sanitize the equipment and the floor while I took the banners down and rolled them up. After we were done, I took a picture of Max in his gear for Kenny, and then we took our jocks and bands off and put them in our bags and started to turn off the lights around the room.

"Do you know who is replacing Bo yet?" Max asked me as we headed for the door to get dressed and leave.

"Not yet," I replied. "I guess we will find out on Thursday."

"What does that mean for our cleaning duties on Monday and Wednesday?" Max asked.

"It means we will need to double up, but we can talk about that more later," I replied. "Don't worry, I got your back."

Max smiled and opened the door, and we went into the hall to get dressed.

After I left John's house, I went and ran some errands and got a late lunch. I debated heading home for a while, but with traffic being a bit bad, I just stopped by an ice cream shop and treated myself to kill some time. By the time I got back over to the house again, it was about ten minutes to five in the afternoon. I stripped down again and put my clothes in my bin and as I walked by Bo's now empty bin, I rubbed his name tag before heading into the dungeon area.

I knelt beside the door in my spot for a few minutes before I heard John's voice over the speaker system.

"Come on upstairs boy," he said. "I am in my office on the second floor."

I got up and started to go up first one flight and then the second flight of stairs. I had been up there a few times and had spent time in the guest bedroom when John's guests were in town earlier in the year, but I had never seen his office. When I got to the second floor, I started to walk down the hall and I saw that the second door to my right was open and the light was on. I walked over to the door and looked inside and saw John sitting down at his desk. John looked up and smiled and told me to come in.

The office was originally a bedroom, but all that was in it was his desk and some shelving. There were diplomas and law certifications and awards on the wall, but behind his desk were the pictures of all the boys he had trained over the years. I noticed that Bo's picture had been moved up here and hung on the bottom row.

"This is your first time in here, right, boy?" John asked.

"Yes, Sir!" I replied.

John turned to the wall of photos. "As you can see, this is my wall of honor. It contains all the boys that have completed their training and are now serving as dutiful subs for their masters."

"I'm impressed, Sir!" I said.

John smiled and stood and walked over to me. "You handled yourself well today. I know you have feelings for Bo and that the ceremony was probably extra special for you both. As I told you, now that he has graduated, you may see him now. I have communicated this to him as well and he is looking forward to talking to you soon. Just be sure that any relationship you forge with him does not conflict with my rules and that it does not interfere with your training or your responsibilities here or to me. Is that understood?"

"Yes, Sir," I replied.

"Good," John said. "Now you are the senior sub. That means you are now responsible for cleaning the second floor. I will show you what I expect in each room in a moment. However, the senior sub also is responsible for draining my cock when he arrives. So, on cleaning days, if I am here, your first duty will be to come up here and get under my desk and suck my load down. Is that understood?"

"I will be happy to, Sir!" I said with a smile.

"I have to say I am impressed with you, boy," John said, putting his hand on my shoulder and looking me in the eyes. "You were very inexperienced when you came to me and I have been impressed how quickly you have grown. You have had a few slip-ups and lapses in judgment recently, but I am still very proud to have you as one of my boys."

"I appreciate that a lot, Sir!" I replied.

"Come then," John said. "Let me show you what to do and then you can leave."

I spent about thirty minutes at John's house as he showed me the cleaning duties I would be expected to do upstairs and also showed me some of the files he had on his previous subs. I got to know the names of some of the doms that had collared his boys and we also discussed Todd's interest in possibly taking me on as well. Once I was done, I walked back downstairs and got dressed, and headed out to my car.

When I got in and started the engine up, my phone went off and I looked down and noticed it was a call from Bo.

"What's up, bubba?" I asked as I answered.

"Not much here," Bo replied. "Are you busy?"

"Not now," I said. "I am just leaving Sir's. He had to walk through my duties as senior sub."

"Oh yeah!" Bo said. "Are you excited about moving up?"

"A little," I said. "But I will miss having you around."

"Well, I am over at my apartment starting to pack some things up for my move this week to Todd's," Bo replied. "Do you want to come over for dinner?"

"Sure," I said. "I'll be right over."

I hung up the phone and drove over to Bo's house after stopping for some gas. He sounded much happier and I figured he was excited to be moving on to a new phase in his life. After I parked, I walked over to his apartment and knocked on the door. When he opened it, he was smiling from ear to ear.

"Come in!" he said.

I had not gotten far in before he wrapped his arms around me and gave me a big kiss.

"Hurry up and take your clothes off so we can make out on the couch sexy," Bo said with a smile. "I've been waiting for this for a while."

CHAPTER THIRTY-ONE

The New Sub

On Thursday, December 10, Max and I went to John's house to witness the initiation of the new sub to replace Bo. John gave us no indication of who it might be, so my first view of him was when he walked in while we were kneeling beside the door. Max and I had our heads bowed, so all we saw were his feet at first. He had some big ones with a dark complexion and a tiny tuft of hair on each toe.

John welcomed him to the dungeon and let him know the cameras were recording everything and then they went over to the table to our right to go over his contract. It all seemed pretty standard from not only my experience but what I had witnessed when Max came on board. Once the new guy had signed the contract, John locked the black and green collar around his neck.

I saw the two sets of feet then move across the room and heard as John looked through the drawers for the right type size of chastity device. John remarked that as an uncut sub, he would have to make sure he was extra diligent about hygiene and washing while in the cage. I then heard the device installed around his nub.

"You are officially one of my boys now," John said. "Please walk over to the wall and kneel in the green square with your head bowed like your sub brothers."

"Yes, Sir," came the response. It was a deep voice with a slight hint of a southern accent.

The new sub came over and knelt with us for a moment while John got things put away and then John came over and stood in front of us.

"Rise, boys, and look up and face me," John said. "Matt, please come forward and introduce yourself."

I stepped forward and turned and got my first look at him. He was a younger Hispanic man with thick dark hair and beard and deep brown eyes. He was chubby like Bo and had some hair on the upper part of his chest with a little treasure trail moving down towards his belly button. He had big hands to go with his big feet and thicker legs as well. All around, he was very attractive, I thought.

"My name is boy Matt," I said out loud. "I am your sub brother and I have been in training under Sir for nine months."

The new sub smiled at me and I smiled back and then returned to my spot. Max was up next.

"My name is boy Max," he said. "I am your sub brother and I have been in training under Sir for three months."

"Mateo," John said, "please come forward and introduce yourself as well."

Mateo took a step forward and turned to face us. "My name is boy Mateo. I will be your sub brother, and this is my first day!"

"Good job boy," John replied as Mateo returned to standing beside us. "Matt and Max will be your family here while you are training under me, Mateo. They are indeed your sub brothers and you should get to know and rely on them. Matt is the senior sub, and he will be meeting with you after you are done here. I will give you his information and I want you to text him when you leave."

"Yes, Sir!" Mateo responded.

"Very well," John said. "Boys, please recite the creed for Mateo."

Max and I responded. "I am a sub in training under the supervision of Sir John. My goal is to serve men in the best way I can and derive pleasure from that service. My chastity cage and collar are a symbol of that service and I desire one day to be in permanent chastity and receive my formal graduation collar as proof of my commitment."

"Excellent job, boys," John responded. "You may leave now."

"Thank you, Sir," we both responded as we turned to leave and close the dungeon door behind us.

"I'm staying with Kenny tonight," Max whispered to me once we closed the dungeon door behind us and were in the hall and getting dressed. "Do you just want me to come by your apartment and we can invite Mateo over there when he is done?"

"Yeah," I said in a whisper back. "That sounds like a good plan."

Once I got home and undressed, I went over and grabbed a beer to relax. I got a text from Mateo just after I sat down on the couch and I asked him to come over and gave him my address. Max knocked on the door a few minutes later and he came in and grabbed a drink and joined me on the couch to play some video games as we waited.

About fifteen minutes later, there was a knock at the door, and I went over and opened it. Mateo was on the other side and looked a bit shocked to see me naked except for my cage and collar.

"Come on in brother!" I replied as I hugged him.

Max smiled and hugged him as well and he looked a bit nervous.

"Make yourself at home, but be sure to strip down," I replied. "Remember, no clothes on inside."

"Oh, right!" Mateo said as he fumbled with the buttons on his shirt.

"Would you like a drink?" I asked. "I have beer, soda, and water."

"Just a coke if you have one," Mateo said as he put his shirt on the ground and kicked his shoes off and dropped his pants and underwear. "Sorry if I am a bit nervous. I am not used to being naked around strangers."

"Don't worry," I said as I brought him his drink. "Nothing we have not seen before."

Mateo managed a half-smile and took the drink from me in one hand and fidgeted with his ass with the other.

"Sir plugged you didn't he?" I asked with a smile.

"Yeah," Mateo said with a grin. "Fucked a huge load in me and locked it in."

"That's all part of the initiation," Max said.

"How long did it take you two to get used to this thing?" Mateo asked as he pointed to his cage.

"Not too long for me," I replied. "Though it took several weeks to get over waking up at night from attempted erections."

"Yeah, it was the same for me," Max said. "I just had to use some lotion around the base ring at first."

"I guess I will just have to deal with it," Mateo said as he came over and carefully sat in the chair across from where we sat on the couch. He adjusted a few times as the plug pushed deeper into his ass.

"How did you hear about Sir's program?" I asked.

"My buddy Hugo is a dom," Mateo said. "I met him several months back and he told me about it and introduced me to John."

"Sir," I corrected him. "Be careful about that."

"Sir," Mateo said shyly. "Sorry about that. I am still learning. Anyway, Hugo has known Sir John for a while and has attended several parties that have been thrown and thought I would benefit from the program."

"Oh, I know Hugo," I said with a laugh.

"You do?" Mateo asked.

"Oh yes," I replied. "He was at Sir's party this summer. Huge, thick cock and he loved to fuck our sub brother that recently graduated named Bo."

"Yeah that sounds like Hugo," Mateo said. "He nearly had me in tears the first time he fucked me. Nearly ripped me in two."

Max laughed, "Now I am curious to meet this guy."

I smiled, "I am sure you will at some point."

"Anyway," Mateo said as he took a sip of his drink, "I wanted to learn more about what it is like to be a sub. The whole chastity thing is completely new to me, but I'm up for a challenge."

"I was like you at first," I said. "But you will adapt quickly. In the meantime, though, we need to talk about a few things and the first is your appearance."

"Is something wrong?" Mateo asked?

"Nothing about you personally," Max said. "You will need to trim your hair and beard a bit though."

"And your groin area as well," I said as I pointed to his thick bush around his cage.

"If you are up for it, I can help you right now," Max said.

"Sure," Mateo said. "I better get in line quick."

"Can we use your bathroom Matt?" Max asked.

"Go for it," I replied. "You will be in good hands Mateo, don't worry."

The two got up and walked back into the bathroom and I heard them talking and the buzz from the trimmer going for a while. When Mateo came back in, his beard was trimmed back a bit and his hair was shorter. Max had also cut back his groin to just a stubble.

"Mateo wanted to try going short with the pubes at first since he is not used to the cage," Max said.

"You look really good Mateo!" I replied. "Quite a sexy sub."

Mateo blushed. "Thanks."

We ran over the basics with Mateo and made sure he had both our contact info. We talked about what to expect and I highlighted some of my experiences over the past nine months, and Max talked about what he had experienced in his time as well. He seemed to get more comfortable as time went along and seemed truly interested in learning quickly and doing the best he could. After about an hour, he had to go, so we wished him well and he left followed by Max shortly after.

The following Monday, we all showed up at John's house for cleaning day. We knelt in our spots till we heard the footsteps of John come down the staircase and some in and stand in front of us.

"Rise boys," John said.

We stood and faced him, and he smiled.

"How is that cage working out Mateo?" John asked.

"Good Sir," Mateo replied. "I am still waking up several times a night, but I will adapt. I know I can."

"Good boy," John replied.

"Matt, please show Mateo the ropes as far as what he needs to do around the house, and then you can come upstairs for your duties," John said.

"Yes, Sir," I replied.

"Boys, in two weeks I will be having my annual holiday party at the house," John said. "This year it will be Christmas-themed since it will be occurring the day after Christmas. Do any of you have conflicts with this date?"

"No, Sir," came the reply from the three of us.

"Good," John said. "Six people have RSVP'd so far, so it should be a nice event. You will be used as the party favors, but you will also be expected to serve the guests food and drink and see to any other need they may have."

"Yes, Sir!" we replied.

"I will work with Matt on the details," John said. "As senior sub, Matt will be responsible for the entire event and ensuring you other subs know what you should be doing."

"Sounds like a plan, Sir," I replied.

"Very well," John said. "You can get started cleaning. Matt, I will await you upstairs when you have got Mateo started."

"Very good, Sir!" I responded.

Once John had left we relaxed a bit.

"How wild do these parties get?" Mateo asked.

"Just be sure you are well cleaned out and ready to be walking funny," I said with a grin. "Especially if Hugo shows up. But in all seriousness, they are a lot of fun."

Mateo smiled and I showed him back into the isolation room and ran down the normal duties he would be doing around the house on cleaning days. Max helped me show him where the supplies were, and we answered any questions he had. After he was set and ready to start, I grabbed what I needed and headed up to the second floor.

When I got to John's office, the door was open. I knocked on the threshold and he looked up and beckoned me in with his hand. As I came in, I looked to my left and saw that the flatscreen TV on the wall was on and it had several cameras showing. I saw several angles in the dungeon on the top row and then images of the various other rooms in the house as well. I could see Matt starting to clean in the kitchen and Mateo was coming up the staircase with a vacuum.

"The whole house is wired," John said to me as he saw me looking. "I like to keep an eye on my subs when I am in here. Plus, the sessions I have with you make good viewing for later."

"Yes Sir!" I replied with a smile.

"Come over here and kneel in front of my chair boy," John said. "My balls are heavy."

I walked around his desk and he pulled his chair out to give me better access to him. He was completely naked already and I knelt in front of him and stroked his thick cock a bit till a bead of precum formed, which I licked off and swallowed. John grabbed the back of my head and forced me down on him to his root, which caused me to gag a bit.

"Still need to work on that gag reflex boy," John said. "But you are doing much better than when you first started with me."

John started to force my head up and down on his shaft and I closed my eyes and focused on my breathing so I could take him better. A mix of saliva and precum started to fill my mouth and dribble down his cock and balls. When he let me up, I went down and licked his balls and brought my tongue up his shaft to savor it all. I could tell he had been sweating today, as he had a good musk built up in his crotch. As I leaned down and swirled my tongue around his balls and shaft, I breathed deep and took it all in.

John looked down at me and smiled. Over the past nine months, I had learned he liked having his balls played with, and I rolled them in my hand as I started to go down on him again. John closed his eyes and leaned back and groaned. I felt his hand on my shoulder and he started to rub it as I continued to work his meat.

I brought one hand up to start to jack him a bit and then brought my face up and over his head to lick and suck on him. He started to flex his legs and groan more and I knew this was a sign he was close. I started to go faster and work his cock with my hand and mouth and was soon rewarded with a large burst of cum that splashed across my beard before I got my face back on his head to suck it down.

"Fuck!" John groaned as he held the back of my head.

He forced me down and I felt more pulses of warm cum hit the back of my throat and dribble down to my stomach. He pulsed at least five or six times before he caught his breath, and I felt his cock start to soften. Releasing his grip on my head, I came off him and used my fingers to collect the part of his load on my beard and savored the taste.

"Well done, boy," John replied. "You may now get up and get to cleaning."

"Thank you, Sir!" I replied with a smile.

I went about getting my chores done upstairs and finished with some time to spare, so I came down to help Mateo, who was in the dungeon dusting.

"How are things going bro?" I asked as I came into the room.

Mateo turned to look at me and smiled. He had been on a small step ladder and was dusting some of the pictures and art hanging on the wall. John had some erotic artwork on the wall that the door to the entrance hall was on and some that extended down the hall to the stairway as well. Pictures of myself, Matt, and Mateo hung over the table that we used to sign our contracts.

"Good!" Mateo replied. "Sir already has my picture hung!"

I walked over and looked. The picture had been taken on Mateo's initiation day and he was standing tall with his feet slightly spread and his hands behind his back. His collar and cage were on full display and he had a slight grin.

"He got a nice one of you!" I replied as I put my hand on his shoulder. "Matt and I are really happy to have you on board with us."

Mateo smiled and turned to finish dusting and I grabbed the disinfectant and wiped down the surfaces of the equipment in the room before starting to put my cleaning supplies away. Max walked down just as I finished.

"Well guys," I said, "I have to head off, are you two ok getting things put away on your own?"

"No problem," Matt said. "We got it covered."

"See you Wednesday!" Mateo said.

I waved and headed into the entrance hall to dress and leave. Bo had completed his move to Todd's over the weekend and had invited me to come by after I completed my duties with John to see his new digs. It was not a far drive and after stopping to top off the gas tank, I walked up to the front door and knocked. Bo opened it and smiled.

"Hey, babe!" Bo replied. "Come on in!"

Bo was in some sweatpants and had a tank top on and hugged me as I came in and he closed the door behind me.

"I hope it's not awkward, but Sir allows me to have comfortable clothes on around the house since I'm his boy now," Bo said. "You'll still have to strip down. If that makes you uncomfortable, I will strip as well."

"Not a problem at all," I said as I started to take my pants down. "We talked about this. You are the alpha sub now around here. Just let me know if there are other rules I need to follow outside of what Sir John requires."

"Will do," Bo said with a smile.

Once I stripped naked, Bo put my clothes in a basket near the door and then I followed him into the living room. Todd was on the couch watching CNN. He looked up and smiled at me when I came in.

"Good to see you, boy," Todd said.

"You as well, Sir!" I replied.

"Bo, can you grab me another soda?" Todd said as he held out his empty can.

"Yes, Sir!" Bo said.

He walked over and grabbed the can and threw it away and got a fresh one out of the refrigerator. After handing it to Todd, Bo came behind me and put his arms around me.

"Is it ok if I show Matt my room now, Sir?" Bo asked.

"Sure, boy," Todd replied. "You two have fun."

Bo kissed my neck and then led me down a hall and into his bedroom. It was a nice size. He had floor-to-ceiling shelving on the wall to my left as I entered with books and various other personal items on some of them. There was still a lot of empty space though. A queen-size bed sat against the opposite wall and there was a window on the wall opposite of the door with a desk below it. Beside the door was a chest of drawers. On the far end of the shelving was a door that led to his closet that was rather deep and had his clothes and tons of room to spare.

"This is a big room!" I replied.

"Right?" Bo said. "I was shocked. I was expecting to get a small little space, but Todd wanted me to feel at home. I have a cot in his bedroom where I can sleep if he wants me in there and I did that Saturday when his boyfriend came over to stay the night."

"How did that go?" I asked.

"It was good," Bo replied. "He and Pat are starting to see each other more, but this was only the second time he has slept over."

"Did you have to do anything for him?" I asked.

"I gave him a morning blow job Sunday, but that was it," Bo replied. "I think Sir just wanted to get him used to me."

"That's cool," I said.

Bo went and sat on the bed and scooted back some.

"Come sit here," Bo said, patting the area in between his legs.

I walked over and sat in front of him and he put his legs around mine and then leaned over and put his hands around my belly.

"There's plenty of room here if you get Sir's collar too," Bo said as he leaned in and put his head on my shoulder.

I smiled as he rubbed my belly. His hand drifted down and reached my cage and I started to stiffen instantly.

"Hey now!" I replied.

"Oh, you calm down," Bo said with a devilish smile. "Don't forget I am the alpha around here now. I have permission to play with you a bit from Sir."

I rolled my eyes and turned to look at him and he moved in to kiss me deeply. I brought my hand up and behind his head as we made out and he continued to rub my cage until I started to leak a bit. He brought his hand up to his mouth and licked the juices off his fingers and then smiled.

"I love how much you leak," Bo replied.

"Well, the company also has an effect as well," I said with a grin.

We continued to make out a bit until we heard a knock on the doorframe and looked up to see Todd staring at us.

"You having fun playing with the sub there boy?" Todd asked with a grin.

"Yes, Sir!" Bo replied as he squeezed my balls and cage.

"Don't torture him too much," Todd said with a wink. "I am about to go lay down for a bit. Be sure to clean up the living room and kitchen before you go to bed boy."

"I will, Sir," Bo replied.

Todd waved at us and then went down the hall to his bedroom. When he had gone, Bo pushed me a bit to get me up and then stood as well.

"Why don't you come and help me," Bo said.

"Be happy to!" I replied.

We walked into the living room and Bo told me to grab the plates and glasses that Todd had out, and I began to wash them in the sink as he straightened things up. When he was done, he came in to check on me.

"When you finish that, please wash the dishes in the sink as well and then dry and stack them, I am going to put the trash out," Bo said.

"Yes, Alpha!" I said with a grin.

Bo winked at me as he slid on some flip-flops to take the trash out and I finished washing things up and drying everything. When Bo came back in, he showed me where to put things away, and then we grabbed some water and headed back to his room.

Bo laid down in bed and had me lay in front of him and he big spooned me as we talked about how his day went. At one point, he wrapped his leg around me, and I felt his cage under his pants rub up against my ass. He started to nibble on my neck and ran his hands over my naked body.

"Are you sure it's ok with Todd to be doing this?" I asked.

"Don't worry," Bo said. "We had a long talk. As long as I am not breaking any of Sir John's rules you have to follow, it's ok. He told me since I have his collar, if he's not using me or wanting to use you, then I do what I want to you."

"Well now," I said with a grin. "What do you want to do to me?"

"I'm content to spoon you, for now, sub," Bo said with a grin.

"Oh, I'm your sub now am I?" I replied with a grin as well.

"At the moment you are!" Bo said as he squeezed me, and I squeezed him back.

We laid there and made out again before passing out.

CHAPTER THIRTY-TWO

The Christmas Party

John's holiday party was scheduled for the Saturday after Christmas. I had met with Mateo and Max and with permission from John, we had decided to decorate the house a bit to get the theme going. We also agreed to wear some red and green Christmas socks that I found as well. They would be beneficial for an idea I had to run by the guys. So, it was that we had scheduled to meet in the dungeon at 10 am that Saturday. I had a few boxes of decorations that I had brought over to the house in my car and I was unloading them when Max arrived first.

"Hey bro," Max said as he waved at me. "You need some help?"

"Yeah," I replied. "I need everything in the back here brought inside."

"Sounds like a plan!" Max said as he started to help.

Mateo arrived soon after Max and between the three of us, we were able to get everything inside. I had garland to hang around the dungeon area and down the staircase and I had Mateo tackle that. Max and I set out the lube and various toys that the guests might like to use on us, and we also laid out hand towels for cleanup as needed as well. I had a few knick-knacks that I had brought as well, such as some tabletop light-up trees and some small wreaths. By the time we were all done and ran the vacuum one last time, the place looked cool at a lowered light level.

"This turned out nice!" Mateo said as he looked around.

"I'm pleased as well," I said. "Come over here guys, I need to show you some things."

The guys walked over to where I was on the side of the room and I pulled out the socks I had brought for us.

They came up over your thigh and were red and green with some Christmas Trees on them. I had ordered them special online and they had our names at the top. Mine said 'Sub Matt', and the other two said 'Sub Mateo' and 'Sub Max'.

"Oh, these are cool!" Max said.

"Well, just wait," I said, pulling out three markers as well. "I cleared this idea with Sir. Keep these markers in your left sock. The guests will give you a hash mark on your ass for every load you take and on your chest for everyone you swallow. The sub that has the most hash marks will get a special present from Sir."

"I'll take that bet!" Mateo said with a smile as he grabbed a marker.

"I think my piggy ass can best you," Max said with a smile taking a marker as well.

"Well," I replied with a grin. "Don't fight over the cock just yet guys. There will be plenty to go around from my experience at these parties."

"Yeah," Mateo said. "Hugo said he will be here, so I hope you two are ready to be split in two."

"Unless he decides you're his bitch," Max replied slyly.

We all laughed and set things on the shelving unit for the moment.

"I brought some salads for lunch if you all are up for it," I replied.

"Salad?" Mateo asked with a grimace.

"Mateo, we are on the bottom diet today," Max said as he poked him. "Nothing heavy."

"I guess," Mateo said, rubbing his belly slightly defeated.

The three of us were sitting on the floor around the table next to the wall eating when John came downstairs to check on us.

"Nice job boys," John said as he looked around.

He had some sweatpants on and a t-shirt, but his hair looked disheveled like he had just woken up.

"Thanks, Sir," I replied as I set my fork down and stood to face him.

My fellow sub brothers joined me, and John walked over to us.

"The first guests will not be here till 4 pm," John said. "So, you have some hours to kill. I would like you to please do a thorough cleaning of the first and second floors after you finish your lunch. I might have some people staying the night if they so choose."

"Yes, Sir," we replied.

"I have ordered some food that will be delivered about 3:30 pm as well," John said. "Matt, please see to it that it is accepted and set out for the guests. I believe you know where the folding tables are at."

"I do, Sir," I replied.

"Very well," John said. "I am going to go get a shower and then take a nap for a bit. Matt, please ensure I am up at 3 pm."

"I will, Sir!" I replied.

John smiled and turned and went back upstairs and we sat down again to finish our lunch. When we were done, we set to work cleaning the house from top to bottom. John's bedroom door was closed, so I made sure to hold off vacuuming up there till he was awake but managed to clean the rest of the rooms as quietly as I could. By the afternoon, the place was spick and span and ready for the first guests to arrive.

After waking John up and running the vacuum on the second floor, I made my way downstairs in time to hear the door chime. It was at that point that I was a bit perplexed as to what to do. I was naked and did not want to answer the door in that state. John saw me in the hall and came over to me.

"Go ahead and answer boy," John said. "The caterer is a friend and knows you will be undressed."

"Yes, Sir!" I replied and I went over to open the door.

A short, bearded man with thick-rimmed glasses smiled at me. He had a few trays in his hand and started to hand them to me.

"Hello, sub," he replied. "Be careful, these are warm. I will grab the other trays for you."

"Thank you, Sir!" I replied.

Max had come behind me and I passed the trays to him and then turned to get the other ones from the delivery man. After we had everything moved to the kitchen, the man handed me a receipt and winked at me.

"You boys have fun tonight," he said with a smile and left.

I had Mateo and Max help me grab the folding tables and chairs from where they were stored, and we set them out on the far wall of the dungeon area away from the equipment. I wanted to keep some distance from the play area and the food. We then set out all the trays and then brought down the coolers of drinks as well. Alcohol was next and before long, we had quite a spread set up.

I looked at the clock and noticed that it was almost 4 pm, so we turned and put our socks on and slid our markers down the back of one of them and then went and knelt in our squares on the floor to await the guests. After about ten minutes, we heard footsteps coming down the staircase and when the door opened, we saw two pairs of bare feet walk by.

"You may rise boys and stand at attention," John said.

When I got to my feet, I saw that Greg was standing next to him.

"Max and Matt, I believe you know Greg," John said.

"Yes, Sir!" we both replied.

"Greg, this is my newest sub, Mateo," John said, reaching out to grab Mateo's shoulders.

Greg smiled and nodded and then John showed him over to the food and they grabbed some meatballs and some cheese and crackers before beginning to talk and catch up. A few minutes later I heard the doorbell chime and another set of footsteps come downstairs. This time Todd came through the door into the dungeon.

"Todd!" Greg exclaimed. "How have you been bud?"

Todd smiled and walked by us and went over to hug Greg. "Doing well my friend."

"I hear you collared yourself one of John's boys," Greg said.

"Indeed, I did," Todd replied. "Moved Bo in and he's already fitting in nicely."

"He's got a nice ass that one," Greg said with a smile. "I'm a little envious."

"Well stop by whenever you want," Todd said. "You can always use it again."

Gregg laughed. "I'll take you up on that!"

Todd turned to grab some food and looked over at me and smiled and gave me a wink. Once he had his plate full, he came over and stood in front of me.

"You ready for today, boy?" he asked.

"We all are, Sir!" I replied.

"Good sub," Todd said. "How about you fetch me a whiskey on the rocks."

"Right away, Sir!" I replied.

Hugo was the next to arrive and as soon as he saw Mateo he grinned.

"I do like the look of that cage on you boy," Hugo said as he came over and squeezed Mateo's cage.

"Thank you, Sir!" Mateo replied with a grimace.

I returned with Todd's glass and turned to see the door open again. In walked Kenny and Jack and John came over and greeted them. I was just returning to my position next to my sub brothers when John moved to the center of the room to make an announcement.

"I'm glad to see you all here," John began. "Dusty is running a little late and said he would be here shortly. I think you all know one another and at least two of my subs here. Their names are on their socks and each has a marker inside one of them. I have a little competition that I am playing with them. If they give you a good blowjob, give them a hash mark on their chest and if you breed them, give them a hash mark on their ass."

"What's the prize for the most loads?" Jack asked with a grin.

"I'll award that at the end of the night," John replied with a grin as well. "It's a secret for now."

The men in the room laughed and started to look at us, but John got their attention again. "As you all know, the boys here are for your entertainment. Please use them as you see fit. They can take your clothes and they will be stored in the isolation room for you. Please mingle and socialize and have a great time. And, of course, Merry Christmas! Make sure your sacks are emptied before the night is done."

Another chorus of laughs and a few cheers came next and then the men started to undress. Kenny was the first to approach me and I helped him as he stripped down. Once I had his clothes, he asked me to grab him a vodka and cranberry and I went to put his things away and fulfill his order. Max and Mateo were busy tending to the other men when we heard the door open again and Dusty came in.

"Well, howdy guys!" Dusty said in his thick, Alabama accent. "Shit, everyone is already naked. I'm late to the party!"

Dusty started to take off his shirt and he snapped his fingers at Mateo who came over and helped him undress and take his boots off. Once he was done, he grabbed a beer from the cooler and walked over to John and Greg to talk.

For the first hour or so, the men mostly mingled and talked. We shuttled between them fulfilling drink orders and cleaning up trash. On one occasion, I looked over to see Max on his knees taking Kenny's piss and Hugo playing with Mateo's nipples, but otherwise, it was a social occasion. Once they had a few drinks in them, though, they started to get a bit more handsy and I was groped on more than one occasion as I walked by.

Mateo was the first to be put on display. Hugo brought him over to the fuck bench and bent him over it and buried his face in the boy's ass. Mateo started to groan, and I can only imagine that Hugo was getting deep with his tongue to open him up. I saw Hugo push his fat fingers into Mateo's ass and start to stroke his cock at the same time. Even though I had seen him hard before, it was still a masterpiece of a dick. He had to be as thick as a beer can and precum started to form on the tip of his sheathed head. He fondled his balls a bit as he worked his way up to three fingers in Mateo before he placed his cock on the entrance to the boy's ass and started to push forward.

"Fuck!" Mateo screamed as Hugo started to split him wide.

"Shut the fuck up!" Hugo yelled as he slapped Mateo's ass.

John came over to me and told me to put a gag on Mateo, so I walked over and grabbed the ball gag from the wall and bent down in front of him.

"Sir wants me to put this on you," I said as I held it up to his eyes.

There were a few tears on his face, and I could tell he was trying hard not to yell.

"Are you sure you are ok?" I asked, a bit concerned.

"I'm good bro!" Mateo struggled to say as Hugo got fully in him and started to slowly pull out. "Please put it on me. I need something to bite down on."

"You got it, bro," I replied, and I fastened it around his head, and he bit down on the ball and closed his eyes.

I moved off as Hugo started to move in and out of Mateo faster. Mateo was grunting loudly even through the gag and I looked over to see Hugo fuck. I felt a hand on my shoulder, and I was startled and turned to see Jack behind me.

His broad chest towered over me and he looked at me with his pale eyes and smiled. "How about you jump in that sling over there boy and I'll give you some dick as well."

"Yes, Sir!" I replied.

Jack followed behind me and once I got up in the sling, he helped me put my legs in the stirrups and locked my wrists in the restraints as well. He then brought my ass forward a bit and then used some lube to work his finger into me. I closed my eyes and bit my lip as I felt his finger rub my prostate and my nub instantly swelled and started leaking.

"I forgot how much you leak there boy," Jack said with a grin as he watched it dribble out over my cage and down my balls.

Jack handed me a bottle of poppers and I took a hit, and he did as well before he put the top back on and then placed his hard cock at the entrance of my ass.

"You know the drill, boy," Jack said looking down at me. "Take a deep breath and keep your voice down."

"Yes, Sir," I replied.

Jack started to push forward, and I felt his cock push into my ass. I groaned a bit, pulled on the restraints on my arms, and threw my head back a bit as he entered me. Jack reached down and grabbed my waist and guided me back onto him. I watched as my suspended legs started moving towards his chest and made contact as he got fully in me and his balls hit my ass as well. I squeezed my ass a bit and felt him in me and he looked down and grinned.

"Someone likes being fucked," Jack said.

He pulled out and using his hands on my waist, he rocked me forward and back using the sling to help him fuck me. I heard the chains of the sling start to clang and the smack of my ass on his groin as he thrusted. I looked over and saw Mateo still being railed by Hugo. The fuck bench was starting to groan and creek as Hugo fucked him hard and Mateo had spit dripping out of his gag and his face was red.

I turned back and looked up at Jack who had his eyes closed and had his face slightly turned upwards. He was fucking me with full strokes, and I felt the slam of my ass as it hit his groin. I grabbed the chains that my wrists were secured to and hung on for the ride. A loud groan caught my attention, though and I looked over to see Hugo leaning over on Mateo's back as his cock was filling him up. Mateo was groaning loudly and covered in sweat, as was Hugo. I felt Jack start to pick up the pace and hammer my ass faster and I looked up to see him grinning down at me.

"Here it comes boy!" Jack said as he slammed his cock home and emptied into me.

I could feel his cock pulsing inside me, and he brought it out just enough that it was rubbing my prostate and sending waves of energy through me as well. I groaned a bit as more precum started to flow out and drip down my balls mixed with a little prostate juice. I closed my eyes and breathed deeply and then felt him withdraw and finger my ass. When I looked up, he had a towel in his hand and was wiping his brow. He then brought it down and wiped my crack and then undid my wrist restraints and let me up.

"Turn around boy," Jack said as I got to my feet.

When I turned around, he pulled the marker out of my sock and put a hashmark on my ass, and then put the marker back. He then gave me a spank and asked me to get him a beer. As I walked off, I saw Mateo on the fuck bench. He looked exhausted. He had a hashmark already on his ass and I saw Dusty rubbing his red and dripping hole in preparation for his next breeding. Near the table where the alcohol was at, Max walked over and smiled. He had a hash mark on his chest.

"You looked like you enjoyed that," Max said. "That Jack fella is hot."

"He's got a nice cock too," I replied with a wink. "I'm sure you will probably find out at some point."

Max licked his lips and chuckled. "That is if Kenny let me. He already fed me one load and wanted me in the sling after seeing you up there."

"Well, the night is still young, bro," I replied as I patted him on the shoulder. "You might get that prize before it's all over. But, from the look at poor Mateo, we might both be out of luck."

We both turned to look over and watched Dusty plowing Mateo's sore ass and then went back to work. I had just grabbed Jack's beer and popped the top off the bottle when Todd saw me and came over.

"You busy, boy?" he asked.

"I need to get this beer to Master Jack, but I'm otherwise free Sir," I replied.

"Good, hurry up and come back over here," Todd replied.

"Yes, Sir!" I said as I hurried over to Jack with his bottle.

As I passed the fuck bench I heard Dusty starting to groan and saw his ass clench as he added another load to Mateo. Mateo groaned loudly and clinched the bench. He looked over at me with a tear running down his face and I stopped for a moment, but he held up a thumbs up at me and then turned to look down again. Figuring he was ok; I continued and handed the bottle to Jack and then took my leave to return to Todd.

Todd led me back into the isolation room and closed the door behind us. He then sat down on a padded chair near one of the cages on the floor and looked at me.

"I just wanted some private time with you, boy," Todd said. "How is your training going?",

"Well, Sir," I said as I stood at attention in front of him. "I have about two and a half months to go before graduation."

"So Bo has told me," Todd said as he leaned back and sipped his drink. "I'm still giving serious consideration to taking you on as a collared boy. I know Bo would like this and you and I seem to click well."

"I would be very honored, Sir," I replied.

Todd smiled and spread his legs open and his low hanging balls fell beneath his hardening cock.

"On your knees boy," Todd said. "Show me how much you like sucking my dick."

I got down on my knees immediately and knelt in front of him. He leaned back a bit more and his cock was fully hard and pointing towards the ceiling. I grasped his balls in one hand and then brought my mouth over and around his head and slipped it in between my lips slowly. Todd groaned and grasped his glass as I swirled my tongue around and down his shaft and used my hands to massage his balls as well.

I heard pops from his feet and looked down to see him flinching and stretching his toes and flexing the joints. He spread his legs a bit more and I got down and started to deep throat him a bit. He placed his glass on the floor and then brought his hand down over my head and guided me as I started to move up and down on him.

I felt his cock pulse a bit and tasted the sweetness of his precum and groaned a bit myself as I brought my tongue up and around his head and savored it. Todd looked down at me and I met his eyes and we both smiled at each other. I took his lower shaft in my hands and started to jack it slowly as I worked the head with my mouth. His chest was starting to heave, and he moved his hands down to my shoulders.

I wanted to drain him good and I had learned from Bo that he liked having a finger placed in his ass, so I started to move down and move my index finger into his crack. Todd moaned and shifted forward and gave me more access and I felt his hole. I pulled my finger back and licked it and then returned to rub his hole with it. This produced even more precum and his legs started to quiver. With a little more spit, I was able to push my finger in and turn it till I found his prostate gland.

I started to rub the gland as I worked his cock with my other hand and mouth, and he started to moan and reached up and rubbed his nipples. He flexed his feet again and I watched as his balls started to move a bit as well. Figuring that was my cue, I applied a little more pressure to his prostate and started to work his shaft and was rewarded with a huge spurt of cum that came shooting out of his cock. His ass clenched down hard on my finger and he groaned loudly.

"FUCK BOY!" Todd yelled as his whole body shook.

I managed to pry my finger loose from his tight hole and I continued to stroke his cock and pull all of his load out to swallow. The last bits sat on my tongue and I swirled them around and savored them as I looked up and saw that he was opening his eyes to look at me. He reached down and grabbed my head and brought me up and kissed me and tasted a bit of his cum on my lips.

"Someone has been telling you some of my secrets," Todd said with a grin.

"Bo mentioned that you enjoyed that from time to time," I said as I pulled back.

"I'll be sure to thank him tonight," Todd said.

I knelt again, and he leaned over and grabbed the marker out of my sock and added two hash marks to my chest.

"I know, I know," Todd said as I looked down and then back up at him. "But, that blowjob deserves two hashes."

I smiled and Todd grabbed his drink and took a few gulps and then sighed.

"Ok, boy," he said. "Get back out there."

"Yes, Sir!" I replied with a smile and I returned to the dungeon area and closed the door behind me.

As I walked over to the food table, I saw Mateo was up and mixing a drink for someone.

"Hey bubba," I said as I gently put my hand on his shoulder. "Are you ok?"

"I am, bro," Mateo said with a smile.

His face was still red from the squinting and intensity of the fuck he had earlier, and he looked a bit disheveled, but his large grin and the glint in his eyes told me he was indeed ok.

"I always think I am ready for Hugo and then you get him in you, and you remember just how big he is and how hard he fucks," Mateo said, still grinning. "I'm gonna learn to take him like a champ one day."

I laughed. "That might take a lot of training."

"You're probably right!" Mateo said with a chuckle.

I needed to take a bathroom break, so I excused myself for a moment. When I returned, I saw Greg in the hallway leading back to the dungeon area.

"Where have you been, boy?" he asked. "I lost track of you."

"Master Todd was using me privately, Sir," I replied.

"Ahh, ok," Greg said. "Well how about you put those lips to work on me. It looks like you have already been hard at it today."

I smiled and got down on my knees in front of Greg and licked the underside of his balls. I could smell his sweat and musk and it got my nub instantly swelling again. Greg leaned against the wall and spread his legs a bit to give me better access and I got my tongue into his crotch and bathed his balls before moving up to start to suck on his hard cock next.

"That's a boy," Greg said as he reached down and grabbed my head and started to face fuck me.

His cock started hitting the back of my throat and I concentrated as best I could to keep from choking. For the most part, I succeeded, but there were a few times I involuntarily gagged and spit ran out of my mouth and down his shaft and balls. He didn't seem too concerned, though, and continued to use my mouth as his personal pleasure toy.

He started to pull on my head harder and his hard cock was deeper in my mouth and I was starting to gag a bit more. He did not let up, though, and assaulted me until I thought I could take no more. It was then that I felt him tense up and blast his cum straight down my throat. I was not ready for it and I coughed right as he did, and it went up my nose and started dribbling out a bit as well. This made me cough more and I ended up with cum all over my beard before he was done.

Greg looked down at me and wiped my cummy nose and then pulled my mouth open and spit. I watched as the liquid came out of his mouth and dribbled down into mine and hit my tongue. He spat it out and then closed and rubbed my face and beard making sure his cum was massaged in. He then slapped my face.

"Good boy," he said as he adjusted his balls.

I got up and he had me hand him the marker and he added a third hashmark to my chest. He then smiled and returned to the room to grab some more food and a drink.

The sex took a brief pause while the men talked and had some more food. When it resumed, Max was on the fuck bench getting railed by Dusty and Mateo was on the cross getting his back flogged by Greg. I, for my part, ended up in the sling and was fucked first by Kenny and then by John before being let up and told to get down on my hands and knees and act as a foot prop for Hugo, who had sat down and was enjoying a cigar with John.

As I sat in that position with Hugo's large feet propped on me, I looked over and saw Mateo's red back as he was strung up on the cross. Greg got him down after spending some time slowly rubbing him down and put him on the fuck bench and started fucking his ass next. After being opened up by Hugo and then Dusty, Greg had no trouble pushing right in. At the same time, Jack moved around to Mateo's head and started to face fuck him. I watched as the fuck bench started to squeak and move back and forth as they used both his holes.

Hugo blew a puff of smoke over me and looked down at me. "How are you doing down there boy?"

I looked back at him and smiled. "Good, Sir. Happy to be of service."

Hugo smiled and blew more smoke in my direction and then crossed his feet on my back and leaned back in the chair and watched the Mateo fuck show continue. I heard a groan and looked over and saw Greg pushing forward and unloading into Mateo's ass. He pulled out and let some of the spurts of cum coat his crack and then he snapped his fingers over at Max and had him get down and lick the cum clean. Just as Max was finishing, Jack grunted and loaded Mateo's mouth up and I heard him cough a bit as it went down his throat.

The men left Mateo on the bench for a while and they sat down and joined John and Hugo for a cigar as well. Max ended up as a footrest for Greg and had his ass pointed at mine and at one point I felt his cage hit mine. I felt some liquid run down my balls and later learned that it was from Max. He had been leaking precum like a sieve and it was everywhere.

John took a deep drag from his cigar and then handed it to Hugo and got up and walked by us over to Mateo. The poor boy was still strapped to the fuck bench and even after being cleaned by Max earlier, some more cum had come out of his ass and was dripping down over his caged balls. He had relaxed and not made a sound for several minutes, but when John lightly started to rub his ass, his eyes popped open and he gripped the bench.

"How's my boy doing there?" John asked.

"I'm ok, Sir," Mateo responded.

"Are you still in the game?" John asked as he moved his thumb down and rubbed Mateo's cummy, stretched hole.

"Ready to serve, Sir" Mateo responded.

"Good boy," John replied as he started to stroke his cock.

It enlarged pretty quickly, and he pointed it at the exposed ass in front of him and it slipped in quite effortlessly. Mateo did not even grunt as John started to fuck him, though his big feet did flex a bit in their bindings. Another waft of smoke came over me from Hugo who was still resting his legs on my back. I looked up at him and he grinned.

"You think you can take me like Mateo can?" Hugo asked.

"A sub's goal is to please his dom," I replied. "My ass is yours if you want it, Sir."

"Good answer," Hugo said with a wink. "We will see."

Inwardly, I was hoping and praying he would not try to fuck me. I pride myself on pleasing a dom, but I was intimidated by the size of

Hugo's cock. Fortunately, by this point, he had dropped at least two loads that I knew of and I was hoping he was satisfied for the moment. I turned my head back to watch Mateo, who was gripping the fuck bench hard and had his eyes closed and squinted as John fucked him hard.

John started to slap Mateo's ass and gripped and groped it as his cock slid effortlessly in and out of his used hole. A froth of cum from the previous loads he received was building up and made a squishing sound as he pounded. It dripped down Mateo's balls and onto the floor and started to make a puddle.

John picked up the pace and was fucking Mateo so hard the bench started to move. Mateo started to grunt at each thrust and I had to admit, I was impressed at his ability to take a pounding. Before long John tensed up, though, and then with a final thrust, he groaned and unloaded into Mateo's ass.

He pulled out and a few spurts hit the back of Mateo's ass and what was deposited started to just dribble out. His hole was so stretched he could not hold anything in.

"Max, get over here and clean your brother out again," John said between pants as he caught his breath.

"Yes, Sir," Max said as Greg put his legs down and Max got up and went over to Mateo.

He licked up and down Mateo's crack and swallowed the cum on the outside and then moved down to his caged balls, which made Mateo moan a bit. When he was done, he moved up and started to put his tongue in Mateo's hole, but Mateo groaned a bit.

"Please don't, bro," Mateo said. "I'm sore."

Max rubbed Mateo's ass a bit and when he stood, John asked him to get him a beer and John returned to his seat next to Hugo to finish his cigar.

By the late evening, the air smelled of cigar smoke and sex. The lights were dim, and the lingering smoke mixed with them to give a nightclub feel to the dungeon. Some light electronic music was playing in the background and the crowd had thinned out a bit. John and Hugo were still sitting and talking. Kenny had fucked Max before leaving and Mateo had finally been let off the fuck bench and was on his hands and knees before Todd who had his feet propped on his back. The rest of the men had left, and I was starting to clean up a bit.

"So, who was the winner?" Hugo asked as he blew some smoke out into the room.

"Let's find out!" John said. "Boys, stand at attention in front of me."

I stopped what I was doing and came over and stood in front of John. Max, who was emptying the trash, joined me and Mateo slowly got up from his crouched position to join us. On our chests, Mateo and I had four hash marks and Max had two.

"Looks like we have a tie for first place so far," Todd replied with a smile.

"Turn around boys," John said.

When we turned our asses towards the men, they saw three hash marks on my ass, two on Max's, and four on Mateo's.

"We have a winner!" Todd replied as we turned back around again.

"Indeed," John replied. "With seven loads, Mateo takes the prize."

"Wait a moment," Hugo said as he lowered his cigar and looked at Max. "You only took four loads boy?"

"Yes, Sir," Max replied.

"I think we need to fix that," Hugo said as he got up and handed his cigar to John. "On the fuck bench boy."

Max looked pale and walked over to the bench and got on it. Hugo strapped him in, and I exchanged a serious glance at Mateo before we both turned back to look at Max. Hugo flopped his hardening cock on the back of Max's ass. His thin furry body looked small compared to the large, dark man and the cock laying on his crack. Hugo grabbed some lube and started to push his fat thumb into Max and Max yelped in response.

"Do you need a gag too boy?" Hugo asked.

"Please, Sir!" Max said, his voice quivering.

Mateo took the initiative and went over and grabbed the gag he had in his mouth earlier and brought it up to Max. He moved in close so Max could hear him.

"Prepare yourself, bro," Mateo said as he strapped the ball gag on Max.

Max bit down on the gag and closed his eyes as Hugo pointed his hard, fat cock at his hole and started to push forward. Max grunted immediately and tried to twist his body to push out the invading member.

"Stop trying to torque your body!" Hugo said as he slapped Max's ass. "Remember, this is for my pleasure."

Max tried to stay still but, as Hugo pushed inside him again he tensed up. I think he realized that he might have met his match.

"Hold on Hugo," John said as he came over to Max.

Hugo pulled out and John bent down, and Max looked at him.

"Are you ok with this boy?" John asked. "Give me a thumbs up or down."

Max grunted and gave him a thumbs up and John patted his head.

"Good boy," John said.

John returned to his seat to smoke and Hugo mounted up and started pushing into Max again. Max groaned and his eyes closed and watered as Hugo pushed his cock into him and split him open. I watched

Max's legs shake and his toes curled tight as he was impaled. Even my ass squeezed a bit involuntarily.

Hugo finally got balls deep in him and he reached down and squeezed Max's waist. Max was still shaking a bit and biting hard on the gag. His grip on the bench was so strong I thought he might break the wood in two.

"Here we go boy," Hugo said as he pulled out and started to fuck Max.

Max was groaning loudly, and muffled cries could be heard through the gag as Hugo railed his ass. He was giving no mercy to the boy and was soon pounding him hard enough that the sound of his groin hitting Max's ass echoed off the wall.

"Damn you got a tight ass boy!" Hugo said as he pounded away.

He used to, I thought as I watched. My nub was swollen and poking through the bars of my cage and I looked down and saw that Mateo was the same way. There was a dribble of precum extending from Mateo's cage to the floor. When he saw me looking, he looked down and saw it too and grabbed the stream and licked it clean.

I looked back over at Max and tears were rolling down his face. I didn't think that he could take much more, but Hugo kept pounding away and it took several minutes before his load finally erupted from his balls and filled Max's ass. He pounded him two more times and then pushed in till he was drained and when he pulled out, I saw that Max's hole was red and raw and cum started leaking out.

Max's body went limp on the bench and let out a huge groan. I came over and removed his gag and he gasped and looked at me through tear-filled eyes with a stare that told me he had just been given the fuck of his life. Mateo walked over and bent down and, using his tongue, started cleaning Max's ass of Hugo's cum. I used my hands to wipe Max's face of the tears on it and ran my fingers across his cheek to comfort him.

"Are you sure you are ok?" I asked in a whisper to Max.

"Totally," Max said with a half-smile. "I would have said something if I wasn't."

I patted his face and then walked back over and stood in front of Sir. Once Mateo was done, John had him get Max up and steady him so he could walk over and stand next to me.

"Well, Mateo wins the prize," John said.

He got up and crossed the room and picked up a small box. He brought it over to Mateo and handed it to him and told him to open it. Mateo removed the wrapping paper and opened the small white box and inside was a one-hundred-dollar bill and a note. On the note, it read, 'free pass from duties'.

"That gives you the right to skip out on a day of cleaning," John said. "Your sub brothers will pick up the slack for you on that day as a reward."

"Thank you, Sir!" Mateo said with a smile.

"You boys did exceptionally well tonight," John replied.

"Indeed, you did," Todd said as well, holding up his glass as a toast and winking at me.

"You may continue to clean the room," John replied.

It took us another hour to get things all cleaned up and put away. By the time we were done, only Hugo and John remained, and they were sitting together talking when we came over to them.

"Can we be of further assistance Sirs?" I asked.

John looked up at me and smiled, "No, boys. Hugo here will be staying the night. You can all go home. Thank you for your service and have a good evening."

"Thank you, Sir!" we all replied, and we turned to leave.

Max and Mateo were in front of me when I closed the door to the dungeon behind us and we started to get our clothes to dress and leave.

"I have to say guys," I said. "You all did a great job."

Mateo smiled as he pulled his pants on and Max just collapsed on the floor.

"You look like you might need a few days recovery," I said to Max.

Max looked up at me and smiled. "I just hope Kenny doesn't expect any more ass tonight. I'm tapped out."

Mateo laughed a bit. "You held up well bro."

"Indeed," I said as I laughed as well.

CHAPTER THIRTY-THREE

Winter Wonderland

Saturday, January 23, 2016, I woke up to find snowflakes falling and some snow accumulating on the ground. For those in more northern climates, this might not seem like a big thing, but here in Atlanta, snow is an uncommon occurrence. We usually only see it a few times a year, and if it is more than a dusting, it can cause havoc since we do not have the infrastructure to handle removing it.

Fortunately, it looked like it was just going to be something to look at and not worry about. It was still cold out, though, so I had not made any plans to do anything for the weekend. I was sitting on the floor in nothing but my cage and collar as usual playing a videogame when my phone went off. I looked down to see a message from Mateo.

"What are you up to today, Matt?" he asked.

"Not much here," I replied. "Watching the flakes fall from the sky out the window and playing some games. How about yourself?"

"Not too bad here," he said. "Gabriel just left here and I am a bit bored."

Gabriel was the name of a guy that Mateo had met two weeks ago when we both went out to the Eagle. We had been hanging out on the upper back deck drinking when a rather fit Hispanic man approached us. The first thing I noticed was his eyes. They were a deep brown, but something about the shape or look of them just made you want to take a second glance at him when he walked by. He had a cropped goatee, short hair, and his tight jeans outlined a nice package as well. I had noticed him first, but when Mateo turned to look at him, the poor boy was speechless.

Gabriel had come up beside Mateo and squeezed his ass and then looked down and saw our collars. Once he saw we were labeled as 'Chastity Subs', it immediately piqued his interest. Mateo was just staring with his mouth a bit open. I swear I could see drool starting to form at the corner of his mouth. Gabriel must have picked up on it too because he smiled and brought his hand up and drew his thumb across Mateo's mouth.

"You like what you see here, boy?" he had asked him.

Mateo smiled and nodded.

"This is my sub brother Mateo, Sir," I stepped in to reply. "My name is Matt. Mateo's usually more talkative, but I think you may have broken him with that grope."

Gabriel chuckled. "Well glad to meet you both and I hope I have not broken you there Mateo. Although, I would sure like to try."

Gabriel gave Mateo a sly look and moved to kiss him and Mateo closed his eyes and returned the gesture. While they made out, Gabriel reached down and started to squeeze and feel Mateo's cage under his pants and Mateo let out an audible grunt in response. Gabriel pulled back and looked at him and smiled.

"Just checking to make sure that collar was accurate," Gabriel replied.

"Yes, Sir, it is," Mateo said as he was getting lost in Gabriel's eyes. "I am about two weeks into a month lock-up."

"Very nice,, boy," Gabriel said as he ran a finger down Mateo's chest.

Gabriel smiled as his finger continued down and when he reached his waist, he started to unbuckled Mateo's pants. He pulled open the fly of his jeans and reached in and pulled Mateo's underwear down and under his cage to reveal his leaking nub. Gabriel ran his hands over the cage and collected some of the precum and brought it up to his lips and tasted it.

"You taste good, boy," Gabriel said. "Are you exclusive to your dom?"

"No, Sir," Mateo responded. "We are encouraged to service all men that are interested."

"Well, I am interested," Gabriel said.

Some of the guys around us started to notice Mateo's caged nub hanging out and Gabriel stepped in a little closer and took Mateo's hand and brought it over his groin. Gabriel must have been getting hard because the look Mateo had told me he wanted to drop to his knees and worship the man's cock right there.

"How'd you like to come home with me tonight boy?" Gabriel asked.

"I'd love to, Sir," Mateo replied.

"Go ahead Mateo," I said. "I'll be ok here."

Mateo looked at me and smiled and Gabriel came in for another kiss as he pulled Mateo's pants back up. When he pulled back, Mateo rebuckled his belt and gave me a wink as he passed by and followed Gabriel down the staircase.

Mateo had told me later that Gabriel was hung like a horse and fed him one load and fucked two into his ass before the evening was over. They had seen each other twice since then and I got the impression that this was turning out to be a more long-term connection.

"You get to service Gabriel again?" I texted Mateo as I paused my game.

495

"Yes!" Mateo replied. "He stayed overnight and my ass is full and happy."

"Well, you are having a damn good day then," I said. "You are welcome to come over if you want. I never mind company."

"Be right there then," Mateo replied.

Just as I was about to turn back to my game, there was a knock on my door. I got up and went over to see who it was and saw Max waiting on the other side. He did not have a jacket on and looked like he was shivering. I opened the door and let him in.

"What the hell are you doing out in the snow without a jacket, bro?" I asked.

Max hurried by me and rubbed his arms a bit while I closed the door behind him.

"I stayed overnight at Sir Kenny's and he kicked me out early cause work called and he needed to go in for something," Max said. "I just stopped by to see if I could visit for a while instead of driving home."

"Sure," I replied with a smile. "Take off your clothes and you can come over here and play some video games with me. Mateo is on his way over as well."

"Oh, nice!" Max replied as he started to take his pants off. "I hope I'm not interrupting any plans you both had."

"Naa bro," I replied as I went into the kitchen to get a drink. "He was just bored. You want a drink?"

Max was just pulling his underwear off and adjusting his cage when he looked up at me. "Yeah, sure. You got a beer?"

"I'll grab you one," I replied. "Go ahead and sit on the couch."

About 45 minutes later I heard another knock on the door and I opened it to let Mateo in. He smiled at me and when he leaned in to hug me, I could smell the sex on him. He had Gabriel's musk all over his beard and I had a pretty good impression there was some dried cum in there as well.

"I think you got some of Gabriel's seed in there bro," I replied with a smile.

Mateo blushed and rubbed his fingers over his beard and then licked them.

"Yeah, I probably do," he said. "It was a wild night."

"So, tell me more about this guy," Max said with a smile as he came over to greet him.

Mateo smiled broadly and hugged Max too.

"I didn't know you were here," Mateo said.

"Eh, I just got here a bit ago," Max said. "I stayed the night with my man. But, seriously, tell me more!"

I chuckled and went to grab Mateo a drink as well as he undressed and filled Max in on his escapades the night before. He had gone out on an official date with Gabriel last night that led to them sleeping together afterward. Mateo had ridden him twice before they passed out and then woke up his new hot Latin lover with a thirty-minute blowjob followed by another breeding before he had to leave. They had also made plans to see each other tomorrow as well.

"So, when is he going to collar you?" I asked with a grin as I handed him his beer.

"Well, it is a bit early for that," Mateo replied. "But, who knows. I've never fallen for someone this quick before."

"That's how Sir Kenny and I were," Max replied. "After the second date, I was all over his cock and balls and I knew he was the one for me."

"Speaking of hot cock," Mateo said looking at me, "how are things going between Sir Todd, Bo, and you?"

"Well, Bo and I are still seeing each other when we can," I replied. "He has settled into his role as Sir Todd's sub, but he also has a lot more autonomy under him than he did when he was in training under Sir John. Sir Todd and I get along well and he has still been hinting at maybe taking me in. But, regardless, I am sure Bo and I will still be seeing each other."

"Well, that's good," Max replied. "Y'all make a cute couple."

"Thanks," I said with a blush.

The three of us sat down to play some games for a while before ordering some pizza for lunch and breaking out some cards to play poker for a bit. By the afternoon, we were all a bit tipsy from drinking and my supply of beer was running low.

"Well, guys," I said as I came back into the living room from the kitchen, "this is the last beer."

"Boo!" Mateo said with a smirk as he crossed his legs on the floor and stared at his cards.

"Now what are we going to do?" Max asked.

"Hold on," I replied. "I may have a lifeline."

I pulled out my phone and texted Rick to see if he was home. I had already told him that he could borrow my vacuum yesterday because theirs was broken.

"I'm here," Rick replied. "Chris is out visiting his mom. Is it ok to come by to pick the machine up?"

"Well," I said. "Yes, but my sub brothers are here and we are out of beer. Do you think you could pick up a 12-pack for us on your way over?"

"Wait, let me get this straight," Rick replied. "There are three tipsy, horny subs over there right now?"

"There are," I replied with a devil emoji.

"I'll be right over with the beer," Rick replied.

"Well, we are set, boys," I said as I put the phone down. "Rick is on his way over with more beer."

"Wait, your hot dom friend Rick?" Max asked.

"The same," I replied with a smile.

I noticed Max's nub react instantly and start to harden a bit in his cage. Mateo noticed the same thing and grinned.

"Well, I'm looking forward to meeting this guy," Mateo replied. "From the look of Max's nub, he must be hot."

Max blushed and covered his cage with his hands and grinned sheepishly.

We continued to play cards for a bit. I could already tell that Max was pretty much a card shark. I had only beat him three times and poor Mateo had yet to win a hand. It was a good thing we were not playing with real money. Max had cleaned Mateo out of the last of his poker chips when there was a knock at the door. I got up and went over and looked through the peephole and saw Rick standing there.

"Hey, Rick!" I replied as I opened the door to let him in.

"Good to see you again cubby," Rick said as he hugged me. "Here's the beer for you boys."

Rick put the box of cans down and Max grabbed it and brought it back into the kitchen. I saw Rick staring at Max's naked ass as he walked by and I patted his belly to distract him.

"Come over here and meet Mateo," I said.

Rick looked over and saw Mateo getting up to come over to him and he crossed over and shook his hand.

"So, you must be the one that replaced Bo," Rick said.

"Yes, Sir," Mateo replied.

"Damn if John wasn't right," Rick said as he bit the front of his tongue a bit and checked Mateo out. "He said he found a really hot boy to take Bo's place."

"Thank you, Sir!" Mateo said with a big smile.

Rick reached behind Mateo and started to rub his ass and his middle finger found its way down to Mateo's hole while I went to help Max put away the beer. When I returned, I found Rick had his finger up Mateo's ass and Mateo was bent over the couch moaning a bit.

"Well, that did not take long," I said with a smile.

"Hey, what can I say," Rick replied. "I'm always horny."

Mateo had his eyes closed and was biting his lower lip and moaning a bit as Rick fingered his ass. Rick then kicked his shoes off and bent down and put his face in Mateo's crack and started to lick his puckered hole.

"Fuck!" Mateo replied as his caged nub jumped a bit and a stream of precum started to dribble out and down to the floor.

Mateo spread his legs a bit as he bent over the side of the couch and Rick spread his ass cheeks and started to get his tongue in the boy's hole. Max's nub was leaking as well and mine was not far behind, so we both sat down and watched Rick go at it while collecting our precum and licking it off our fingers.

Rick started to drop his pants and his cock popped out of his underwear fully hard and dribbling precum. He spat on his hand and stroked his shaft and then went back in Mateo's ass a few more times with his tongue before spitting on it a few times as well.

"Mind if I take a ride boy?" Rick asked.

"No Sir," Mateo replied. "I'd love for you too."

Rick smiled and pointed his cock at Mateo's ass and pushed forward. The fucking Mateo had earlier in the day had already loosened him up and he took Rick's cock easily as it slid in him. Rick groaned as he got balls deep and his groin hit Mateo's ass.

"Damn, boy," Rick said as he groped and rubbed Mateo's ass and waist. "Your ass is amazing."

Mateo grinned and flexed his ass muscles a bit which gripped Rick's dick and sent a pulse of energy right through Rick's groin and up his spine.

"That's a boy," Rick said in reply. "I'm gonna load you up good."

Rick pulled his shirt off and tossed it at me and started to pound Mateo, who let out a huge grunt as the first thrust shoved him into the couch. I picked up Rick's shirt and breathed in his scent and fingered the head of my nub under my cage and started to feel the precum collecting underneath. Rick's pecks flexed a bit and the fur on his chest bristled as he started to build up steam and fuck Mateo hard. The smack of his groin against bare ass echoed across the room and Mateo gripped the cushion and started to bite it a bit.

Rick continued to pound his ass and the couch started to move. I smiled and walked over and sat on it for some stability before turning to face Rick as he continued to assault Mateo's ass. Rick was building up a sweat and I saw it start to bead on his chest and the hair on his body started to moisten. He was in the zone and had his eyes closed and was slightly looking up at the ceiling.

"God damn this is a good ass, boy!" Rick yelled as he pounded.

"It's all for your pleasure, Sir!" Mateo responded between groans.

I looked over at Max and he was groping his cage and fingering his nipples. He was just as turned on as I was. I suspect if we had been uncaged like normal males, we would have shot our loads already by now. Still, the scene was hot and in our semi-drunk state, we were mesmerized a bit by the alpha male rutting in front of us.

I knew Rick was close when he opened his eyes again and looked down at Mateo's ass. He gripped Mateo's waist and started to fuck even harder till I saw his chest swell up and he forced his cock deep into the ass in front of him and he groaned loudly.

"Take that load boy!" Rick yelled as he closed his eyes again and lowered his head to his chest.

He was breathing heavily and held Mateo tight on his cock as he drained it deep inside him. After a few minutes, he had regained his composure and started to pull out. Max immediately ran over to him and got on his knees and Rick turned to let Max suck his cock clean of his remaining load. Mateo opened his eyes and looked at me and smiled and mouthed the words, "fuck that was good". I smiled as he took a deep breath and pulled himself upright again.

"Thank you for your load, Sir," Mateo said as he turned to Rick.

Max sucked the last of Rick's cum off and stood as well and Rick put his hands around both of their waists and looked at me.

"You know getting you in John's program was the best idea I ever had," Rick replied with a grin.

"I see that!" I replied as I raised my beer to him.

Rick asked me to grab him a towel and I brought one back to him with a beer as well. He sat down and talked with us until he finished it and then he got up and got dressed and grabbed the vacuum to head home.

"You can come by and get this tomorrow," Rick said to me. "I'll load your ass up then."

"Sure thing, Sir," I replied with a smile.

After Rick left we all sat down to play some more cards. Mateo slowed down his drinking so he could sober up enough to drive home, but Max and I continued till we were pretty much in a fog of alcohol. I can get handsy when I have been drinking and I started to grope Max a bit who was sitting next to me and he was leaning on me and rubbing my belly. Seeing that we were pretty much done playing, Mateo smiled and put his cards down, and announced he was going to go ahead and leave. I gave him a pouting face in return, but he came over and hugged us both and then got up to leave.

"Just be careful getting home in the snow," I replied as Mateo pulled his pants on.

"I will. Don't worry bro," Mateo said.

Once he zipped up his jacket we each hugged him and then I closed the door behind him.

"Kenny just messaged me that it was ok for me to wander back over to his apartment, so I best be going as well," Max said.

"Ok, bud," I replied. "Thanks for coming over and just be careful on those steps out there. They can get slick."

"Will do!" Max replied as he hugged me and left.

After closing the door, I walked over to the couch and collapsed on it. I had just about nodded off when my phone went off again.

"How's your day going babe?" was the text that I received from Bo.

Doing my best to type in my current state, I replied, "Ok. The boys were over here for a while playing cards and Rick came over and bred Mateo before borrowing my vacuum to leave. I'm drunk now."

"Well, that is random and hot," Bo replied with a smiling emoji. "Do you want some company? Sir has given me the evening off."

"Sure," I replied. "The door is open and I'll be on the sofa."

I must have passed out after sending the last text because the next thing I remember was Bo kissing me and rubbing my belly. I opened my eyes to see him as he pulled away from my lips and smiled at me. I was still getting used to seeing him in clothes. After almost a year of never wearing any at home, it had just become second nature to me. He had taken his jacket and shoes off but was still in his sweatpants and t-shirt.

"Hey babe," I replied with a grin.

Bo moved down to the end of the couch and picked my legs up and sat down and put them in his lap and started to rub my feet. It felt good and I closed my eyes and groaned a bit in response.

"Looks like you tied one on today," Bo replied as he looked back at me.

I cracked my eyes open at him and grinned and burped loudly.

"Woops!" I replied as I started to laugh.

Bo's expression was priceless. He had this surprised look on his face and then it turned to laughter immediately.

"Well, alrighty then!" Bo replied.

I rubbed my belly and flexed my foot as he rubbed it.

"I'm glad you came over," I replied.

Bo smiled and put my foot down and crawled over me until his face was over mine.

"I missed you," Bo said as he came in to kiss me again.

We started to make out and I pulled my legs apart so he could put his knees on the sofa. His hands roamed over my body and I felt his cage under his pants hit mine a few times as we shifted around. I wanted nothing more than to pull his cage off and take his cock into my ass, but I knew that could not happen, so I took what I could get at the moment.

Bo broke our embrace and put his head next to mine and started to rub my head. I closed my eyes and hugged him and I nearly passed out again before I felt him rub my face again and I opened my eyes to see him staring at me.

"You are drunk," Bo said with a smile.

"Sorry, babe," I replied. "I'm not being a good boyfriend I guess."

Bo laughed and returned to the end of the sofa and started rubbing my feet again.

"Sir's been talking about you recently," Bo said.

I opened my eyes and propped a pillow under my head so I could see him better and looked down at him.

"Oh?" I replied. "I hope it was good things."

Bo laughed. "Yes, silly. He and Pat broke off seeing each other two weeks ago. They are still friends, but it just did not work out for them. Since then, he has been a bit more affectionate with me and has mentioned collaring you more than once."

"I would like that," I replied.

"Me too," Bo said as he squeezed my feet. "The only thing is would you be upset being the beta in the house?"

"What do you mean by that?" I asked.

"It's something Sir mentioned the other day when we were talking about you," Bo said. "He sees me as his alpha sub around the house now. I have a lot more privileges than I did when I was under Sir John, but he said if he brought you in, he would like to have a more subordinate sub like you are now. He said you would be the beta in the house."

"If it meant we could live together, then I would be ok with that," I replied. "I'm ok with you being the senior sub in the house."

Bo laughed. "Well, we can talk about it more when you are sober. For the moment, why don't we go back in the bedroom and lie down so I can properly spoon you."

"Deal," I said with a grin.

Bo followed me back into the bedroom. The alcohol was hitting me hard and I needed to piss bad as well. I told him to wait for me on the bed while I drained my bladder. One thing that you learn quickly when you are in chastity is that caged boys always sit to pee. It is just a lot less messy that way. However, when you are drunk, even sitting can be a challenge. I managed not to piss on the floor, though and when I came back in the bedroom, Bo was naked and turned towards me.

"Come on over here sexy bear," Bo said as he held his arm out.

I walked over and rolled into the bed and scooted my ass up against his body. I felt the metal of his cage as Bo shoved it into my crack and then wrapped his arms and leg around me. He put his head on my neck and started to kiss me and nibble on my ear. He knew that always got a reaction out of me and I groaned a bit and grabbed his hand and squeezed it hard.

"I'm looking forward to using that strap-on on your ass again," Bo said. "That was hot watching you cum."

"It felt good too," I replied. "I also loved having you in my mouth during your graduation ceremony. You do have a nice cock."

"Nub babe," Bo said with a smile. "Don't forget your training."

"I know," I replied as I closed my eyes and scooted up into his groin.

His cage was rubbing in my crack and I felt some precum start to form and coat my ass. I knew we had to be careful, but I was drunk and horny and I pushed my luck a bit. Bo knew better though and pulled away from my ass.

"Got to be careful there babe," Bo said as he kissed my neck and upper back. "Rules are rules."

"I know," I said with a groan. "Hold me tight."

Bo grinned and bear-hugged and spooned me until I passed out.

CHAPTER THIRTY-FOUR

Meeting Alex

By the middle of February, I had been in my cage for five months total without a manual release. John had milked me every one to two weeks and I had found ways of dealing with the waves of horny energy that sometimes came over me, usually in the morning when I woke up. But, I had started to think of the cage as a part of me for the most part. I barely ever woke up at night and with the aid of a leather strap I had purchased, I was able to keep the cage nice and firm against my body when I was at work and it never bothered me. Overall, I was very proud of myself.

Of course, the other thought I had was that it was only about a month till my training would be finished. My cage would be removed one last time for a manual release and when it was put back on, I did not know when or if it would be coming off for another one. It scared me a bit but having been around so many subs that had trained with John and successfully found their life in permanent chastity, I also knew that if that was something I chose, I could do it.

Bo had told me that he and Todd had talked some more over the past few weeks about taking me in, but I still had not heard anything definitive. So, I was a bit nervous when Bo let me know that Todd wanted me to come over for dinner one Saturday night to talk. I did not know what to expect as I drove over to his house in the dark. If he did not want to take me in, I did not have any other offers at the moment and I was unsure of the future.

When I walked up and knocked on the door, Bo opened it and greeted me. He was in some khaki pants and a button-up shirt and looked very nice.

"What's the occasion babe?" I asked as he closed the door behind me.

"You'll see," Bo said with a smile as he kissed me. "Go ahead and strip and kneel by the door here. Sir will come for you shortly."

"Ok," I said with a smile.

Bo walked down the hallway and disappeared around the corner and I took my clothes off and folded them neatly and put them in a basket near the door with my shoes. I got down on my knees and put my hands behind my back and bowed my head like I usually did at John's and waited. About five minutes later, I heard Todd come down the hall and I saw his boots in front of me.

"You can rise, boy," Todd said.

I stood and faced him and he was dressed in slacks and a dress shirt as well. He even had on some nice cologne that smelled good. I was starting to wonder what was going on.

"I'm glad you could make it," Todd said. "Bo has been cooking all afternoon for you and has quite a nice dinner ready. Follow me."

"Yes, Sir!" I replied as I followed him down the hall and around and into the dining room.

The room was brightly lit by a chandelier above and there was a white linen cloth spread out over the table. There were three place settings set out formally with several forks, spoons, knives, glasses, and plates. There was a place setting at one end of the table which had a larger chair with armrests and two on either of the longer sides with simple chairs behind them. It all looked very intricate.

"Oh wow, Sir!" I exclaimed. "This is nice!"

Todd smiled. "As you know, I don't allow non-collared boys to use the furniture in my home, but for this one evening, we have set you a place here on the side of the table. Please stand behind the chair and I will tell you when you can sit."

"Yes, Sir," I replied as I walked over and stood behind one of the chairs on the side.

Todd walked around and pulled the larger chair out from behind the foot of the table and then sat down. Bo came in soon after with some food on a tray and set it in the middle. He then returned to the kitchen and came back out with several smaller trays as well. There was a roast in the middle with baked potatoes, steamed sliced carrots, green bean casserole, some sliced fresh fruit, and freshly baked rolls as well. It smelled as good as it looked.

Once Bo had brought the last plate out, he stood behind his chair and faced me.

"This looks good boy," Todd replied. "You can serve me now."

Bo smiled and grabbed Todd's plate and set about filling it up with food. He then got his plate and did the same. Once he did so, he sat down, and then they both looked at me.

"You may now take your plate, fill it and sit to eat boy," Todd said to me.

"Thank you, Sir," I replied.

The meal was indeed delicious. I had no idea Bo was such a good cook and I complimented him on several occasions. After we finished eating, Bo brought out some bourbon for Todd and filled his glass, and then cleaned the plates and food from the table. I sat there and watched and felt bad about not helping, but Todd had told me to sit quietly after we had finished dinner, so I did as I was told. When the table was clear, Bo returned to the table and Todd pushed his chair back a bit and looked at me while he sipped his drink.

"When is your graduation, boy?" Todd asked me after several minutes.

"Saturday, March 12, Sir," I replied.

"A little less than a month away," Todd replied as he swirled the remains of his drink in the glass and then set it down.

"As you are aware, I have been talking to my boy Bo here about you at length," Todd said. "I am aware of your relationship and I fully support it. However, I have had to think long and hard about whether I want to take on another boy or not."

"I understand, Sir," I replied.

Todd smiled and sat back in his chair. "When I first took Bo on, I treated him as a member of my family, but as a sub, he had duties and responsibilities around the house and to me that he had to attend to. Although I had not intended it at first, over these past few months I have become quite fond of him and have allowed him more freedoms than he had originally."

Bo smiled and looked at Todd and he returned the glance and winked at him.

"He is still my boy, but we have altered his chastity role a bit. He will be let out four to five times a year, upon good behavior of course, and be allowed to orgasm normally. I had quite a lot of fun with him last week when I removed his cage and got to see just how long I could keep him hard and on the edge before going over. A bit of torture I am sure, but it was still hot to watch."

Bo blushed. "Thank you, Sir."

"I still would like to explore permanent chastity with a boy as well, however," Todd said. "There are certain aspects of denying a boy the right to his nub that I find intriguing and stimulating and I think with a second boy I could do that as well. So, I have decided to offer you this position if you wish to take it."

I started to smile a bit, but I was also nervous. Bo had hinted before with me about this type of relationship, but I was also unaware that he was no longer completely permanently caged.

"Should you choose to join my family boy, Bo here will be the alpha sub and you would be the beta sub," Todd continued. "You both would be responsible for the house duties and seeing to my needs, but you would be permanently caged and I will explore certain kinks and roles with you that I may not do so with Bo and vice versa. By no means would Bo be over you in any way, it would just be a different type of service to me."

"And Bo and I could still be boyfriends?" I asked.

"Of course!" Todd said with a laugh. "You'll be a part of the family and free to live together and be intimate in your way together as well. You can use those strap-ons to your heart's consent as long as my needs are put first, that is. I am sure things will evolve and I do not know how the roles may change in the future, but I like you boy and you seem to be a sub that I would enjoy having around the house."

"Thank you, Sir," I replied. "I have enjoyed getting to know you as well."

"Well, what are your thoughts boy?" Todd asked.

I looked over at Bo and he smiled at me and I smiled back. I took a deep breath and gave it some thought for a moment.

"Sir, I really love Bo and I would love to be able to live with him, but more importantly, I think you are a great dom that is caring and fair," I replied. "I would be honored to join your family.

Bo smiled large enough that his cheeks started to show some dimples and Todd grinned as well.

"I am really happy to hear this, boy," Todd replied. "I will be there next month for your collaring and you can move in with me as soon as you are ready afterward."

"Thank you, Sir," I replied.

"Now, please help Bo finish straightening up this room and I will return to my room to get undressed and relax," Todd said. "I will ask you to head home after you are done, though. I have some things I want to do with Bo tonight."

"I understand, Sir," I said with a smile.

Bo and I stood as Todd did and he turned to leave the room. After he had disappeared down the hallway, Bo came over to me and gave me a big hug and a kiss.

"I'm so happy right now I could cry," Bo said.

"I'm looking forward to it myself, babe," I replied. "This next month is probably going to drag by now."

"Well come on and help me clean up," Bo said. "I need to get back and start servicing Sir as soon as I can."

The following Monday, I was at John's house as usual. After greeting Max and Mateo, I headed upstairs to the second floor and found John typing up some documents for work. He looked up and smiled and beckoned me over and slid his chair back so I could have access to his crotch and I got on my knees and sucked on him till he blew down my throat. After he was done, he patted me on the head and told me to stand at attention.

"I have something I need some assistance with, boy," John said.

"How can I help?" I asked.

"A new boy named Alex has been referred to me as a potential replacement for you after you graduate." He said. "I had dinner with him Saturday night and he seems like he might be a good fit; however, he was hesitant to move forward and requested that he speak to a current sub in the program. I would like for you to coordinate a meeting with him and answer any of his questions."

"I would be happy to help, Sir!" I replied.

"Thank you boy," John replied. "You did a good job helping Max decide to move forward and I feel sure you can size this new potential up and let me know if he would be worth my time."

"I'll do my best, Sir," I replied.

"Very well, I will text you his contact info," John said. "Please have this done this week and report back to me no later than this weekend."

"Yes, Sir," I replied.

"You may go about your duties, then," John said as he motioned for me to go.

I went back out into the hall and proceeded to complete my cleaning tasks for the night. When I was done, I came downstairs and found Mateo wiping down the surfaces in the dungeon and Max was putting his supplies away.

"Brothers, can I have a word with you two?" I asked.

"Sure thing," Max replied. "Let me put this vacuum away and I'll be right there."

"What's up?" Mateo said as he walked over to me.

"Nothing much, I just wanted to give you both a heads up on a special task for us this week," I replied.

When Max returned to the room, he came over and joined Mateo and I continued.

"Sir asked me to reach out to a new potential sub that might take my place after I graduate," I said. "As he would be working closely with both of you after I am gone, I wondered if you wanted to help me."

"Sure thing!" Max said. "I remember how much meeting you and Bo before I joined helped put my mind at ease. It would also be nice to meet him now before he is initiated."

"Yeah," Mateo replied. "Count me in as well."

"Ok guys," I said. "Well, Sir said he would text me the contact info for him. Once I have arranged everything, I will let you both know. Sir asked that this be handled by this weekend, so I will try to get this done as soon as possible."

"Sounds good bro!" Max replied with a smile.

When I got home, I checked my email and noted the message from John that had Alex's phone number and email. I wondered if it would be awkward getting a call from a stranger, but I also felt like an actual call might be the best way to get a meeting scheduled sooner, rather than later. I called the number listed and it rang a few times before a deep voice answered.

"Hello?" Alex said.

"Is this Alex?" I replied.

"It is, can I help you?" Alex asked.

"This might be a bit awkward, but I guess the best way to handle this is to get straight to the point," I said. "My name is Matt and I am a sub under Sir John. He told me you had met with him recently and although you were interested in his program you were still unsure about it."

"Oh yes!" Alex replied. "I met with him this past weekend. He seemed like a nice guy, but it sounds like a demanding program."

"I get that," I replied. "Believe me I had the same nervousness when I first met with him as well. Would you like to meet with me this week? I can have my other two sub brothers there as well and you can ask any question you might have and get to know us a bit."

"Sure," Alex said. "You up for dinner tomorrow?"

"That would be great," I replied. "Where would you like to meet? Your place? A neutral place? My place? You let me know."

"Not here," Alex said. "I don't mind meeting you at your place. I think it would be more private that way and I would feel more comfortable asking about things."

"Very well then," I replied. "How about you come over here at 7 pm tomorrow. I will order some pizza and we can all relax and talk openly."

"That sounds good," Alex said.

"I'll text you the address and we will see you tomorrow," I replied.

"See you then!" Alex said before hanging up.

I immediately messaged Max and Mateo and told them to be at my place as soon as they could after work so we could be ready for Alex's arrival. They both said that it was no problem and I started to clean up the place a bit to make it presentable for my guest.

Tuesday evening, I got home around 6 pm and about thirty minutes later Max and Mateo were walking through the door as well. We ordered the pizza so it would arrive soon after Alex was supposed to be there and we cracked open some beers and sat down to play some games while we waited. At about ten minutes to seven, I heard a knock at the door and I looked through the peephole and saw a young man on the other side.

He was probably just out of college if I had to guess. Thinner guy with dark shaggy hair and some scruff on his face with a long dark goatee. He had some oversized clothes on that made him look a bit disheveled and he was about my height. When I opened the door, his eyes widened and he blushed when he saw me naked.

"Oh wow!" Alex said. "What is going on here?"

"Don't be alarmed," I replied. "Subs in the program are not allowed clothes inside. I hope that does not freak you out."

"Umm, ok," Alex said as he walked inside. "It's just a little weird."

Mateo and Max approached him from the living room and extended their hands to greet him. He kept staring at their cages as he shook their hands and stumbled his words a bit as he said hello.

"I'm Matt," I replied as Alex turned back to me after I closed the door. "I'm the one you spoke with on the phone."

"Oh ok," Alex said as he reached out and I shook his hand.

"I don't have to get naked too do I?" Alex asked.

I laughed. "No, you are not a sub in the program, so you are fine like you are, but I would be happy to take your jacket."

"Thanks," Alex said as he took off the long coat and handed it to me.

"Would you like a beer?" Max asked.

"Sure, that would be great," Alex replied.

"Come over here and sit in the living room," Mateo said. "Might as well get comfortable."

Alex was still hesitant. I am sure this was a shock to take in all at once, but he smiled and followed Mateo into the living room and sat in one of the chairs. Mateo plopped down on the sofa and Max joined him there after bringing Alex a beer. I walked over and sat across from Alex in the other chair after putting his coat away and he cracked open his can and took a sip.

"First off Alex," I said. "Please know you are among friends. We would never divulge anything you say here to Sir or anyone else. Please feel free to ask us anything you want and we would love to get to know you better as well."

"For sure," Mateo replied. "How did you meet Sir anyway?"

Alex smiled and put his can in his lap and leaned back in the chair a bit.

"Through a friend of mine," Alex said. "I have always been mostly bottom when it comes to sex. I had a boyfriend in college that was pretty dominant and we got into some BDSM play. He introduced me to like-minded guys and one older daddy bear told me about his friend John that he thought I would be interested in. So, he set up the meeting and that is how it happened."

"I got ya," I replied. "So, this is still pretty new to you then?"

"I mean, yes and no," Alex said. "I know I am young, but I have been sexually active since I was 15 and I can be pretty kinky."

"You sound similar to the way I was when I started last fall," Max said.

"Yeah, so I met with John and he seemed cool and all and we discussed some of the things he trains boys to do," Alex said. "But, I will be honest, the whole chastity thing seems a bit much. I don't want to offend as I see you all have them on, but I have never worn one."

"Is there anything about it that specifically concerns you?" I asked.

"Well, it is the whole idea that I would not have access to my dick," Alex said. "I mean I jack off three times a day sometimes."

Mateo started to laugh. "Dude, preach. I was the same way."

"But you still locked yourself up?" Alex asked.

"For me, it was about trying to change my mindset," Mateo said. "I had played around with chastity on my own before but giving up control to another was something I was interested in and there is no greater thing to give up than access to your nub."

"Nub?" Alex asked.

"That's what we are required to call our genitals," I replied. "It is all part of the program to help you to reorient how you see yourself and others.

"Ok," Alex said.

"You should only go through with this program if you are truly committed to challenging yourself to submit to others," I replied. "You still have your own life, but there are rules to follow and you have to want to learn what it truly means to be a subordinate."

"I guess it is just a lot to take in at once," Alex said.

"I get that," Max said. "I was fortunate that I had a dominant man in my life already before I started the program. He helped and encouraged me and the things I have learned in the program have brought me much closer to him and we have had a lot of fun exploring the dom/sub dynamic."

"And you don't miss cumming?" Alex asked.

"Well, yeah I do," Max said. "I'm still a young, horny guy. But I have found that being a sub for another man and finding new ways to please him pushes my buttons. It comes down to what you want out of a relationship."

"I do want to explore more and push my boundaries," Alex said. "I hope I am not coming off as a jerk or anything, but I just don't have a lot of experience."

"Well, first off, you seem like a cool guy, so please be at ease," I replied with a smile. "And it is completely natural to be nervous at first. If you took the chastity aspect out of it, did anything else Sir talked to you about scare you off?"

"Actually, no," Alex said. "It sounded pretty hot and I would love to learn to be a better sub."

"Then what I suggest is to try chastity for a bit and see what you think," I said. "You might find it's interesting and you want to explore after all."

"That is fair, but I'll need to get a device," Alex replied.

"I'll lend you one that I started with," I said. "Try wearing it tonight when you get home and sit down while you have it on and think about what you want and where you see yourself."

"I can do that," Alex said with a smile.

A knock on the door told me that the pizza was here and Alex volunteered to greet the delivery man since we were naked. He brought the pizza over to the kitchen and we relocated there to continue our discussion.

"So, if I were to accept John's offer, would you all be in the program with me?" Alex asked between bites of pizza.

"You would be with Mateo and Max here," I replied. "I graduate next month and will be leaving the program."

"Oh, nice!" Alex replied. "Congratulations."

"Thanks," I said with a smile. "It's been a long year, but I have learned a lot."

"So, none of you regret the decision to train under John?" Alex asked.

"Not in the least," Max said. "Sir is fair and firm and I have learned a lot about my boundaries and experienced a lot. I would say I would not be the sub I am today if I had not started training under him."

"Yeah," Mateo said. "I have only been under Sir since December, but even in that time, I have learned that what I thought I knew about being a sub was only the tip of the iceberg. It's much more about attitude, discipline, headspace, and commitment. You have to want this body and soul for it to work."

"Well, you all seem nice," Alex said. "I don't know where this decision will land, but I would love to hang out with you all more in the future regardless."

"Absolutely," Max replied. "Always up for new friends."

"Hold that thought," I replied as I put my pizza down and left the table.

I went back into my bedroom and pulled open the top drawer. In it, I had placed the fabric bag that contained the first cage I had bought last year that got me started down the journey to where I was today. I had cleaned and put it away and had not pulled it out since John had locked my current metal cage on me. I brought it back into the kitchen and laid it on the table in front of Alex.

"That's the cage I started in," I said. "It's been thoroughly cleaned, but I think it would be a good place for you to begin."

Alex wiped his hands on a towel and then opened the bag and removed the device.

"There are four base rings in there," I said. "Hopefully, one will work for you for the best comfort."

"Wow," Alex said as he inspected the device. "So, do you think you could show me how it works?"

"You want to put it on?" Max asked.

"Sure," Alex replied.

Max got up and washed his hands at the sink and then came over and bent down in front of Alex.

"Stand up and drop your pants," Max said.

"Umm, ok," Alex replied as he stood from the chair and undid his belt.

He lowered his pants and underwear and revealed his genitals. He had a nice set of balls and his shaft and head were visible.

"I'm more a grower than a show-er," Alex said, a bit embarrassed.

"Nothing wrong with that," Max replied. "That helps some."

Max tried one base ring and then moved to a larger one when that did not work. When he found it made a good fit, he pulled Alex's balls through the second ring, Alex shuttered.

"You ok bud?" Max asked looking up at him.

"I'm good," Alex said with a smile. "Just a shiver."

Max smiled and pulled the cage out and put Alex's soft member in it and then brought the post attached to the base ring through it and then put the lock through the post and clicked it closed. He then adjusted Alex's balls a bit and made sure everything fit well.

"I think that fits you better than it ever did on me," I replied with a grin.

Alex reached down and felt the device and I saw his shaft starting to swell in the confines of the cage. He was already getting turned on from the feel of it.

"Oh wow," Alex said. "There is not much room there for my dick to grow."

"The point is to inhibit erections," I replied. "A good fitting device will allow you to swell to fill it, but that is it. You might feel a little pain behind your balls, but over time, you will get used to it."

Alex sat back down and continued to play with the device and Max returned to sit down and finish his dinner.

"How long did you go at first?" Alex asked me.

"A few hours in my first official session under someone else," I replied. "It takes a while to get used to the feel of it and I will warn you the first time you try to wear it at night is a bitch. You will be up constantly due to failed erection attempts, but your body will adjust."

"Yeah, before long you will forget it is even there," Mateo said with a smile.

Alex let go of the cage and pulled his pants up and then turned to us.

"How long do you think I should go?" Alex asked.

"Tell you what," I replied. "I will seal the keys in an envelope and see if you can wear it till you go to bed tonight. That should give you a little experience. If you can make it that far and you decide to consider Sir's offer, text him this week and ask him to help you out. He can run you through some test sessions as a key holder and give you advice as well."

"Ok," Alex said. "I'm still nervous, but I'm willing to give it a go."

"That's the spirit," Max said with a grin. "Before long you'll be one of us."

Alex smiled back and finished his dinner and then we went into the living room. He was continuing to feel and adjust his crotch and so I figured we might need to do something to distract him.

"How about we play some video games for a while?" I asked.

"Sure!" Alex replied. "That would be fun."

We all sat down in front of the TV and played for a few hours and Alex forgot all about the cage on him for a while. We also got to talk a bit more with him and he seemed to become more at ease with us and chill out a bit. I thought he would make a good candidate for John. He was raw and needed a lot of coaching and molding, but I intended to tell John to continue to work with him. Of course, it also drove home the fact that soon I would be graduating and a new chapter of my life would be beginning.

CHAPTER THIRTY-FIVE

Concluding My Contract

On Friday, March 10, 2016, I finished work and started driving home. It was not until I was behind the wheel and started to relax after a long day at the office that it hit me that tomorrow was my graduation. I had gone through a year of service under John and had just completed six months continuously in my chastity cage. Tomorrow, I would be given one last manual release from my nub and then the lock would go on permanently. No more manual releases again for the foreseeable future after that.

It was a daunting thought, but surprisingly, it was not upsetting. I had come to embrace my cage as part of me and, frankly, did not want it removed. Don't get me wrong, I wasn't going to turn down one more manual release, but I had learned to cum from anal stimulation and a good prostate milking could tide me over in between. I also had come to enjoy serving and servicing dominants. Hearing them growl, seeing them tense up, watching cum explode from their cocks, and witnessing the energy flow over them and the pleasure they received because of my help was intoxicating and something I craved.

In many ways, I had rewired my brain and learned to find joy and pleasure through service. I credited John with a lot of that progress. He had been kind to me, but firm. I had been exposed to a lot of kinks and learned that some things I thought were hard limits for me were not so hard, and there were some things I did not enjoy that I had not experienced before. He had helped me push my boundaries and I had learned that some pain could be pleasurable. But, I also had to credit myself. I took a huge leap into this program and if I had not been committed, I don't think I would have been as successful. Of course, my sub brothers and their support had a lot to do with it as well.

All these thoughts were going through my mind on the way home and when I pulled into my parking lot I turned off the engine and sat there for a moment. Only the sound of my cell phone going off distracted me and brought me back to reality. I looked down and saw it was from Chris.

"Are you done with work yet?" he asked.

"Yup, I just got home," I replied.

"Change into something comfortable and come on over, Rick has a surprise for you," Chris said.

"Ok," I replied, a bit puzzled.

I had no idea what Rick had done, but I went inside and changed out of my work clothes and put on some jeans and a t-shirt, and then headed back over to their apartment. When I arrived and knocked on their door, Chris greeted me.

"Hey babe," Chris replied as he reached out and gave me a big hug. "Are you excited about your big day tomorrow?"

Chris and I had gone out to Woofs the weekend before to have some drinks and catch up. I had told him about my graduation ceremony and how I was a bit nervous but excited. I also filled him in on Todd's offer to collar me and the prospect of moving in with him and Bo.

"I am," I replied with a smile as I came in.

I started to undress as Chris closed the door behind me and once I was naked I followed him over to the kitchen where he was cooking some things. I heard the toilet flush in the bathroom down the hall and then the door opened and Rick appeared. He was in his boxers and a t-shirt and looking hot as usual.

"There's my sexy sub," Rick said as he came behind me and hugged me. "How are you?"

"I'm doing well," I replied. "I'm guessing Chris filled you in on all the details that we talked about."

"Yup," Rick said as he walked over to the refrigerator and grabbed a beer out. "I've met Todd before. He is a good man. I think you will enjoy living with him. How are you and Bo doing?"

"Good," I replied with a smile. "He's the first serious boyfriend I have had in a very long time and I am looking forward to moving in with him."

"Y'all make a cute couple," Chris replied as he looked over at me.

"So, what is this big surprise Chris told me about?" I asked.

Rick smiled and sat down at the kitchen table and opened his beer. "You just wait, boy. That is coming. But we are treating you to dinner, so come over here and sit down. Grab you a drink if you want one."

I smiled and grabbed a beer out of the fridge and sat down across from Rick.

"What you got cooking?" I asked.

"Spaghetti with meatballs, green beans, and some garlic bread," Chris said. "I know it's your favorite."

"Mmmm," I replied as I rubbed my belly.

Chris was right. It was a personal favorite of mine and one of the first things I cooked when I was a kid. My grandmother taught me a lot of different recipes and techniques as I grew up, but that was the first and it was still something I loved to make.

"When do you move over to Todd's?" Rick asked.

"I'll be moving next weekend," I said. "My lease is not up till the end of the month, but I wanted to move in as soon as I could and Bo is already arranging our room so my stuff can fit. What I won't be bringing over I will just put into storage."

"That sounds like a plan," Rick replied. "Just let us know if you need help."

"I will," I said with a smile.

Chris finished up cooking and brought over the plates of pasta and sauce and the side dishes. It all tasted wonderful and I noticed he had used my grandmother's recipe for the sauce that I had given him. It was a good thing that I didn't have clothes on as well, as a few times the sauce got on my chest and it would have stained my shirt horribly. That is pretty typical of me, though. I rarely come out of a meal unscathed from stains. When we were done, Chris cleared the plates away and Rick disappeared for a moment. When he returned, he had a large, wrapped box in his hands.

"Here is your surprise Matt," Rick said with a grin. "This is something special from Chris and me to mark your graduation. We are proud of you and how much you have dedicated yourself to your training but remained the nice guy you always have been."

"Aww," I replied. "You guys are going to make me cry."

Chris came behind me and squeezed my shoulders. "Go ahead and open it!"

I pulled off the wrapping paper and opened the box and inside was a nice leather vest.

"Oh, this is nice!" I said.

"Will look good with your harness at the Eagle on leather nights," Rick replied.

"It will!" I said. "Thank you two so much."

I gave each of them a hug and a kiss and then put the vest back in the box and closed it.

"God, this is hitting me," I replied. "I'm going to be a mess tomorrow."

Chris bent down and put his arms around my neck. "You'll be ok bubba."

We all had another round of drinks and talked for a bit, but I wanted to get home and get a good night's rest, so I bid farewell to them and headed home to prepare for tomorrow.

I woke up the next morning and noticed that I had kicked the covers off me. I looked over and saw the light streaming in from the crack in the curtains and it fell right on my cage. It was almost as if mother nature was reaching out to touch me and remind me what day it was. I stretched my arms out and took my CPAP machine off and pulled myself out of bed. When I picked my phone up, I noticed a text from Bo. He was wishing me luck today and told me he could not wait to see me this afternoon.

After I took my shower, I trimmed up my hair, beard, and pubes and then took a look at myself in the mirror. It was still hard to believe that it was a year ago that I started this journey. I smiled and wandered into the living room and sat down to play some video games for a while to pass the time. I made myself a salad for lunch as I had no idea what Todd had in store for me after graduation and I knew I was going to get fucked at least once today.

When I finally got dressed and made it over to John's house, it was about twenty minutes to two in the afternoon. I walked into the hallway and started to undress and realized this would be the last time I would be doing this. I reached over and rubbed my nameplate and figured, if things worked out, Alex's name might be there later in the week.

When I opened the door to the dungeon, the banners were already hung. I looked across the room and saw the one that said 'Graduation Day' hanging over where the Saint Andrew's cross was and to my right were the colored banners with the names of the subs that had graduated and that of their masters. I closed the door behind me and looked down to see Mateo and Max looking up at me with big grins on their faces. They were already in their jocks and armbands and were sitting cross-legged in their respective squares on the floor.

"Hey Matt!" they both said.

"Hey guys," I replied with a smile.

"It's your big day!" Max said. "I hope you are ready!"

"Yes I am," I said. "Let me go get my gear on and I'll be right back."

"Ok," Mateo said.

I crossed the dungeon and entered the isolation room and opened my bag that had my name on it. Inside was my leather jock and armbands and I put them on and looked at myself in the mirror on the wall before adjusting a few things and then heading back out to sit down next to my sub brothers.

"I love this jock!" Mateo said as we sat there.

"It is quite nice," I said. "It's yours to keep when you graduate."

"That's what Max told me," Mateo replied.

"You got any plans this evening?" Max asked.

"Nothing at the moment," I replied. "I left things open as I did not know what Sir Todd might have planned for me."

"That makes sense," Max replied. "Both of us want to take you out to dinner at some point though."

"Yeah," Mateo replied. "We are going to miss you around here."

"That sounds like fun," I said. "We will set something up soon."

At about five minutes to the hour, the sound of a bell echoed through the room through the speaker system and we got up on our knees and bowed our heads and waited. Several minutes later the sounds of two men coming downstairs could be heard and we saw their feet cross in front of us and stand still.

"You can now rise boys," John said.

I got to my feet and looked up and saw John to my left and Todd to my right. I grinned and Todd smiled back and then I looked at John.

"Boy Matt," John began. "You have completed your year in service to me. I have watched you grow and become a very experienced sub, worthy of a good master and one I am very proud of. Are you now ready to proceed to the next step in your journey?"

"I am, Sir," I replied.

"Come forward," John said.

John grabbed the leather blindfold from the table just behind him and came up to me and fastened it over my eyes and around the back of my head. I took a deep breath and felt his hand on my arm as he led me over to the far side of the room and turned me around. He raised each of my arms and fastened my wrists to restraints on the Saint Andrew's cross and then bent down and did the same to my ankles. Once I was restrained, he moved away.

I sat there a moment in the darkness, unable to see and listened to the breathing of the man in front of me, my trainer for the past year, and a man I had come to respect.

"Boy Matt," John said. "The contract you signed with me had a stipulation that you would be in chastity during the entire year. You have worked yourself up to longer and longer periods fully caged and you have done this of your own free will to show that you are committed to being the best sub you can be and put the needs and pleasure of a dom above your own. Your cage is a symbol of your service and role. You have just completed your final lock session that lasted six months and have now earned a manual release."

I felt John reach down and pull the front codpiece off my jock. I then felt his hands as he grabbed my cage and started to remove the security screw and then pulled the device off my nub and balls. Cool air moved across my free genitals and my shaft recoiled a bit. John reached down and started to rub my nub soon after, though and I felt it start to fill with blood.

"Your sub brothers have been your support base throughout your journey Boy Matt, and they will now be called upon to witness your next step," John said. "Boys Max and Mateo, please come here."

I heard my sub brothers walk over and then John spoke. "What is the service creed boys?"

We all replied. "I am a sub in training under the supervision of Sir John. My goal is to serve men in the best way I can and derive pleasure from that service. My chastity cage and collar are a symbol of that service and I desire one day to be in permanent chastity and receive my formal graduation collar as proof of my commitment."

Boy Matt, do you wish to continue and take the next step in your journey and enter into permanent chastity and receive your formal collar from your new master?" John asked.

"I do, Sir," I replied.

"You understand the commitment you are taking on and you do so under no coercion and of your own free will?" John asked.

"Yes, Sir," I replied.

"Boy Max," John said. "As his sub brother, I will now task you with providing Boy Matt with his last manual release he will receive before his permanent cage is installed. Are you prepared to do this?"

"Yes, Sir!" Max replied.

"Boy Matt," John said. "For the last time. Do you agree to submit to one last manual release from your sub brother before your permanent cage is installed?"

"Yes, Sir," I replied.

"Step forward Boy Max and perform the release," John said.

Another cool breeze blew past my body and then I felt the hand of Max on my balls. I jumped a bit and I felt Max rub my leg to calm me. I realized that this was probably the first time he had ever seen me uncaged. I wish I could have looked down and watched, but the sensation was heightened in my blindfolded state.

I felt his lips on my head and then felt him start to stroke my shaft. I breathed deeply and my body reacted automatically as the tissues fully engorged with blood for the first time in six months. The head of my nub was sensitive and I felt Max lick it as the precum started to flow out almost instantly. He started to stroke me and I squeezed my ass a bit and shifted in my restraints as the nerve ending sent electricity through my body.

I was fully hard and Max started to stroke me faster. Only my head was in his mouth and he did a good job of helping to stimulate a response but not go overboard. I knew that John was pretty strict on a manual release being different than a pleasant blow job. Still, he was pretty skilled and I felt that deep feeling in my balls and knew that I was close. I groaned a few times and started to strain against my restraints. At that instant, I realized this might be the last time I would feel another man stroke me. It might be the last time I felt a full, complete orgasm. It might be the last time I came into another man's mouth with a full erect shaft. It was all too much and I was going over the edge.

"Fuck!" I yelled as I felt the cum explode from my nub.

Max continued to jack my shaft a bit till the waves of energy subsided in me and he sucked the head one last time to get the full load out of me before letting go. I felt my nub fall and start to soften and I took a deep breath and felt a bit lightheaded.

It was quiet in the room for a while. I knew that Max was sharing my load with Mateo. They were kissing as I had done with Max when Bo graduated and my cum was being shared between them before being swallowed. I felt even closer to them now than I had been before.

"Boy Matt," John said. "Master Todd is here and has expressed interest in collaring you and bringing you into his family. Do you agree to this?"

I smiled. "I do, Sir."

"Master Todd, you may now install Boy Matt's permanent cage," John said.

I felt Todd's hands on my balls. The base ring was put around them and then the metal cage reattached and relocked with its security screw. I was my complete self again. My cage was back on and I felt at peace.

I felt Todd remove my blindfold and as it came down, his smiling face was in front of mine.

"I'm proud to have you as part of my family, now Matt," Todd said. "Your cage is just a symbol, but I know you are more than this, and I promise to respect and care for you."

Todd leaned over and kissed me and then stepped back.

"Your formal collar will now be installed," John said.

Todd came forward and removed the lock on my collar and took off the silver tag I had worn for a year. He then stepped back and John brought over a jar that contained my new gold tag.

"As you know, inside this jar your new permanent tag sits within five loads of your new master's cum," John said. "It has been marked with his DNA as a symbol of your bond with him."

Todd reached in and took the tag out and shook it a bit to let the fluids drip off and then he brought it over to me. It read 'Boy Matt / CHASTITY SUB / Collared by Sir Todd' and on the back, he had written something else that he showed me, 'My Beta Boy'. I smiled as he attached it to my collar and reinstalled the lock.

John walked over and grabbed the shot of vodka that would mix with Todd's cum loads in the jar. He poured it in and swirled the jar around and then gave it to Todd who brought it up to my lips and tipped it forward. I felt his juices slide over my tongue and down my throat and I swallowed them all.

"Boy Matt," John said as Todd stepped back. "With the acceptance of your new collar, you have completed your contract and are no longer my sub. Your new master is Todd and his rules will now govern you. Master Todd, you may consummate this relationship."

Todd came to me and started releasing my wrists and ankles from their restraints as John walked back to sit down. Once I was free, Todd took my arm and guided me over to the fuck bench and I got on it so my ass was on display for him. I felt his hands rub over my cheeks and he continued up to my lower back and rubbed it a bit. He then reached down and kissed the small of my back before grabbing some lube and fingering my ass.

Todd was gentle and slow as he pushed his fingers into me. I felt one, two, and then three enter me while he stroked himself till he was fully hard. He then placed his cock at the entrance to my ass and pushed forward. I felt his head enter my hole and I groaned as I felt the shaft enter and fill me. His cock was the perfect size. The sensation was overwhelming and I closed my eyes and took a deep breath.

Once Todd was fully in me, I felt his hands on my lower back again and he was rubbing it and then moved around to grab my waist and started to thrust back and forth. He was slow and deliberate. This was not a common fuck, he wanted me to enjoy it and feel our bonding and I groaned as I felt his cock penetrate me and rub against my prostate. I was precumming and it was dripping to the floor and flexed my feet and cracked the joints in my toes as he moved back and forth.

I started to hear Todd breathe faster and he picked up the pace of his thrusts. He grasped my waist firmly and I started to hear the smack of his groin against my ass. I felt my body pushed forward a bit on the bench as he pounded and there was a slight creak and groan as he fucked. I gripped the bench, opened my eyes, and bit my bottom lip in preparation for what was to come.

Todd started fucking harder now and the slapping sound started to echo in the room. I started to grunt with each thrust and I almost thought I could feel his cock as it swelled within my ass signaling the end was near. Todd growled loudly as the orgasm overtook him and he pushed forward and delivered his load deep inside me. His balls rested on my ass and I felt them jump a few times as he pulsed. When he was done, he slowly pulled out and then fingered my ass a bit before moving away.

"Thank you, boy," Todd said as he helped me up.

"Thank you, Sir," I said with a smile.

I walked over to John and extended my hand and he grasped it.

"Sir, you have been more than a mentor to me," I said. "Thank you for all your guidance and training."

"You are most welcome boy," John replied.

I then walked over to Max and Mateo and gave them hugs as well before turning back to John.

"It's time to add your name to your banner, boy!" John replied as he handed me a marker.

I walked over to the banner and added my name below Ryan and Johnny's. I then handed the marker to Todd who put a 'x2' next to his name and smiled.

"Two for two, back-to-back," Todd replied.

"Well, you took the cream of the crop," John said as he put his hands on my shoulders.

John then turned to Max and Mateo and addressed them next.

"Boys, please clean up the room, and then you can leave," John said.

"Yes, Sir!" they replied.

"Todd and Matt, please follow me upstairs," John said.

I winked at Max and Mateo as I walked by them and I followed John and Todd upstairs. When we got to the main floor, I saw Bo on his knees on the floor in his cage and collar. He smiled and stood and came over and embraced me after the men walked by.

"Congratulations babe," Bo said as he kissed me.

"Thanks," I replied with a smile. "Ugh, this is a lot to take in."

Bo grabbed my hand and squeezed it and we walked over into the dining room where John and Todd were sitting at either end of the table. Bo and I sat on either side and John smiled.

"I have a little treat for you boys," John replied. "Fresh homemade ice cream made at a local dairy by a good friend of mine. It's the best you will ever have."

John opened the containers in the center of the table and passed around bowls. I took two heaping spoonfuls of the creamy vanilla treat and tossed some sprinkles and chocolate chips on top from the bowls of toppings that were laid on the table around it. As I put the first spoonful in my mouth, I savored the taste. John was right. The milkfat in the cream was delectable and it truly was some of the best I ever had.

We all sat there for a while and talked. John was very complimentary of my service over the past year and noted on several occasions he will be very sorry to see me go. Todd updated him on my plans to move in and we discussed how I was feeling. It was a wonderful end to a graduation ceremony I would never forget. When we were done, we all got up and John hugged me one last time, and then Todd and Bo prepared to leave.

"You want me to come over to your apartment after?" Bo asked.

"I would love that," I said.

"Ok, see you shortly," Bo said as he kissed me.

I returned downstairs and found the dungeon area clean and quiet. Max and Mateo had left already and there was a slight scent of disinfectant in the air. I walked over to where our pictures were hanging and stared at them a bit.

By the end of the day, my photo would be moving upstairs to hang in John's office. By the end of tomorrow, a new sub will have signed his contract on the table below me and taken his place in my yellow square on the floor. By Monday, my bin will have been reassigned and Max would be taking over as senior sub. Time was moving on and I needed to as well. I had a whole new journey to embark on and I was very excited to see where it would lead.

I reached up and felt the gold tag and lock marking me as a true sub and collared boy and I smiled. I was very proud of myself. I turned one last time to look at the dungeon and then left through the door for the last time.

EPILOGUE

Life as a Collared Sub

Spring had come to Atlanta again. The days were getting longer and the pine trees were spreading their yellow pollen far and wide, covering everything in the process. I opened my eyes and saw some of the morning light coming through the sides of the shade that was pulled down. I was on my back and Bo's arm was over my chest. He was still sound asleep and his head was on my shoulder. I carefully pulled my CPAP mask off and the sound of the forced air continued for a moment till the machine automatically turned off. I brought my hand down on his arm and squeezed it. Bo began to stir and as his eyes opened he looked at me and smiled.

"Morning babe," Bo said as he lifted his head and kissed me. "How did you sleep?"

"Not bad," I replied as I ran my hand through his hair and down his face.

"What time is it?" Bo asked.

I turned and looked at the clock next to our bed and it said it was 8:15 am. Todd did not usually wake till 8:30 am on weekends. Saturday and Sunday were normally my mornings to wake Todd with his morning blowjob or fuck, depending on his mood. Bo usually had the weekday mornings and I took care of making Todd his breakfast and other household chores before I had to go to work.

"A little past 8 am," I replied. "We have a few minutes to cuddle before I need to go tend to Sir."

"Good," Bo said as he kissed me again and his hand ran down my chest.

He played with my balls a bit and my nub started to swell in its cage. He liked to tease me, but I could do the same to him as well if I wanted to. I turned to him and embraced him putting my legs around his. Our tongues explored our mouths and I ran my hands through the hair on his upper back and down to his furry butt. Our cages met and my precum mixed with his as we moved around.

We often took the time to be intimate in the morning, even if it was early. Todd even allowed us to use the strap-ons with permission and Bo had gotten good and being able to milk my prostate with it, but I was still learning to do the same to him. I missed being able to fuck and cum like a normal man, but we made it work, and servicing and pleasing Todd made up for any frustration we might have. In the few weeks, I had been his boy, he had treated me well and I had become pretty greedy when I got my turn to drain his balls. His loads were so tasty, his scent was intoxicating, and he always gave us lots of attention afterward in appreciation.

When we finally broke our embrace, I sat up and rubbed Bo's belly and he groaned a bit.

"Set the alarm for me so I can be sure to go get breakfast started," Bo said.

"I will," I replied. "I'm off to go take care of Sir."

"I hope he breeds your ass today," Bo said. "You are always in a better mood when he does."

I chuckled and kissed him one more time and then went out into the hall and down to Todd's room to wake him.

An hour later, Todd was in the shower washing up after fucking my ass twice and I had wandered into the kitchen to check on Bo. He was in his shorts and tank top working on some scrambled eggs and sausage and it smelled wonderful. I was still naked and my hair was a bit of a mess. As the service sub and true beta around the house, I was either naked or in a jock, though I could use the furniture as a collared boy. Bo was allowed clothes, but sometimes he stripped down when the mood suited him or when Todd told him to.

I walked into the kitchen and he reached around and felt my ass. His finger brushed by my hole and he brought it up to his lips and licked it and smiled.

"Yup," Bo replied. "Tastes like Sir's cum."

I grinned. "I hope you are going to wash that finger now."

"Don't worry babe," Bo said with a laugh. "I will."

Bo turned to wash his hands and handed me the spatula to turn the eggs.

"We have a visitor coming by at 10 am," Bo said.

"Who is that?" I asked.

"Alex," Bo replied. "Master John's new sub. He is coming by for his interview."

"Oh, nice!" I replied. "I will be glad to see him again."

"He's just interviewing me and Sir, but I will be sure that he gets to see you before he leaves," Bo said with a wink. "Sir has some things he wants you to do out in the garage today. But don't worry. I will come out and help you after Alex leaves as I have tasks I have to perform as well."

"Sounds like a plan," I replied.

"Something smells good in here!" Todd said as he came into the room.

He was in his jogging shorts and I saw he had trimmed his beard. He looked refreshed and attractive as usual. He kissed me and then walked over to Bo and did the same while groping his ass.

"Everything is ready, Sir," Bo said. "I just need to plate it."

"That's my good boy," Todd said as he grabbed some coffee and walked into the dining room to sit down.

Bo brought him his food and then came back and made his plate and sat down next. As I brought my plate over to the table, I looked at them both as they started to eat. My sexy Sir to my left and my handsome boyfriend and fellow sub to the right.

I was a very lucky boy.

ABOUT THE AUTHOR

L. D. Cub is an author of LGBT books and gay erotic fiction based in the United States. Most of his material involves the BDSM scene and chastity play and explores consensual relationships between adults over the age of 18. His stories have been published online and can also be purchased as an e-book or physical paperback as well. If you would like other formats or have feedback, please contact him at any time at the Twitter handle @LockedStories.